SILENTCIDE 3

FREEDOM QUEST

Freedom is elusive. The quest is perilous.

A SUSPENSE THRILLER BY

RICHARD EBERT

Encircle Books™
The publishing imprint of
Encircle World Photos, LLC
Saint Paul, Minnesota

ISBN: 979-8-9895711-6-1 (Hardcover)
ISBN: 979-8-9895711-7-8 (Paperback)
ISBN: 979-8-9895711-8-5 (E-book)

Library of Congress Control Number: 2025928211

First Encircle Books™ edition: May 2026

Printed in the United States of America

Encircle Books™ is a trademark of Encircle World Photos, LLC

Cover photos: El Morro Fortress - Richard Ebert; Eyes – Adobe Stock/Whitestorm
Cover design: Rafael Andres
Author photo: Lisa A. Crayford

Author website: www.RichardEbert.com
Author email: Author@RichardEbert.com

140 Online Photos for Silentcide 3

140 online photos show *Silentcide 3* action scenes
in 20 cities in 8 countries.
Each photo annotated by a footnote number in the book.
Photos and descriptions by Richard Ebert.

Three Ways to See Photos

Author website: RichardEbert.com. Look for *Silentcide 3* cover.
Click "140 Silentcide 3 Photos."
Scan QR code at the end of a chapter.
See entire photo gallery:

Scan QR code below

PROLOGUE

Monday

One clandestine kiss in a closing elevator during the Republican National Convention destroyed his life. Steven Oakley was plunging toward rock bottom. The inevitable crash would be catastrophic, followed by decades of federal incarceration.

The disgraced CEO stood up at the ostentatious conference table and buttoned his Escorial wool suit coat with feigned dignity and control. His signal was clear. This insufferable meeting was over.

The lead attorney mirrored his client's actions with a practiced smile of reassurance. At $2,400 an hour, the son of a bitch could at least be sincere. "Don't worry, Steven. Tomorrow's procedure should be very routine and discreet. We should have you in and out in a few hours."

The word *procedure* was euphemistic for the arrest, booking and arraignment on a nineteen-count criminal complaint. Being told not to worry was insulting and condescending. At least the attorney had negotiated a deal allowing him to surrender at the regional FBI office. He would avoid the perp walk with bowed head and handcuffs. Promises were also made about circumventing the media frenzy.

But these small accommodations wouldn't prevent the twenty-four-hour news cycle from generating more sensational headlines. The press vultures were unrelenting in shredding his reputation's carcass.

Oakley avoided eye contact with the $11,000-an-hour group of partners, associates and paralegals huddled around the table. A smaller defense team in Washington, DC, watched on a bank of oversized monitors. Their individual roles were unclear. Together, they were draining the initial eight-million-dollar retainer. Their lust for billable hours was insatiable.

Elsewhere, corporate attorneys were ousting him from the company, defending against shareholder lawsuits and struggling to save billions in cancelled defense contracts from several countries. Divorce lawyers were also busy jostling for personal assets. His wife had vowed to leave him penniless. And with any luck, the court would set bail in the low millions.

Steven Oakley strode with faux dignity across the law firm's marble foyer, endured the indiscreet stares of elevator passengers during the forty-nine-floor descent, and hustled through the ornate lobby. His waiting chauffeur nodded, smiled and held the glass door while popping open an oversized umbrella.

Within three steps, a bitter wind rendered the umbrella useless against the needles of rain. After another step, his calfskin loafer sank into a puddle. By the time he reached the sanctuary of the limousine, his perfect coal-black hair was a matted mess. The leather car seat was saturated. He drained water from his shoe.

"Sorry for the inconvenience, sir," the chauffeur said as he wedged the Bentley Mulsanne into downtown gridlock.

Without acknowledging the apology, Oakley asked, "Did you arrange for the delivery?"

"Of course, sir."

Knowing the twelve-block ride might consume twenty minutes, the executive scrolled through emails and text messages. Most spewed venom. Two were recurring death threats. He succumbed to morbid curiosity by watching a CNBC video clip on the rear-seat entertainment system. The talking heads trashed him while displaying charts of his company's collapsing stock price. The market cap had dropped $52 billion.

The chauffeur impeccably timed the prearranged pit stop at the iconic Pike Place Fish Market. As the limo pulled curbside, a young man with an orange bloodstained apron and a backward baseball cap rushed out to deliver a bundle wrapped in white butcher paper.

Ten minutes later, Oakley was inside his penthouse condominium with a commanding view of the Seattle Waterfront.[1] Far below, couples strolled along the piers without a care in the world. Gondolas swung around the 175-foot Ferris wheel. Tourists were exiting the aquarium after hours of fun. They were all oblivious to his crisis.

Oakley unwrapped the package. He smiled for the first time since the scandal broke. Inside were succulent Brussels sprouts, a pound of morel mushrooms and three clusters of king crab legs. He'd fondly remember this decadent meal in prison.

He lifted a Waterford lowball from the china cabinet, dropped in a large square ice cube and poured two generous ounces of Booker's. The uncut, 121-proof bourbon didn't have a chance to open up before being guzzled. He welcomed the assault blazing down his throat.

Equally soothing was the steam shower until his mind drifted toward the tryst with US Senator Vickie McLoren. What a disaster! Their high-stakes conspiracy had been flawless. The initial results exceeded expectations, and their ultimate goals were within reach.

But a drunken one-night stand triggered a chain reaction of ruin. The sex – from what he could remember at least – was mediocre at best. What was he thinking? While drying off, he stared at the culprit responsible for the impulsive and errant decision.

Steven Oakley admired his mid-fifties physique. He was in remarkable shape except for chronic sore knees from too many years of jogging and racquetball. Now they were the least of his problems. He slipped into silk pajamas and tied the sash around a cashmere robe.

Returning to the kitchen, he filled a large roasting pan with water, placed it on the stove and turned the gas on high. He poured another whiskey and swirled the amber despondency with his index finger. The storm had passed, the clouds had parted, and the sunset over Elliot Bay[2] was sensational. Golden hues glistened across the water.

As he took a sip, a single drop of blood splashed into the bourbon and spread like gasoline hitting water. After a sniffle, the back of his hand caught the flow. He stuffed a tissue from the kitchen island into his nostril. It was obviously time to adjust the humidifier setting.

He loved this penthouse. The aerospace company purchased it when headquarters were relocated to Arlington, Virginia, to be near the Pentagon, politicians and lobbyists. The local condo's expenses were justified to accommodate his frequent visits to the Seattle factory, one of the largest buildings in the world. Today, the board of directors issued a thirty-day eviction notice on the condo. No doubt his prison cell would be smaller than the butler's pantry.

A pained sigh escaped his tight lips. Why had he allowed greed to rob him of his pinnacle of success?

Without warning, blood gushed from the open nostril. He pinched his nose, leaned back and grabbed more Kleenex. Nausea rumbled. Vision blurred. The room spun as an explosion ruptured his brain. As his knees buckled, he flailed to prevent a collapse. Gallons of boiling water cascaded as he crashed, scalding the scream from his gaping mouth.

With raw fingers as pink as crab claws, he yanked the cell phone from the robe.

Upside down. Wrong side. Excruciating pain. Password rejected. Panic. Hit Emergency Call.

"911, what's your emergency? ... Hello, this is 911. Is anyone there? ... Hello?"

◆◆◆

WASHINGTON, DISTRICT OF COLUMBIA

A diamond bracelet slid across Vickie McLoren's wrist as she pulled back the curtain, revealing the Washington Monument[3] a few blocks away. Glorious. When she first saw the obelisk as a teen, this tribute to the nation's first president was inspirational. Over four decades, that inspiration evolved into aspiration and then an obsession. She was going to be the first female president of the United States. The goal was assured.

Two weeks ago, the dream died.

As the curtain closed, McLoren pivoted back into the primary bedroom of the George Washington Presidential Suite at the Willard InterContinental.[4] The historic hotel – nicknamed Residence of Presidents and located in the shadow of the White House – had been her epicenter of power. After becoming the Republican presidential nominee, a torrent of big donors, politicians, dignitaries, ambassadors, and even heads of state came here to kiss her ring. Most would have kissed her ass if she weren't such a lady.

This had once been her throne. Now the three-room, two-bath suite was her gilded cage.

McLoren grabbed another panettone shortbread from the dinner tray and cursed as crumbs sprinkled across her Christian Dior suit. Before climbing back onto the king-size bed, she adjusted the tight gray wool around the waist. She felt bloated. *Let's be honest, girl, you're getting fat.* Too many calories on the campaign trail, from fine cuisine to fast food to rural cooking in church basements.

Why had she even bothered to maintain her exalted dress code today? The only visitors expected were room service and the rotation of US Marshals. They monitored her house arrest 24/7. The US Attorney General had assigned the Marshals because of their neutrality. The FBI, Secret Service and Capitol Police faced intense political and media attacks for not stopping McLoren's "alleged" crimes.

One unannounced visitor stopped by a few hours ago. Her former campaign manager, designated chief of staff, and loyal friend since grad school dropped off two boxes hidden during the FBI raids. Written in black ink on top were the words "For US Senator Vickie McLoren – PERSONAL."

Technically, McLoren maintained that title until the Senate Select Committee on Ethics delivered its findings. Then the entire chamber – a group of divisive politicians who couldn't agree on the virtues of motherhood, apple pie or puppies – would vote unanimously for expulsion. They had bipartisan disdain and condemnation for poisoning four of their congressional colleagues.

If she resigned, the ethics report might not go public. But senatorial grandstanding was inconsequential compared to the attorney general's intentions. He had vowed to pursue charges for the three murders of US senators plus the attempted murder of another, all in the first degree. Even worse were the domestic terrorism charges for the staged Russian missile attack at the National Mall during her campaign rally. The maximum penalty was death.

Vickie McLoren felt flushed. Armpits damp. Her skin ablaze.

Damn hot flashes. When is this shit going to end?

She raced to the thermostat and turned it down to 65°. As she yanked off her dress, the zipper caught in the ankle monitor. While hopping on one foot, she got dizzy and stumbled back to bed. After gasps for breath, a few sips of water and another shortbread for sugar, she felt reasonably better.

The unopened boxes loomed beside her. She knew what was inside. One held diaries and logs chronicling every day since McLoren announced her presidential bid. The other contained news stories of major milestones and events. The collection was going to be the foundation of a ghostwritten memoir titled *Becoming Madam President*. The publishing company had already rescinded its seven-figure book deal.

Wanting to relive her glory, she opened a box and immediately regretted the impulse. On top was the *Washington Post* headline from two weeks ago: "Conspiracy to Steal White House." A snot-nosed cub reporter from Des Moines had written the sensational article after unraveling the plot. Featured above the fold was a grainy photo of the senator kissing Steven Oakley in a closing elevator.

McLoren spat at the image of her accomplice. "Bastard!" she seethed. "You said the plan was foolproof. Who's the fool …"

Excruciating stomach pain stopped the rant. "Oh my God!" With sweaty palms, she clutched her extended abdomen. The fetal position was defenseless against the torment. Rapid heartbeats pounded in her ears.

"Ethan! Help! Help me!" Her yell became a whimper. "Please." She cursed the inattentive marshal in the next room.

Desperate, she tried standing but collapsed. Her organs were ablaze. Her body was chilled. She wanted to scream again, but terror and bloody froth waterboarded her throat. While crawling toward the door, red splotches ravaged her arms. The bolts of agony were unbearable.

She reached up for the door handle but failed to grasp it. Her hand was convulsing. With final determination, she grabbed the handle and headbutted the door. Lying on the other side was the marshal.

His lifeless eyes were open.

Prologue: Seattle, Washington and Washington, District of Columbia

---

Photos 1–4

CHAPTER ONE

PHILADELPHIA, PENNSYLVANIA

Tuesday

Chris Davis worried about his sister. Michelle Barton was lethargic as they trudged along Arch Street in downtown Philadelphia. Her long sandy-brown hair was unkempt. Her slouch belied her athleticism. Eight weeks of grief were etched into her face over the violent death of Ansel Meehan, their former foster brother.

Conflicted emotions ran deep. Michelle was in denial about Ansel's betrayal. She mourned the loss of their romance. She cursed herself for getting him killed in Seville.

Worst of all was the guilt. Every day she chastised herself for not heeding her older brother's warnings. Through choked tears she often lamented if she had listened to Chris – even once – Ansel might still be alive.

Blaming herself was wrong. Chris took no satisfaction in being right.

The depth of her anguish was perplexing. They were trained to suppress the psychological impact of death. The skill was essential for an assassin. There had been a few times during their career when remorse for killing caused prolonged despondency. Michelle always bounced back. She was resilient.

This time was different, very different.

Every effort to ease her pain failed. He suggested grief counseling. "That's for wusses," she declared. "I can handle this." Yet she was sinking deeper into despair.

Chris took an abrupt left turn along a head-high brick wall and entered an arched double gate.

"No." Michelle was emphatic. "We don't have time for this."

"Sure we do. This will only take a minute."

"We're going to be late."

Ignoring her protest, he paid their entry fee and walked along the herringbone-brick path of Christ Church Burial Ground.[5] The eighteenth-century cemetery contained two acres of irregular headstones and cement burial vaults with faded names of the forgotten, plus the graves of five signers of the Declaration of Independence. A few steps away was the colorless marble slab marking the final resting place of Ben Franklin and his wife.[6]

Michelle approached, swayed with sorrow, and laid her head against her brother's shoulder. They stood in respectful silence.

While the siblings were growing up, their mother often took them on field trips to historical sites. She wanted them to be cultured, a trait she considered lacking in their South Philly neighborhood. Mom was especially excited to bring them here so they could see the source of the maxims and proverbs she often quoted. Mom had rambled on and on about this Founding Father's accomplishments and wisdom, no doubt hoping to create an aspirational role model for two fidgeting children.

Chris was ten and Michelle eight during that visit to Franklin's grave. The timing was seared into his memory. The field trip was the day before they killed their abusive stepfather in self-defense while trying to stop him from murdering their mother. The double homicide left them orphans and sparked twenty-eight years of oppression.

Chris debated what to say about the deaths of Ansel or Mom as they stood in the cemetery. Nothing seemed appropriate. They wallowed in their private torment, ignoring the family of five who were posing for a selfie.

He pulled out pocket change, found two pennies and gave one to his sister. With a moment's hesitation, Michelle threw the coin atop the grave among dozens of others left by tourists. His penny rolled off the gravestone and wedged into a crack between brick pavers. He decided against retrieving it. The gesture was what counted.

Michelle broke the somber mood. "Seriously, Chris, we've got to get going. Right now."

They left the burial ground at a brisk pace. After crossing the street, the siblings glanced at the block-long green space of Independence Mall.[7] Basking in the sunlight were the Liberty Bell Center and Independence Hall. For decades, these two landmarks had symbolized Michelle's hope for freedom from a lifetime of dominance and control. That dream was still elusive. Although their worst tyrant died yesterday, the siblings expected the next decades of misery to start in a few minutes. That possibility was dreadful.

When reaching the William J. Green Jr. Federal Building,[8] they lingered in the plaza of the ten-story office complex despite being late for the impromptu morning appointment. Chris was nervous about the mandatory meeting yet said with assurance, "We can do this. Are you ready?"

Michelle's deep-blue eyes were dull. Her wholesome appearance had lost its color. He gave his sister a consoling hug. She quivered while clutching his lean frame. Two deep sighs later, she said with tenacity, "It's game day. Let's go."

They cleared the security checkpoint and hustled into an elevator. A large man stuck his hand between the closing doors, nodded a greeting, and stood in the corner. His posture was stiff. The jacket was too bulky for the warm autumn weather. Chris sensed what was coming.

His suspicions were confirmed when the elevator reached the eighth floor. A battery of Glock 19Ms was aimed at their heads. A special agent screamed, "FBI! Hands up. Step forward." The man in the elevator waved his 9mm pistol to hasten their exit.

The rapid-fire instructions continued. "Down on the floor. Spread-eagle. Interlock your fingers behind your head. You know the drill. Do it! Now!"

Chris and Michelle lay across the foyer of the regional FBI office. One arm was yanked behind his back. A handcuff was slapped on and ratcheted until his skin pinched. Chris heard the double lock applied before the second arm was hog-tied. Michelle was also being manhandled. They were frisked and yanked to their feet by the handcuff chain. The brutal action tore at his wrist.

Weapons were holstered as the siblings were led down the hall past the room where they had attended meetings for the last several weeks. Michelle was pushed toward a door marked Interrogation. She glanced back at Chris with trepidation. There was no way to know if or when they would see each other again.

In an instant, her vulnerability disappeared beneath a professional veneer. Her shield was up and impenetrable. He knew she could handle whatever happened.

Chris was shoved into a cramped room with three barren walls and secured to a metal table. The door slammed and locked. The stillness was foreboding. A camera blinked overhead. Surely, people were watching from behind the one-way window. He resisted the urge to wave.

His reflection in the tinted mirror was grim. The tousled blond hair, white eyebrows, pale skin and androgynous facial features appeared ghostly, yet his aquamarine eyes remained intense. Wanting to display confidence, he sat upright, refused to fidget, and waited patiently.

An hour passed. Two. Michelle was probably being grilled first. The sequence didn't matter. They had spent hours rehearsing. Their answers would naturally flow to stymie even the best interrogator.

Telling convincing lies was a core competency thanks to a decade of training.

The door swung open and ricocheted against the wall. Chris didn't react as an uptight, mid-forties woman stormed in wearing a shapeless black suit and bland white blouse. She was thin, bordering on gaunt – not from eating too little or exercising too much, but from overwork. Her graying black hair was coiled into a bun, revealing a large forehead etched with stress. The only jewelry was a thin silver wedding band. She was pissed.

A stack of files skidded across the table in front of Chris. He speculated they were a prop designed for intimidation, along with the firepower at the elevator and the handcuffs. Another bullying tactic was to stand rigid with hands on her hips. She loved demonstrating her control.

"For the record," she recited for the overhead camera, "my name is Special Agent Sloan Hamilton with the FBI Philadelphia field office and head of the Sicarius Task Team."

Her small group was mandated to spend twenty-four months dismantling what remained of the international assassin network. They were also told to identify and arrest all clients who ordered hits. When Chris first heard the ridiculous name she had selected, he scoffed. Sure, Sicarius was Latin for assassin, but most people couldn't remember, spell or correctly pronounce the task team's name.

During the prior three years, Hamilton had been instrumental in uncovering pieces of the assassin network. Her tireless contribution led to the simultaneous takedown of many of the players eight weeks ago, including the arrest of the siblings.

Soon afterward, the case and her former boss were reassigned to Washington, DC. Now thirty people at the J. Edgar Hoover Building were sorting, categorizing and analyzing the confiscated files, inventorying the seized property and gathering more evidence to prosecute the prisoners. Others were investigating the killings of the senators.

The DC headquarters had all the resources, political capital and accolades. The Sicarius Task Team was Hamilton's consolation prize. Chris knew she was bitter about being snubbed.

Hamilton demanded, "State your name for the record."

"Chris Davis."

"And your real name?"

"Daniel Ritchie," he answered but was perplexed. No one had called him that since childhood when their deaths were faked, their names were changed, and they were banished to an Amish farm for a decade to learn how to become silent assassins.

Special Agent Hamilton glared from behind oversized black glasses perched on a Roman nose. She yanked back a chair and sat to confront her adversary.

Chris remained calm. "Am I under arrest?"

"No, you're only being questioned."

"If that's the case, then under the law, I assume I'm free to go?"

Hamilton leaned close. He smelled coffee on her breath. "Don't delude yourself. You've never been free. Your ass has been mine since we arrested you eight weeks ago in Seville. Your recent privileges had strings attached, remember? They're contingent on your full cooperation with this task team. So I'd advise you to keep cooperating."

"Would you mind if I got my advice from a lawyer?"

Hamilton pushed back. Her brow twisted. "Sure, go ahead. Then I'll arrest you again, tear up the conditional immunity agreement, and make it my mission to get you a lethal injection."

Chris was playing her to perfection. His only hope of getting out of this situation was to appear submissive, compliant and innocent. To sell the ploy, he shuffled and waited ten seconds before sighing with resignation. "What's your first question?"

She tried to suppress a smirk. "Tell me what you know about Steven Oakley."

That was an unexpected opening salvo. "You already asked me about him when the scandal broke a couple weeks ago. Your boys in DC also quizzed me. What else can I say? Oh, I know, I've heard he's a bad kisser."

"Cut the crap." Her jaw tightened. "You ready to be serious yet?" She waited for his apologetic nod before continuing. "Did you ever work for Oakley?"

"Not knowingly."

"What's that mean?"

"It means if he co-conspired to have those senators killed, then he might have contracted other hits. But I don't know. We were never told client names."

"Who'd want him dead?"

"Probably plenty of people."

"How about Senator Vickie McLoren?"

"Sure, she has a motive to knock off her accomplice."

"That's not what I meant."

Chris acted perturbed. "Listen, how 'bout we stop dancing around and get to your point, Sloan."

The bags under her eyes twitched. "No, you listen to me. You'll no longer call me Sloan. The name's Special Agent Hamilton. And I'll ask the questions, you provide the answers. Got it?"

He had her rattled. "Sure, whatever you say."

A glint of superiority flashed across her exhausted eyes. "Why did you two kill Oakley and McLoren?"

"Really?" He was taken aback. This interrogation was not going where he expected. "Why do you think we did that?"

"Because they were poisoned last night only hours apart. That's the hallmark of silentcide killings."

"And where did they die?"

"They were both in Washington."

This was damning news. A train from Philly to DC was less than a couple of hours. Although circumstantial, the FBI could argue the proximity provided ample opportunity for the crimes. Hamilton was acting determined to pin anything and everything on them. He asked, "Is this my chance for a rebuttal?"

"Be my guest," she said smugly.

"Okay, let's think about this. Number one, Michelle and I spent weeks trying to save the senators, not kill them. So why would we murder the people who did? Number two, if you already know they were poisoned, then it's not our MO. Silentcide is the art of undetected killing, remember? If we did it, you'd need at least two weeks of tox work to confirm how they died."

Unconvinced, she pressed on. "Let's assume for one fleeting second I believe you. Who else would want them dead?"

"That's obvious to both of us. The one person who'd benefit most by having Oakley and McLoren murdered is the same person who orchestrated their plot to kill the senators." He proclaimed, "Irene Shaw." She was the seventy-two-year-old owner of a Philadelphia law firm and the founder of the assassin network. Irene had also been the autocrat over Chris and Michelle since childhood.

"Then let's talk about Irene."

Here we go. The main event. "What about her?"

"Have you seen her recently?"

"I've told you repeatedly, I have no idea where she is," he said, reminding himself not to refer to Irene in the past tense.

"Well, I do." Hamilton paused for dramatic effect. "She's in the morgue." Her voice crackled during the announcement, as if disappointed. The task team's ultimate goal was to arrest Irene Shaw. Capturing the high-profile fugitive would've been Hamilton's crowning achievement. Her dream died when Irene did.

Chris feared the siblings had replaced one living hell for another unless they had committed the perfect crime.

Hamilton broke the prolonged silence. "Cat got your tongue?" She was toying with him.

"Irene's dead?" Chris faked a broad smile. "That's awesome! How did the wicked witch die?"

"Stop the bullshit, Chris. We have your fingerprints on the scalpel you used to slit her throat."

Hamilton glowed with fiendish pleasure while Chris managed his breathing and eye blinks. She was lying. Yesterday, the siblings had sprayed their fingers with latex before killing Irene on the operating table at a plastic surgery clinic. Leaving behind latent fingerprints should have been impossible. But nothing was impossible. Maybe he should have wiped the weapon down with surgical disinfectant. *Careless? No, she's bluffing. She's got nothing.*

Hamilton glanced at her Timex watch. "Let's speed this up, shall we? I have a meeting soon." With a Cheshire smile, she declared, "You're under arrest."

"On what grounds?"

"On the grounds that Michelle confessed to killing Irene Shaw."

No fucking way.

As Hamilton recited the Miranda rights, Chris realized the gambit of turning themselves in as if they had nothing to hide had failed. Despite ending Irene Shaw's reign of terror, they were still screwed for life.

Chapter One: Philadelphia, Pennsylvania

Photos 5–8

CHAPTER TWO

When Irene Shaw was killed yesterday, Wolfgang König felt compelled to pick up the pieces.

The de facto head of her assassin network gripped the steering wheel of his late-model Ford F-150 with a massive fist, picked the gumline of a crooked tooth, and scowled at the idiot driver admiring the Harrisburg skyline from across the Susquehanna River.[9] His thick black eyebrows pinched with disgust while blasting the horn. The former college linebacker, decorated Army vet and ruthless mercenary refused to be late.

Frustration boiled at every red light until reaching a brick, Colonial-style duplex.[10] A dummy corporation had purchased the 2,100-square-foot, late-Victorian home long before Wolfgang was recruited. Irene considered the safehouse a tolerable driving distance from her mansion and law firm in Philadelphia. And the two Amish farms used for assassin training were only forty miles away.

When the FBI seized those properties, Irene took sanctuary in this capital city of fifty thousand. She believed this was the perfect place to hide in plain sight. The exterior was humble, yet the interior was lavish. Even in exile, Irene demanded luxury.

Wolfgang cursed the lack of parking on State Street at Irene's hideout. Cars filled every space in front of the similar houses. "To hell with it," he mumbled while parallel parking in front of a yellow fire hydrant. He threw a counterfeit handicap sticker on the dash and stabilized a pistol in a shoulder holster beneath his suit coat before exiting the truck. A crippling pain shot through his spine. He gasped and powered up the stairs and across the porch.

Pierre opened the configuration of locks from inside the reinforced doors. He was Irene's ever-present butler, cook, man-servant and occasional boy toy. Wolfgang didn't know the scrawny twerp's last name. Pierre tried to convey a brave face, but his red eyes were moist. "Welcome, Mr. König." His voice crackled with emotion. "I can't believe Ms. Shaw is …"

Unbelievable. He might be the only person mourning Irene. Deal with him later. "Yup, it's a tragedy. A real tragedy."

After an awkward pause, as if waiting to be consoled, Pierre struggled to regain his professionalism. "I'm so sorry. Where are my manners? Please come in. May I get you anything?"

"No. Just remember what I told you to do when they get here."

"Yes, sir. I assume you'll conduct your meeting in Ms. Shaw's office?"

"Of course." Wolfgang had expected to be seated in the living room, but her study would be more ominous. He had dreaded facing his former boss when she held court there.

The banister creaked as they climbed to the second floor. Irene had converted two bedrooms into an office, featuring wall-to-wall cherry cabinets, smoked-glass sconces, a pretentious chandelier, and a double-knotted Turkish rug on the bamboo wood floor. An expensive interior designer must have selected the knickknacks; they lacked Irene's panache.

Sprawled across a white camelback sofa was Irene's dog, the love of her life. The Afghan hound raised his head with anticipation, scanned the men with chocolate-brown eyes, and lowered his snout with a whimper.

"Nice seeing you too, Brutus," Wolfgang said in jest.

Before Pierre could close the door, the fifty-five-pound purebred leaped off the couch and followed with his tail between his legs.

Wolfgang stared at the burgundy leather executive chair and hesitated before sitting. He was officially at the helm. When they were in Granada, Spain, Irene had promised him control of her assassin enterprise once Vickie McLoren became president. Irene had wanted time to harvest the glory and riches as DC's newest power broker.

A couple of days later, however, the shit hit the fan when the FBI implemented an international takedown. Wolfgang spent the last eight weeks in damage control. Although the network was now decimated – people were either arrested or in disarray – he was in charge without Irene hovering over his every move. A broad smile crossed his ruddy cheeks.

A laptop was on the desk. It was a different model than the company-issued laptop he recognized sitting on the credenza. The latter was worthless. Wolfgang had implemented a system-wide wiper attack on all company records, computers and software moments after the first raid. Maybe tech nerds from the FBI's Computer Analysis and Response Team could retrieve something useful, but that was doubtful.

Irene's personal laptop, however, could prove invaluable. He turned it on and wasn't surprised to learn he needed a password or fingerprint biometrics. She was a sophisticated and cautious old coot. When the wooden stairs groaned under heavy footsteps, he closed the cover and pushed the laptop aside.

There was a timid knock on the door, followed by Pierre's request to enter. "Your guests have arrived, Mr. König." The manservant carried two handguns as if they were live grenades, placed them in front of Wolfgang, along with a stag antler switchblade and a teal leather purse. "May I escort them in now?"

Irene's bodyguard Frank and chauffeur John walked in wearing black suits, white shirts and conservative ties matching Wolfgang's. They stood at attention. Frank made eye contact. John's eyes were downcast.

The pair had snubbed Wolfgang when he started working for Irene eleven years ago. They begrudgingly showed more respect as he rose through the ranks. Now he demanded fear.

Wolfgang inspected the thirteen-inch WWII stiletto and marveled at the Italian craftsmanship before snapping open the blade. Light danced across the stainless steel. "Why do you still carry this toothpick?" he asked Frank.

"It was my grandfather's."

"Golly, family heirlooms are so nice, aren't they?" With a heinous roar, Wolfgang hurled the switchblade. The bayonet point slammed into the rug and gyrated between Frank's polished shoes. To his credit, the bodyguard didn't recoil. Wolfgang's rigid jaw clenched.

He picked up a SIG P229, pulled out the magazine and ejected the 9mm round in the chamber. The hollow-point bullet rolled across the desk. He disarmed the second pistol and slammed it down. Irene would've had a conniption fit at the scratch in the antique inlaid wood. Wolfgang screamed, "What the hell's the matter with you two?"

Neither henchman dared to answer the rhetorical question.

"Frank! Why weren't you on duty yesterday protecting Irene?"

"I planned on it," the bodyguard said. "I really did. But she, uh, gave me the day off. In fact, she insisted."

"Why the hell would she do that?"

"Because, well, she didn't want me to see her face post-op."

Frank's excuse was credible. Irene refused to be seen when not at her physical best. Yesterday, she had insisted on getting a nip and tuck by her favorite plastic surgeon in Philadelphia. This meant violating her own rule of never being predictable when hunted. Contrary to her adamant belief, Irene Shaw was vincible. Vanity was her Achilles' heel.

"You should've gone anyway," Wolfgang admonished the body-guard, knowing full well no one disobeyed Irene's orders. The consequences for disobedience were unpleasant.

Wolfgang swiveled his accusations. "John, look at me, goddamn it." He bored his deep-set eyes into the chauffeur. "I assume that's Irene's purse. It has a padlock on it. Do you have the key?"

"No, Ms. Shaw taped it to her wrist before surgery."

"That's great. Just great. You saved the purse but not her?" he raged. "What the hell were you doing at the clinic while she was being killed? Reading old *People* magazines?"

The brute blanched. His fingers twitched. "Well, yes, I was waiting in the lobby … but only 'cause they wouldn't let me in the operating room."

"You mean they didn't listen to your *pretty please*? Damn it, that's where you belonged. It was your job." Wolfgang hoped he heard the past tense. "So what happened?"

John shuffled. "I was tranquilized."

"How?"

"By a pregnant woman."

"A pregnant woman? Seriously? For Christ's sake. Did you recognize her?"

"No, it all happened so fast."

"That's crap! You were trained to detect and neutralize a threat." Wolfgang considered the people who wanted Irene dead. The list was long, but there was one prime candidate. "Could this mystery woman have been Michelle Barton?"

"Maybe, I don't know." Fear beaded on John's temple. "It didn't look like her."

"Of course not, you idiot. She's a master of disguise." Wolfgang shifted toward Frank. "Do you know where Chris and Michelle are now?"

"As far as we know, they're still in FBI custody."

"Which means you're clueless."

Frank barely nodded.

Damn siblings. They ruined Irene's enterprise and were probably squealing to the feds.

Wolfgang yanked at his short black hair. This conversation was pointless. He had enough of Tweedledum and Tweedledee. He yanked his SIG Sauer out of the shoulder holster and pulled back the slide to engage the single-action trigger. The sound echoed through the room.

"John, on your knees. Now!"

The chauffeur stared at Frank as if asking for help. He also glanced toward the door and considered bolting. Both were futile. He dropped to one knee. Seconds passed before he lowered the other. He moaned with resignation and terror.

Wolfgang's voice was calm and grim. "You know what's about to happen here. I can do it one of two ways. The first requires your buddy to clean up the mess. And you don't want to create extra work for Frank, do you?"

Wolfgang removed a gelcap from his shirt pocket, picked off some lint and handed it to John. "Here. Put this into your mouth and bite down … hard. It'll all be over soon. I promise."

The chauffeur took the pill, stared at it and began mumbling. This wasn't the first time Wolfgang had seen a confirmed atheist find God.

"Do it!"

John placed the capsule on his tongue but didn't close his mouth.

Wolfgang thrust the handgun closer. "Would you rather have this between your teeth? I said bite … down … hard. Now!"

With squinted eyes, a twitching face and trembling hands, the chauffeur complied. Wolfgang heard the capsule snap.

Two seconds of agonizing anticipation passed. Three. Four. Five. "Nothing's happening," John whimpered.

"Sure it is. Just be patient. According to the packaging, that Tylenol Extra Strength should reduce your stress headache for up to six hours."

John collapsed with relief.

"Stand up, you ninny. You're not dying today. And more good news. According to actuarial tables, you shouldn't die for another forty years … unless you screw up again."

"Thank you, Wolfgang. Thank you. Thank you. This'll never happen again."

"It better not. And I have just the job to prove it. Remember Anna Monteiro, Chris's bulletproof girlfriend? Do you think you can do what – God, it's been at least six – what six others died trying to do in the last few months?"

In late June, Anna Monteiro had been the target of a routine silentcide commission until Chris Davis became infatuated, decided to protect her and went rogue. The results were devastating. In retaliation, Irene wanted them killed.

The chauffeur struggled to accept the perilous assignment. "Wolfgang, I wasn't trained as an assassin."

Wolfgang raised the SIG Sauer again.

"But, yes, I think I can do that. No, wait, I can kill her. No question about it."

"Excellent. This will be a loving memorial for Irene, so make it messy. I want Chris to suffer for what he's done."

Wolfgang handed them their handguns without the mags. "Meeting adjourned," he declared. "Oh, and one more thing. From now on, you gentlemen will call me sir or Mr. König."

John rushed out the door. Frank lingered behind. "Congrats on your trip yesterday, sir," the bodyguard said, trying to suck up. "From all the news stories, it was a huge success."

"Except for the collateral damage of the US marshal," Wolfgang said. "Senator McLoren didn't seem the type to share her shortbread."

"And how did the teen do?" Frank asked, referring to Jacob Conners, an eighteen-year-old silentcide assassin trainee who Wolfgang was mentoring.

"Better than expected. I couldn't tell if the death trap he set in

Seville a couple of months ago was skill or a lucky one-off. But after yesterday in Seattle, he shows potential. I just hope something doesn't bite us in the ass."

"I hope so too, Mr. König." Frank took a longing glance at the switchblade before leaving.

Wolfgang was uncertain why Oakley and McLoren had to die. Irene had insisted they be killed simultaneously. He assumed she was covering her tracks. But maybe someone else wanted them dead too. The answer was moot. He chased the unproductive question from his mind.

"Now what?" Wolfgang mumbled to the sound of someone knocking. "Come in."

"I've prepared a little something for you, sir," Pierre said while delivering a cheese and sausage plate with a chilled Bud Light in a Philadelphia Eagles beer coozie.

Eating like this could be habit forming.

Wolfgang grinned while loosening his tie. He no longer had to wear Irene's noose around his neck.

Chapter Two: Harrisburg, Pennsylvania

Photos 9–10

CHAPTER THREE

Tuesday

Three hours after enduring a humiliating incarceration process, Michelle Barton was pushed into a ninety-six-square-foot hellhole at the Federal Detention Center. Her cellmate was oblivious. The emaciated woman clutched the stainless-steel toilet and ground what remained of her blackened teeth. Needle marks and scabs covered her arms. A leg bounced. Wheezing, sobbing and a violent cough reverberated off the peeling walls.

Michelle inched around the woman, sat on the edge of a cot and crouched. She nibbled, bit and ripped off a cracked fingernail. The tear was deep. Sucking on it stung. The taste was metallic. She pressed the wound on her knee until the bleeding stopped. A red stain marred the baggy orange jumpsuit. She shifted away from a protruding bed coil.

Michelle had been naive.

Chris was adamant they should run after killing Irene. He was confident they could avoid being caught for years, perhaps decades. Escape was better than immediate imprisonment. Even if the authorities caught them, the outcome would be the same. At least they could enjoy freedom while it lasted.

But she was tired of running, frankly tired of everything. A fugitive's life was no life of peace. Michelle was desperate for peace.

In hindsight, desperation clouded her judgment. She was certain they remained valuable to the Sicarius Task Team. Sloan Hamilton depended on their help to dismantle the rest of the assassin network. Voiding the immunity agreement and prosecuting them for Irene's murder would be counterproductive, especially with no evidence. They had been careful. Any accusations would be circumstantial at best. All they needed to do was convince Hamilton they were innocent of killing Irene Shaw.

For an hour yesterday, the siblings had debated the pros and cons of running versus surrendering. Their conversation was often heated until Chris acquiesced.

This morning, within thirty minutes inside the interrogation room, Michelle grasped her flawed logic. Hamilton didn't give a damn about the homicide of Irene Shaw. The siblings had killed her career aspirations. They had unleashed her wrath. Sloan Hamilton wanted revenge, regardless of the facts or consequences.

Worse yet was the hollowness consuming Michelle. After watching Irene bleed out, she expected to feel something, anything … maybe joy, relief, satisfaction or retribution. But there was nothing. Decades of Irene's brutality weren't erased. They weren't absolved from sixteen years of silentcide killing. Ansel, her former foster brother and lover, did not come back to life. And freedom remained a childish fantasy. The siblings were going to pay an exorbitant price for vengeance for the rest of their lives.

The drug addict vomited into the toilet. Michelle saw her future.

✦✦✦

The cellmate did not regain consciousness when two US marshals approached. An obese officer demanded, "Barton. Stick your hands through the slot. Now!"

Michelle cooperated while being handcuffed. The pair escorted her through a tunnel leading back to the William J. Green Jr. Federal Building. No one spoke while riding the elevator reserved for prisoners. Two FBI agents took custody. They returned her to the interrogation room, secured her wrists to a metal table and left without a word. The foul air reeked of sweat and fear.

Hamilton was probably ready for round two. This time, Michelle would say nothing except repeat her demand for a lawyer. An irony struck her. The only good thing about Irene was her outstanding defense team. Shaw's law firm always seemed to make legal problems disappear. Michelle would love to have that caliber of counsel now. She doubted that a court-appointed attorney could save her.

A door buzzer announced the entry of a late-fifties man. On his elongated face were deep frown lines intersecting with forehead grooves. His brown, Ivy League haircut receded on the left. The five-day-old facial hair was meticulously groomed. His voice was commanding. "Michelle Barton?"

"Yes."

"Good. I'm in the right room. Don't get up." With a dismissive flair, he leaned against the wall. Oversized tortoiseshell glasses magnified his stare. With arms tight across the chest, he was crushing the tailored sport coat, Oxford shirt and pocket square. If he intended to appear casual by not wearing a tie, he failed. Michelle's first impression was this guy was a cross between a corporate executive and an ex-Navy SEAL.

Michelle tried ending the awkwardness. "Are you my attorney?"

"Hardly." With a halting hand gesture, he added, "Let's remain quiet until your brother arrives, shall we?"

That's insulting. She couldn't tell if he was misogynistic, arrogant, or just plain rude.

Ten minutes passed. Fifteen. He kept glancing at an expensive dive watch. The man was getting agitated, obviously unaccustomed to waiting. His large ears flushed. Michelle relished the payback.

"Christ almighty," he bellowed to an agent when the door opened. "It's about time."

Chris walked in with his head down wearing a matching prison jumpsuit. He appeared vulnerable until seeing Michelle. He mouthed the words, "Are you okay?"

She forced a nod.

The man told the agent, "Remove his handcuffs. And hers too."

"Are you sure?"

"I wouldn't ask if I wasn't. Just do it." He grew impatient until Chris was seated, she was uncuffed, and the agent left the room. He stepped forward and towered over her brother.

"So you're Chris Davis?" he asked with superiority. "You must have one helluva PR firm."

"What's that supposed to mean?"

"It means you're nothing like I expected."

"What did you expect?"

The man's arms flailed with exaggerated excitement. "To see an assassin extraordinaire. The legendary silent killer." His hands stopped. "Instead, you're a wimp. My prepubescent lawn care kid looks more ferocious."

Chris formed a fist. Michelle prayed he could contain his anger. The man's insults were a tactic to establish dominance. A single outburst would relinquish control.

With unwavering confidence, Chris said, "My appearance is an asset, a tool that doesn't alarm the hunted. Bravado like yours is a liability."

The man blustered. "An asset? Really? Is that what you call your boyish blond hair and pasty white skin?"

"At least I don't try hiding them like those ugly pockmarks under your scruffy beard."

The man cocked his head and laughed as if he had enjoyed the first serve in a long tennis tournament. "I like you."

"I can't say the same about you," Chris volleyed back. "So why don't you sit down and let's get started. And include my sister in the conversation. We're a team."

"Excellent idea. Just give me a minute before we chat." The man stared at the one-way observation window. "Turn off the camera, please. That includes any microphones." The light on the overhead camera turned red. "Now pull the shade. We want total privacy." He draped the sport coat over a chair. "There, that's better."

Michelle asked, "Can anyone hear us?"

He shrugged his broad shoulders as if it didn't matter and made a production of rolling up his sleeves, revealing well-defined arms. She wasn't impressed. He sat down, facing off across from the siblings.

"Comfy?" Chris asked.

"No, not particularly, but this won't take long."

"That's good to hear."

The man ignored the sarcasm and was about to start his agenda when he saw Michelle's finger. "You're bleeding. Do you want medical attention?"

She hid her hand below the table. "No, I'm fine."

"You sure? I can at least get you a Band-Aid."

Chris exchanged a glance with Michelle. "She said she's fine. She doesn't need your fake chivalry."

The man revealed a polished smile. The rows of teeth disappeared the instant he said, "Just trying to help."

"We don't need it." Chris went on the offensive. "So explain why you're not wearing a visitor badge or ID card."

"You're observant." He made a sham of checking his pockets. "It appears I left my credentials at home."

"That's bullshit. Are you a lawyer or from the FBI?"

"Neither."

"Then who the hell are you?"

"My name is Mason Webber with two Bs." He folded his hands on the table. "And I understand you two kids are in trouble with Mom after being very naughty yesterday."

Michelle felt Chris bristle at the condescending language. *Keep your cool, brother.* To his credit, he remained quiet.

"But I have an assignment that may interest you. If you cooperate, there's a chance your federal charges may be dropped and your current predicament may go away."

Chris shook his head with growing irritation. "Using the word *may* twice in one sentence doesn't suggest much certainty."

Webber's cocksure smile returned. "'Nothing in life is certain …'"

Michelle finished the quote, "'Except death and taxes.' We know. We're well-versed in Ben Franklin quotes." She leaned across the table. Michelle was livid. "You want us to kill someone, correct? Probably a high-value target."

"I didn't say that."

"That's what you're implying. What else would be worth wiping our slates clean?"

The tension was thick. Their expressions were combative. Chris intervened. "Why don't you just tell us about the mission."

"*Mission* is an interesting choice of words. I called it an assignment."

"Enough with the word games, Mason Webber with two Bs. Tell us what you want."

With arrogant smugness, he said, "That's confidential, on a need-to-know basis, and you don't need to know yet. You'll be briefed when you get there."

"Where's there?"

"That's also classified. All you need to know is you'll fly out tomorrow."

"That's not much information."

"Too bad. That's all you're going to get. And we need your answer now."

Chris couldn't resist. "Who's we? What three-letter acronym do you work for?"

The cocky smile returned. "You don't need to know."

Michelle had enough of this son of a bitch. She sat back and frowned. "We'll pass, thank you very much. We're done here."

Webber eyeballed Chris to see if he concurred. Her brother was motionless. She couldn't decipher whether his silence was defiance, agreement or support of her.

Webber jumped to his feet. The chair skidded across the room. He ripped off his glasses, slammed his palms on the table and lurched his six-foot brawn within inches of the siblings. "I don't think you shitheads understand. Your FBI immunity agreement is being torn up as we speak. You'll soon be prosecuted for every crime you've ever committed, real or imaginary. You're facing life in a federal max prison."

He turned his rage onto Chris. "And you, pretty boy. If you're lucky, you'll become someone's bitch on day one. If you're unlucky, an entire gang will share you every day. After decades of that, you'll welcome the death penalty."

The siblings remained unified with their brazen stares.

"Christ almighty, you two are unbelievable." Webber paced the cramped room. He picked the suit coat off the floor, brushed off the dust and dirt, and hung it on the door hook. His fury exploded. The chair ricocheted against the wall before he lunged back into position. A rapid pulse surged through his carotid arteries. "Why is this so damn difficult? I'm offering you a get-out-of-jail-free card. Take it!"

Five seconds of silence lasted an eternity. Michelle had expressed her abhorrence to the proposal. It was Chris's turn. She expected solidarity. To her chagrin, Chris asked, "Can we talk about it?"

Webber grinned like he had won the first set of the match. "Sure. You have ten minutes."

CHAPTER FOUR

PHILADELPHIA, PENNSYLVANIA

Tuesday

As soon as the door shut, Chris embraced his sister. Hugs provided the support and comfort they needed to get through the worst of times. Michelle clung longer than normal. With a deep sigh and an extra squeeze, she let go.

She pushed aside drooping hair, a telltale habit when she was nervous. Her eyes were hollow, her lips pursed, and a tear formed in the corner of her eye. She looked like hell. "Are you okay?"

"Yup," she said but didn't mean it.

He struggled to find something to say. "How's the finger?"

She formed a fist to hide the wound on her lap. "It's nothing."

"You sure? Let's see it again."

"I said it's fine, Chris. Let it go. We've only got ten minutes, for God's sake. Let's not waste time talking about my damn finger."

Michelle took a second to recover from her overreaction. She stared at the camera. The light was still red. "Do you really think this room is secure?"

"I doubt it. So be careful not to say anything incriminating."

She snapped again. "Stop being condescending."

"Relax, will you?" He put his arm around her shoulder. "Pull yourself together. I need you thinking here with me."

With elbows on the table and hands rubbing her face, she struggled for self-control.

Chris knew her anger wasn't personal. She had been edgy since Ansel was killed. But coddling her could make things worse. "I've got an idea." He turned the chair around, faced the blank wall and hunched over. Michelle followed his lead. "Now let's whisper." He cleared his throat. "But before we get too far, I need to ask you something."

"What's that?"

He fidgeted before spitting it out. "Sloan Hamilton claimed you confessed this morning."

Michelle's eyebrows rose in disbelief. "You don't buy that crap for one damn second, do you?"

"No, of course not."

"Then why are you even asking me?"

Chris stammered. "Well, ah, because if she tried tricking me, then maybe she said something to you that I should know about."

"She didn't have the chance. After thirty minutes of her ranting and raving, I lawyered up. That's when she slapped on the cuffs again."

"She does have a gift for interrogation, doesn't she?"

"No, she has bugs up her ass. And they're us."

Chris laughed a nervous laugh.

Her grin faded away. "Okay, can we switch gears to our immediate problem? Who's this Webber guy?"

"I've been thinking about that. He's got to be someone important to just stroll in here, unless he's one of Hamilton's tricks. But if he's legit, I'm guessing CIA. Maybe from the Special Activities Center. Their SOG operatives do all the covert raids, sabotage and targeted killings."

"I'll bet they have good people, right?"

"From what I hear, sure. They're the best of the elite. Why?"

"If Webber has all those great resources, why does he need us?"

"Probably for our silentcide skills."

"Come on," she said with skepticism. "They must have plenty of guys who can do what we do."

"But maybe not with our twenty-six years of training and experience. If the target is really high value as you said, and a typical assassination would create a political firestorm, they might want specialists to conduct an undetectable kill."

"You're delusional. It's not a silentcide mission, Chris, it's a suicide one. They don't want to use their own guys and then have to put new stars on the CIA Memorial Wall. That's why they're recruiting us. Don't you get it? We're expendable. What better way to ensure deniability. Dead men tell no tales."

"You think so?"

"Absolutely. That guy is no better than Irene – maybe worse. That witch died only twenty-four hours ago, but she reincarnated into this Webber guy with two Bs."

"He is a pompous ass, isn't he?"

"I can deal with pompous, arrogant alpha males. But he's dangerous. He's bulldozing us into a trap to get us killed. I'm telling you right now, I'll have no part of him or" – she made air quotes – "his assignment."

"So what are you going to tell him?"

"Aren't you listening? My answer is no."

"But if we don't cooperate, we'll go directly to jail without passing go."

"Maybe, maybe not. But I'll take my chances with Hamilton, thank you very much."

"You know she's gunning for us."

"Of course she is. But she has nothing, nada, zilch … a big fat diddly squat."

Chris shuffled his feet as he lowered his voice. "She claims my fingerprints are on the scalpel."

Michelle whispered back, "She also told you I confessed. Look,

Hamilton will lie about anything. She's desperate. But her claims have to be proven in court."

"Maybe she can't prove Irene's murder. But she has lots of evidence on other things we've done. Hell, she'd take us down for jaywalking if it got us back to prison."

His sister's round cheeks twitched. "Does that mean you're going to take Webber's assignment? You really want to do this?"

"Of course not. But this might be our last get-out-of-jail-free card."

"You do remember Webber's bullshit about death and taxes, right?"

"Sure, there's no guarantee. But having even a slim chance is better than none. I don't see we have a choice."

"I do. And my mind's made up. No way."

Frustration boiled. *Why's she so damn stubborn? She must understand.* "Look, yesterday I let you talk me into surrendering to Sloan. That's turned into a disaster. It's my turn to insist we follow my instincts."

Michelle bristled. "Insist all you want, but there's no 'we' here. If you really want to do this, go ahead. I won't stop you. Just count me out."

Chris heard himself sounding desperate. "Okay, how 'bout we compromise. Let's say yes now and learn more about the mission in a few days. If it's what you think, then we can always say no. Or maybe we'll find a way to escape."

Michelle held up her index finger. The bleeding had stopped. "Shh. Just stop talking. Please."

She struggled with her thoughts in an uncomfortable silence. When she raised her head, her deep blue eyes were clear and her expression was relaxed. She glowed. "Chris, listen to me … very carefully. And don't interrupt, okay?"

He nodded, hoping she had an alternative.

"If you decide to go with Webber, that's on you. I just hope you don't regret it. But for me, it's different." She rubbed her forehead. "God, how do I say this?"

A gasp filled her lungs, followed by a loud exhale. "For almost three decades, Irene made us do terrible, terrible things. I've always hated her for it. But truth be told, I hated myself more. Despite all our justifications and denials, what we've done is unforgivable. You know it and I know it."

The color left her lips while forcing a weak smile. She reached out to hold his hand. Her fingers were icy. "But now Irene's dead. And I just realized something. The only freedom I'm ever going to get is the freedom of choice. I know that's not saying much. And yes, I'll probably rot in jail. But at least now I'll have the peace of my own free will. So I'm not killing anymore. Can you understand that?"

Chris had never admired his sister more. But was she willing to suffer the lifelong consequences of her conviction?

CHAPTER FIVE

Michelle flinched when the buzzer sounded and Mason Webber burst through the door of the interrogation room. "There's no way that was ten minutes," she protested.

He tapped the crystal of his watch. "Darn, this must be running fast. Sorry about that. Well, I'm here now. Let's finish our chat." He repeated the spectacle of draping the sport coat on the chair.

Michelle stifled a giggle. Dust and hair covered his back sleeve.

Webber mounted the chair as if getting on a horse. "Have you kids reached a decision?"

Chris seethed at being called a kid again. "We're still talking about it, Mr. Company Man," he said, referring to the CIA's nickname.

Webber studied Chris. "Are you always this obstinate?"

"Are you always this egocentric?" Chris's pretentious insult came across as a weak attempt to prove he was Webber's equal and not a slug from South Philly.

"We're going to have to work on that mouth of yours."

"Good luck with that. You're going to be very busy."

Michelle considered intervening but allowed the bucks to finish their standoff.

With controlled irritation, Webber said, "Tell you what. Let's stop the saber-rattling and have a civil conversation."

Chris said nothing. She sensed her brother was savoring the

minor victory of making this jerk blink first. "Sure," he finally said, but his tone came across as "fuck you."

Michelle guessed their civility would be short-lived. Probably under a minute.

"Good. Then let's proceed." Webber's hands rested on the table, yet his arrogance rose. "This is simple, really. All I need is an answer to my proposal."

She expected Chris to decline for both of them and was surprised when he hesitated. The extended pause was troubling. *What's he waiting for?* Michelle tried sending him a telepathic message to look at her. When he did, he seemed apologetic.

Chris turned to Webber and said without conviction, "I'm in."

"Good." Webber turned to Michelle. "And you?"

She was stunned. How could Chris ignore – no, frankly disregard – her decision? He always had her back. Always.

Reality crept in. Perhaps he wasn't abandoning her. He was grasping at straws to save his own definition of freedom. And Webber was his last chance, albeit a shitty one. She could still make her own choice.

"I'm not doing this." Her statement was emphatic.

Webber lowered his head, gave it a dramatic shake, and stood up to tower over them again. With arms across his chest – apparently his favorite power pose – he spoke with restraint. "Let me explain how this works. You're a package deal or my proposal is off the table, comprende?"

To his credit, Chris didn't try reasoning with her or object to her refusal. His silence spoke volumes. He appeared willing to let her make the final decision for them and would accept the consequences.

Webber grew impatient. "Come on. This is so easy. You either both do this or, as I said, you'll serve life in a max prison, maybe supermax. No, I have a better idea. I'll save the taxpayers a lengthy trial by throwing you into a dark box somewhere."

Michelle spiraled into a quandary. She couldn't justify condemning her brother to life in solitary confinement by clinging to her new-found principles. It wouldn't be fair. The guilt would be intolerable. Maybe she could say yes while keeping her vow not to kill again. The odds were low but worth taking. If they stayed together, they'd find a way to survive. Solidarity gave them strength and was core to their bond. She hoped to God her brother was right this time.

"Okay, I'll do it," she said.

Chris reeled around in astonishment. "You don't have to do this for me."

"I'm not. I'm doing this for us."

"You sure?"

"Yes. End of debate. Move on."

"Good," Webber said with self-satisfaction. "Now let's go over some ground rules. If at any time you don't cooperate, meet my expectations, or try to escape, the deal's history with severe ramifications. You must remain silent – and I mean totally silent – before, during and after the assignment. And if something happens to you in the field, well, your ass is grass with complete deniability. Any questions?"

Michelle recoiled. The odds of surviving this "assignment" were dismal.

Chris remained defiant. "You're such a sweet talker. You must be The Company's number one recruiter."

"Let's stop calling it The Company, shall we? That's a ridiculous nickname fabricated by thriller novelists."

"I can think of several other words to call 'it,' none of which you'd like. What do you call your employer?"

"That's not important. But maybe we do need a name for us." Webber snapped his fingers. "I know, let's call us The Club. That has a lovely ring of camaraderie, don't you think?"

"No," Michelle answered.

With a dismissive hand gesture, he said, "Good, then it's settled."

Chris's anger boiled over. "Goddamn it. Show my sister some respect."

"What's your problem?"

"My problem is your misogynistic bullshit. You just waved off my sister like she's nothing. You'll always show her respect. Every single damn minute. That's my ground rule. Without it, we're done."

Michelle was awed.

Webber appeared to respect Chris for the first time. "Message received" was all he said while their eyes remained fixed. She could tell her brother refused to look away.

Webber broke the deadlock by reaching into his coat pocket. "To button things up, I have some paperwork for you to sign."

Chris emitted an exasperated sigh. "Oh boy. Is this the part where you slap down some legal doc the size of a house mortgage?"

"Nope, just a simple hand receipt." He placed a quarter sheet of paper on the table. "Here."

> Chris Davis and Michelle Barton agree to work with the US government as a NOC under the direction of Mason Webber and will not disclose any information about or the activities of this relationship to anyone without proper clearance.

Michelle asked, "What's a NOC?"

"The acronym stands for non-official cover."

"I still don't get it."

"Remember when I said your ass is grass with complete deniability? That's a NOC." The conceited bastard chuckled while giving them a pen. "Sign and date it."

The siblings hesitated in shared trepidation. They were signing their lives away but didn't have a choice. She was surprised when Webber snapped a photo of them on his cell phone. "Why did you just take our picture?"

"For my scrapbook. I couldn't resist." He retrieved the hand receipt and smirked before slapping his knees. "Well, I think we're finished here." He swung the sport coat over his shoulders as if donning a cape. "I look forward to working with you two. It should be fun."

"Not a chance," Chris mumbled as the spook turned his back.

Webber was about to knock on the door to be let out. "Oh, one more thing. I try to maintain a friendly relationship with the FBI, so we also have an agreement. In your free time, you'll keep working with Special Agent Hamilton and her Sicarius Task Team. I insist on your full cooperation, comprende?" He didn't expect an answer. "I know, why don't I invite her in so you can tell her yourself. Sit tight."

When Webber stepped out, Chris leaned over and stroked Michelle's arm. "It's not too late. You can still say no."

"I'm fine. We're doing this together."

"You sure?"

She wasn't sure. "Yes, Chris, this is final. Stop asking me already."

"Thank you," he said with an appreciative and relieved smile.

She removed his hand. "We'll see if you can thank me when this is over."

The lock buzzed again. Webber held the door as Special Agent Sloan Hamilton entered. The gesture felt patronizing. She assumed a defensive position: feet together, hands on her hips and back against the wall with a cold stare.

Of course, Webber spoke first. "I'm happy to announce that Chris and Michelle have accepted my proposal. They've also graciously agreed to continue with your task team in their spare time."

"How often is that going to be?" Hamilton asked.

"I honestly don't know. But in consideration for their help" – Webber raised a finger to accent each point – "their arrest is void, their conditional immunity is intact, you'll restore their previous privileges, and you'll extend them every courtesy as valuable members of Sicarius."

His unexpected leniency shocked Michelle. There had to be a catch.

Hamilton was furious. "That's a load of crap. These two murdered Shaw yesterday and probably had a hand in killing Steven Oakley and Senator McLoren too."

His calm voice was disarming. "Sloan, I've read your team's investigative reports. You have no evidence that any of that's true. Absolute jack shit. Even your speculations are baseless."

Michelle thought she heard her brother's subtle sigh of relief. Maybe they should've refused Webber's assignment and taken their chances with Hamilton. It was too late for that now.

Hamilton pushed back again. "But they're a flight risk."

"After our little chat, I think they clearly understand the consequences for disappointing me. So let's keep this simple, shall we? You do your job and I'll do mine. And with their help, everyone wins. How's that sound?"

Hamilton's face was blotchy while struggling with contempt.

Webber couldn't resist the urge to keep goading her. "Of course, if you prefer, I'm sure you're replaceable. But it would be a shame for the FBI to lose someone with your experience and talents. Are we on the same page now?"

Hamilton's eyes squeezed shut. Her nostrils flared. She caved. "Yes, sir."

"Good. Chris and Michelle, I'll send you details of where to meet tomorrow. In the meantime, I'm sure you three have plenty to talk about. Enjoy the rest of your day."

When he left, the air was sucked out of the room.

Michelle dared to speak. "Who is that guy?"

Hamilton glanced at the overhead camera. The light was still red. "An asshole."

Chris laughed. "That much we know. Is he CIA?"

"I have no idea. Neither does my boss. All I've been told is to do whatever he says."

Hamilton must've determined this banter was unprofessional. She yanked down her black jacket as her persona returned. She was back to being an FBI agent. "Regardless of Webber's bluster, you're still at the top of my list for Irene Shaw's murder. I know you did it and we'll prove it. So don't get too comfortable."

Michelle knew Hamilton would be unrelenting in the investigation. She wished someone less capable was at the helm.

"In the meantime," Hamilton continued, "I need some information before you leave."

Chris interrupted. "Can we get out of these prison peels first?"

"No, you look good in orange. And soon that'll be your daily uniform." Hamilton was back in control. "For starters, who would take over for Shaw?"

Michelle answered, "Irene was the driving force. No one can really replace her. Besides, I doubt her network is very active, especially after yesterday. But if someone tried, I suspect it would be Wolfgang König."

Chris added, "I agree. As we told you, he was introduced to us as the Preceptor, which was Lionel Jørgensen's old title."

"Well, thanks to you, we discovered where Irene's number two was buried," Hamilton said. "A couple of days ago, forensics ID'd Jørgensen's remains in a grave on the Amish farm."

Michelle winced. She assumed they also uncovered the bodies of their foster mother Mamm and the teenage orphan Rachel who they tried to rescue. But asking about them would be incriminating. The siblings didn't need to be accused of two more deaths.

Hamilton asked, "But where's König?"

"Not a clue," Michelle said. "For all we know, he could still be in Spain."

"That's not helpful."

"Here's something that might be," Chris said as if deciding to be cooperative. "I've been giving this some thought."

"What is it?"

"We all agree Senator McLoren was behind the plot to kill off the senators to get the presidential nomination, right? And Oakley's role was to supply the money to pay Irene. In return, her sugar daddy expected business favors from the White House and personal ones from the Lincoln Bedroom."

Hamilton's brow tightened. "You're stating the obvious. Is this going somewhere?"

"Yes, bear with me. What if they were puppets in a larger scheme, so they had to be silenced. And that's why Irene was killed too. Figure out who is really pulling the strings and you're the hero."

The FBI agent gave the theory a second of consideration before shaking her head. "Stop yanking my chain. The reality is Shaw was covering her tracks by having McLoren and Oakley poisoned. Then you two just happened to kill her on the same day."

Hamilton was too smart to fall for Chris's red herring. *Nice try, brother.*

"Look, you two. I need something new, something big and something tangible. Preferably client names. And lots of them."

"I'll tell you for the tenth time," Chris said. "We were never given the names of clients who commissioned silentcide kills."

"But knowing you, you spent lots of time trying to ID them. So start talking. Now! Right now!"

Her demand sounded desperate. Hamilton was probably being squeezed hard, minimized and set up to fail. Michelle felt empathetic. She could relate to the unrelenting pressure to satisfy impossible expectations. The fear of failure was all-consuming. It corroded every thought and assaulted every organ. Stress was toxic.

Chris's flippant response was, "Aren't you busy enough with three murders?"

"Shut up, Chris." Hamilton pivoted toward Michelle. "We followed up on your lead to meet with Dr. Nathan Yasin, but he shut us out. Won't say a damn thing. Certainly, as Irene's number three for decades, he knows all the secrets. Can you get him to talk?"

"That's unlikely."

"Why? If he was half the mentor and father figure you've claimed, surely he'll confide in you."

"No, Dr. Yasin blames me for getting his family killed. He thinks I betrayed him. I'm the last person he wants to talk with."

"But you could at least try. How about if I arrange a phone call?"

Chris interjected. "That's a non-starter. He wouldn't take the call."

"What part of 'shut up' don't you get?" Shifting back to Michelle, Hamilton asked, "Is that true?"

"Without question."

"Okay, I couldn't offer him immunity. He was too central in Shaw's assassin network. But if he cooperated, I could talk to the AG about reducing his sentence."

Michelle shook her head while pushing some hair behind her ear. "Knowing him, that's meaningless. Dr. Yasin is old and broken and probably resigned to dying in prison. In fact, I'm guessing he'd welcome it sooner rather than later."

"Then how can you make this happen before he takes everything to the grave?"

Michelle considered a few options before saying, "There's only one way, but the chances for success are slim to none."

"I'll take those odds. Name it."

"I'd have to see him in person."

"You mean in Saint Paul?"

"Yes. And it'd be best to meet in a neutral setting where he doesn't feel threatened."

"Consider it done as soon as you get back from Webber's field trip."

That assumes we come back from Webber's field trip.

CHAPTER SIX

Cambridge and Boston, Massachusetts
Wednesday

Anna Monteiro's attention drifted as the CFO stood at the front of the conference room using a laser pen to highlight his PowerPoint presentation. The board members and corporate officers were riveted on the dismal quarterly numbers. But Anna couldn't stay focused, once a core competency. She hadn't recovered yet. Far from it. She was making some progress, at least that's what she tried telling herself. But that was a lie. She was sinking into an inescapable morass.

Her lawyers argued in court that she was a victim of Stockholm syndrome. This defense helped them broker a plea deal to reduce federal charges down to a single misdemeanor. Maybe their claim explained why she had developed a bond with Chris. Maybe not.

A psychiatrist diagnosed her with latent daddy issues. He said sleeping with a bad boy was payback to her straitlaced and wealthy yet emotionally absent father. That had an element of truth. But she didn't know Chris was an assassin when they first hit the sheets on a Caribbean cruise. At the time, she thought he was wonderful, the kind of man she always wanted but never expected to find. The sex stopped when she learned the truth. The sole reason she stayed with him was to stay alive.

Anna was convinced she suffered from post-traumatic stress

disorder. Who wouldn't have PTSD after being shot at three times? Her doctor prescribed Xanax for the anxiety. After a few days of feeling drowsy and loopy, plus getting breathless while running, she flushed the pills down the toilet.

She discovered the best medicine to forget those hellish five weeks with Chris and Michelle was to stay busy. She immersed herself again as chief marketing officer at Longfellow BioSciences.[11] The struggling biotech in Cambridge specialized in immunotherapy technology to fight cancer. Anna was passionate about their mission.

The people at work were supportive when she returned from the ordeal. But many gossiped behind her back. The cruel social media posts would never disappear from the internet, but at least there hadn't been any new ones in weeks. And her friends had distanced themselves. Their abandonment hurt.

Anna had one true friend left: Liz Walker. The chief operating officer's curly red hair seemed ablaze while her animated green eyes and waving hands explained the progress of restarting the cancer clinical trials. Her report and enthusiasm captivated every board member around the table. The damage inflicted by Big Pharma would take a long time to repair. But if anyone could lead Longfellow BioSciences out of the ashes, it was Liz.

Liz was also Anna's confidant, advisor, moral support and occasional drinking buddy. Their relationship began in high school. Whenever Liz was around, Anna forgot the past and welcomed the future. As soon as the board meeting was over, however, Anna's protective shield dropped, letting in a flood of ugly memories.

Anna hunched over a bench inside the company locker room while lacing up pink Asics. With the backpack secured and earbuds in place, she turned on her MP3 player. Most of the songs on the runner's playlist were 140 to 145 beats per minute, an ideal tempo for an all-out exercise. The first tune was "Eye of the Tiger" by Survivor. She hoped the music would drown out the malaise. That seemed unlikely.

She cranked up the volume while racing out the door. A foot slapped the pavement on every drumbeat. Her arms pumped. Oxygen surged. By the time she raced along Broad Canal Walk[12] in Cambridge, endorphins were creating a sense of well-being.

The euphoria crashed on Memorial Drive.[13] An excruciating pain crippled her calf like a butcher knife twisting deep into muscle.

She cursed getting older. Ever since turning forty-one, Anna's endurance began dropping. Extra pounds on her hips and thighs were adding bulk to her small athletic figure. Her olive complexion had become a garden for new wrinkles. The short black pixie haircut no longer was cute but frumpy. Her dark brown eyes were challenged to read small print. And she was tired, chronically tired, and not just from a lack of sleep.

Anna hung on to the green guard rail and did stretches to relieve the pain. Admiring sailboats floating along the Charles River[14] was soothing. The skyline of Boston's Back Bay was impressive on this flawless autumn day before sunset. Despite nodding or waving to passing joggers, bikers and walkers, she felt isolated and alone.

After being arrested in Sausalito, California, eight weeks ago, she had longed to be alone. Her mother had stayed at her Boston brownstone home for weeks. Every day was a blur of police, FBI, lawyers, courtrooms and doctors. Her father had hired bodyguards who shadowed every movement. Someone was constantly asking how she was doing or if she was okay. It was stifling until a week ago when everyone left.

In retrospect, all that commotion gave her less time to think. Now she dreaded quiet. Prolonged silence unleashed the agony of her dead ex-husband, good friend and unborn child. They had all died in less than a month. The grief and anger were gut-wrenching.

Anna pulled out a tissue, wiped her eyes and blew her small nose. With a sigh of despair, she resumed running but at a slower pace.

While passing the MIT campus, her calf stiffened and twinged. She stopped, drank water with electrolyte powder, massaged the tenderness and cycled through leg swings, jumping jacks and lunge stretches.

A middle-aged man jogged by wearing a zipped jacket. Anna waved, but he didn't wave back. Probably in his own little world. He wasn't one of the regulars she passed along the Charles River. His eyes were hidden by oversized sunglasses, he was unshaven, and a long blond ponytail flopped from side to side. She guessed he might be bald beneath the Red Sox baseball cap. Not a good look. She dismissed a gnawing premonition.

When she came up to the Harvard Bridge, the man was sitting below a traffic light, tying his shoe. Very odd. She had spent ten minutes doing stretches yet had caught up to him within two blocks. An inner alarm went off. He did not raise his head when she passed, but she sensed him monitoring her.

Despite the sore calf, she picked up the pace along the bridge. She dared to look back. He was following, step for step. Her heart raced. Cars flew by on the right. A guardrail constrained the left. The river was below. There was no place to go but straight on the narrow walkway. She felt trapped despite her speed.

Toward the Boston side of the bridge, she looked back again. He was about twenty yards away. Something was familiar. Not his face. Not his clothes. *That's it! His stride!* A runner's stride was as unique as a fingerprint. This guy had been following her for days wearing different disguises. Now he was coming in for the kill.

Anna made an evasive move on the pedestrian ramp. She darted around the curves in a panic and smashed her hip on a railing. The pain was crippling. She stumbled when reaching the Charles River Esplanade[15] and sprinted along the path as fast as she had after being shot at in Québec City and Montreal. Chris had saved her before. This time she was going to die.

"Help! Help!"

No one was near except the approaching assassin. This path was always jammed with people, but not when she needed to be rescued.

A bullet would soon penetrate her back … maybe into the spine or through a lung. She pictured herself collapsing, bleeding, gasping for life. She quaked with the anticipation of death.

Ahead was an old man on a park bench. He stood when he heard her scream. What could he do to save her? He pulled a gun. The muzzle rose. He took aim. It was an ambush.

A playground fence prevented an evasive right turn. The river was on the left. They had her surrounded. She dove in at the first sound of gunfire.[16]

Water poured into her gaping mouth. The cold was shocking. Wet clothes and the backpack pulled her under in the strong current. Sewage stench assaulted her nose. She stroked and kicked but doubted she could outswim the hail of bullets.

Behind her was a huge splash. The jogger was in pursuit. His cap was gone, his blond hair was askew, and pieces of disguise dripped off his face. He was swimming fast, gaining distance with every stroke.

"Anna!" he screamed. "Stop!"

She prayed to go faster, but her body was cramping. She was exhausted, gasping for breath. She pivoted to fight him off. She punched and bit while her legs flailed to avoid sinking. He blocked every defensive move before pinning her arms together. She was hysterical.

He said in a calm voice, "Anna. Please stop. Chris sent me to protect you."

The words were difficult to comprehend. She didn't believe him. It must be a trick to deceive her. "Prove it!" she screamed.

"Your favorite wine on the cruise and at the brownstone was Cakebread."

Only Chris knew that. She collapsed in the man's arms. He held her afloat while treading water.

"What happened to the old man?" she gasped.

"Probably dead. But he wasn't old. He was obviously sent to kill you."

"Am I safe?"

"I think so, at least for now."

"Oh, Jesus! You mean there might be more after me?"

"I honestly don't know. Listen, I have a burner phone on shore. It's pre-programmed with Chris's phone number. Give him a call. He'll know what to do."

"Thank you so much. What's your name?"

"Roundy," the young man said.

"I can never thank you enough." She gave him a kiss on the cheek.

He flashed an engaging grin and began dragging her toward shore.

She thought the threats to her life had ended eight weeks ago. That was wishful thinking. A bullseye was still on her back. Was it only a matter of time before someone tried killing her again?

Chapter Six: Cambridge and Boston, Massachusetts

Photos 11–16

CHAPTER SEVEN

Harrisburg, Pennsylvania

Wednesday

Wolfgang König's attention swiveled away from Irene's files at the Harrisburg safehouse when he heard the whispered words "Target approaching." The middle monitor along the back of the credenza showed Anna Monteiro running on the Charles River Esplanade in Boston.[17] Her pace was fast. Her face was red. Her destiny was sealed.

For not being a trained assassin, John had done many things right so far. The chauffeur had created a convincing disguise. He had leveraged Anna's known routine for running, had determined her direction when she left from work, and had hurried into position on a bench at what appeared to be an ideal kill zone. His bodycam gave Wolfgang a front-row seat.

"Just breathe," Wolfgang coached him. "Take your time. Let her get closer."

"I've got this," John said, trying to sound confident, yet his voice was shaky.

Seconds passed before the camera rose. The suppressed barrel of a SIG P229 entered the bottom of the screen. The pistol popped. The muzzle flashed. A shell casing flew. The visual jerked upward as John flinched from the recoil. Three rapid gunshots. Three successive thwacks. The picture swirled before a violent thud. Only the blue sky was visible.

"Goddamn it! No!" Wolfgang pounded Irene's credenza. "What the hell happened?"

He thought a woman was screaming. *Was Anna hit? Was she dying?* He strained to hear. His Adam's apple lurched.

Two anxious minutes passed. An elderly woman's face entered the monitor screen and hovered. With a horrified expression, she said, "I think he's dead. Someone call 911."

Wolfgang's clenched fists pressed against his forehead. *What the hell's with Anna? Why doesn't she die?* He replayed the attack. *Such an easy target. Nobody could've missed that shot. There's a runner behind her. Is that a gun?* He froze the frame and zoomed in. *Who is that guy? A private bodyguard? Someone from Phonoi?* Wolfgang didn't know all the people in Irene's violent-killer division. Until recently, he had only managed Thanatos, the division named after the winged god of nonviolent death.

He took a screenshot, printed it, and stared at the mystery assailant. *It's not Chris. Too tall. Too well built. But not surprised if he's still protecting his girlfriend. Damn bastard.*

Wolfgang jumped out of the chair and cursed the bolt of chronic back pain. As he paced around the study, he vowed to see Anna and Chris dead. Michelle too. They had collapsed Irene Shaw's network. There was zero doubt they also killed Irene. The trio's deaths were now his mission.

Equally important was Irene's personal laptop on the credenza. It was a pot of gold. The key to financial freedom. A promise of an instant and carefree retirement at forty-one.

Months ago, in a rare moment of giddy candor after the staged bombing in Washington, DC, Irene had let it slip she expected to profit from dramatic stock market swings from the ensuing chaos. Her goal was a quarter billion dollars. That treasure trove – maybe lots more – was waiting to be collected … if he could open her damn laptop.

He had guessed a few obvious passwords. None worked. He

couldn't risk too many wrong entries. A Google search suggested the laptop would lock up after ten unsuccessful tries and wipe the drive clean. All the network's sophisticated software tools – including those for password recovery – were in the FBI's hands. He had sought help from several trusted facilitators who were not in prison. They were the tech-savvy members of Irene's enterprise. None responded. Maybe the butler knew.

He bellowed "Pierre" until there was a gentle knock on the door.

The manservant entered the room. He was probably in his mid to late twenties. The houseboy had a blanched complexion, unkempt pompadour-style hair, and a rumpled uniform. Wolfgang speculated that the runt hadn't eaten in three days.

Pierre's lackluster amber eyes widened as he surveyed the ransacked room. Books and knickknacks were in disarray. Art was on the floor. Furniture was out of place and some was overturned. A corner of the expensive rug was flipped up. The butler grimaced when noticing the hammer and screwdriver above the jimmied drawers of the credenza.

Wolfgang had been frustrated while trying to open Irene's file cabinets. The safehouse had state-of-the-art security and a cache of weapons but was ill-equipped to operate as headquarters. He didn't even have access to a fifty-dollar lock pick set.

Pierre asked with hesitation, "Are you looking for something, Mr. König?"

"In fact, yes."

"I wish you'd asked. I have the keys," he said while removing a set from his pocket.

Of course he does. "Do you have a key for the padlock on Irene's purse?"

"Yes, sir, I have backup keys for all her designer handbags." That was when Pierre noticed the destroyed purse on the camelback sofa. "Oh my God," he squealed. "What did you do? That was a nineteen-thousand-dollar Hermès Birkin 30 bag."

That would've been nice to know before I slit it open, Wolfgang thought. But the jackpot inside was worth it. The wallet was full of credit cards issued to a fake identity. In a velvet pouch were her diamond necklace, bracelet, watch, earrings and ring. The jewelry had to be worth a fortune. He couldn't crack into the cell phone without destroying the data, but it graciously displayed the two-step verification code for resetting the password of her alias bank account. The total of her savings, checking and two CDs was $262,000. That was a great start. But the contents of her purse were chump change compared to the riches hiding in her computer.

"Don't worry about the damn purse," Wolfgang said. "Do you have the password to Irene's laptop?"

The butler looked perplexed. "No, sir."

Wolfgang's palm rested atop the firearm on the desk. "Are you sure?"

"Yes, sir." With a conciliatory tone, he added, "But I hope you know I'm here to serve you in any way that I can."

He obviously wants to keep his job. "Then start by searching this house. And I mean turn it upside down. Don't stop until you find something resembling passwords."

"Yes, sir," he said as casually as if taking a meal order. Irene had taught him to remain calm, submissive and professional regardless of the pressure. "Anything else?"

"Tell Frank to get his ass up here. Then send Jacob in next."

"Of course, sir." Pierre nodded with respect, began backing out, and added in a timid voice, "Mr. König, if I may make one suggestion."

Wolfgang barked, "What?"

"There's a buzzer under the desk to summon me. Or, if you wish, I can install an app on your phone so you can reach me anytime, day or night. Ms. Shaw found these features very helpful."

"Good to know." Wolfgang waved him off.

Perhaps he should've told Pierre about John's death. They had served Irene together for years. *No, not yet. Why risk worsening his grief?*

Wolfgang had barely paged through another file folder when Frank was at the threshold. "You wanted to see me, Mr. König?"

"Yes, get in here."

Irene's bodyguard stood at attention. His suit was in sharp contrast to Wolfgang's casual business attire.

"Your buddy's dead," Wolfgang declared.

Frank seemed dispassionate, as if expecting the news. "That's a bummer" was his monotone response. He appeared numb to death after fifteen years with Irene. Or maybe he considered showing emotion a sign of weakness.

Wolfgang quipped, "I guess the actuarial tables for John's life expectancy were wrong." Frank remained straight-faced. Obviously, Wolfgang's attempt at gallows humor went over like a lead fart.

"How'd he die?"

"He was shot by this man." Wolfgang flipped the assailant's photo across the desk. "Do you know him?"

"Nope."

"Take a good look, a really good look."

Frank studied the blurry freeze-frame. While handing it back, he said, "I'd probably recognize him if he was one of ours. It could be a disguise, but it's kinda hard to see. How'd it happen?"

Wolfgang didn't have the time or inclination to describe John's last moments. "I'll send you the full video. Study it, discreetly ask around if you need to, but ID that shooter. Got that?"

Frank nodded, but his face telegraphed his belief this was a fool's errand.

"There are two more things I want you to do. One, find Chris and Michelle. If they're in prison somewhere, I'll have someone on the inside take them out once and for all. Two, go strong-arm

Irene's managing partner, chief financial officer and assistant at the law firm. Have them cough up any of her personal passwords or thumb drives."

Frank's eyebrows rose in confusion. "Nobody works there after the FBI shut it down."

Not the brightest bulb on the tree. "Thanks for that newsflash. Just find them and do whatever it takes to get their cooperation."

"Yes, sir. Is that all?"

"Isn't that enough?"

Frank shuffled before he spoke. "Can I ask you something before I leave?"

"What!"

"This might not be the right time, but uh, well, I didn't get paid yesterday."

Unbelievable. "You're right. This is a crappy time to whine about that. Go talk to HR. Now get the hell out of here."

Jacob Conners must have been listening outside the door. When Frank left, the cocksure teenager strolled in. The apathetic expression on his oblong face was accentuated by a pig nose, caterpillar eyebrows, elephant ears and a black buzz cut. He wore a dirty white T-shirt. The soiled jeans were slipping down his narrow hips, exposing the waistband on his briefs.

Wolfgang was disgusted. "You look like shit. There's no excuse for dressing like a punk. So clean up your act. In fact, have Pierre take you shopping for some decent clothes."

Jacob's lip snarled. "I'll be damned if I'll look like that dude."

"You'll be damned if you don't follow orders. Now wipe that shit-eating look off your face, stand up straight and stop swearing, or I'll kick your ass."

Why did he tolerate this last orphan from the Amish farm? Jacob showed potential as a silentcide assassin and had a couple of big successes. But, during the last several months, he had mutated into a rebellious, slang-spewing teenager, and the bullshit was driving him crazy.

"Listen carefully. I want you to go to Irene's mansion …"

Jacob interrupted. "But, like, the FBI took it."

Why does everyone keep stating the obvious? "So be careful."

"Whatchu mean?"

"You're a bright boy. Figure it out."

Jacob bristled at being called a boy but wisely said nothing.

"Now shut the hell up so I can tell you why you're going. Ready to listen? I want you to find anything that looks like passwords for a computer, file or website."

Jacob couldn't resist jumping in again. "Bruh, for real, like wouldn't the FBI already have 'em?"

"Maybe, but the feds are sloppy. Besides, the passwords are probably well hidden, so keep digging until you find something. Got that?"

"Bet, that's easy," he said with too much confidence, then demanded, "Key to the truck."

Wolfgang fished them out of his pants pocket.

Jacob grinned while catching them as if receiving a touchdown pass. "Need gas money too. I'm broke."

Wolfgang reluctantly pulled a twenty from his wallet.

"Need forty," Jacob said, extending his palm.

When did I become a damn den mother? "If you want a bigger allowance, you'll have to earn it. Do something useful. Start by taking the damn dog out for a walk."

"You gotta be joking." He epitomized teenage rebellion, more aptly called total insubordination. "After what I did in Seattle, you want me to, like, walk the dog?"

"What did you expect for killing Steven Oakley? A trophy? Get off your dead ass, turn off that damn video game, and start helping around here."

"That's Pierre's job."

"It's also your job if I say so. Now go."

Jacob sulked out of the office. *Good riddance, you little shit.*

Wolfgang returned to the monitor. The Boston shootout live feed was still on, but the picture was obscured. Someone must have covered John's body. He listened to the police chatter for a few minutes, hoping to learn Anna's fate. When the cops began making bets on game one of baseball's divisional playoffs, he turned the video off and opened his email.

He spent five minutes composing the simple email message. The header read: Kill Chris Davis, Michelle Barton and Anna Monteiro. The bounty was fifty thousand apiece or two hundred thousand for the hat trick. Hopefully, he'd have Irene's money by the time the three were buried.

The time-consuming part was gathering photos and writing background information about the three targets. Irene's assassins were accustomed to getting detailed electronic files for every commission. Gathering and assembling the intel was part of the facilitators' job; Wolfgang had never done it before. But providing the briefing was essential because the assassins were always segregated. Nobody knew the siblings, except maybe by reputation. And they'd be clueless about Anna.

Another laborious task was deciding who would receive the encrypted email. Wolfgang had a backup file in the cloud of all personnel, sanctioned resources and clients in case of a crisis like the FBI raid. He also knew who had been arrested. Others were required to check in periodically with their status. He maintained all this information on a spreadsheet.

He limited the email distribution to those he trusted to get the job done and keep their mouths shut. Six names fit that description. A half dozen seasoned pros were plenty of firepower to terminate the three biggest pains in his ass.

His laptop dinged, signaling a new email. His Pavlovian response was to check his personal inbox. The subject line was Irene's Next Assignment.

Wolfgang's jaw tightened. How did someone get his personal email address? It had never been used for business. Was this email legit or an FBI trap to trace him? He searched for the sender's address and discovered the domain name was registered to an untraceable shell company.

His inclination was to zap the email from the inbox and the trash folder. But he was curious. Previewing the message in the reading pane was safer than opening it. It read:

Hello Wolfgang –

Hope you are well. My sincere condolences on Irene's untimely passing. She was an admirable and accomplished woman. However, her death does not end the commitment she made to see this assignment through to completion. As her business manager, that obligation is now yours. After you acknowledge receipt of this communiqué, I'll forward instructions.

I look forward to hearing from you. Have a nice day.

Sincerely,

The Commander

Wolfgang flashed a finger at the screen. *No one talks to me like that anymore.* He was free from control and refused to take a knee for this asshole, regardless of who he was.

As he trashed the email, his military injury spasmed again. The tinnitus in his ears spiked. The ringing was deafening. He tapped two Tylenol Extra Strength gelcaps into his palm, popped them into his mouth and, with a swig of water, washed them down. After staring at the bottle, he took a third.

He remembered.

Life was good for his first two decades. No, better than that. Life was grand. Then everything went to hell and kept getting worse. Somewhere along the line he must've made a pact with the devil. He recalled the first time Satan came calling to collect his soul.

Chapter Seven: Harrisburg, Pennsylvania

Photo 17

CHAPTER EIGHT

Eighteen Years Ago

At 0430 hours, Private William Mathews stepped out of a barrack resembling an oversized outhouse and into the frigid air of Parwan Province in northeast Afghanistan. He was Bill to his family in Philadelphia. However, after arriving at Bagram Air Base a few weeks ago, his nickname became Doc Whiskey because his Army specialty as a medic was pronounced "sixty-eight whiskey."

He shivered in formation with the rest of his battalion and awaited orders. The day before, they were told how the US and the Northern Alliance had crushed the Taliban and took control of Kabul weeks earlier. But intelligence reports concluded Osama bin Laden and his leaders, plus about two hundred al-Qaeda fighters, had escaped to Shah-i-Kot Valley.

The soldiers were told to be proud. They were chosen to be part of the first US conventional force to fight in Afghanistan. This was their opportunity to destroy the savage terrorists responsible for 9/11.

The mission briefing didn't sugarcoat the risks but explained that a convoy of three hundred Pashtun militants would drive into the valley from the south to lead the ground assault. The two US infantry battalions named Task Force Rakkasan would be airlifted in along the eastern valley perimeter to block the enemy from escaping through the mountain passes into Pakistan. They'd be supported by eight Apache helicopters.[18] In advance, commandos would neutralize al-Qaeda defenses on the mountain ridges.

When asked if artillery would be deployed, the briefing officer claimed the terrain couldn't support it. His comeback was the brass expected al-Qaeda troops to surrender or run like the Taliban had as soon as the battle started. Operation Anaconda was supposed to last three days or less.

Everyone was pumped yesterday. This morning, Bill smelled fear oozing beneath the fifty pounds of full battle rattle worn by every man.

When given the command to board the helicopter, the soldiers from 1st Battalion marched single file up the back cargo ramp resembling alligator jaws.[19] They strapped into two rows of red jump seats shoulder to shoulder. An M4 carbine was wedged between their legs. As the tandem rotors of the massive CH-47 Chinook whirled, the copter rattled as if falling apart. Some tried yelling at each other, most wore earplugs and stared blankly, others tried napping, and a few paled while gritting their teeth. One blanched young man stifled tears.

The helo, along with five others, lifted off the tarmac. Bill felt the g-force when the Chinook made a tactical turn. The intense shaking kicked up dust and dirt. An earthy smell assaulted his nose. He tried distracting himself with the exposed pipes, wires and hoses weaved into the hull's steel skeleton. But during the ninety-minute flight, Bill kept recalling the fateful days that led to this one.

He was twenty and a junior at Penn State studying for a BS degree in biology. A full scholarship made it all possible, although he worked part-time in a local clinic for the cash and résumé-worthy experience. Coach Paterno said he had NFL potential. That was high praise for a linebacker coming from a football program nicknamed Linebacker U. During a goal-line stance against Minnesota in Beaver Stadium, Bill had stopped a running back from scoring yet suffered a debilitating ACL tear.

After surgery and a year of intense physical therapy, his knee recovered. But poor grades and an unwillingness to play sports cost him the scholarship. He quit school mid-semester. For nine months, he slept late at home and partied till dawn before becoming desperate.

On a lark, he walked into an Army recruiting center. They told him he had to commit for four years, but they would train him as a medic, and the GI Bill promised full college tuition. There hadn't been a US war in about a decade, so the risk-reward ratio seemed excellent. He signed up.

Bill squirmed beneath the flak vest, trying to get comfortable. He pushed up the drooping night vision goggles on the helmet. He did a mental inventory of the Unit One Pack on his back, hoping he had placed all essential medic supplies inside. He said a prayer. Nothing stopped the memories.

Five days after enlisting, he was in bed at his new girlfriend's apartment. She had little personality, but she was warm. While she was in the bathroom, he turned on the TV in time to see United Airlines Flight 175 crash into the World Trade Center's South Tower. They spent days riveted to live coverage. Shock and horror made him furious.

The subsequent six months were a whirlwind of pressure. Following ten weeks of basic training at Fort Jackson, he spent sixteen more at Fort Sam Houston for medic's Advanced Individual Training. When assigned to the 187th Infantry Regiment, he learned about mountain tactical warfare. But being molded into a soldier happened so fast he'd barely bonded with anyone before being shipped out. Maybe he knew by name ten of the thirty men who tensed up when hearing the announcement they were landing in five minutes.

The Chinook made an unexpected bank to the left. The infantrymen gasped and held on as the chopper looped around to reverse direction. In the heavy fog, the pilot had missed the southern valley entrance.

Nausea gripped Bill during the fast descent. The door gunners readied their M240 machine guns. Four wheels bounced twice when the helicopter came in hot. The men ran down the ramp and into a cloud of swirling dust. Enemy bullets appeared from nowhere. The fuselage was riddled with holes before the big bird lifted off. Bill dove for cover behind a boulder. He couldn't breathe through the debris plugging his nose.

The ground was ice-caked mud, the sky cloudy and dark, the wind was howling, the temperature couldn't be above 15° F, and confusion was rampant.

They had been told to expect Afghan civilians and warned combatants might be in the mix. But the valley was deserted. The assault was coming from the high ground. The enemy was entrenched on the mountain. His team were sitting ducks. They had just landed at the pointed end of the spear, the worst part of any battlefield.

Mortar rounds arced in the sky, whistled toward them and exploded in clouds of smoke. Machine-gun fire was unrelenting. An artillery battery opened up, raining down certain death. An Apache helicopter swept a crag and engaged with its 30mm Bushmaster Chain Gun but was repelled by rocket-propelled grenades. Where the hell were the Pashtun militants and bombing support? They were supposed to be the cavalry.

Bill couldn't move. He couldn't think until hearing the scream, "Medic!" The soldier was pinned down. Enemy fire filled the gap between Bill and his wounded friend.

A jihadist fighter unleashing bullets was standing on a ridgeline about two hundred meters away. Bill raised his M4. He locked the enemy in his sights and told his brain to fire.

Nothing.

The paralysis was reminiscent of buck fever the first time his father took him hunting in McKean County, Pennsylvania. His heart pounded, his hands shook, and his clammy palms made it difficult to hold the carbine.

Bill heard his father's coaching in the tree stand. He imagined a ten-point whitetail deer. He regulated his breathing while squeezing the trigger. The 5.56x45mm NATO bullet dropped the combatant. For the first time in Bill's life, he had taken a human life.

For twelve hours, Bill fought gallantly. He lost count of the al-Qaeda fighters he killed emerging from mountain caves, bunkers and trenches. His legs and back ached from dragging the wounded to safety, then treating their lacerations, trauma, hypothermia and hemorrhaging from gunshot wounds and shrapnel. His hands were blood-soaked.

Near sunset, all he remembered was curling into a fetal position as a fragmentation grenade dropped near him. At night, a Pave Hawk CSAR chopper extracted Bill. When he regained conscious-ness, a medical team subjected him to endless diagnostic tests.

A doctor told him he was lucky to be alive. Most of his injuries were minor: cuts, burns and several broken bones. The good news was the flak vest absorbed most of the shrapnel, protecting his vital organs. However, the blast velocity had damaged his spinal cord. The physician hoped for an incomplete injury, meaning the paralysis in his lower extremities would improve when the swelling rescinded around the lumbar and sacral nerves. Recovery would take months, maybe a year, maybe longer. Or he might never recover the feeling below his waist.

An hour later, a major was at his bedside. His enthusiasm was sickening. The officer assured Bill he'd receive a Purple Heart and maybe the Bronze Star Medal for heroism and bravery. There was fleeting acknowledgment of the wounded Bill treated. Instead, the major kept congratulating him on how many al-Qaeda soldiers he killed. His unabated praise was reminiscent of his father's proudest moments every time Bill posed behind a fallen deer.

Drugged, distraught and depressed, Bill lost his dream of saving lives. Something dark and sinister replaced his passion. Now, he had the rage to kill. The fury threatened to consume him.

Chapter Eight: Shah-i-Kot Valley, Afghanistan

Photos 18–19

CHAPTER NINE

Wednesday – Present Day

Anna Monteiro slumped on a park bench[20] alongside the Charles River, clutching an EMS blanket so it wouldn't slip off her shoulders. A towel covered her wet hair. Flashing strobe lights on several Boston police cars cast eerie blue lights flickering across first responders, investigators and curious onlookers. The whooshing from the oxygen mask was hypnotic. The plastic smell was horrid. She couldn't stop shaking.

Sergeant O'Neill placed a gentle hand on her back before squatting down to eye level. The act of genuine concern made Anna flinch. "Feeling any better?"

Anna shrugged.

The stocky woman sighed while rubbing her eyes. The police officer had always been professional, thorough and tenacious yet compassionate while investigating other acts of violence against Anna in past months. "I'd really hoped all this crap was behind you. It obviously isn't." After another deep sigh – this one sounded disapproving – she added, "I respect your decision not to go to the hospital. But do you still want to go home rather than someplace that might be safer?"

Anna removed the mask. "Yes. I used a paramedic's phone to call my parents. They'll be there in about an hour. And my father is going to hire bodyguards again. He thinks they'll arrive in the morning. Now I just want to crawl into my own bed."

"I understand. I've arranged for a couple patrolmen to take you home. Shifts will keep you safe until your private security takes over." Sergeant O'Neill paused before removing her ever-ready spiral notebook from her back pocket. "Sorry, but I must ask. Did your dad say if any bodyguards were on duty at the time of the shooting?"

"He said no."

"And you're totally sure Chris Davis wasn't involved in this?" The cop's stare resembled a polygraph examiner expecting to detect a lie.

"As I said, I haven't talked to or seen him since he started on that FBI task team." That answer was true. During the last conversation with Chris, Anna was delighted the siblings received conditional immunity in exchange for helping the task team dismantle Irene Shaw's network. However, the news had pissed off Sergeant O'Neill. She wanted them to rot in a cell. Was she fishing for any reason to pin this shooting on Chris so he'd go back to prison?

"Fine, I'll call the Philly FBI to establish his alibi. And you still have no idea who either shooter was?"

Anna shook her head, hoping the poor light in the waning minutes of dusk concealed her omission about Roundy. But the sergeant made her nervous by writing down every word.

The policewoman said, "Well, maybe we'll get a good image off the CCTV. Perhaps the FBI will be willing to run it through its facial recognition. I've heard their database contains over six hundred million people."

They probably couldn't ID Roundy while he was wearing his disguise. But maybe when he ran away without it? What would happen if the truth came out that she lied? Anna had to know the risks. "If you find the second shooter, will he be in trouble?"

"Maybe, maybe not. We'll see. But it's not good that he fled the scene."

"Well, I hope you can find him so I can thank him. He saved my life. He should get a medal." She sensed she was overplaying her innocence. *Could the officer detect the deceit?*

Anna pretended to be distracted as a coroner's van arrived on the scene. The dead man was still on his back. Only his legs were visible beneath a sheet.

The sergeant wasn't distracted. She kept probing. "Is there anything else you remember that might be helpful?"

"I've already told you and that homicide detective everything that happened."

"I'm sure you did. But sometimes a victim's memories improve after the initial shock wears off." Her insinuating tone implied she knew Anna was holding back information. "We'll talk again tomorrow at my precinct office, okay?" Sergeant O'Neill patted Anna on the knee. "Now go home and get some rest."

Anna sat in the back of a patrol car while being driven to her brownstone[21] on Commonwealth Avenue in Boston's Back Bay. When stepping out, she was haunted by the crazed hedge fund manager who had shot out the window and the sniper who had tried killing her on the doorstep months ago.

Gotta move out of this damn house soon. Very soon. Too many horrid memories.

While two policemen sat in the living room, she ran upstairs to her bedroom, stripped off the stinking, wet clothes and soaked in a hot shower. Despite the heat, she kept shivering.

Without taking time to dry off, she pulled on a robe, sat on the side of the clawfoot tub and used the burner phone Roundy gave her to call Chris. "I was just attacked again," she blurted when he answered.

"I know." His calm voice was in sharp contrast to her hysterics. "Roundy's already filled me in. Are you okay?"

"No, goddamn it. I'm not okay. I'm not the least bit okay."

"Anna, breathe. I'm here for you."

She gulped down staccato breaths as her lips quivered. Slowly, the panic subsided enough to talk. "Who's Roundy?"

With an apologetic tone, Chris said, "You know better than to ask me that. Let's just call him a friend."

"Well, thank him for me, will you? And thanks to you for saving me again. But how'd you know I needed help after all this time?"

His voice was monotonic. "Because someone killed Irene a couple days ago."

The realization was difficult to process. *Irene's really dead? Then why isn't he ecstatic?* "That's awesome news, right?"

"You're right, that is awesome news," he said without inflection.

"Did you do it?"

Chris didn't answer. The evasiveness suggested he wouldn't admit anything over the phone, yet his message was clear. She'd have to wait for the details.

"But why didn't you give me a heads-up that Roundy was protecting me?"

"Because I didn't want to worry you. Besides, I assumed you'd reject him like you did your father's bodyguards. You can be a bit pigheaded sometimes."

"Up yours, Davis." It was now clear Roundy had been watching over her for at least a week, maybe longer. She dared to ask, "Am I safe now?"

His hesitation gave the dreaded answer before he spoke. "No, it's probably worse."

"Oh, Jesus."

"Listen, you're probably fine as long as the police are at your house."

"How'd you know that?"

"Because Roundy is still on the job. How long are they staying?"

"Until my bodyguards show up in the morning."

"Okay, I'll tell Roundy to back off when they get there. But you can call him anytime, day or night, if you need him. His number's on your phone."

"Can't I just call you?"

"No, don't call me at this number again. Besides, I'll be gone for a while."

"How long?"

"I don't know."

"Where are you going?"

"I don't know."

"Damn it, Chris, why can't you just give me a straight answer?"

"I'm really sorry, but that's the way it has to be for now. Look, when I return, I'll call you on this burner phone. So don't let the police get it. In the meantime, you're in survivor mode again. Remember all the rules I taught you for staying alive. That includes staying off your personal phone so no one can track you."

"That's not a problem. It's at the bottom of the river."

"Even better. But if you use another phone, assume whoever you're calling is being monitored."

Anna's fingers whitened as she grasped the porcelain tub. "I'm not sure I can do this all over again."

"You can. I know you can. You're strong." His confidence was reassuring until he added, "Besides, you don't have a choice."

Her face paled. "Oh, Jesus. I'm scared. Terrified. And what about the police? They've been asking a whole bunch of questions. You remember Sergeant O'Neill? She's a bulldog for the truth. She keeps asking about the second shooter, and she wants me in her office again tomorrow."

Chris asked what she had told the police. When she finished explaining, he said, "That's good. Perfect, in fact. Were there any witnesses?"

"Not sure. It all happened so fast. But I did see the police talking to some people in the crowd."

"Don't worry about that. Just keep repeating the same story."

"But if O'Neill learns the truth, can I be charged with aiding and abetting a felon or, even worse, as an accessory to murder? If I'm implicated in anything, my plea deal is toast."

"I doubt it. You're the victim here. Act like one."

"That'll be easy," she said, but nothing about this horror was easy.

"Listen, I have to go. But before I do, one more piece of advice. Find a safer place to stay until this blows over."

"How long is that going to be?"

"I honestly don't know."

His words resonated like a death sentence.

Chapter Nine: Boston, Massachusetts

Photos 20–21

CHAPTER TEN

Philadelphia, Pennsylvania and
Wrightstown, New Jersey

Wednesday–Thursday

Michelle rotated her injured index finger, signaling Chris to finish the phone call. "Hurry up," she whispered, drowned out by the roar of two motorcycles racing through a yellow light on Arch Street in downtown Philadelphia.

He nodded in frustration. "I'm sorry, Anna. I really gotta go. Take care. Bye."

As he pushed End, Michelle asked, "How's she doing?"

"Not good. Not good at all." He seemed distraught and helpless.

"But at least she's safe?"

"For now, anyway. But if Wolfgang is seeking revenge against us for killing Irene, he'll keep trying. And Anna is the most vulnerable. God, I wish I was there for her."

She patted her brother's shoulder. There was nothing to say or do to lessen his anguish, but maybe her gesture sufficed to express empathy.

Chris forced a smile of appreciation. He pulled the SIM card from the burner phone, snapped it in half and threw the pieces into a trash can outside of the Federal Reserve Bank.[22]

They dodged traffic while crossing the intersection. After clearing security at the William J. Green Jr. Federal Building,[23] they dashed through the lobby and exchanged uneasy glances while riding the elevator up to the FBI offices. Special Agent Sloan Hamilton had called another impromptu yet mandatory meeting.

There were no guns in their faces when the doors opened, yet two agents flanked the head of the Sicarius Task Team. One of their suits was stretched from too much food and too little exercise. Hamilton wore her classic FBI uniform: all black except a white blouse. Her surly demeanor never changed.

"I thought we were done for the day," Chris said. "Kinda late for another get-together."

"Shut up, Chris," Hamilton demanded while an agent grabbed his arm.

Michelle said, "We've got to meet with Mason Webber in ninety minutes."

"Screw him," Hamilton responded.

"But his departure time isn't optional," Michelle countered with increased concern and urgency.

"And neither is this." Hamilton's determination was unrelenting. She motioned to the other agent. He told Michelle to step back into the elevator.

As Chris was being led away, he asked, "What's this all about?"

"I've got a few questions about the Boston shooting involving your girlfriend."

"Holy shit! What happened?" were the last words Michelle heard before the doors closed.

During the elevator ride, she worried about her brother and what Hamilton knew or was fishing for about the attack on Anna. Michelle was escorted down a hall where four women of about her age wore identical wigs. They were under the watchful eye of two policemen from the Federal Protective Service.

"Are you Michelle Barton?" one of them asked. She nodded. "Put on this rug, hold this sign, and wait over there with the others. And no talking."

One woman acknowledged her with raised eyebrows. The cheap perfume was god-awful. Her excessive makeup failed to conceal blackheads and pimples. The other women studied the floor. The agenda was clear: they were headed to a lineup.

Michelle's pulse elevated. She immersed herself in relaxation training. She succeeded as a policeman tapped his earpiece and said, "Yup, we've got a quorum." A downbeat later, he added, "Will do." He opened a door. "Ladies, please enter according to the number on your sign, hold it across your chest and stand shoulder to shoulder against the wall facing the window." He perfected their spacing and gave each an index card. The stifling room was hot and foul.

An intercom voice boomed, "Number one, step forward and read the first line on your card."

Suspect number one said, "Yes, hi. My name is Linda Madison. I have a ten o'clock appointment."

The faceless voice said, "Now read the second line."

"Is there a bathroom nearby?"

Those sentences were everything the disguised Michelle had said to the plastic surgeon receptionist on the morning Irene Shaw was killed. In fact, those were the only words the siblings had uttered at the clinic. They'd been silent while subduing the doctors and staff.

When Michelle's turn came, she recited the lines without the slight Scandinavian accent she used that day. She tried to convey an attitude of disinterested impatience while the other women took their turns.

Suspect three was asked to read the card again before they were dismissed. Obviously, the lineup was inconclusive, or better yet, the receptionist picked the wrong person.

Nice try, sucker breath, Michelle thought with a grin.

She was led back to the FBI floor and told to have a seat in a stiff upholstered chair that may have been fashionable in the seventies.

Fifteen minutes passed. Each moment risked their being late for Webber's meeting. Her biggest concern was about her brother.

When Chris walked down the hall beside Hamilton, Michelle tried reading his boyish face. The twinkle in those aquamarine eyes telegraphed he was okay.

Hamilton was snarly. "You two can go. Have a wonderful time on Webber's field trip. And when you get back, or should I say *if* you get back, I'll have enough evidence to throw your asses in jail forever."

"Thanks, Mom."

Michelle telepathically begged her brother to stop taunting Hamilton, but he kept going.

"We'll be good with Dad while we're gone. And we'll try sending you a postcard."

"You know what, Davis? You're a jerk."

"We love you too."

When the siblings exited the building, they shared what had happened. The consensus was they were in the clear ... for now. Michelle said, "I'm surprised Hamilton already knew that much about the Boston shooting."

"I'm not. It's pretty obvious the police, probably Sergeant O'Neill, called her."

"You don't think maybe Anna said something –"

Chris cut her off. "Not a chance. Not a chance in hell."

Maybe he was right, but maybe Anna had slipped up. Michelle thought better than pushing the point.

They raced three blocks down Arch Street. Center City was ominous at night. Too many dark corners harboring seedy characters intent on crime versus sharing brotherly love. Michelle's angst stemmed from the unknown about what Webber expected them to do.

They arrived at the designated address with five minutes to spare. In disbelief, they stared at the narrow, eighteenth-century brick building with dormer windows and a steep roof. This was the Betsy

Ross House,[24] where the famous upholsterer had sewn the first American flag. *What an odd place for a rendezvous.*

An Uber with blackout windows pulled up. They tried waving it off as a late-thirties brute exited the car. His chiseled face was stonelike. There was a nasty scar across the bridge of his crooked nose. A streetlight reflected off his polished bald head like a lighthouse beacon. His body fat measured less than ten percent. Despite the unseasonable chill, he wore a golf shirt displaying ostentatious muscles. His ego and arrogance were also on steroids.

The siblings were instructed not to bring luggage, not even toiletries. Michelle had insisted Chris follow Webber's orders. She wasn't surprised or offended when they were ordered to put their hands on the hood and spread-eagle. The pat-down was quick and professional, yet Chris hovered with concern. The man dropped their laptops, phones, wallets, watches and shoes inside a black garbage bag.

A woman emerged from the historic house wearing Puritan clothes – a linen skirt and jacket, white apron with a matching coif covering her hair. Michelle was astonished Webber had recruited the Betsy Ross impersonator. Without a word, she grabbed the bag with the siblings' possessions and hurried back inside. Michelle doubted the overhead security camera had captured the exchange.

Mr. Macho Man opened the car's back door, pointed and grunted a command to get in.

"Hi there, kids," Mason Webber said while leaning over the passenger seat. "You're punctual. That's a good start. You might get your stuff back, but maybe not. And later we'll fit you with swell new footwear. Sorry, Michelle, but they won't be a designer brand. Now remain quiet until given permission to talk, comprende?"

This man is such a misogynistic ass.

Chris blurted out, "Aren't you going to introduce us to your friend?"

Webber ignored the question by turning up the volume of "One

Day More" from *Les Misérables*. For over an hour, he wallowed in top tunes from musicals and operas, often waving his hands like a conductor. Chris fell asleep.

Michelle nudged her brother as the car turned off the New Jersey Turnpike. On the horizon, bright lights reflected off the cloudy night sky. Webber stopped the music as the driver picked up a BlackBerry. She had heard rumors that the government still used the antiquated phone brand for secure communications.

The driver tapped some keys, waited a couple of seconds and said, "Unit 9254 is approaching. Requesting clearance." After another pause, he added, "Thank you." He gave Webber a nod.

The guards waved them through the front checkpoint of McGuire Air Force Base before they proceeded to a hangar. A reinforced door rattled open as they approached and closed with a resounding thud. No one was inside. There was an overpowering stench of floor cleaner. Dominating the steel shed was an enormous gray military plane.

"What is this beast?" Chris asked, one of the few times she'd seen him in awe.

Webber said with pride, "A C-17 Globemaster III. Isn't she a beauty?"

Outside the car were two pairs of tactical boots. They matched those worn by the two men. "Put 'em on. I hope they're the right size," Webber said as if he couldn't care less. "I don't want you to stub your precious little toes inside the plane."

As the siblings laced up, the driver unloaded duffel bags, luggage and what appeared to be aluminum gun cases from the car trunk. Without effort, he carried the heavy loads during two trips into the plane.

Mason Webber stood motionless. He was characteristically stern, but casual from the neck down in a worn leather jacket and khaki pants. He was growing impatient. "Ticktock. Hustle up. Gotta go." When the loading was finished, he directed the siblings to move.

Walking up the aircraft's back cargo door was like being swallowed by Jonah's whale. Tethered to the steel floor were armored trucks and a tank, plus piles of crates stacked up to the twelve-foot ceiling. It was intimidating to sit among the two rows of twenty-seven jump seats lining each side of the aircraft. They were the only passengers.

Of course, Chris couldn't resist being a smart aleck. He turned toward Webber. "Is there dinner on this flight?"

"Yes, I believe tonight's entrée is French cuisine."

"Great. How 'bout beverage service with some pretzels?"

Webber tired of the banter. "Plug in your damn headset and shut up."

Michelle chuckled at how often Chris had been told that in the last couple of days.

The pilot's voice was piped into her ears as the plane's gigantic back cargo door closed. "Welcome, folks. Please buckle up. We're about to taxi. Travel time is approximately nine hours. I'm sorry to say there is no movie. So, as you've heard many times before, sit back, relax and enjoy the flight."

That seems unlikely, she thought while staring at the giant front tire of an Army transport truck. *This view is going to get old fast.*

The subdued lighting and drone of the engines lulled the three men to sleep. Chris snored. Michelle was restless. Two hours later, the female loadmaster approached her. The master sergeant leaned over. "There are a couple of bunks behind the flight deck. Would you be more comfortable there?"

Webber opened one eye. "She's fine right where she is. But I'd love to have a blanket and pillow." He gave Michelle a pompous smirk.

The bastard.

During the night, Michelle never saw the pilots. She assumed this was by design. The foursome was traveling as ghosts. This realization heightened her apprehension about the stealth mission. The stakes must be enormous.

In the morning, after Michelle used her finger to brush her teeth, the loadmaster asked if she'd help prepare the MREs. Michelle was clueless while staring at the four plastic bags of breakfast cold-weather meals.

Inside each Meal, Ready-to-Eat bag were brown, vacuum-sealed packages containing oatmeal, a breakfast skillet with hash browns, and instant coffee. Pouring in hot water and stirring with a plastic spoon made these tastebud-tempting delights come to life. On the side were tortillas, cheese spread, a protein drink and sugar cookies. At least the cookies were edible.

After the paper trays were removed, Webber struck his power pose in front of the siblings. "We'll be landing soon, so let's chat for a few minutes. First, let me introduce you to Shawn."

The brutish driver lifted his fingers in bored acknowledgment.

What a wussy name. No wonder he's worked so hard to be a tough guy.

"Shawn will assist with your assignment," Webber continued. "You'll always follow his orders as if they came from me. If you don't, then his orders are to, uh, manage the situation."

Shawn flashed a sinister wink.

"Two, your wallets are back in Philly. You won't get passports, driver's licenses or credit cards. You don't exist as far as the government is concerned. If you're pulled over by local authorities for any reason — even spitting on the sidewalk — we'll abandon you. There's no *nemo resideo* creed here."

So much for leaving no one behind.

Chris asked about health benefits.

Webber wasn't amused. "None, so I suggest you stay healthy." He cleared his throat, signaling Shawn to unlock a soft-sided zipper portfolio and remove two manila file folders. "Three, in a minute I'll hand you these. Notice they're marked Classified. Take that very seriously. Study the information inside. Memorize everything,

These briefing packages will not leave the plane."

Michelle raised her hand. "Do they fully explain the assignment?"

"No, you'll learn more when the time is right."

Chris said, "Those files look pretty thin. Before any commission, we always received detailed information about the target and their health, business, industry and schedule."

"That's nice, but you've had a job change, remember? Anything else? No?" He handed each of them a folder. "Here you go. Read fast. We touch down in a few minutes."

Michelle opened hers. Inside was a 3x5 color photo of a lean man whose handsome features resembled a distinguished statesman. His brow was pinched, his eyes glared, and his cheekbones were pronounced. Too much sun and booze had produced leathery skin and a bulbous nose. He radiated power and influence.

The first six words typed on the document were: Dimitri Yegorov is a Russian oligarch.

Chapter Ten: Philadelphia, Pennsylvania and Wrightstown, New Jersey

---

Photos 22–24

CHAPTER ELEVEN

The cargo plane's landing gear descended with a hydraulic whine and locked in place with a thud. As the engine's thrust slowed, Chris's anxiety rose. The "briefing package" in his lap was a quarter page of scant information. The intended target was ominous. He squirmed beneath the seatbelt harness.

Dimitri Yegorov was the sixty-one-year-old chairman of Iskop, an abbreviation of the Russian word *iskopayemoye*, meaning fossil. The non-state, multinational petroleum and natural gas company had a revenue of $95 billion USD (8.65 trillion Russian rubles) and net income of $7.6 billion. His traceable net worth had been $5.2 billion prior to sanctions but not including vast hidden assets.

Yegorov was described as an influencer of state policy, a trusted advisor and longtime friend of the Russian president, and godfather of his niece. When Chris read "Securing Dimitri Yegorov is of great importance to the national security of the United States," he understood the word *securing* was a euphemism for assassination.

Chris stared at Webber in disbelief. The cloak-and-dagger man was smug. After savoring the siblings' reactions to the gravity of their situation, he said with a sinister tone, "Welcome to The Club, kids. Won't this be fun?"

Chris tried to appear composed but failed. Michelle's pale complexion contorted. Yegorov wasn't a routine scumbag assigned by

Irene Shaw. He was an integral part of Russia's inner circle. A botched success or failure could be tantamount to an act of war.

Michelle was right. This is a suicide mission.

"I'm sure you have lots of questions, but now is not the time." Webber nodded to Shawn. The buff lapdog snatched up the briefing files and disappeared behind the tethered truck. "So buckle up. We're about to land at Aviano Air Base. And in case you're wondering, that's about one hundred kilometers north of Venice."

The C-17 Globemaster III landed on the tarmac, taxied across the airfield and came to a stop. Reverse thrusters moved the enormous plane backward before the engines shut down. The lowering cargo ramp revealed another empty hangar except for a black Fiat Tipo Cross hatchback. Of course, the windows were tinted. Shawn loaded the nondescript car in minutes, sat behind the wheel and waited for his boss to get comfortable. Webber adjusted the passenger seat to rob Chris of legroom. They drove off the military base without clearing customs or undergoing an immigration check, another demonstration of Webber's clandestine clout.

"Where're we going?" Michelle dared to ask.

Webber stared out the windshield at the midday sun. "You'll find out in about eleven hours. If you get hungry, there should be sandwiches and bottles of water in a paper bag at your feet. Eat sparingly. That's your lunch and dinner. And one important rule for the trip: absolutely no talking, comprende?" He inserted earbuds, folded his hands and leaned back. A tune from *42nd Street* was barely audible, the first of countless instrumentals he listened to during the ride.

The drive on the motorway was monotonous, creating too much time for wandering gloom. Attempts to redirect his focus on traffic and scenery were short-lived. As the passing road signs displayed city names in northeast Italy, Slovakia and Croatia, Chris tried picturing their locations on a map. The game offered fleeting distractions.

The two pit stops at petrol stations were a welcome relief for the legs and bladder but did nothing to ease the sense of peril.

Every kilometer was cramped drudgery. The burning, unanswered question was: *With all the CIA's resources, why did Webber choose us for this assignment?* There was one logical answer: *We're expendable.*

Near midnight, a whiff of the Adriatic Sea woke Chris. He lowered the window to savor the cool breeze. The sky was dark and threatened rain, yet lights from boats and distant waterfront towns twinkled across the inky water. Shawn rubbed his eyes in a final attempt to endure the grueling drive. Chris enjoyed seeing the boor's vulnerability to exhaustion.

After forty minutes of winding along a coastal road through quaint seaside villages, and less than a kilometer after passing a yellow sign marking the entry into Perast, Montenegro,[25] Shawn tapped the brakes, strained to see, put on the car's hazard blinker and clicked a garage door opener above the visor. A metal gate swung to the side. As he inched down a sloping driveway, the metal gate returned to the locked position.

Webber raised his hand toward Chris and Michelle in the backseat. "Wait."

Shawn bounded out, dashed down a flight of stairs and disappeared on the side of a narrow stone house. An exterior light came on, followed by several on the first floor. When he returned, he nodded toward Webber and began emptying the trunk. Chris's offer to help was rebuked.

The house was suspended in a bygone century. Exposed wooden beams lined the plaster ceiling, hints of mold discolored the mortar of the rough stone walls, the furniture and appliances were archaic, and the few modern amenities were rudimentary. A musty odor was pungent.

Webber was equally unpleasant. "Your rooms are on the third floor. Chris, you're on the left, Michelle on the right. Get some sleep. Tomorrow you go to work."

The siblings exchanged uneasy good nights.

Chris entered a dank bedroom with a small desk and an unstable nightstand next to a rusted single bed. Two suitcases sat on the warped wooden floor. One contained toiletries and nondescript clothes that appeared too big. The other was a hodgepodge of materials for creating disguises. The pile resembled a ghoulish Halloween costume box.

Chris drew back a yellowed linen curtain and pushed open double-sided windows. Three tiers of clay tile roofs and a pair of old church bell towers overlooked the Bay of Kotor.[26] Gentle waves lapped against the seawall. Tethered boats bobbed along the waterfront. Although the picturesque village was serene and magical, he expected a sleepless night. After crawling into bed and pulling up a threadbare blanket, he fixated on the ceiling and worried about Anna.

✦✦✦

Before sunrise, Shawn pounded on the door. "Wake up, damn it. Report downstairs. Now!"

Chris plodded to the first floor wearing yesterday's clothes. Webber sat at a rickety kitchen table pouring Turkish coffee from a copper cezve into a delicate porcelain cup. Chris was served tepid tea in a chipped mug.

When Michelle arrived, Shawn served everyone a quarter slice of a quiche-like pie filled with spicy meat and spinach. On the side were a wedge of goat cheese, two deep-fried doughballs, a grape leaf roll with rice, and a couple of yogurt dollops. The breakfast was delicious, yet Chris felt like a death row inmate eating his last meal.

When the dishes were cleared, Webber announced, "Playtime is over. Time to get down to business." He produced a laptop and spun the screen toward the siblings, showing a gleaming white yacht with four decks above the waterline, a helicopter on the bow and a swimming pool in the stern.

"This is the *Grand Dutchess*, Dimitri Yegorov's 210-foot mega yacht. This forty-five-million-dollar beauty has a crew of fifteen, seven staterooms, plus an owner's suite on the upper level that's thirty-eight feet wide. Shortly after leaving Marina Port Vell in Barcelona, the vessel's AIS transponders were deactivated. Despite going dark, our satellites have tracked it for twelve hundred nautical miles. The *Grand Dutchess* will dock at the Port of Tivat on the outer Bay of Kotor early this afternoon. The luxury marina caters to the social elite and their dinghies measuring up to five hundred feet long."

Before continuing, Webber said thanks to Shawn for refilling his porcelain cup. "If Yegorov stays true to his previous visits, he'll spend a few days throwing lavish parties. There's a huge contingent of super-rich Russians living in the area. Then he'll probably sail to Turkey, another safe haven for big-boy Russian yachts. So here is your assignment." He paused for dramatic effect. "You have seventy-two hours to determine the best silentcide techniques."

"That's bullshit." Chris objected less to the mission – he had assumed the goal since reading the briefing package – and more to the deadline. "Making a death appear from natural causes takes time, lots of time. An expedited commission was a week. We typically had several weeks. Three days is impossible."

Webber returned a defiant stare. "Up your game, Davis. This is the major league."

"No, it's a bush league. Why not just send in a sniper? All he does is extend a bipod, shoot from hundreds of meters away, then sips cocktails by five. Silentcide is the art of undetected killing. One takes brawn, the other brains. It's the difference between boxing and chess."

"You done with your little rant? Because you can stomp your feet and hold your breath all you want, but the timeframe won't change. You have seventy-two hours."

"Then for God's sake, at least give us something more to go on than that pathetic briefing."

Webber deflected the insult with a click of the mouse, displaying a directory. "You'll both be given a laptop with this cache of extensive intel." The file names were: Company Info, Career, Political

Affiliations, Investments, Family, Medical Records, Food & Drink Favorites, Daily Habits, Sinful Habits, Montenegro Friends, Yacht Specs & Floor Plan, Crew Dossiers, Satellite Archives and Live Drone. Chris was impressed but refused to admit it until reviewing the reports.

"By the way," Webber said, "the internet has been disabled. Let Shawn know if you want to conduct a search."

Michelle raised her hand. "We often use pharmaceuticals to exploit the medical maladies of our targets."

Webber replied, "Just tell me what you need."

"I'm sure you have ground rules," Chris said. "What are they?"

"Glad you asked. You're free to go anywhere unescorted, but you must always wear a Garmin GPS tracking watch and a disguise. You'll be given a smartphone that's been locked down to only allow calls and texts to our pre-programmed numbers. They also have an interactive GPS map and a few apps that may come in handy. There are two scooters in back for transportation. Anything else?"

"I seem to have misplaced my wallet," Chris said. "Can we have some money?"

"Your care packages will include two hundred euros in small denominations." Webber scanned from side to side as if ready to field another question. There weren't any. "Well then, before we break huddle, I have a final pro tip. Yegorov travels alone, trusts no one, never leaves the yacht, and has armed guards securing him 24/7. That could be a bit problematic, don't you think?"

No shit.

The siblings retreated to their bedrooms. Chris spent a couple of hours absorbing the intel. The information quality exceeded anything he had received from Irene's facilitators. The live drone surveillance was impressive. The 3D images could even detect the weapons being carried by the patrolling guards on the yacht.

There was a gentle knock on the door. Michelle was unrecognizable. She had long black hair in a braided ponytail. Sunglasses reflected atop a complexion riddled with acne. The bodysuit added thirty pounds beneath her drab blouse and paisley pants. "I gotta get out of here. Can we take a walk?"

"Sure. I'll meet you downstairs in a few minutes."

Chris slapped on a reddish-brown shaggy wig and mustache with a goatee. He used a foundation and a bronzer for a rugged tan, a brow pencil to darken the eyebrows and enhance his crow's feet, plus a blend of two blushes to create puffiness below his now hazel eyes. A bulky sweater beneath a denim jacket helped broaden his shoulders and chest.

They walked in silence down a long, uneven staircase wedged between walls and clinging vegetation until reaching the water-front promenade.[27] Limestone mountains surrounded the idyllic village. The Venetian-style, three-story buildings were built with beige stones, white shutters and orange roofs. Several were former seafarers' palaces. Two islets floated in the shimmering bay.[28] The warm sunshine was soothing.

"I can't do this," Michelle declared, breaking the silence. "I just can't."

"Lower your voice, will ya?"

She leaned into his ear. "I vowed to stop killing. Now this ass-hole wants us to off a Russian oligarch in three days. It's ludicrous. I should've listened to you when you wanted to run after killing Irene. I'm sorry. I'm really sorry." With increased desperation, she pleaded, "But we can still run before it's too late, right?"

"No, we can't. Listen, it's one thing to outrun the FBI in the States. It's ten times harder to hide from the CIA in Europe with no money, no credentials and nowhere to go. We don't stand a chance. And Webber was serious about throwing us into a deep dark hole if we don't comply. I don't know who this guy is, but he's obviously very connected and powerful. He makes Irene Shaw look like a bumbling fool."

"So we've replaced one evil master with someone worse?"

"Yeah, pretty much," he concluded. "But don't worry. We'll get through this together. We always do."

Michelle leaned against his shoulder while struggling to control her emotions.

"Let it out," Chris said with compassion.

"No, I'm okay."

"I said let it out."

She raised her head. "I'll be fine."

He sensed Michelle was embracing their reality, compartmentalizing her feelings and preparing to get back in the game. She was comfortable sharing her self-doubts with him but also capable of suppressing her insecurities as a consummate professional. And confidence was key to their survival. But they'd need more than confidence to stay alive.

Chapter Eleven: Perast, Montenegro

Photos 25–28

CHAPTER TWELVE

Eastham on Cape Cod, Massachusetts
Friday

Hints of reds, oranges and yellows shimmered in the trees. The ocean breeze was crisp and clean. A grasshopper made a hasty retreat. Anna Monteiro raised her face into the sunshine and listened to songbirds, struggling to be distracted. Her troubled thoughts persisted.

She glanced at the Three Sisters of Nauset.[29] The near-identical lighthouses had white cedar shakes that flared like petticoats. Their lanterns resembled black pillbox hats. They were Mom's favorites of the fourteen lights on Cape Cod. Anna had hoped the national park would bring her comfort. It didn't.

Her head pounded, her gut ached, her eyes burned, and her calf muscles wouldn't stop twitching. Caustic fear had corroded her ability to perform simple tasks without suffering traumatic flashbacks or dark bouts of mourning. She was nervous and emotionally numb. There was little hope things would improve, only expectations they would worsen.

Two fiftyish bodyguards flanked her. They wore windbreakers emblazoned with a security company logo to conceal their weapons. Their heads swiveled on high alert. They were a constant reminder of her peril.

A rare smile crossed her face as Liz Walker approached the concrete path. Her boss's shoulder-length red hair and bangs danced in the wind. The Longfellow BioSciences COO wore a pantsuit with practical dress sneakers. No doubt she had left work in Cambridge to make the hundred-mile drive and would return to work after their meeting. Only a best friend would make such a sacrifice on short notice.

When Liz spotted Anna, she waved and quickened her pace. A bodyguard intervened. With an extended hand, palm out, he demanded, "Stop!"

Liz halted in confusion.

"She's okay, Stuart," Anna said.

"But your father's orders are to frisk …"

"I said she's okay. So please step aside."

"Yes, ma'am."

Liz sized up both men and hung back until Anna opened her arms. Liz rushed forward for a heartfelt hug. Anna savored the affection and support.

Liz whispered, "Are you okay?"

Anna sighed, pushed back, stared into Liz's worried green eyes and moaned, "No, I'm not okay. I'm not the least bit okay. I'm an emotional train wreck. I feel like dead weight struggling to survive. So would you do me a favor?"

"Sure, anything."

"Never, ever ask me that question again." The rant intensified. "I hear it all day, every day. I always lie by saying I'm fine. But I'm not. So assume my life is a living hell until I tell you otherwise."

Liz was speechless.

The anger deflated from Anna's shoulders. "Jesus, I'm sorry. I shouldn't have snapped at you."

"There's nothing to apologize for."

"Yes there is. You drove all this way and the first thing I do is bite your head off. I'm sorry. Thanks for coming."

"No problem. You'd do the same for me."

Liz was right. Anna would do the same. "Now I've gotta ask. Were you followed?"

"I don't think so."

With a sharp tone, Anna said, "You're either sure or you're not."

"You're kinda freaking me out here. This feels like a spy novel."

"It's worse because it's real. You get very, very paranoid after being shot at so many times."

Liz's white complexion paled despite her rose blush. "Nobody followed me."

"Good." Anna's hypervigilant radar detected people entering the grounds, jeopardizing their privacy and maybe her safety. "Let's go for a walk to Nauset Light. It's a beautiful lighthouse about a quarter mile from here."

They set off on a narrow, well-groomed path shielded from Cable Road by a canopy of overgrown trees. An occasional leaf drifted to the ground. Piles of fallen leaves rustled and crunched underfoot. Anna loved autumn strolls. This was her favorite season. Today, her nerves were fried.

One bodyguard took point. Stuart followed close behind.

"I've got to tell you," Liz said after a few minutes of silence. "I first got worried when you didn't show up for work, then spooked when your letter mysteriously arrived at home."

"My older brother delivered that. I couldn't think of another way to ask you to meet here."

"You couldn't call, email or text?"

"No, not without being traced."

"Can people really do that?"

"Absolutely. They already have, multiple times. So my life depends on keeping my location secret."

Liz digested the gravity of what she heard before changing the subject. "I saw on the news about the shooting on the Charles Esplanade. I had no idea that was you. That must've been terrifying. What the hell happened?" Liz listened in horror as Anna explained. "Did they catch the second shooter?"

"No, and I hope they don't."

"Why not?"

"One, he saved my life. Two, the police would probably arrest him for murder. And three, and this part you have to keep absolutely secret, promise?"

"Of course. We've always kept each other's secrets."

"The shooter is a friend of Chris who agreed to protect me."

"No way! You're still talking with Chris? I thought you ended that months ago."

"I did, but he's still watching out for me."

"But why?"

Anna's irritation boiled to the surface. "Damn it, because someone is still hell-bent on killing me, that's why. But now it's a vendetta for the murder of Irene Shaw, that woman I told you about who controlled Chris and his sister since they were kids."

While struggling to manage blowing curls, Liz hesitated to ask, "Is it over now?"

"No, not according to Chris."

"My God. What are you going to do?"

"The first thing I did was move out of my brownstone and into a Cape summer cabin near here that belongs to friends of my folks. Now I'm living with Mom, Dad, a brother and rotating shifts of bodyguards."

"That sounds clubby," Liz said with a tense chuckle.

"You have no idea. It's suffocating."

"Well, don't worry about work. Take off all the time you need."

"I appreciate that, but it'll be a while. My attention span is about five whopping minutes. I can't focus on a thing."

"No hurry. When you feel up to it, maybe you can ease back in by working remotely."

Anna stomped a foot in frustration. "Liz, you still don't get it. I can't work remotely. They'd find me in a heartbeat."

Struggling to find a solution, Liz said, "Can't the police do something?"

"They're investigating the last shooting, but that won't help me much going forward."

"How 'bout the FBI?"

"That's the role of the task team Chris and Michelle are on, so hopefully they can do something. But that could take months, maybe longer."

"What are you going to do in the meantime?"

"That's one of the things I wanted to talk about." Anna paused, debating how to say it. Hoping not to enrage Liz, she blurted, "I'm thinking about going back with Chris."

Liz's feet locked mid-step. Her green eyes widened. "Are you out of your damn mind? He's an assassin, for God's sake."

"Shhh, keep your voice down, will ya? But yeah, he is, and those skills are what've kept me alive."

Liz's brow creased. "Isn't that the job of these two guys?"

Anna looked back. "Hey, Stuart, give us a little more space, will you?" When the bodyguard dropped back, Anna said to Liz, "In theory, yes, but they're no match against the people after me."

"I assume they're armed, so why not?"

"Look at 'em. Do you really think they could handle ambushes like what happened in Québec, Montreal and Boston? I doubt it. But Chris did."

"That's great, and you know I'm thrilled you survived, but Chris is toxic."

Anna's neck cords tightened. "Don't say that. You don't know him."

"Is that the Stockholm syndrome talking?"

"Oh, please, that was a legal defense to keep my ass out of jail."

"So you do have feelings for him?"

"I did, but ..."

Liz interrupted. "You do, don't you? I can see it on your face."

"No, I just want to keep breathing."

"Cut the crap. It's me you're talking to. There's more going on here. What is it?"

"Okay, here's the thing." Anna pulled the jacket tight across her chest. "Chris is the only person who really knows what I'm going through and how to handle it. But just as important, maybe more so, he's also a great listener and compassionate."

"You mean he's good in bed."

"No, damn it."

Liz flashed that knowing bestie smile.

"Well, okay, yes, he was," Anna admitted with an embarrassed giggle. "But that's not it. He's the only man who cares more for me than himself. He's my selfless champion."

"Why do you need some guy telling you how good you are? I tell you that all the time."

"It's not the same and you know it. You've been married to a wonderful guy for what, fourteen years? He's always there for you, always supportive. I have no one. And, uh, well, Chris would sacrifice anything for me."

"Anna, this isn't a dating app. Give me one good example of what the hell you're talking about."

"Okay, sure, I wasn't going to tell you this, but he saved Longfellow."

"Say what?"

"Yeah, I know for a fact he bribed Robert Nole to have Fármaco buy out Longfellow when it was near bankruptcy. And later, when that asshole started suffocating the life out of your company, Chris bribed him again. That's when Nole grandly announced" – Anna flashed air quotes – "'Longfellow BioSciences is a welcomed new member of Fármaco's pharmaceutical portfolio and will have a critical role going forward in our mission to cure cancer.'"

Liz struggled to process the information. "I can't believe this." She raised her eyes. "That's why Nole did the surprising one-eighty?"

"Exactly."

"How did Chris bribe him?"

"I don't know. I was afraid to ask."

"But why would he do that?"

"Because he believes in me and, by extension, my passion for your cancer technology and our shared dream of saving people."

"That's awesome, it really is, but what's he get out of it?"

"Nothing. In fact, he didn't even tell me about it. His sister did. That's the kind of guy he is."

"Why didn't you tell me about this before?"

"Because I didn't think you'd understand."

"You're right. I don't." Liz stepped in front of Anna, stopping her at the path leading to Nauset Light.[30] She reached out to hold hands. "Listen, I've known you for over half of our lives. You're a sister to me. But frankly, I can't understand or relate to anything you're going through. And I have no idea how to help."

Anna squeezed her friend's fingers. "You already have by being here."

"That's fine, but are you looking for my blessing to go back with Chris?"

"No, I'm not even sure he'll take me back after I ratted him and his sister out to the FBI."

Liz cocked her head in confusion. "You mean getting back together wasn't his idea?"

"No, we haven't even talked about it."

A bicyclist sped toward them on the road. A helmet and sunglasses obstructed his face. He reached into the handlebar bag and pulled out a black metallic object.

"Gun!" the front bodyguard screamed while pointing his pistol. Stuart tackled Anna. She hit the ground. Skin ripped from her palms. A stone embedded in her knee. Suart's body weight was crushing.

The biker swerved, lost control, skidded across the asphalt, tumbled, and slammed into a wooden fence. Liz froze in fear.

The man writhed in pain as the bodyguard pressed a shoe against his neck and frisked him. After searching the grass, fenceline and bicycle, the bodyguard sheepishly admitted, "It was just a cell phone."

Anna sobbed.

This was a false alarm. But what about the next time? Is there a bullet waiting for me?

Chapter Twelve: Eastham on Cape Cod, Massachusetts

Photos 29–30

CHAPTER THIRTEEN

Friday

Wolfgang propped his ostrich cowboy boots on Irene Shaw's cherrywood desk at the Harrisburg safehouse. He was engrossed in *Collectible Automobile Magazine*. The article was fascinating. It showcased the top ten celebrity car collectors. Of course, Jay Leno was number one. The value of his cars and motorcycles exceeded fifty million dollars. Surprisingly, Jerry Seinfeld was third. Apparently, being a successful comedian meant laughing all the way to the bank.

Wolfgang slipped into a recurring fantasy about what he'd do after acquiring Irene's fortune locked in her laptop. He didn't want a big house – too much to clean and maintain – or a trophy girlfriend – too much to tolerate and maintain. Perhaps some travel would be nice, especially to a Caribbean island during Pennsylvania winters.

The ideal investment would be to collect cars, especially the classics from the fifties – tailfins, shiny chrome and bright colors – and muscle cars from the sixties – two-seaters, powerful V8s, fast and sexy street machines. He imagined buying neglected barn-find vehicles, restoring them to factory condition, and attending car shows, or just driving around while watching people watch him.

There was a knock on the office door. "What is it?" He dropped his legs to the floor, sat up straight, shoved the magazine into a drawer, and grabbed a file to appear busy.

"I have lunch for you, sir," Pierre said.

"Come in."

The young manservant carried a banquet on a silver platter with Brutus by his side. The Afghan hound's eyes were fixated on the food. The double California burger was stacked with fresh lettuce, homegrown tomatoes, red onions, two strips of bacon and American cheese topped with Thousand Island dressing, all wedged between a fresh sesame seed bun. Bock beer was in a frosted mug. The first onion ring was fantastic. Crispy outside, juicy inside. Perfection. Irene's incessant raving about this boy was justified. Eating his food was the best part of the day. Everything else sucked.

"Can I get you anything else, sir?"

"Not for now," Wolfgang said with his mouth full. He threw a pickle spear to the dog.

"Very well." Brutus pranced behind the retreating butler. "Oh, by the way, Jacob would like some of your time."

"Tell him to wait ten minutes," Wolfgang said while savoring another bite. He now understood why Irene was cranky when he interrupted her life's little pleasures. He used a cloth napkin to dab away the burger juice dripping down his chin stubble.

The news this morning wasn't good. Frank claimed he couldn't identify the runner who shot John the chauffeur at the Charles Esplanade. Wolfgang questioned how hard he tried. Frank also said his "friendly chats" with the law firm's managing partner, chief financial officer and Irene's former assistant failed to produce her passwords, even after "significant persuasion."

Another disappointment was only three of the six assassins handpicked to kill Chris, Michelle and Anna had responded to his email. He was dumbfounded why the others weren't motivated by the generous bounty. The reason became obvious. Wolfgang didn't have the clout he had when Irene was behind him. No one ever said no to Irene Shaw.

Jacob Conners burst through the door. The teenager was still dressed like shit.

Wolfgang stood, gripped the pistol on the desk for intimidation, and screamed, "You will never, and I repeat, never enter this room without knocking. Got that?"

"Uh-huh." The twerp's startled stare resembled a mugshot.

"That's yes, sir."

"Yes, sir."

"And when I tell you to start dressing like a human being, I expect you to do it. In fact, you will always follow my orders." He rotated the gun toward Jacob. "Or else." Wolfgang couldn't believe he was relegated to disciplining this brat. Whatever happened to managing the vast network Irene had promised him? "What do you want?"

Jacob grinned. "A big burger like that."

Good God almighty. "Too bad. I assume you want to tell me you found Irene's passwords at her mansion."

"No, but I tried, bro. Like, I really did. I looked yesterday afternoon and night and like two hours this morning. The place is a total bust. The FBI must've took everything. Maybe vandals too. There's beer cans and red Solo cups like all over."

"Did you find anything at all?"

"Yeah, a hidden panel in Irene's bedroom." Jacob snickered. "The closet was filled with like S&M stuff and like real skanky sex toys."

Wolfgang cringed at the mental image of a seventy-two-year-old dominatrix. But why not? She was also an alpha female with her clothes on.

The mobile on the desk rang. Caller ID said Frank's Cell. Wolfgang swiped Accept and placed the phone to his ear. "What do you want?"

A sultry woman said, "Why didn't you answer my email?"

Taken aback, Wolfgang scrambled to identify the voice. He knew it from somewhere. "Who the hell is this?"

"Why, The Commander, of course. I had hoped your lack of response to my email was merely due to some oversight."

"Screw you. I won't do your assignment. We're out of business."

"Oh dear, what an awkward situation. There will be consequences." A hideous cackle followed before the line disconnected.

Adrenaline pumped through his tight chest. Fingernails dug through his short black hair.

"You okay?" Jacob asked.

"Get out," Wolfgang yelled. "Now! And close the damn door."

How did that woman get this burner number? Who the hell is The Commander?

A synapse from his youth fired in his brain. Wolfgang and his younger brother grew up watching classic Disney movies on VHS. The caller's synthesized voice, cadence and vocabulary sounded like Maleficent, the mistress of evil from *Sleeping Beauty*. This was no accident. The Commander was imitating the animated villain who resembled Irene.

Irene had dominated Wolfgang since they had met eleven years ago. He shivered.

The phone call felt like her cold dead body was still in control.

CHAPTER FOURTEEN

Philadelphia, Pennsylvania
Eleven Years Ago

"Tim is dead," wailed the mother of William Mathews.

"Nooo!" Bill screamed, melting in denial and grief in the 103-degree Afghan heat. "What happened?" The sandblasting wind made it difficult to hear. He rushed behind a rusted corrugated shed, squatted, and stuck a finger in his ear. "I asked what happened?"

The satellite phone delay was infuriating. Mom's tearful explanation was difficult to hear over the static. "He was mugged and murdered last night while walking home."

Bill's younger brother was the gifted sibling. Tim was a month away from a master's in electrical engineering from Temple University and had a lucrative job offer.

Mom had always worried Bill would be the one to die young. Her worry was justified. Bill would've exchanged his wretched thirty-year-old life for his brother's. Tim had a bright future. Now that future was gone.

Bill spent a day trying to secure a sanctioned leave. When unsuccessful, he went AWOL and flew home from Baghdad where he had worked for a private military company for almost six years. After Operation Anaconda in Afghanistan, his yearlong recovery had been grueling. Although his physical health improved, but not without lasting disabilities, his mental health declined. He couldn't hold a job or his booze.

Six months after President Bush declared "mission accomplished" in the Iraq War – which sparked chaos and civil war – Bill was recruited to become a medic for armed mercenaries who protected convoys in Iraq. At last, someone wanted him.

The pay was good, up to $300 a day. The reenlistment bonuses were generous. But the real money came when he partnered with Colombian mercenaries to sell medical supplies and drugs on the black market to Iraqi insurgents. Countless palms were greased along the way, all at the expense of the Department of Defense.

Bill's share of the profits helped support his widowed mother. She never asked where the money came from but was always grateful. He also paid for his brother's education so he would graduate debt-free. That dream died when Tim bled out in North Philadelphia. The mental image was crushing. The anger was suffocating.

Bill dreaded walking up the stairs of his boyhood home.[31] He stood on the sagging wooden stoop, hesitated, and opened the front door. Mom collapsed in his arms. Her hair was a mess, her house-dress was wrinkled, and her eyes were puffy and bloodshot. Despair had etched grooves on her face. The deep wrinkles weren't there when he saw her two years ago at Dad's funeral. "Promise never to leave the country again," she kept saying. "You're the only family I have left."

Tim's girlfriend was also devastated. Torment had swallowed her charm, beauty and wit. Her quivering pain was dreadful to watch. Every attempt to provide comfort was meaningless. In hysterics, she pointed to a modest ring on her finger. "We were engaged. We were going to tell everyone at Tim's graduation." Two bright futures died with a single bullet.

Bill regretted visiting the crime scene. There was a faded brown stain on the sidewalk in front of a mini market.[32] Someone had tried washing away the blood of the brother he loved. Apparently, death was bad for a retail business.

The police were worthless. No witnesses, no suspects, only speculation that the assailant was a drug addict, a transient, or a gang member who wanted to kill someone white. "You just have to be patient," the cop said. "It's under investigation. We'll find whoever did this, I promise." But the exhaustion in the homicide detective's eyes promised otherwise. It was obvious Tim's death would soon become a dead end.

Days of incessant media coverage and public outrage were evaporating in the revolving news cycle. Bill generated lots of leads with neighborhood posters and a reward. According to the police, a few tips were credible, but none generated a viable suspect. The detective's tone suggested he resented the extra work Bill had created.

The celebration of life was a blur of sympathy and condolences. For two hours, well-intentioned people struggled with ineffective words of compassion. No one provided solace. Bill was the last to leave the funeral home. He approached the open coffin, stroked his brother's hair, caressed his cheek and held his rigid hand. "I will avenge you."

During the first week of Bill's intensive investigation, he spoke with ordinary people – neighbors, students and passersby, as well as store employees and customers. For the next ten days, he switched to the dark side – junkies, hookers, homeless and gang members. Everyone was clueless, either from apathy, fear, loyalty or they genuinely didn't know.

On day eighteen, Bill got a break. He spotted a skinny street punk hustling money from rolled-down car windows before the customers drove nearby to get their dope. When he approached, the punk ran. He didn't get far. Bill slammed him against a dumpster.

"Why'd you run?"

"Why ya think? Don't need no shit from a stinkin' pig."

"I'm not a cop, just want answers." Bill shoved Tim's picture in his face.

Terror or guilt enlarged the punk's pupils, but he said with defiance, "Don't know nothin' 'bout no shooting."

"I never said anything about a shooting." He bashed the punk's head against a wall. "What do you know?"

"I said nothin', so go fuck yahself."

Brandishing the Ruger LCP was persuasive. Bill had a name and address in fifteen seconds.

The same pocket pistol rested in his lap while sitting in the car outside of Pit Bull's home.[33] Although dilapidated – the roof sagged, paint was peeling, windows were broken, the padlocked front door was boarded, and exposed wires dangled – this had to be Pit Bull's parents' rowhouse; no street soldier could afford it. While waiting, Bill debated whether to beat out a confession first or just shoot the bastard and be done with it.

When a mail truck pulled up, he ducked and peered over the dash as the carrier dropped off a package. Bill had an inspiration. *Why sacrifice yourself? Maybe there's a way to get revenge without being caught.* When the coast was clear, he used a towel to lift the package from the step. He sneaked it into his mom's basement and went to work.

He spent thirty minutes removing the packaging tape. Inside was a wireless game controller for an Xbox 360. He smiled. *Of course Pit Bull was a gamer.*

Bill found a druggie's discarded syringe, soaked it in excrement overnight, and wedged the tip of the hypodermic needle into the base of the gamepad. Now all he needed was luck. Hopefully, a deep finger prick would allow sufficient E. coli bacterium, plus whatever other germs and drugs were on the needle, to enter the bloodstream to cause septicemia. At first, the sepsis symptoms might resemble the flu. But if left untreated, the infection could lead to organ failure, shock and death.

Within ten days, Pit Bull was dead. A week later, an FBI SWAT team rammed the front door of Bill's mother's house at two in the morning. After agents threw him to the floor at gunpoint, he was shackled, arrested, booked, and jailed at the Federal Detention Center.

The FBI's interrogation ended when Bill demanded a lawyer. By the second day, a public defender hadn't arrived. He was despondent when roused from his bunk, handcuffed and trudged to a private attorney-client room. Ten minutes elapsed before the locked door opened.

In strolled a stunning bejeweled woman wearing flashy high heels and a black dress that hugged every curve. Her perfume was sensual. Judging from the silver-white, tied-back hair and the veins on her hands, she was older than Bill's mother. However, her body was better than most women half her age. She was tall, slender and alluring, yet also composed and in control. She was a force to be reckoned with and feared.

"Mr. Mathews?" she asked in a sultry voice.

"Yes. Are you my public defender?"

She cackled. "Heaven's no. My name is Irene Shaw. I own the state's largest defense law firm."

Bill said sheepishly, "I'm afraid I can't afford you."

"You're right. You can't." She hiked up her skirt while sitting down, flashing her long legs. "But this meeting is pro bono."

"Thank you. Thanks a lot. But is it safe to talk?"

"Of course, dear. I'm a bit of a celebrity around here. There's no way they'd betray my privacy by listening to our initial consultation, so don't fret." She opened a file folder. "Let's get started, shall we? Apparently, the FBI arrested you on suspicion of murdering Mr. Roger Coronado."

"If that's Pit Bull's real name, the guy was a worthless gangbanger. Good riddance to the little shit. I'm not sure what all the fuss is about when the cops haven't lifted a goddamn finger to find my brother's killer."

"Oh dear, I heard about Tim. So tragic at such a young age." Her saccharine condolences vanished as her tone became ominous.

"Let me tell you what all the fuss is about. That 'little shit' was an undercover DEA agent."

Bill gasped. "You jerking my chain?"

Irene ran a manicured red fingernail across the paperwork. "And it says here you're being charged with first-degree murder of a federal officer while performing law enforcement activities. My, my, my." She stood and paced the confining room. "If I remember correctly, you're facing life in prison if you're lucky, and the death penalty if you're not."

He sat transfixed while grasping his fate.

With a scolding inflection, she said, "Stop looking at my ass. Let's keep this strictly professional, shall we?"

"I wasn't … really," he stuttered. "I'm sorry."

She flashed a provocative smile. "No problem, Billy. I'm sure it won't happen again."

After an awkward pause, Bill mumbled, "I can't believe this. I really can't." He stared into her steel-blue eyes. "Do they have any evidence?"

"Let's see here now." She flipped the page. "The FBI claims to have a witness willing to testify."

"Who?"

"Some street hood you muscled. He gave you up as part of a plea deal to avoid juvie time as a drug mule. According to his statement, he said the gang suspected Mr. Coronado, aka Pit Bull, was a narc. They figured you'd be happy to take care of their problem. In short, it appears you were set up."

Un-fucking-believable. "But that punk didn't know my name. How did the feds find me?"

"That was easy. In the last few weeks, you've made a spectacle of yourself by talking to everyone within a five-mile radius of your brother's murder."

He winced in disbelief. "But that little snot's testimony will never stand up in court, right?"

"Maybe. I'd agree he's hardly a credible witness. And his testimony would be circumstantial at best if taken alone."

"You mean there's more?"

"I'm afraid so. Apparently, Mr. Coronado told the intensive care doctors about pricking his finger. Then, with a little good old-fashioned forensic work, the FBI found your partial print on that game thingy."

"It's called an Xbox wireless game controller."

Irene's temper exploded. "I don't give a shit what it's called. And never, ever correct me again. Understand?"

"Uh-huh."

"That's yes, Ms. Shaw. That's how you'll always address me."

"Yes, Ms. Shaw."

"That's better." The decibel level lowered. "Now then, as I was about to say, leaving your fingerprint was sloppy. But it was very, very clever using E. coli as a murder weapon. Most resourceful. I'm also impressed by your medical background, killing prowess at war and your mercenary resume. We always need someone with your talents."

"Who's we?"

"That will be disclosed later, much later. For now, I have a job offer. In exchange, I can make the evidence and that runt witness disappear. Soon after the case is dismissed and the charges are dropped, something tragic will happen to you. When you're a new man, I'll put your talents to work." Her scarlet lips pursed. "But once you're in, you're always in. There's no such thing as quitting."

Bill hesitated to ask, "What exactly do you want me to do?"

"I'll have HR send you the full job description." She slapped the table. "Jesus Christ, Billy, figure it out."

Oh God. She wants me to silently kill someone like I did to Pit Bull, maybe kill many. Is this for real or some kind of trap? If real, it's better than dying in prison. "But I'm not sure I can just vanish. I promised to take care of my mother."

"Ah, that's so touching." She covered her heart. "If I had a son, I'd want him to be just like you." Her expression chilled. "But here's the reality. You can't do Mom much good behind bars for life. And yes, if you join us, you'll never see her again." With an insincere smile, she added, "But to make things a bit easier, I'll have my staff avoid probate, transfer your handsome bank account to her tax-free, plus slip in a wonderful signing bonus."

"And what about Tim's killer? Can you do anything to help there?"

Not a hair dared to move as she shook her head. "No, dear. We both know that'll never be solved. It's time to say goodbye to him too." She leaned close enough to see tiny pores hiding below heavy makeup. Her aggression was intimidating. "Now it's decision time. This offer is good for thirty seconds." She studied her diamond watch as if counting each second.

"Do I really have a choice?"

"Of course you do. But it seems to me there's only one that's viable."

Bill was trapped. Frankly, he didn't give a shit about what happened. His life was worthless no matter which way he turned. With a sigh of resignation, he said, "Okay, yes."

Irene's fingers cupped a diamond earring. "Can you speak up, dear. My hearing's not what it used to be."

What a load of crap. This old coot never missed a damn thing. "I said yes."

Her hands rose in triumph. "That's wonderful. You'll love joining our team. You'll have so much fun."

I doubt it.

Irene began leaving before making an about-face. "Oh, by the way, you'll have to dump your ridiculous name. Billy is weak and so unbecoming. Let's see, what shall I name you?" She searched the ceiling for the answer. "I know," she said with delight. "You'll be called Wolfgang. I like that. It's perfect. Just the kind of manly name people will fear."

When the guard opened the door, she strolled out as if expecting thunderous applause after the last curtain call.

Her leaving was the best part of being around Irene Shaw.

Chapter Fourteen: Philadelphia, Pennsylvania

Photos 31–33

CHAPTER FIFTEEN

Monday – Present Day

The Old Town of Budva[34] was wedged on a narrow peninsula, encircled by imposing stone walls and fortified by watch towers, embrasures and a citadel facing the Adriatic Sea. Most of the external defenses and internal charm reflected four centuries of Venetian rule. Glistening high above the orange rooflines was the belfry of Sveti Ivan Church. Michelle's elevated view of Stari Grad was spectacular, yet she battled to stay awake.

Three days of surveillance had been grueling. Exhaustion and stress begged for sleep. The final report to Mason Webber was due in two hours. In her opinion, they would not deliver what he wanted: a detailed plan to silently kill Dimitri Yegorov. Chris disagreed. He was emphatic Webber would be impressed.

"Where you at?" Michelle asked her brother after accepting his phone call.

"Sitting outside the luxury shops at Porto Montenegro.[35] I'm watching that catering company making deliveries again to the *Grand Dutchess*. Good news. The average time between loads to the yacht is eight minutes. And they leave the truck unlocked. That's a huge opportunity."

"If you say so," she said, but determined it would be impossible to taint only the food the Russian oligarch would eat.

"You still monitoring the yacht's second officer?"

"Yeah, and I don't know where this guy gets the stamina. He sure makes the best of his time off. He partied all night in the clubs and discos, and now he's partying again on Ričardova Glava Beach[36] next to Old Town with his new Russian friends. Most are wearing very small bikinis." Michelle raised her binoculars. "It appears he's extra friendly with one of them, because they just groped their way into a changing booth."

"What's that tell us?"

"Well, I haven't figured out how to compromise him yet. But one thing's crystal clear. He's a drunk," Michelle concluded. "He was buying vodka by the bottle at the clubs. And he's drinking again this morning. If this guy really is head of the yacht's security, I'll bet his protocols suck."

"That explains why the late-night guards are slouches. Most of the time they stood around the stern talking, smoking and sipping from a flask."

Michelle was encouraged. "Does that leave the bow vulnerable for a breach?"

"Yes indeedy, if it's a pattern. And it also exposes the copter. Listen, I'll see you later. I'm going back to finish our report."

Michelle started the scooter for the twisting drive back to Perast, passing through a valley, in a tunnel and along a rugged coastline. Traveling for an hour was plenty of time to worry about the meeting with Webber.

The siblings' normal routine during a silentcide commission was to research, observe and brainstorm for a week or two until agreeing on the best approach. Then they'd develop an ideal game plan complete with contingencies before waiting for the right moment to strike. Their honed process and teamwork had been a recipe for success. Irene rarely wanted details in advance. She only cared if the target died by the deadline without repercussions and when the client paid their bill.

Everything about this assignment was different and destined

to fail. The stakes were astronomical, the target was elusive, the timeframe was impossible, and Chris had developed a fanatical need to impress Mason Webber. He spent hours analyzing intel and creating a PowerPoint. The presentation was glutted with scenarios. Most were subpar, a few showed potential, and none were vetted. She kept stressing quality over quantity. Chris wouldn't listen. The report kept ballooning into a well-organized hodgepodge of raw ideas.

Michelle reached a scenic overlook.[37] She squeezed the brakes, skidded to a stop and straddled the scooter. At the base of a barren limestone mount, and hugging the shores of a placid bay, was another medieval fortified town. Kotor appeared serene when viewed from a distance.

She struggled to remember when she had been at peace. One time came to mind: when they first thought Irene Shaw was dead and she allowed herself to make love to her foster brother. Those fleeting days were filled with joy. The mutual infatuation was intoxicating. Ansel's kisses, caresses and sensual embraces promised happiness free from oppression and killing.

That utopia was shattered when their nemesis resurfaced and Ansel betrayed the siblings. But God how she missed Ansel, despite his faults. She blamed herself for his death. The waves of emotional pain were relentless. She also mourned losing the future she always wanted but never thought she'd have.

But tasting the dream made it real. Liberation was possible. It was not too late. Now was the time to act. She could ignore the consequences and run. She would not be denied freedom again.

With resolve, she throttled the scooter. Wind caressed her cheeks. Accelerating around curves was invigorating. Her unknown destiny was exhilarating. The decision was right.

Thirty minutes later, Michelle arrived back at Perast. She couldn't abandon Chris and subject him to Webber's wrath for her escape. Freedom at her brother's expense was unconscionable.

✦✦✦

Michelle watched as Chris pretended to be confident while setting up his laptop on the unstable table. He insisted on presenting. "You can add color commentary if needed."

Being relegated to second fiddle wasn't offensive. She felt no compulsion to prove herself to Webber. As the staircase groaned, her advice was, "Relax, brother. You'll be great."

"Hey there, kids," Webber said in his typical condescending greeting while entering the kitchen. "You ready for the big unveiling?"

Chris's voice cracked. "Yes, sir."

"Good." Webber tugged his shirt cuff away from his watch. "Let's wait for Shawn to join us, shall we?"

There'd be hell to pay if we were two minutes late. Why does Shawn get a pass? And what does that buff jerk do all day besides shave and polish his head? He rarely leaves his room.

Webber sat, rolled up his sleeves and showed uncharacteristic patience until the lapdog walked in. There was no apology for being late. Shawn gave a nod and stood against a countertop behind his boss.

Michelle wanted to yell, *Come. Sit. Stay. Atta boy. Good dog.*

"Okay," Webber said, "we're good to go. What've you got?"

Chris turned the laptop to show the title page.

Webber stopped him cold. "Oh, dear God, a PowerPoint? You're kidding, right? Are you some kind of staff weenie?"

Shawn stifled a chortle.

Webber's rant continued. "I refuse to sit here while you read a bunch of bullet points." He looked at Shawn. "Scrub this shit off his computer when we're done." He turned back to Chris. "Sit down, shut up and let me go through this, then we'll talk." Shawn leaned over Webber's shoulder to read along.

Michelle wanted to console Chris, but there was nothing she could do. They avoided eye contact, but she sensed his humiliation.

The presentation was organized by vulnerability: yacht, security, crew, helicopter, deliveries, guests, target routines and medical maladies. The last slide ranked the options by potential success.

The men were stoic as they clicked through the slides. Their stone faces resembled seasoned poker players. When Webber lifted his head and removed his glasses, he glared at Chris. *This is going to be bad.*

Chris dared to ask, "Well, what do you think?"

What came out of Webber's mouth was unexpected. "I admire your work ethic and ingenuity …"

A compliment?

"… but not your focus."

Of course there was a but.

"I asked for your best silentcide techniques, not everything you could think of. There are some good ideas here, but no detailed plans about …"

Chris interrupted. "But we didn't have enough time."

Webber snapped back. "You had plenty of time to waste on this report. Now let me finish." He said to Michelle, "The last vulnerability section was very good. I assume that's your work. I like how you described the pharmaceuticals for exploiting Yegorov's medical conditions. Scoring them on discoverability by a medical examiner or forensics lab was a nice touch."

"Thanks," Michelle said. "But there's one big problem with all of them."

"What's that?"

"Delivery. We haven't had time to find a non-invasive way to target Yegorov with any drug compound. The man's a ghost."

"He's been a ghost ever since his brother" – Webber used air quotes – "'accidentally' fell from a ten-story building." With a grin, he added, "That's a popular way for Russian oil executives to retire early."

Michelle ignored the shared laugh of the two jackasses. "We're working on how to breach security to board the yacht. So far that's risky. Ideally, we'd be invited on."

"Excellent conclusion." To accentuate his delight, Webber slammed the laptop closed and pushed it aside. "Great minds think alike. That's why you'll love our plan. I'll let Shawn tell you all about it in a minute."

Shawn stood tall and smug, as if he had tolerated the bumbling of the dumb kids in class and now the teacher had called on the star pupil.

Webber turned toward Chris. "You'll learn your role later. Go get some sleep for a couple hours. You'll need it. This all happens tonight, and it's going to be a very long night."

Chapter Fifteen: Budva, Tivat and Perast, Montenegro

Photos 34–37

CHAPTER SIXTEEN

Kotor, Montenegro

Monday

Michelle deliberated until mustering the fortitude to repel the guilt. She walked through the Sea Gate, an arched entry into Kotor. Looming above a pillory was a limestone clock tower.[38] She sensed Webber's chastisement. He had given a strict time to complete the task. She was already running late.

She took a moment to get oriented in Trg od Oružja.[39] Canopies and flags accented the Renaissance buildings of Arms Square, including the seventeenth-century Rector's Palace and a Venetian armory. Tourism season was waning. Mostly Montenegrins were peering into shop windows or enjoying the sun-drenched afternoon at the outdoor cafes and restaurants.

The small medieval town was a triangular labyrinth of narrow cobblestone walkways. Getting lost would be easy, yet the enormous defensive walls prevented wandering off too far. With a sigh of regret, she glanced again at the interactive phone map and started moving in what she hoped was the right direction. While she hurried through the tunnel-like streets flanked by stone facades, the sun was blocked, the temperature dropped, and the GPS signal became unreliable.

She hated Webber. How dare he assign her this disgusting task. And Shawn was repulsive, especially when he said with superiority, "She's just another local tramp who services rich visiting Russians.

These women get passed around like trading cards. So don't worry about it. She'll love the extra money."

Throughout their careers, she and Chris had an ironclad rule: never involve a civilian in a silentcide commission. It was not only risky but unethical, and they had precious few principles to preserve. These men had no scruples. None.

Michelle stopped cold. The view was quintessential Kotor. On the left was a Juliet balcony[40] with a cast-iron railing covered with flower boxes. Laundry danced in the breeze on a clothesline strung across the cramped passage. Attached to the limestone brick wall was a decorative streetlamp.

What got her attention were two women. The tourists were fingering cheap dresses hanging outside a narrow doorway.[41] A young shopkeeper dashed out smiling, chatting and hoping to make a sale.

Michelle turned around and, while pretending to scroll on the phone, checked her disguise in the reflection. When the voices drifted off, she strengthened her resolve to advance.

The shop wasn't much of a store. It was a dingy room with a few racks of handmade clothes and trinket jewelry. The shopkeeper was sitting on a folding chair stringing plastic necklace beads. She was in her late twenties — maybe older — but her makeup-free Mediterranean complexion was years younger. A scrunchie held a long black ponytail. The modest floral sundress didn't conceal her tall, lean frame. With a radiant smile, she stood and said in Montenegrin, "Dobar dan. Mogu li vam pomoći?"

"Good afternoon. Do you speak English?"

The woman shrugged, giggled, and formed the letter C with her thumb and index finger. "Little bit. Better understand than speak. Me help you?"

"Are you Ljiljana Milošević?"

"Da," she said with an apprehensive nod.

Michelle delayed the inevitable by asking, "Am I pronouncing that correctly?"

"Me know you?"

"No, you don't." Michelle closed and locked the door. She unzipped a fanny pack and flashed the two-inch barrel of a Black Widow mini revolver. "Sit down."

Ljiljana's brown eyes widened as she complied.

Michelle exchanged the five-shot gun for the phone and showed a photo of Dimitri Yegorov. "You know this man?"

She shook her head. "Ne."

"Look again. He's invited you to his yacht tonight as his escort, correct?"

Her leg began bouncing. A worn sandal tapped on the dusty floor. "Me no understand."

Michelle slowed her cadence while speaking louder. "You are his escort tonight."

"Ne, ne."

"Don't lie to me," Michelle threatened while revealing the handgun again.

Ljiljana raised her palms in submission. "Dobro, dobro. Me do nothing wrong."

Of course she wasn't doing anything wrong. Ljiljana was a broke single mom trying to survive. One night with a disgusting Russian probably exceeded a month of selling crap to tourists.

"I'm not judging you. Honest. But you need to do something for me." Ljiljana flinched as Michelle reached into the fanny pack again. "It's simple and worth ten thousand euros."

Ljiljana's face flickered with awe as two stacks of one-hundred-euro notes were placed on the worktable.

"This is half," Michelle said. "You get the rest tomorrow if you cooperate."

Ljiljana studied the money with a frightened expression. "Ah, what me do?"

"Whatever you'd normally do during Yegorov's parties." She paused. "I assume that includes sleeping with him."

Ljiljana's pretty features twisted. "Many, many times. The man is – what you call? – a pig."

Michelle empathized. She remembered being sexually assaulted by her drunken stepfather for years. Those scars never healed. She powered through the ugly memories. "I'm sorry. Now listen carefully. When Yegorov falls asleep for the night, pull open the bedroom curtains facing land, then walk off the yacht."

"Just pull curtains?"

"Yes, but they must be the shoreside windows. And only when he's sleeping. Got it?"

Ljiljana struggled to decide. Seconds passed. She swept the money away. "Na. Na. Can't. Won't. Too easy. Something wrong."

Michelle's inflection softened to ease the panic. "Nothing's wrong. It is just that easy."

"Na. He find out. Men will hurt me. Please take money. Leave me. Please leave."

What Michelle was about to do was despicable. Involving innocent children – worse yet, threatening to hurt them – was another sibling taboo. But Webber and Shawn had insisted she cross the line if needed.

Michelle showed a photo on her phone of an elderly woman and a child having fun on a swimming pier in the adjacent town of Dobrota.[42] Ljiljana's mother was babysitting her four-year-old son.

"Nikola! Na!"

Chapter Sixteen: Kotor, Montenegro

Photos 38–42

CHAPTER SEVENTEEN

Monday

Chris admired the intuitive design and lightweight feel of the HK M110A1 CSASS. The compact, semiautomatic sniper rifle appeared new. There was no way of knowing, however, if anyone had ever been on the wrong end of the barrel.

He placed the weapon on the brittle floral tablecloth and began field stripping. After arranging the pieces, he tested the moving parts and inspected them for corrosion and residue. The lubricant's pleasing aroma was smothered by the wafting smell of garlic sauce Shawn was preparing for scampi buzara. The he-man had a death grip on a dented aluminum pan while fixated on the archaic stovetop. His jean-covered ass was two feet away. The incessant whisk beating was irritating.

When Chris finished reassembly, he started the stopwatch on the phone and repeated the process. For someone who abhorred rifles, he thought his speed of two and a half minutes was at least respectable.

Webber tucked his legs beneath the small kitchen table. A plate of hors d'oeuvres rested in his lap. He seemed peeved. "That's pathetic," he bellowed at Chris after swallowing a wedge of goat cheese. "Bad guys won't wait while you fiddle around. Do it again."

Screw you, Chris wanted to say but didn't.

As if hearing the rebuke telepathically, Webber stood to display his formidable height. "I said do it again."

Chris complied but was fed up. He performed the final function check by yanking back and releasing the charging handle, pulling the trigger, and listening for the metallic snap. "You know, instead of doing this forever, it would've been nice to zero it in at least once."

Shawn remained focused on the stove. "Don't worry. I did that for you. The scope is fine."

That's ridiculous. Chris didn't doubt the quality of the Schmidt & Bender 3-12x50 scope. But firing a few rounds to sight the weapon was critical. Shawn knew that. Debating the point was worthless.

When he cooled down, Chris examined the two 7.62×51mm NATO cartridges on the table. They had been modified with hollowed synthetic tips. "And what did you say was in these again?"

Webber finished chewing a red grape. "An experimental nerve agent."

"Does it have a name?"

"It does." Webber's expression telegraphed he had no intention of revealing it.

Chris inspected one of the rifle cartridges. "You sure there's enough chemical or gas or whatever's inside to do the trick?"

"Yes, but it requires two." Webber pointed to a cartridge. "So call this one trick" – he pointed to the other – "and that one pony."

These men are asses.

As Chris removed his gloves, Shawn saw another opportunity to state the obvious as if Chris were a rank amateur. "When you're done wearing gloves tonight, make sure you pocket them. They are a cesspool of DNA and fingerprints."

Chris was infuriated. "Just what the hell do you do all day besides be arrogant and cook?"

Shawn pretended to be offended. "What, you don't like my cooking?"

"No, your cooking's great. It's you I can't stand."

Webber intervened. "Okay, kids, sticks and stones. Stop the bickering."

"No, I won't stop," Chris insisted with clenched fists. "Why should I tolerate his bullshit when Michelle and I've been doing all the work? And why did you put us through three days of hell when you had no intention of using our silentcide recommendations?"

Webber was unfazed by the tirade. "We wanted to see what you came up with."

Shawn chimed in, "And everything we saw in your cute Power-Point sucked the big one. That's why we're going with my plan A."

Chris bolted to his feet and was about to do a David and Goliath with Shawn – a fight that would have ended poorly – when Michelle burst into the house. She threw off the scarf and wig. Teeth prosthetics bounced and skidded across the kitchen floor.

Webber sniffed golden-yellow cheese rolled in a thin slice of dry-cured ham. "How'd it go?" he asked before popping the appetizer in his mouth.

Her face was red. Eyes were ablaze. "Terrible!"

Shawn wiped his hands on an apron and placed them on his hips. "That mean she's not cooperating?"

Michelle pivoted. "What choice did she have? Of course she'll do it."

"Good," Shawn said.

"No, there's not a damn thing good about this." She turned her venom toward Webber. "Promise me if Ljiljana does what you asked, you'll pay up and leave her son alone."

"I can't promise anything until we see what happens tonight."

"Besides," Shawn said, "who cares what happens to her? She's nothing."

Michelle lunged toward Shawn. "And you're a bastard." Spittle hit his face. "She's a young single mom, for God's sake, just trying to eat and take care of her son. And how dare you make me threaten her little boy?" Her finger wagged. "You will not, I repeat, you will not touch a hair on his head regardless of what she does or, so help me God" – her finger resembled a gun – "I'll put a hole in your shiny bald head."

CHAPTER EIGHTEEN

Tivat, Montenegro

Monday–Tuesday

Yegorov's yacht party was scheduled for eight. Chris and Michelle left Perast at five forty-five. They wanted to arrive at the designated coordinates at dusk. Despite the warmth, Chris was chilled during the scooter ride wearing a T-shirt and shorts. But he was sweating beneath the oversize backpack wedged between him and his sister.

Traffic on Jadranska Magistrala – the two-lane artery through the coastal town of Tivat – was gridlocked. They were behind schedule when they drove up through a neighborhood. When the pavement ended, they snuck along a dirt road through a twenty-five-acre tract of undeveloped land and hid the bike beneath scrub brush. The three-quarter moon made it easy to see but also to be seen. To camouflage themselves, they put on black tactical gear, gloves and hooded masks. Only their eyes were exposed.

At an elevation of ninety-eight feet, Porto Montenegro[43] was visible while they were standing. At least three hundred vessels – ranging from fishing boats to yachts of all sizes and a three-masted sailing ship – were docked along the marina's piers. Yegorov's *Grand Dutchess* dwarfed them all.

There was a problem. The thick vegetation was great for concealment but blocked a prone shooting position. They stomped down the tall grasses to create a firing lane and lay shoulder to shoulder.

Michelle took the caps off the Steiner M22 field binoculars. "Distance 835 meters." She faced Chris. "That's what, about …"

"About half a mile."

"That's far. Are you comfortable with that?"

"No, I'm not comfortable with any of this. But Shawn made me feel a whole lot better when he said Yegorov's yacht is much bigger than the broadside of a barn. He's such a jerk."

Chris assembled the rifle, created a flat spot among the rocks for the bipod, peered through the scope and cursed. So many variables would impact accuracy. This would be easier if he had created DOPE calculations for the rifle and ammunition in advance.

He opened a simple ballistic calculator on his phone and entered information such as bullet caliber, style, weight and velocity, plus elevation, temperature, wind speed and target range. The resulting table suggested a bullet drop of 27.8 MOA. That was about twenty-two feet. And that didn't consider how a synthetic tip would perform. This was a damn guessing game. He dialed in the scope. Too bad there wasn't an adjustment for luck. He tapped the comm pack in his ear. "Shawn, we're set up."

"Copy that." Shawn was somewhere nearby but refused to disclose his location. So much for teamwork.

Michelle zoomed in on the pool at the stern. "It looks like the crew and caterers are about ready. The first guests should arrive soon." With a dramatic huff, she lowered the binoculars. "Why are we going through with this? There's still time to ride outta here and not look back."

With a frustrated sigh, he said, "We've been through this, haven't we?"

"Yes, but now it's real. I have a bad feeling about this plan and an even worse feeling about Webber and his court jester."

"As I've said before, if we bail, the CIA and the FBI won't stop until they track us down."

"Yeah, but if we kill a billionaire friend of the Russian president, and maybe start a superpower war, how many other bad guys with big guns will be after us?"

"Relax. It won't come to that."

"How do you know?"

Chris didn't respond, but he also didn't get up to leave.

Ten minutes of tension passed. Michelle seemed distracted by more troubled thoughts. "What if this is all a ruse?" she asked.

"What do you mean?"

"You know how Webber was so complimentary about my medical malady recommendations?"

"You mean the only presentation section that got an A+?"

Michelle ignored his attempted levity. "What if Shawn circled back and forced Ljiljana to give Yegorov one of my drug compounds?"

"Shawn's a lowlife, but I don't think that low."

"And you're naive. Remember how Webber said great minds think alike when I said the only way to safely deliver the drugs is by getting invited on board?" Michelle panicked. "That's what they've done. I'm sure of it. That'll make Ljiljana a murderer. She'll never recover from that … ever. And that assumes the Russians don't retaliate by killing her."

"That's not going to happen," Chris said. "But what could we've done to avoid it?"

"I should've asked Ljiljana to get me on the yacht. Better yet, I should've replaced her."

"You really would've subjected yourself to that rich deviant? No way."

"It would've been better than ruining her life." Michelle paused. "Mine's already ruined."

Chris was unsure how to counter her damning self-assessment. What he managed to say provided no comfort. "Well, I guess it's a moot point now."

A trickle of guests arrived on valet-driven golf carts, followed by a steady stream. As they walked up the gangway, white-gloved crew members greeted them with flutes of champagne. "There she is," Michelle announced. "Ljiljana's approaching the yacht."

Chris repositioned the rifle scope. Ljiljana didn't resemble a poor single mom, more like a starlet at the Oscars. The figure-clinging red dress had a thigh-high slit, and the daring neckline left little to the imagination. Long black curly hair cascaded over a sparkling necklace and bare shoulders. Red stilettos accented her seductive strut. A charming smile heightened her flawless beauty. She was stunning. "You sure I'm looking at the right woman?"

"Wow! I can't believe the transformation. No wonder Yegorov keeps inviting her back."

"Ljiljana just boarded the yacht," Shawn said through their earpieces. "I'll keep monitoring and update as needed." Ljiljana had been told to wear black opal earrings fitted with a microphone. Of course, only Shawn could hear the transmissions.

Soon the party was in full swing. Through the third-deck windows, Chris saw flashing disco lights illuminating a growing crowd. Many were dancing to the steady beat of club music orchestrated by a manic DJ. Other clusters were talking, laughing, drinking and eating catered canapés around the outdoor pool. Two guards with sidearms stood watch. They were far more disciplined than the previous night.

Michelle hunched over her cell phone, cupping the screen to conceal the light. She was trying to determine Shawn's position on the map. "Uh, do you realize you'll be shooting almost directly over a police station?"

"That's not good," he said while eliminating one of their planned escape routes.

"No shit."

A few minutes later, the sound of falling rocks behind them startled Chris. "Hear that?"

"Yup," she whispered on high alert.

They strained to listen. Nothing. Nearby shrubs rustled. Chris considered aiming his rifle toward the suspicious noise. But a long gun was often worthless at short range. Besides, Webber only gave him two bullets. He needed them both for the assignment. "It'd be nice to have a pistol. But Webber kept saying I wouldn't need one."

Michelle pulled out her Black Widow pocket revolver.

He scoffed. "What good is that peashooter going to do?"

"Would you rather throw rocks when we're attacked?"

They crouched together, coiled to strike. The fight-or-flight response surged through his veins. How were they compromised? He was confident his sister could handle one assailant, but what if there were more? They didn't stand a chance. And if the intruder was a neighborhood child or dog, they would jeopardize their position and mission.

Michelle was the first to laugh as a domestic Balkan goat[44] emerged. The farm animal stared, bleated twice, sniffed, and wandered off. The comic relief felt great.

Fifteen minutes passed, then thirty and an hour before either of them spoke. "Goddamn it," Michelle said. "Take a look at the bow end of the top deck."

Next to the owner's suite, Ljiljana and Yegorov were holding on to the railing of his private balcony. She was pointing toward ripples near the water's surface. Michelle asked, "Are there dolphins around here?"

"How should I know?"

She peered through the binoculars again and Chris through his scope. The situation had deteriorated. Yegorov was kissing her neck and groping her bottom. Ljiljana stood rigid while tolerating his lust. He grabbed her hand and led her inside the lion's den. The bedroom curtains closed. "The bastard!" Michelle spat. An hour later, the couple arrived at the pool arm in arm. Yegorov pranced around while displaying his trophy for all to admire.

Chris wasn't sure when Michelle fell asleep, but he let her rest. They were sleep-deprived. Waiting – for hours and sometimes days – was one of the worst but most essential parts of the job. An idle mind conjured up what could go wrong, especially with a crappy plan like Webber's.

"It's the essence of easy," Shawn had said to Chris with his cocky attitude. "When the bedroom curtains open and Ljiljana leaves the yacht, I'll send a supersonic, armor-piercing round through the bullet-resistant glass of the owner's bedroom. Then, you fire two supersonic bullets through the smashed window. They'll disintegrate on impact, and the nerve agent will disperse before Yegorov gets out of bed." The plan was as subtle as dancing elephants in a closet.

At two o'clock the music stopped. The glittering lights around the pool flickered on and off. A throng of people soon began disembarking. A couple stumbled down the gangway. Many weaved along the pier. One woman on her hands and knees vomited into the water. Most waited in a queue for golf carts to take them back to their parked cars.

For two more hours, the crew cleaned up the yacht while the guards patrolled the decks. Yegorov and Ljiljana were nowhere in sight. Tired of waiting, Chris asked Shawn, "What's the status?"

"I'm not sure you want to know," he said over the comm pack.

"What's that supposed to mean?"

"Well, maybe you want to know, but I'll spare Michelle's virgin ears. Suffice it to say they're enjoying each other's company in his bedroom."

Michelle flashed the finger.

Twenty minutes of tense readiness were numbing until the moment arrived. A bedroom window curtain opened. A fleeting shadow passed by the second one. Shawn's voice made Chris flinch. "That's the signal, guys. Ljiljana's headed out. Stand by for action as soon as she clears the yacht."

Chris began his sniper-readiness routine. *Recalculate the temperature. Judge wind speed and drift.* Two clicks on the scope. *Control diaphragmatic breathing. Relax the muscles. Clear the mind. Sight the target. Anticipate the command.*

"She's at the top of the gangway," Michelle whispered.

Chris timed her descent. He released the safety. His index finger slipped into the trigger guard. He waited.

Michelle kept monitoring Ljiljana's movements through the binoculars. "She's on the pier. Now she's walking beside the yacht. She'll pass the stern in twenty seconds."

Chris felt pressure on the trigger.

"Ten seconds." His sister paused while he waited. "Five seconds." Another pause. "She's clear."

"It's showtime," Shawn announced. "Ready?"

"Yup." Chris's answer was faint. He focused.

"Remember, you'll follow my shot."

Chris visualized the bullet's path into the bedroom window.

A shot rang out.

Chris snickered. *The dumb son of a bitch missed.*

"Oh my God!" came a muffled scream from Michelle.

Chris saw the bedroom window shatter before he heard Shawn's second shot. He squeezed the trigger. His bullet blasted. The rifle recoiled. The spent cartridge flew. He sensed he hit the target.

As he prepared to send the next round, the top of the yacht exploded and disappeared in a roar of fire and smoke. A blinding flash. Shards of steel and glass pierced neighboring yachts. A black mushroom plume blocked the moonlight. Debris splashed into the bay like hailstones. Glowing embers resembled spent fireworks. A flaming ball of navigation equipment slammed onto the pier, wobbled and rolled, and dropped into the bay with a splash.

Chapter Eighteen: Tivat, Montenegro

Photos 43–44

CHAPTER NINETEEN

Tuesday

Seconds before the yacht exploded, Michelle was horrified when Ljiljana was shot, clutched her chest and catapulted into the water. A single high heel marked the spot where a bullet blew her away. "You bastard!" Michelle prayed Ljiljana would climb a pier ladder and emerge unharmed. She didn't. She was gone. "You damn bastard!"

Chris pointed to his ear and mouthed the words, "Off. Turn your comm off." He waited before asking in confusion, "How the hell did Shawn blow up the yacht? Or did my bullet do that?"

"I don't know. I don't know." Michelle was frantic. "What I do know is he just killed Ljiljana."

"From the bomb?"

"No, he shot her in cold blood beforehand."

"You sure?"

"Yes, I'm sure, damn it. I'm one hundred percent sure. Nobody survives an armor-piercing round to the chest."

Chris shook her shoulders … hard. "Stop it! Hear me? Right now. If they blew up the yacht and killed Ljiljana, then we're next. We're the patsies for all of this."

The yacht's shrill fire alarm sounded. A pajamaed crew member ran down the gangway, followed by two others. One was barely dressed. The other clutched her robe.

Michelle struggled to suppress her anger. The fury was blinding.

"Get your shit together," he demanded.

She tried – pounding her fist on the ground – until remembering a survival maxim taught on the Amish farm: "Fear gets you killed. Calm keeps you alive." Her face contorted. She squeezed her eyes. The hyperventilating slowed. She floundered for restraint. With a final gasp of recovery, she was under control and aware of the surrounding perils. Neighboring house lights were coming on. People on balconies were watching or filming the chaos at the marina. Anyone could be a potential witness. Time was running out. "Now what?"

"Like you wanted before, we get the hell out of here and don't look back."

"Finally."

They grabbed their gear and jumped to their feet. A bullet shattered a sapling. They rolled into a washout shielded by rocks.

"Holy shit," Chris muttered with wide eyes. "You okay?"

"Yeah," she gasped. "Where the hell did that come from?"

"Not sure. I, uh, I think from behind us."

Michelle threaded the binoculars through a thick bush. "There's a road up there. About 140 meters. It's a perfect elevated position."

"So we can't reach our scooter."

"Got that right. We'd be dropped in our tracks. You think it's that son of a bitch Webber?"

"Who else? Shawn's shots were from the southeast, and he's probably coming in fast."

"And if we go downhill," Michelle said, "we'll walk right into the police station." A patrol car was leaving the parking lot. Their lights were flashing. Sirens from distant first responders pierced the early morning silence. A fireguard boat sped toward the burning yacht.

"That leaves one way out." Chris picked up the rifle. "Ready?" Michelle grabbed the backpack. "Stay low."

They crouched for six feet before another bullet ripped through tall grass and ricocheted against a boulder. She fell, slamming a knee on rocks. The tactical pants' kneepad softened the blow, but it hurt like hell. She grimaced.

Chris pulled her into a ravine. "We're trapped. Either him or us. Gotta find him, fast, so I can take him out."

Michelle used binoculars and Chris his rifle scope to search the higher ground. The moonlight – drifting in and out of wispy clouds – cast haunting shadows on the trees. Too many crevices in the tangled vegetation offered places to hide. Finding Webber seemed impossible. He could be anywhere. They scanned the landscape for ninety seconds before Chris got excited. "I think I've got him."

"Where?"

He pointed. "Look for a boxy white building on the upper road. It's some kind of electrical utility shed."

"Where?" She was getting frustrated. "Okay, I see it."

"Good. Now watch for a moving reflection on the roof."

She saw a small, mirrorlike circle reflecting the yacht's fire below. As it swept back and forth, the reflection disappeared and reappeared.

Chris declared, "I swear to God that's his rifle scope." He shouldered his weapon again.

"But I don't see a gunman. You sure?"

"Not exactly, but my instincts say yes." He stabilized his grip and sighted his target.

"It could just be a utility light."

He ignored her.

She tried a different deterrent. "But you've only got one bullet …"

Before she could finish, Chris fired the shot.

A rifle fell off the roof. Two arms dropped and dangled over the side.

Chris spat. "Good riddance, Mr. Mason Webber with two Bs."

"Awesome!" They exchanged a high five.

"Thanks, but we gotta move before the lapdog gets here."

"Wait," Michelle said. "I've got an idea. Let's throw our tracking watches downhill about ten yards. When Shawn comes searching that way, we'll ambush him."

"Grand theory, but he probably has his big boy pistol. And your twenty-two is no match for his nine mil."

"Got a better idea?"

"Yeah, let's throw them as far as we can. While he's wandering around down there, we'll get out of Dodge fast."

They ran like hell toward a bordering neighborhood. Michelle lost her footing but recovered. Thistles scratched her cheeks. A tree branch swatted her head. She stumbled over a hidden log. Chris pulled her up. They kept racing.

The GPS hoax didn't fool Shawn. His pounding footsteps were close. "Stop," he yelled. "Cops coming. Gotta get out of here."

"What's with this guy?" Michelle asked while panting.

"Maybe using a drone or night goggles. Either way, we're being lit up like Christmas trees."

"How do we outrun that?"

Chris ditched his rifle. "We run faster."

Michelle threw the backpack.

They reached a crossroads. The cramped streets were flanked by bland, two-story houses with slender balconies facing the sea. Untamed vegetation, a few garden plots, and an occasional palm tree choked the minuscule backyards. The siblings surveyed down and straight before racing uphill. Within a few steps, a German shepherd attacked. A metal fence stymied him. Saliva drooled from the fangs during manic barking. Overhead, a man shouted, "Zovem policiju! Zovem policiju!"

Shawn was gaining ground with a pistol at his side. "Please stop. I won't hurt you."

Michelle yelped, grabbed her knee and began limping. "Can't make it."

Gasping for air, Chris conceded. "Gotta take a stand. Quick, behind that car."

They huddled behind the hood. Michelle steadied the mini revolver with both hands.[45] A showdown was imminent.

Shawn's pace slowed. He knew where they were. "For the last time," he said, sounding winded, "come out. Make this easy. Please."

Chris mouthed the words, "Do it."

Michelle pulled back the hammer with her thumb, jumped up and fired a .22 Magnum round at Shawn's insipid face. Bang!

Shawn flinched but didn't duck. "They're blanks, Michelle." He aimed his Glock. "Now please give yourselves up. I won't hurt you. Promise."

Chris lunged from the other side of the car. Shawn reached into his pocket. Electricity shot through Michelle's body. Crippling. Excruciating pain. She was paralyzed. After collapsing on her back, she saw Chris twitching face down on the road. His arms and legs were shaking.

Shawn dropped a knee on her brother's neck, yanked back his arms and zip-tied his wrists. He manacled her arms in front. As the shock lessened, he dragged her up. Her left foot was ablaze. Tears rolled down her cheeks. "What the hell was that?"

"There're tasers in your boots. Trust me, I didn't want to use them. This isn't what you think."

"Bastard," Michelle cursed. "You don't want to know what I think."

As they were led at gunpoint toward the Fiat, Michelle was convinced Shawn was going to drive up Mount Vrmac and put a bullet through their heads.

Chapter Nineteen: Tivat, Montenegro

Photo 45

CHAPTER TWENTY

Dubrovnik, Croatia

Tuesday

Chris's left wrist was bound to the steering wheel with a rope as the sunrise streamed through the windshield, irritating his exhausted eyes. He admired an enormous medieval tower and formidable defense wall[46] whizzing past the side window of the Fiat hatchback. If only he were a tourist with a camera around his neck instead of a captive fearing imminent death.

The sunshine nudged his sister awake. She bolted upright in the front seat, noticed her zip-tied hands and swiveled her head. "Where are we?"

"Dubrovnik in Croatia," Shawn answered from the back seat while holding a Glock 17. "That's Old Town on the left. You should visit if you get the chance. They filmed a lot of *Game of Thrones* there. You'd love it."

Screw you, Chris thought.

Shawn had been mute during the two-hour trip, except for driving instructions. They were in the home stretch. "Turn right at Pile Gate.[47] Good. Now straight for about three hundred yards. Okay, slow down. It's the two-story house on the right with the cast-iron fence. That's it. Pull into the car park. Turn off the engine." Shawn waited until the street was clear. He exited the car, zip-tied Chris and led them through the arched front door at gunpoint. Michelle was limping.

Mason Webber was sitting on a living room couch, sipping orange juice and reading a Mitch Rapp novel. His posture was relaxed in khaki pants and a worn Notre Dame sweatshirt. "Hi, kids. Busy night, huh? But not what you expected."

Chris leaped forward. "Fuck you!" Shawn restrained him.

Webber put down the book. "Yeah, I had that coming."

"I shot you."

Webber examined his body. "Nope, not me."

"Then who?" Chris screamed.

"Would you like something to drink? Maybe juice, coffee or tea?"

"Answer me. Who did I kill?"

"A yacht security guard." He finished the juice. "Yesterday, we got intel the second officer was fired for incompetence. His replacement was hell-bent on upping security. We noticed an immediate improvement in discipline with the guards on the yacht. Unfortunately, we never saw the sniper because our drone failed last night."

Chris pivoted to Shawn. "Then how did you keep finding us in the field? You weren't wearing night goggles."

Shawn pointed to the siblings' feet. "There're GPS trackers in your boots."

Of course, there were redundant trackers in case we escaped. How stupid to wear those damn things.

The typical condescending Webber said, "But I hear you made a helluva shot."

"What if I'd been out of ammo like you planned?"

"Lucky for you, the explosion happened before your second shot, because otherwise" – he shrugged – "yeah, things would've been dicey. Sorry 'bout that."

Michelle's anger burst open. "Are you also sorry for killing Ljiljana, you bastard?"

He leaned back into the cushion. "Looks can be deceiving."

"Stop the crap. I know what I saw. Her chest exploded."

The bathroom door opened. Ljiljana walked out wearing faded jeans, a T-shirt, and a damp towel wrapped around her head. Her scrubbed face was attractive and competent. She smelled of lilac soap. "Thanks for concern, Michelle. You really sweet. But I'm fine."

"But I saw …"

"The blood was, I think, you Hollywood call a squib bag," she said in broken English. "After fall off pier, I extracted by SEALs. It must look like I die so Russians won't try find me."

"But what about your son?"

"No idea who little boy is. But, as you Americans say, he real cutie pie."

Webber stood. "I'd like to introduce you to Nina Kováč. She's an outstanding operative from Slovakia and was pivotal in this assignment." He sat and crossed his legs.

"So you're the one who set the explosive?" Michelle asked.

"Yes," Nina said while removing the towel and running her fingers through long tangled hair.

"But why?" Chris asked. "Even our bad silentcide ideas would've been more targeted with no collateral damage."

"No worries," Nina said. "Bomb designed with directional blast up, not down. We want to destroy owner's suite, not rest of ship. Besides, I wait over two hours for crew to be sleeping on lowest deck before setting timer on detonator."

"And you'll be happy to know," Webber added, "our portside man reported everyone escaped. Only two crew had some smoke inhalation, and one guard had minor burns."

"But how did you smuggle the explosives on board?" Michelle asked. "Certainly not in that dress."

Nina's laugh was charming. "That dress so hideous, no? And heels gave me blisters." She pointed to sore toes inside old sandals. "SEALs deliver bomb. I pull up from water to bedroom balcony during party."

"That was risky," Chris said.

"Yes, me almost caught by security guard. But Dimitri Yegorov saw him first, grab my butt and yell to guard go away. Old pervert like groping too much."

"What? Why would Yegorov help you?" Michelle asked.

"I let Mr. Webber explain."

Webber said to Shawn, "Cut their restraints, will you?" He motioned to the opposite sofa. "You kids have a seat. This'll take a few minutes."

As they rubbed their wrists, Shawn asked, "Now can I get you something to drink, like maybe a beer?"

Chris said, "Something stronger."

"Me too," Michelle echoed.

Shawn chuckled. "I'll see what's in the kitchen." He handed the gun to his boss.

Chris was distracted as Nina pulled out a long green string from her hair. She mouthed the word *seaweed*.

Webber cleared his throat to get the siblings' attention. He leaned forward with locked fingers. "What I'm about to tell you is classified. You mustn't tell anyone, ever, comprende?"

They nodded.

"Good. I'll need your signature on another hand receipt." He gave them a handwritten page. "It says you understand this information is classified and you'll keep it confidential." Webber took a photo of them as they complied. "Okay, here's the skinny. Yegorov is alive."

The siblings glanced at each other in disbelief before Michelle said, "Did the SEALs extract him too?"

Nina spoke up. "I wish. Be easier for I. No, near end of party, we go back to bedroom. I shave his arms, legs and wax face. He keep asking for bikini wax. So gross. Then makeup, wig and padded dress. He ugly woman but do job. He sneak out when party crowd leave ship, then take golf cart away."

Chris asked, "But won't the gig be up without a body?"

"You're going to like this part." Webber's smug expression radiated self-satisfaction. "Remember his brother who was pushed off a balcony? Well, they're identical twins. We exhumed Fyodor's body from St. Petersburg, removed his teeth, dismembered him and charred the body parts. Then the SEALs released them in the bay when the bomb went off."

These guys are good. But I'll be damned if I'll admit it. "But why the elaborate scheme?"

"It's simple. After Fyodor was killed, Dimitri worried he'd be next. He was very eager for a deal. In exchange for asylum in the US, a new identity, government protection for five years, and return of his sanctioned billions, we'd fake his death for information vital to national security."

"What information?" Chris asked. "Or is that on a need-to-know basis again?"

Webber flashed his irritating grin. "Right, it's classified."

Michelle chimed in, "But what good are billions going to do him if he's in hiding?"

"That's his problem, as long as we get what we want."

Chris wasn't buying any of this. "How do we know this isn't all bullshit? All you've ever done is lie to us."

"I suppose you want proof of life?"

"Absolutely. Just call me a doubting Judas."

Everyone laughed. At least Nina was nice enough to cover her giggle. Michelle leaned over to her brother. "I think you mean doubting Thomas."

"Whatever." He resented being a laughingstock.

Webber fished a BlackBerry from his pocket and put the call on speaker.

"Yes, Mr. Webber," a deep male voice said with the sound of a driving car and traffic in the background.

"Everything good?"

"No problems, sir."

While Webber explained the reason for the call, and the man translated it into Russian, Shawn delivered two bloody marys. With a hushed tone, he said, "Sorry, no olives or Worcestershire. This is the best I could do. But the Russian vodka is Beluga." He flashed two thumbs up. "Very good."

He was right. The first sip was delicious and, best of all, generous with the booze.

The call was put on video, and the driver handed the phone to Yegorov. Webber asked in a cheerful voice, "Dimitri, how's it going?"

The translation came back as, "Trip too long. Shitty car."

Webber rubbed his chin stubble in frustration. "I have someone here who has three questions to verify you're alive."

Chris asked the chairman of Iskop for last year's revenue and income for his petroleum and natural gas company. The answers were correct. Too easy. Chris wanted his last question to trip up an imposter. He blurted, "What floor did your brother Mikhail fall from in Moscow?"

Without waiting for the translation, the Russian oligarch erupted in English. "Fyodor was brother's name, not Mikhail. He pushed from tenth floor in St. Petersburg, not Moscow. You know that. Now go fuck yourself."

"Okay, that's enough," Webber said. He disconnected and zeroed in on Chris. "Why'd you have to be such an asshole? We need his cooperation."

"'Cause I still don't believe you. The only picture we've seen of this guy was on the transport plane. How do we know it's really him?"

Webber was losing patience. "Then Google him."

Shawn offered his phone. "No, I want Nina's phone." Within a minute, the images resulting from the browser search resembled the man in the car. Chris conceded Yegorov was alive.

"Satisfied?" Webber asked.

"Yes, but not happy."

"That's fair."

Michelle jumped in. "So answer this. Why did you make us worthless pawns in your master plan?"

"First off, this wasn't my plan. It was Shawn's. He was the quarterback. I was just the coach."

Seriously? No way! Chris eyeballed Shawn.

With a slight head tilt and apologetic expression, Shawn said, "Sorry, guys, that I was such a prick. I mean that. I'm really sorry."

Webber continued, "Second, this was a test."

"Of what?" Michelle asked.

"Of you two. We vetted you in advance. But you can only learn so much that way. The true test is in the field under duress. We wanted to learn your skills, work ethics, willingness to follow orders, where you draw a moral line, and about your silentcide techniques. We learned a lot. You passed with flying colors."

Chris's defiance melted into pride. *They're impressed with us.* "So does that mean we get our full immunity now?"

Webber shook his head. "No, this wasn't your actual assignment. It was only a test. We need your help with something else."

"Oh, come on." Chris was getting pissed again. "We did everything you asked."

"Please just hear me out. You see, there's been a long string of very high-profile deaths recently using silentcide techniques."

"You're talking about the senators and that aerospace company CEO?" Michelle asked.

"They're the obvious ones, yes. But we suspect others around the world. We also believe there's more to come."

"But Irene is dead," Chris interjected. "And so is her assassin network. Shouldn't that be the end of things?"

"Our intel is saying the threat is still very real. That's why we'd like your silentcide insights to neutralize the plot."

With a hint of hope, Michelle asked, "That mean you don't want us to kill anyone?"

"No, just the opposite."

Chris sensed his sister was thrilled with that answer. "Who are the people you want protected?"

"That's a long list right now. We're still narrowing it down. So will you help us?"

"You have a strange way of asking for our help," Michelle said. "If you had just asked nicely in the first place, we probably would've been willing."

"Fair point, but we had to be sure. So what's your answer?"

Chris was skeptical. "If we help, do we get full immunity?"

"If you earn it. But you can't just go along for the ride. Immunity isn't a participation award."

Michelle exchanged a hesitant glance with her brother before telling Webber, "I still think you're a bastard."

"Don't deny it." He cracked a playful smirk. "But my parents were married."

She rolled her eyes at the sophomoric humor. "Despite that, I guess I'm in."

Chris pondered his decision. They had been suckered before. "Under two conditions."

"What's that?"

"You'll only tell us the truth from now on."

"You got it. What else?"

"Stop calling us kids."

Webber's laugh was genuine for the first time. He stood, extending his hand. "Deal?" They shook on it. "Good. Here's what happens next. Finish your eye-openers. Hell, have another one if you wish. You earned it. Then you're welcome to take a shower."

Nina scrunched her nose while making a sidebar to Michelle. "Warn you. No conditioner or detangler in there. Only very big jug of cheapo shampoo."

Webber continued. "Your luggage from Kotor is in a bedroom, so you can change into clean clothes. After that, Shawn's making breakfast."

"How's eggs Benedict with Istrian pršut sound? That's a Croatian prosciutto."

Michelle licked her lips. "Sounds awesome."

After the banter, Webber said, "I'm sure you're tired, but there's plenty of time to sleep during our long drive back to Aviano Air Base and home to Philly. Until we need you again, keep working with Sloan Hamilton and whatever the hell she calls her FBI task team. But not a word about what happened here, comprende?"

The siblings nodded.

"Any questions?"

Chris raised his hand. "Can you tell us now who you guys work for?"

With an apologetic head shake, Webber scratched short hair behind oversized ears. "Sorry, but I can't."

"But you just promised to always tell us the truth."

"I did, and I meant it. But not telling you something isn't the same as lying. There's a lot of what we do that's classified."

Webber clearly harbored many secrets. It was obvious few if any of those secrets would be revealed. Chris accepted that reality. At least their relationship seemed to be on better footing. "Okay, then I have another question."

"Go for it."

"Can we make one stop along the way back to the air base?"

"What for?"

"It's not that we don't trust you now, but we'd like to buy our own boots."

Chris's humor got a laugh, but he remained anxious.

If Webber's test almost killed us, how treacherous will the real assignment be?

Chapter Twenty: Dubrovnik, Croatia

Photos 46–47

CHAPTER TWENTY-ONE

Wednesday

For days, Anna Monteiro had hibernated in a Philadelphia hotel room. The bed was unmade, clothes littered the floor, odorous food trays were piled in a corner, and the curtains stayed pulled tight. The junior suite was suffocating. In the past, she had always been a neatnik; she would never have fathomed wallowing in a pigsty.

She longed for those ten-hour days pursuing her passion to help cure cancer at Longfellow BioSciences. But her vocation was gone for fear that going to work, or making a call or typing an email, could prove fatal.

Anna had tried replacing the emptiness by reading but couldn't concentrate. She binged on quiz shows and soaps in the morning and endless reruns at night while battling insomnia. Worry consumed most hours. She mourned what she had lost and hated what she had become.

Screw it. Fresh air and exercise will help. Get off your damn butt. Go for a run.

She sprinted along the Delaware River waterfront at Penn's Landing.[48] Bodies of water – rivers, lakes and oceans – had always been her happy place. Yet the flawless blue sky and warm sunshine were powerless to bring joy or comfort or hope. She was hypervigilant while tourists snapped photos of *Moshulu*, the world's oldest four-masted sailing ship.[49]

A burner phone rang. She dug it out of her jeans. With an excitement she hadn't experienced in three months, she said, "Hello?"

"Hi," Chris said. Hearing his voice was reassuring. "How you doing?"

She despised that question but camouflaged the truth. "Doing fine. Are you back yet?"

"Yeah, Michelle and I got into Philly about an hour ago."

"That's great." With a broad smile, she started backtracking on the promenade toward her hotel a thousand feet away. "Sorry if I sound out of breath. I'm out for a run. Was it a good trip?"

"I'm not sure I'd call it good, but it was successful." He sounded tired.

"That's great," she said, regretting the redundancy. She sounded like a giddy schoolgirl. While hustling past a World War II submarine and a Spanish-American War cruiser,[50] Anna became incapable of small talk. *Damn it, just ask the question before you lose your nerve.* "Say, I was wondering if I could come by for a visit."

There was an excruciating pause. "I'm, uh, kinda surprised you want to. When we talked a few weeks ago, you made it very clear we were done. Did the Boston shooting change your mind somehow?"

"I guess that's part of it." She tittered. "But you know how fickle women can be."

"Well, maybe if you want to, you know, get together somewhere down the road, then let's think about it."

Anna tensed while blurting, "How 'bout later this afternoon?"

"What? Where are you?"

She tried deciphering his inflection. Was he excited, put off or upset? "I'm staying at the Penn's Landing Hilton."

"Seriously? That's a few blocks from here. You want me to come there?"

Okay, he's agreed to meet. That's a start. "No, I'd rather see your place if that's okay. What's your address?" After adding it to a burner, she said, "Got it. Be there in about an hour." She hung up before he could change his mind.

Anna dashed into the hotel, rode up the elevator, entered her room and went into the bathroom. The mirror was not flattering. Her short black hair was stringy, and her underarms failed the sniff test. There wasn't time to shower. She brushed her teeth, squirted in red-out eyedrops, buried puffiness under concealer, dabbed on colored lip gloss, and searched for the least-wrinkled clothes before packing.

She considered using Uber. However, if she waited too long, she might chicken out. A warped wheel on the roller bag rattled for six blocks over cracked and uneven sidewalks. When arriving at the two-story brick rowhouse,[51] a panic attack was imminent.

Chris opened the blue front door. He had changed during the last twelve weeks. Or had her memory of him changed? He appeared thinner, older and stressed. His blue-green eyes were dull, his complexion was milk white, he was unshaven, and his pale lips were agape while staring, not at her but at the luggage. "I didn't know you planned on staying," he said in a monotone.

Michelle brushed past her brother, ran down the steps and embraced Anna. There wasn't a hint she harbored resentment for Anna turning them in to the FBI in Seville. All Anna felt was sisterly affection.

"How you doing?" Michelle whispered in her ear.

"I'm a mess." Tears dampened Michelle's long sandy hair and shoulder. The quivering wouldn't stop. When the wave of emotions lessened, Michelle invited her in. Chris followed behind.

The living room was clean but sparse. The mismatched furniture was functional. The awkwardness was thick. After a few seconds of silence, Michelle said, "Tell you what. I'll go grab us something to drink. How's that sound?"

More seconds passed before Anna dared to face Chris. His posture was stiff, bordering on defensive. This wasn't the reception she expected. "Are you mad at me?"

"Surprised, yes. Confused, maybe. But not mad. What're you doing here?"

"I don't know, I really don't." *This was a mistake, all a terrible mistake.* She summoned the courage to babble. "Yes, I do know. You're the only one who understands what I'm going through. Sure, my family and Liz love me and try to be supportive, but they just don't get it. I'm in a deep dark hole and can't get out." She swayed with anxiety. "And I'm scared, Chris. I'm always scared. Only you can protect me like you did before."

He seemed distant and unsympathetic. "Well, I just spoke to Roundy. He doesn't think Sergeant O'Neill is onto him. So I'm sure he'd be willing to …"

"I don't want Roundy," she shrieked. "I want you!" *That came out wrong.* She began to plea. "Please let me stay, if just for a few days."

After a deep sigh, Chris said with a calm that contrasted her panic, "Anna, you've said many times you don't want me around. Given all that's happened, I understand your reasons. I really do. So I'm not sure how to act when you suddenly reappear."

She shrieked, "I'm not sure how to act either, but I'm desperate. Please."

His shoulders sagged, but he didn't respond.

Now I've lost my dignity too. She grabbed the luggage handle and headed toward the door.

"Hey, wait." When she turned around, he remained indecisive. "You know, I can't protect you like I did before. That FBI task team is a full-time job. And we'll probably travel more." He paused, struggling with his thoughts. "But it's safer here than your Boston brownstone, that's for sure." He paused again. She sensed his conviction building. "So if you want to stay until the danger is over, well then, I guess you're welcome. But you'll need something to defend yourself with when I'm gone."

"Like what?"

"We need to buy you a gun."

Chapter Twenty-One: Philadelphia, Pennsylvania

Photos 48–51

CHAPTER TWENTY-TWO

Wednesday

After a twenty-minute ride on the SEPTA subway, Anna and Chris emerged at Allegheny Station,[52] a world away from the waterfront beauty of Penn's Landing. He said the neighborhood's nickname was the Las Vegas of Drugs, but she was aghast. His warning hadn't prepared her for the squalor.

The elevated train tracks[53] above Kensington Avenue created a shadowed market for addicts. Many moved in drug-induced stupors, others slouched in contorted positions, a few babbled incoherently, and an emaciated man was tying a latex tourniquet on his extended arm while corner boys peddled their eight-dollar bags. Littering the street were seeping garbage bags, windswept trash, beer cans, head-bobbing pigeons and syringes. The stench was repulsive. She breathed through her mouth.

Anna clutched Chris as they hurried past boarded storefronts, vacant lots filled with encampments, gang graffiti and lewd stares. Only seedy bars, a smoke shop, liquor stores, pawnshops and a nail salon were thriving. A convulsing woman with few teeth grabbed for Anna's shoes.

Trembling, Anna begged, "Let's get out of here."

"We're almost there," Chris said as they turned onto a side street.

Earlier, he had convinced her there wasn't time to buy a gun through a licensed dealer. Too much red tape for a background check and especially for a concealed carry permit. Besides, a legal purchase might flag the FBI or the Boston police. He trusted this guy to sell clean guns discreetly for reasonable prices.

"But what's he doing in this hellhole?" she asked.

"That's easy. A third of Philly's drug violations happen in this square mile, so it's a bonanza for Mark's gun sales."

Chris knocked on the steel door of a narrow, two-story brick row-house with barred windows.[54] Vicious dogs barked and scratched. A security globe whirled. "Give me a sec," came over the intercom. A minute later, a scruffy big guy with full-sleeve tats gave Chris a bro hug, gave her a cursory glance, and welcomed them in. There was a massive gun on his hip.

Dominating the dark living room were a recliner and a sixty-two-inch TV displaying a battle game frozen mid-action. Three Rottweilers with bared fangs growled and foamed while clawing their cage. "Down, girls," he shouted to the dogs. "Don't worry about them. They're pussycats."

Like hell they are.

Mark led them to the basement, entered a digital code, pulled back a vault-like door and flipped on the overhead light, revealing a doomsday arsenal of weapons. Anna was petrified as she walked into the windowless room.

"Now then," Mark said from behind a counter, engaging with Chris, "what can I do you for?"

"As I told you over the phone, Anna needs a handgun, preferably new and untraceable. I'll let her explain."

She tried but couldn't talk.

"Go ahead," Chris said.

"Well, I uh, I've had lots of people shoot at me lately." An anxious giggle bubbled out. "I'm not safe at home or work or even outside because Chris can't always protect me. So I'm scared to death." She flailed her hands. "Oh, God no, that's the wrong way to say it. I just want to stay alive. But I hate guns. I can't trust myself with a gun. I've never even shot one."

Unexpected compassion crossed the gun dealer's brutish face. "I'm guessing it's safe to say you're a beginner."

Anna giggled again. "Yeah, that's for sure."

"Okay, I'll take it slow until we find you something, okay? And ask anything you want along the way."

Mark showed her three 9mm pistols: SIG P365, Smith & Wesson Bodyguard and Springfield Hellcat.[55] He described them as small, concealable and suitable for her hand. They were intimidating. She picked up the Hellcat. "It's heavier than I thought. Is it safe?"

"Yes."

"Is that because the safety is on?"

"No, number one" – he pulled back the slide, showing the empty chamber – "as you can see, it's not loaded." When he released the slide, Anna jumped back at the snapping noise. "Number two, it doesn't have a traditional safety, okay? It's built into the trigger. So don't touch the trigger until ready to shoot, okay?"

"What's that thingy on top again?"

Mark demonstrated three times how to chamber a round. Anna kept struggling to pull back the slide. She didn't have the dexterity or strength or both. Frustration and embarrassment made her seek Chris's help.

"Let's be practical," he said to Mark. "She's never going to be comfortable with a pistol slide."

"It'll get easier when it's broken in and she's had practice," Mark countered.

"Or if she had our muscle memory with pistols. But she doesn't have time for that. The threat is now. Right now. And she'd be dead before figuring out how to rack the first round."

Anna flinched at how fast she'd be killed trying to defend herself.

Chris continued, "Wouldn't a small revolver be easier? It's basically aim and shoot. Sure, there are fewer rounds. But if she needs more than five or six, she'd be toast in a shootout."

"Damn it, please stop saying that?"

"What?"

"How fast I'm going to die."

"I'm sorry. That's not what I meant. But you need something super easy, so if a bad guy is coming at you, you just keep pulling the trigger until he's down."

Mark added, "I agree. You also have to consider recoil, okay? A .38 Special might be best for that." He pulled out a Ruger LCR-X[56] and gave it to Anna. "This snub-nosed revolver is compact, lightweight and reliable, similar to what cops trusted for years. How's that feel?"

She held the gun outward. "A lot better than the other ones." Her hand was shaking.

"Here, let me show you how to hold it," Chris said while manipulating her fingers. "Always, and I mean always, keep this index finger above the trigger guard like that until ready to shoot. Now, tuck that thumb down and grip with your other hand, pressing your thumbs together. Perfect. Now hold out your arms and cover your target with the sight."

"The what?"

"Center that bump at the end of the barrel in the middle of this groove here. That's it. Now pull the trigger slow and steady."

"I'm so nervous."

"You're doing fine."

Anna held her breath, hunched her shoulders and emitted a whimper as the trigger snapped and the cylinder rotated. "How was that?"

"Fine for the first time. But it helps if you keep your eyes open." Both men laughed.

"Stop making fun of me."

Chris got serious. "Sorry, I'm not. It'll take some practice, but at least now you've got the basics." Turning to Mark, he asked, "Would you recommend hollow points?"

"What's that?" Anna asked.

Mark explained, "It means the bullet mushrooms as it spins inside the body, okay, tearing up everything in its path."

"Jesus, that's awful."

"But that's what gives it stopping power," Chris said.

Anna selected the Hornady Critical Defense hollow point cartridges with tips resembling pink lipstick tubes. Chris loaded the revolver with five rounds and handed it back to her.

She cringed. "What the hell am I supposed to do with that?"

"Carry it, now and forever. That was the whole idea, remember?"

As Anna wedged the Ruger inside her runner's pack, Chris paid Mark in cash.

Now she had three things to worry about.

Will the damn thing go off around my waist? Will I ever have to use it? If I do, will it keep me alive?

Chapter Twenty-Two: Philadelphia, Pennsylvania

Photos 52–56

CHAPTER TWENTY-THREE

Thursday

Special Agent Sloan Hamilton was always tardy. She considered fifteen minutes late to be punctual. While the siblings cooled their heels in a task force meeting room at the FBI Philadelphia field office,[57] Michelle assessed her brother's mood.

Normally, Chris would be chatty while waiting. Or he'd complain while tapping his fingers. Not this morning. He was slouching and withdrawn. His sullen mood had started when Anna showed up yesterday, worsened by the time he threw a blanket on the couch so Anna could have his bedroom, and was worrisome during the wordless breakfast. He answered Michelle's repeated concerns with, "Nothing's wrong," "I said I'm fine," or "Just leave me alone already, will you?"

Hamilton burst into the room, dropped a legal pad and bulging file folders on the decades-old conference table, sat down in a huff and began clicking a ballpoint pen. An errant strand of gray-black hair dangled over enormous oval glasses. Her suit was wrinkled and a ribbon bow tie drooped. She seemed haggard and edgy, and it was only eight fifteen in the morning. "Welcome back," she said without sincerity. "Our office pool had even odds you wouldn't make it back alive from your field trip."

Michelle couldn't decipher if the macabre humor was supposed to be funny – or hell, maybe the office pool was real – but there was no way she'd disclose how close they came to being killed. She said with a teasing lilt, "I won't ask how you bet your money."

Ice woman didn't react to the quip. Instead, she asked, "What did Webber have you do?"

Chris scowled. "That's classified."

Hamilton's ire pivoted toward him. "I see. And who is this guy, anyway?"

"That's also classified," he said with a defiant smirk.

Chris and Hamilton reached an impasse in record time. Michelle tried intervening. "Webber asked us to keep working with you and your task team. So maybe we should discuss your priorities."

Of course, her brother insisted on pushing the woman's buttons. "Or tell us what brilliant things your task team's done in the last few days."

"You really want to know?" Hamilton asked as her agitation escalated. "Okay, fine, I'll tell you. Yesterday we found the car you drove the day you killed Irene Shaw. And you'll never guess where it was." In mockery, she glared back and forth. "Give up? At the bottom of the Schuylkill River. I can't imagine how it got there, can you? But I am sure it's chock-full of evidence. And when forensics finds it, I'll be thrilled to tear up your FBI deal and throw your asses in jail."

Chris said with defiance, "We both know that's not going to happen."

"Now that's a bet I wouldn't make. But until then, you'll keep doing your jobs, got it?"

Hamilton's disclosure about the stolen car surged through Michelle. They had been diligent. And a polluted river had a wonderful way of corrupting evidence. But the maxim of forensic science was "every contact leaves a trace."

They could find something. And this woman is hell-bent on proving we killed Irene. Will Webber's promise of immunity overrule her threats? Or are we going to be nailed?

Michelle buried her doubts before body language could broadcast her guilt. She had to mediate again before the confrontation spiraled out of control. With a conciliatory tone, she said, "Agent Hamilton, we're sorry this meeting's gotten off on the wrong foot. We're genuinely here to help. Tell us what we can do next."

Hamilton took a final shot at Chris. "Why can't you be more like your sister?"

Let it go, dude. For God's sake, let it go. Fortunately, he remained quiet.

With a huff of victory, the FBI special agent swiveled away – giving him the cold shoulder – and faced Michelle. Her tone switched from combative to professional. "I've got a full plate this morning, so we're going to keep this short and sweet. I'm sure you remember our last conversation about Dr. Nathan Yasin."

"Of course. But as I said before, he won't tell me anything about Irene's network."

"No, that's not right." Hamilton flipped through her notes until finding a highlighted quote. "Your exact words were, 'The chances for success are slim to none unless you saw him in person.'"

"Okay, that sounds like me. Why?"

"Good, because I've arranged for a meeting in Saint Paul."

Remorse flooded Michelle at the prospect of seeing her mentor again. Dr. Yasin undoubtedly blamed her for the deaths of his son, daughter-in-law and grandsons. Their conversation would be gut-wrenching, assuming he spoke at all. "When's the meeting?"

"Tomorrow afternoon. Our flight leaves tonight at five."

"We're going together?"

"Of course. What'd you expect? This is my investigation. So stick around when we're done here and I'll tell you the questions I want you to ask."

This woman is clueless.

Hamilton focused on Chris. "And you'll report to the task team in ten minutes."

"Okay, but what for?"

"Because your next assignment is to ID anyone from Irene's network who attends her funeral tomorrow."

"You're kidding, right? Nobody will show up for that."

"Why not?"

"There isn't a person on earth who mourns her death. Besides, anyone who has ever seen a cop or FBI show knows you guys monitor criminals' funerals. It's a total waste of time."

"Then I hope you enjoy the hymns, because you're going."

Chris rubbed his eyes and covered his face before sitting upright and locking in on Hamilton. In a calm, noncontentious way, he said, "Fine, I'll go. But in return, can you hear me out for a minute and stay open-minded? Please."

With a sweeping hand gesture, Hamilton said, "The floor's yours." She sat back to listen. Her fuse was obviously short.

"Okay, rather than waste time on things like Yasin and the funeral, I think you should focus on the bigger picture."

"What's that supposed to mean?"

"Remember when I said Senator McLoren and Steven Oakley might've been puppets in killing the senators and trying to steal the White House? Well …" He paused for dramatic effect. "What if the White House was the mastermind?"

Hamilton's eyes flared as the pen skidded across the table. "Cut the crap. That's the most asinine thing I've ever heard."

"No, think about it. This summer, every poll showed President Starling had a zero chance at a second term. Now, with elections twenty-six days away, he's a shoo-in. It's predicted he'll sweep every battleground state."

"Not so fast," Hamilton said. "The polls are notoriously wrong."

"Sure, but not this time. And why? Because after Senator Vickie McLoren was thrown out of the race for poisoning the senators, her weak replacement had no time, no funding, and no political support to campaign properly. So voila!" He emphasized his conclusion with outstretched hands. "A guaranteed second term for President

Starling. Then McLoren, Oakley and Irene were silenced to tie up loose ends."

Hamilton's square jaw tightened. "Do you come up with this kinda shit just to screw with me?"

"I know we've had our differences."

"That's an understatement."

"But I'm serious. Do you want that kind of man to stay in the Oval Office? If you give me the resources, I can unravel this. That's where I should focus."

This theory was new to Michelle. Was it just another head fake on Hamilton? Based on his passion, he seemed serious. Chris was the most analytical person she knew. He always spent an inordinate amount of time uncovering the names of silentcide clients. Maybe his speculation had merit.

Hamilton didn't buy it for a second. "Why don't you focus on what I tell you to focus on? Could you do that for a change?"

He shrugged. "Okay, well, I tried."

"You tried jerking my chain again. Hope it was fun for you, because it wasn't for me." She stacked and straightened the legal pad and file folders, a clear signal the meeting was ending. "Now then, is there anything else — anything valuable — to discuss before we break huddle?"

Michelle debated bringing up the news. She knew Chris opposed her advice, but she'd kept telling him the consequences would be severe if Hamilton discovered it later. "I think Chris has something else to tell you."

He shot venomous disapproval at Michelle's betrayal. Hamilton goaded him on. "Now what? Maybe a new Area 51 theory?"

He vacillated before blurting out, "Anna Monteiro is staying with us for a while."

Hamilton's eyes narrowed to slits. "How'd that happen? Did you coerce her?"

"No, she just showed up yesterday," Michelle said.

"What on earth for?"

"Because she didn't feel safe in Boston," he answered.

"And she's safer with career killers? That makes no sense. Besides, it violates her probation."

Chris countered, "No, she wasn't convicted of a felony, so there's no probation. She pled down to one minor misdemeanor, remember?"

"Then it must be against her plea agreement."

"No again. The only requirements were that she remain crime-free and continue cooperating with the FBI. It said nothing about staying away from us, nor does our agreement with you."

"Why would those docs specify she stay away from assassins? She couldn't get away from you fast enough before."

"That sounds like a lack of foresight on your attorneys' part. Not our problem. It's all perfectly legal."

"Well, not for long. I promise you this. I'll find a way to kick her out."

Chapter Twenty-Three: Philadelphia, Pennsylvania

Photo 57

CHAPTER TWENTY-FOUR

Philadelphia, Pennsylvania

Thursday

Wolfgang was oblivious to the fast-food wrappers on the muddy floor mats of his Ford F-150, and to the dangling evergreen air freshener that had lost the battle against stale cigar smoke. He was heads down, chuckling at the antics of *Spy vs. Spy*.

He had laughed at the pair of bungling espionage agents ever since grade school. The slapstick comic strip was his favorite part of *MAD* magazine. Cuban artist Antonio Prohías drew the best panels. Wolfgang wondered if the original cartoonist's artwork was for sale. They'd be ideal to add to his shopping list after acquiring Irene's fortune from her locked laptop.

He glanced over the steering wheel. Finally, one car remained in the parking lot. He threw the magazine aside, gave the shoulder holster a reassuring pat, gingerly exited the truck to avoid a back spasm, and dashed across the street. After rubbing his eyes until they were red and watering, he rang the doorbell and buttoned his sport coat.

An elderly man opened the door. His thick white hair, conservative tie, pressed black suit and mournful expression gave him a dignified yet solemn appearance. "I'm sorry, sir, we're closed for the day. But I'm Brian Savannah, the director and owner. Can I help you regarding a loved one?"

Wolfgang faked quivering lips. "Yes, my mother died in hospice a few hours ago, and I don't have a clue of what to do next."

"I'm so sorry for your loss. Please come in."

The reception hallway had fleur-de-lis blue carpet, crisp white walls with wainscoting and shell-shaped sconces, upholstered sofas and chairs, and Queen Anne furniture with strategically placed Kleenex boxes. Elegant viewing rooms were on the left and right. They passed a chapel with cherrywood pews and a chandelier hanging from the vaulted ceiling on the way to Savannah's office. "Please have a seat." He pointed to the visitor's chair while rounding the desk.

"I have a better idea." He pulled out the SIG P229. "Let's remain standing."

"Oh, Christ!" Savannah screamed. Wolfgang relished the terror on the funeral director's face. The man trembled while raising his arms in submission. "Please don't hurt me. Please! I don't have any cash. Just take anything you want, then leave."

"Thanks for your generous offer. I'll remind you of that later. Am I correct you have Irene Shaw staying as your guest?"

"What're you talking about?"

"Irene Shaw. According to the obits, you're handling her arrangements."

"Yes," he answered weakly. "She's in the reposing room."

"That sounds lovely," Wolfgang said sarcastically. "Bring me to her. Now!"

Savannah kept glancing backward as they walked down the hall and entered a dimly lit, intimate room with a couch and several plush chairs facing a luxurious mahogany casket. The funeral director lifted the lid's upper half with respect.

Irene was elegant. She would've been thrilled with the mortician's work. Her hair, skin and makeup were flawless. The scarlet lipstick was classic Irene. She appeared at peace and serene despite the power suit. A designer silk scarf covered her slit throat. Wolfgang belly-laughed. She was clutching a rosary.

Savannah worked up the nerve to say, "Okay, you've seen her. Will you please go?"

"Not yet. Remember when you said I could take anything I wanted? Well, I want her hand."

In wide-eyed horror, he asked, "You what?"

"Yes, her right hand."

"Dear God, no. That violates the ethics of four generations of …"

Wolfgang shot Irene in the chest. The act was not as satisfying as the fantasy, but it got Savannah's undivided attention. "Brian, Brian, Brian. This can go one of two ways. Either you cooperate and it's all over soon, or you'll become the next dearly departed. What's it going to be?"

"Okay, okay, okay," he whimpered. "But there's a problem."

"What's that?"

"I don't have tools to sever bones."

"Are you kidding me?"

"No, in my business, we have tools to put body parts back together but not to take them apart."

"Then I suggest you improvise. Fast."

Savannah fidgeted in desperation. "I may have something in the garage."

The floor was spotless beneath a polished black hearse and transport van. Over a pristine workbench were rows of labeled mason jars containing screws, nails and various hardware. Glistening tools hung on a pegboard by type, size and shape like disciplined soldiers during an inspection. Everything was too meticulous. Wolfgang assumed Savannah had obsessive-compulsive disorder. The mortician chose a reciprocating saw, inserted a battery pack, and vacillated before selecting a twelve-inch, stainless-steel, fine-tooth blade.

Wolfgang's OCD suspicions were confirmed when the funeral

director refused to perform the surgery in the reposing room for fear of soiling the carpet and the need for safety garb. He pushed the casket trolley into an elevator, descended to the basement, and approached a door marked Preparation Room.

He flipped on the lights. Surrounding two long steel tables were white cabinets with lower drawers and upper rows of colorful plastic bottles filled with God knew what. Beside the porcelain sinks were two box contraptions with hoses. The commercial cleaner stench was repulsive. The embalming room gave Wolfgang the creeps.

Savannah donned a disposable gown, latex gloves, a mask and a plastic face shield. He secured a black garbage bag over Irene's chest and rolled up her sleeve. When the blade began cutting, Wolfgang turned away. He had seen far worse during his career as a medic, mercenary and assassin. Yet somehow Irene was demanding respect.

The grinding and cursing lasted five minutes.

"Here you go," Savannah said with disgust while holding a Ziploc bag.

The white plastic ID band on her wrist was laughable compared to the diamond-studded bracelet she had always worn and treasured.

"We done?"

"Nope, not yet. I saw online you have a crematorium on site. Let's go for a demonstration."

"But cremation goes against the family's wishes."

"I guess mistakes happen, right? Besides, she has no family. And trust me, nobody cares. Now move." He reinforced the command with a thrust of the gun.

Savannah steered the cart down the hall, elbowed a wall-mounted door switch, and wheeled the casket into a room dominated by an industrial-size steel furnace with protruding pipes and a smokestack. He tapped keys on the control screen and pushed a green button. The exhaust system whirled. The flames whooshed.

"We ready?"

"Hardly," Savannah answered. "The retort must preheat to at least fourteen hundred degrees. In the meantime, I have a few questions."

"Fire away." Wolfgang was disappointed the pun wasn't appreciated or at least recognized.

"Any battery-powered medical devices in the deceased?"

"I'm clueless."

Savannah consulted the screen again. "It says here she has a belly button ring. Do you want it?"

"Eww, God no."

"Okay, and who should I say authorized the cremation?"

"Brutus, her dog." This joke was also ignored. *This man has no sense of humor.*

With a deep breath of tolerance, Savannah said, "Protocol is for the deceased to be in a cardboard box and unclothed."

"So, if I catch your drift, you want to resell the casket. That's fine. Keep the extra profit. But let's maintain her dignity."

While the funeral director used an overhead body lift to position Irene into a cardboard box on a different cart, Wolfgang sat on a corner chair and played solitaire on his phone. The first two games were a bust. He got a decent score on the third try.

"Okay, we're ready now," Savannah announced.

"Excellent!" Wolfgang relished the moment Irene Shaw was pushed through the door of hell.

For the first time in eleven years, he experienced a sense of calm.

CHAPTER TWENTY-FIVE

Thursday

During the ninety-minute drive, Wolfgang tapped the steering wheel, bobbed his head and swooned to Elvis Presley classics. The late fifties were the best era for the King of Rock and Roll. When he had more money than God, he'd drive a reconditioned hotrod to Memphis. A highlight of Graceland would be seeing the iconic pink 1955 Cadillac Fleetwood Series 60 called Elvis Rose.[58] That would be a memorable experience.

Wolfgang turned down the music when entering Lancaster. He glanced fondly at the cooler on the passenger-side floor. Inside was the biometric authentication needed to crack open Irene's laptop. Soon he'd be rich.

He wasn't worried the funeral director would talk. The man was terrified. If he dared to report the incident, there wasn't any security video left behind to corroborate the story. No, Brian Savannah seemed smart enough to pocket the extra profit and, if asked, contend the cremation was an unfortunate mix-up. He was even nice enough to make copies of Irene's death certificate for free. What great service.

Gravel crackled beneath the tires as the headlights turned off and the truck inched into the driveway. The rusted windmill creaked as always. Cow manure stench seeped through the window. The house was dark.[59] Nobody was around.

Perhaps returning to the Amish farm was a mistake. Memories of eleven years as a silentcide instructor flooded his brain. This was a hideous place. But the drive from Philadelphia was shorter than going on to Harrisburg. And the old white farmhouse offered far more privacy than the crowded safehouse to do what he dreamed of doing.

Ghosts of killings past lingered in the moonless dark. He turned on a flashlight and stepped out where teenager Rachel Phillips was killed by a shotgun blast while trying to escape. In front of the barn,[60] senile Lionel Jørgensen – Irene's number two and former husband – had been shot in the head by Jacob Conners. Ansel Meehan's sniper bullet had ended Mamm's life at the top of the rickety steps.

Wolfgang shivered in the warm humid air. He wondered if the feds had discovered their graves. Out of curiosity, he would check in the morning.

A sign on the front door declared the FBI and Department of Justice had seized the property. The warning hadn't discouraged local teens who rebelled against Amish traditions. Party paraphernalia littered the outdated kitchen. A stench of beer, cigarettes and mildew permeated the air.

He lit the propane lantern suspended above a small dining table with bench seating. The sink was rusting where the cast-iron pump dripped. Someone had ripped a wooden cabinet off the wall. The elbowed exhaust pipe was missing from the wood-burning stove. This house had always been rustic but clean. Mamm would be horrified to see how fast it had deteriorated.

But he had never been nostalgic. Wolfgang didn't care about his past. Too many nightmares. What was important was the future. And now was the turning point toward a rich full life. Anticipation surged.

He raced back to the truck for the cooler and knapsack. After sweeping debris off the worn plastic tablecloth, he opened Irene's laptop. The damn thing took forever to boot up. He'd be hosed if the battery wasn't charged. The house had never had electricity, and the generator was finicky.

Now was the moment of truth. The cursor blinked in the password box. He took out Irene's hand, placed her index finger on the sensor and held his breath.

Wolfgang leaped up, spun around and hooted with joy as the screensaver revealed a blurry photo of an Afghan hound. Brutus had never looked so good. He kissed the ugly beast.

He fumbled with the touchpad while scrolling through the file names. Most were unimportant. Plenty of time to explore them later. His pulse quickened while clicking on Financial Files. The parent folders read: Domestic Accounts, Offshore Accounts, Swiss Accounts and Bitcoin Accounts. "Jackpot!"

The front door shattered. "FBI! FBI!" A flashbang rattled across the floor, exploding into swirls of smoke with blinding light. The deafening ringing muted the commands. "FBI! Get down! Now!"

Wolfgang grabbed for anything to prevent falling. The table collapsed, the bench flipped and his head slammed on the gritty floor. Fear and confusion were disorienting.

The strike force team was a blur. "Don't move!" Floating white circles obstructed his view of rushing shadows. "Stay down!" The barrel of an M4 carbine assault rifle hammered his shoulder. "I said don't move, goddamn it." A boot on the neck was suffocating while manic hands searched for weapons. "Got a gun!" He was kicked in the ribs followed by a crushing blow to the groin. Wolfgang curled in agony. Pain stole his breath.

"Damn sissy!" The other two men laughed. "Stop moaning. You're acting like a little girl."

The furniture was righted. He was lifted off the floor, punched in the gut and forced to sit on the bench. His hands were held on the table. A tactical baton was extended. Without warning, the long metal rod crushed a pinky finger.

Teeth clenched, eyes watered and his spine convulsed. A vicious scream mixed with choking gasps.

"Now do we have your attention?" The menacing voice came from the opposite bench.

Wolfgang struggled to see. First in focus were the yellow FBI letters across a tactical armor vest. He confronted the assailant. A black ski mask covered the man's face. The green eyes were sinister. Wolfgang glanced at the other combatants. Their fingers hovered over the trigger guards. Two assault weapons pointed at his head. These men weren't dressed as FBI SWAT. The imposters were poised to kill.

Wolfgang garbled his words. "What you want?"

"We've come to deliver a message. The Commander isn't pleased. Twice you were nicely asked to cooperate. Instead, you were very rude. Tsk, tsk, tsk. Perhaps now you'll reconsider." He pulled an envelope from his vest and threw it in Wolfgang's face. "You will do this assignment or …" The man jumped up, leaned over and pressed his body weight on the shattered finger. "Or our next visit won't be as pleasant." He yanked the pinky backward. "Can I tell The Commander you accepted?"

Excruciating torment prevented a response. He nodded.

The assailant gave the finger an extra tug. "That's good. Very good."

A heartbeat later, a rifle butt battered his chest. He catapulted onto the floor.

The men chuckled.

While Wolfgang convulsed in the fetal position, he spotted the laptop upside down in the corner. He panicked. *Where's Irene's hand?*

After a violent kick to the head, Wolfgang's world faded to black.

Chapter Twenty-Five: Lancaster County, Pennsylvania

Photos 58–60

CHAPTER TWENTY-SIX

Thursday

"Enough already. Go home," the last FBI task team member said while peering over Chris's cubicle. He nodded but was reluctant to leave. He had been researching a plot theory all day but kept hitting dead ends. He typed a final thought, shut down his desktop, and followed the agent out of the building. He wasn't allowed to be in the FBI office unattended.

Chris dreaded facing Anna alone while Michelle was in Saint Paul with Special Agent Hamilton. He spent two hours eating overpriced sushi, scrolled random internet sites for ninety minutes while sitting on a bench at Independence Mall,[61] and meandered for another fifteen during the three blocks to the siblings' temporary home. When he opened the door and the living room was empty, he was relieved.

The sense of relief disappeared in the kitchen. On the table was a place setting for two with wineglasses and an unopened bottle of Cakebread Cabernet. A Post-it® Note on a Tupperware bowl read, "Dinner inside. Heat up if hungry." The beef stroganoff was brimming with bacon bits, his favorite. He resisted and popped the top of a cold beer.

As the refrigerator door slammed, the condiments rattled. He dropped into a chair, took a sip and pressed his fists against his forehead. *What the hell's she doing?* Her reference was obvious, but not her intent.

This was the wine and meal Anna had served at her Boston brownstone about three and a half months ago when their mutual infatuation was electric. He reminisced when she flirtatiously asked, "Wanna be childish?" before their passion beneath a comforter. *God, everything was perfect.*

Hours later, they learned her friend had overdosed, shattering their bliss. He would never reveal he had intended the lethal drug for Anna when she was a silentcide target during the Caribbean cruise. Chris still felt agonizing remorse for the unintentional killing of Jessica, a single mom with a four-year-old son.

Nothing had been the same after that night. While dangerous events spiraled out of control, Anna pushed further away. She rejected him regardless of what he did. Then she left him with only a meager thanks for keeping her alive. Later, when cornered by the FBI, she betrayed them. Was he willing to repeat that cycle?

"Hi," Anna said when entering the kitchen. She was wearing his robe without makeup. She smelled freshly showered. "Have you eaten yet?" she asked as if expecting excited praise.

"Yes" was his sullen response.

"That's okay." She struggled to maintain the smile. "We can have the stroganoff tomorrow night."

"Did you go out and buy this stuff?" he asked with an edge.

Taken aback, she answered, "No, I called in the orders and paid with cash when they were delivered."

"Are you carrying your gun?"

She was startled by the second question. Stepping back, she pulled the terrycloth across her chest. "No, was I supposed to?"

"Absolutely. That's why we got the damn thing. What if it hadn't been me down here?"

"I hardly think the first thing a bad guy does is raid the fridge. But if you want me to go get the *damn thing*, it's beside the bed."

Stop being a jerk. "That's okay for now," he said, using a softer tone. "But please always carry it when I'm not home."

"Sure. Whatever."

An uncomfortable lull followed. He worried she was going to walk away … again. If she did, she was justified. Instead, she asked, "Want to tell me what's wrong?"

He debated whether to tell the truth. *No way. Don't go there.* "It's Sloan Hamilton. She's driving me crazy."

"Why?" Anna pulled back the adjoining chair. The robe slipped away from her knee as she crossed her legs.

He instinctively stared, chastised himself, diverted his focus and played with a spoon. "Because she has us on wild-goose chases. Like dragging Michelle to Minnesota to talk with Dr. Yasin."

"Yeah, she told me about that when she came back to pack before her flight. She wasn't happy."

"No kidding. It'll be a disaster. And I'm supposed to attend Irene's funeral tomorrow."

"What on earth for?"

"On the one-in-a-million chance some idiot from her network shows up that I can ID. It's nuts. Who'd be that dumb?"

"But at least you get to watch the ogre being buried."

"Fat consolation. Irene's already mentally buried." *She may be dead, but the emotional scars will live forever. Goddamn that woman.*

Anna's voice snapped him out of his hatred. "Can't you reason with Hamilton?"

"No, that's just it. I've tried. Like this morning, I begged her to let me focus on the big picture, but she laughed at me."

Anna pulled the chair closer. Her bare foot was inches away from his leg. "What's the big picture?"

"Who really masterminded the poisonings of the four senators and then silenced Senator McLoren and Steven Oakley?"

"I'm sure you have a theory?"

"Of course I do. Ready for this?" He leaned toward her as if sharing a secret. "It might've been President Starling. I think it was his way of eliminating his congressional enemies and presidential rival to ensure a second term in the White House."

Her eyes widened. "Jesus! That's serious." The top of her nose pinched.

"No shit. I'm not sure I'm right, but you'd think Hamilton would at least give me the resources to explore it."

Sitting upright, Anna proclaimed, "Well, I can help."

"What do you mean?"

"Think about it. We were a great team when we found Senator Rosa Phillips in Denver and Irene in Seville. And Lord knows, I've got nothing else to do. So put me to work."

"You sure?"

"Sure I'm sure." She accented her words with waving hands. "Why not?"

"Well, okay, as long as you don't do anything that's traceable."

Her laugh was infectious. "Did you really need to tell me that? This isn't my first rodeo."

Two hours disappeared in a minute. They brainstormed for ideas, wrote them on a legal pad and divided up the tasks. The teamwork was invigorating.

"It sounds like a plan," she declared with enthusiasm while stifling a yawn. "I'll dive in first thing in the morning."

"Great." He loved seeing her energy back and the sparkle in her dark brown eyes. This was the smart, driven, accomplished and humble woman he admired. Yet his emotions remained conflicted. "Now go get some sleep."

The robe peeked open when she stood. There was no effort to close the gap. Perhaps she didn't notice. Perhaps it was intentional. He gnawed his lip, willing her to walk away before he said or did something stupid.

"Can I try asking you something again?" She didn't wait for his response. "Before I asked you what's wrong. You never answered the question."

"Yes I did. What'd you think we've been talking about?"

"Don't misunderstand. I'm excited to be working on this. But what else is eating at you?"

"Nothing," he said without conviction. "Unraveling the plot is what's important. Not for Hamilton, but for me."

Was she reading his soul? He broke eye contact. He had vowed never to lie to her, but just did, and she knew it.

With an almost imperceptible sigh, she said, "Okay then. Good night."

He was mesmerized as she walked away. At the staircase, she glanced back and smiled before disappearing.

Why is she really back? Does she just want a competent bodyguard? Sure, you idiot. Don't confuse protection with desire. Why else would a wealthy, attractive, professional Ivy Leaguer want an impotent assassin from South Philly?

Chapter Twenty-Six: Philadelphia, Pennsylvania

Photo 61

CHAPTER TWENTY-SEVEN

Friday

One of the Sicarius Task Team members studied the dual video monitors — occasionally switching camera views — while Lance, the lead agent, slurped on a thirty-two-ounce Coke and wrestled with a lamb gyro sandwich from a food truck. The FBI surveillance van reeked of tzatziki sauce, garlic and onions. Chris sat on a narrow bench behind the two leather command chairs, waiting for the directive to enter the nineteenth-century Cathedral Basilica of Saints Peter and Paul.[62]

This stakeout of Irene Shaw's funeral was ridiculous. Nobody from her assassin network would show up. If they did, a lone blue van sitting in a near-empty parking lot would be a huge red flag. But his opinions were rejected. Also rejected was his request to be armed. "Felons don't get to play with guns," he was told. He resigned himself to follow orders, resisting the urge to say "I told you so" when the folly was over.

Of course, Sloan Hamilton hovered over the operation from her laptop in Saint Paul. Her modus operandi was to delegate the responsibilities and micromanage the details. Her judgmental and anxiety-ridden face was ever-present in the corner of a monitor.

Lance announced, "Got a black minivan jumping the front curb," as a glob of tomatoes and cheese dropped in his lap.

With a flick of a joystick, the camera zoomed in on the vehicle.

"Savannah & Sons Funeral Home, Celebrating Life for Generations" was stenciled on the side panel. A white-haired man wearing a three-piece suit jumped out carrying a small box and left the engine running.

Lance announced over the radio, "Everyone on alert!" followed by an internal command of, "Switch to camera two with audio."

The monitor showed the man arguing with what appeared to be a bishop based on the red skullcap and flowing robe. The sound kicked in mid-sentence: "... totally unacceptable. We were expecting the deceased in a casket."

The man was panting after running up only nine steps. "There was a mix-up. Here are her ashes."

"But there are spiritual benefits for the grieving ..."

"Sorry. What else can I say? Cancel if you want. Gotta go." The man bolted.

"That was odd," Lance said, using a napkin to clean off his pants. "Get a facial rec ID on that guy." He swiveled the chair while lifting an earcup off his wireless headset. "Davis, time to get in there. And discreetly get a vibe on that box if you can."

Chris marveled at the copper dome, the Neo-classical brownstone façade, and the four massive Corinthian columns before entering a bronze door.[63] There was lingering confusion in the vestibule over the urn marked Irene Shaw on a strip of blue painter's tape. The simple pine box was hardly worthy of internment in a pauper's field. *How the mighty have fallen.*

Chris followed an usher into the nave[64] radiating with golden hues. The view was spectacular. A magnificent dome was adorned with religious paintings and stained glass. Surrounding it were four paneled semi-domes suspended by imperial columns. Over the marble altar was an ornate canopy. While he passed eight side altars, the church echoed from footsteps along the white-and-green checked marble floor. He slid into an empty walnut pew near the front.

The lack of attendance was laughable. One row of people showed up for Irene's final big day. They were all elderly professionals wearing expensive suits. Curiously, one had his arm in a cast while another had bruises covering his face. Chris whispered into the comm, "Don't recognize anyone in the first row. Suspect they're from Shaw's law firm."

"Copy," came the response. "Direct your bodycam toward them when you can. I want better facial closeups." When the church bell pealed outside, the lead agent issued a general alert. "Heads up, people. It's showtime."

A refined woman approached the lectern, tapped the microphone and cleared her throat. "We are here today to celebrate the life of Irene Shaw." She brushed away a tear. "What can I say about her?"

Ask me. I'll tell you plenty. None of it's good.

"Irene was a pillar of society, a giving philanthropist and a defender of the accused. She always had an endearing smile, a gracious heart and a passion to help others in need. She was a beautiful soul." The woman grimaced with sorrow. "Irene will be sorely missed by all who loved her. Our only solace is we know she's in the welcoming hands of Our Lord Jesus Christ."

God, this is painful. Irene must've written this crap.

"Now please stand and face the back of the church."

The procession stood ready, waiting for the bishop to finish a blessing while sprinkling holy water on the urn. Chris thought a wooden stake would be more appropriate. Overhead, the marvelous organ with thousands of pipes played a solemn intro before a baritone soloist began singing "Ave Maria" in Latin.

First down the aisle was a deacon swishing a thurible. The billowing incense was noxious. An adult altar server carried a huge golden cross. He was followed by Irene's urn atop a cart; one wheel squeaked. Behind the bishop were two men, presumably pallbearers who had no casket to usher in. Everyone had his head bowed and hands clasped in reverence.

When the procession reached the bronze gates at the altar

railing, they genuflected. The discolored cloth beneath the urn was straightened. The bishop and servers entered the sanctuary while the pallbearers moved toward the empty front row. That was when Chris saw a menacing reflection in the golden cross.

He swiveled. A masked assailant wearing black tactical gear raced down the center aisle. "Gun!" Chris screamed.

Panic erupted as an AR-15 assault rifle discharged. The cross crashed, the deacon fell, and the bishop cascaded into a cloud of skidding incense. Muzzle flashes. One pallbearer slammed into the cart – scattering Irene's ashes – while scrambling behind the front pew. Screams. Two from the law firm raced out the side. Unrelenting blasts. Others dropped down for safety. Racing footsteps. The lawyer with the arm cast stood frozen for a millisecond until a bullet to the chest blew him backward.

"Shots fired! Shots fired!" Chris yelled to the task team as he wedged into the kneeler. Slugs pierced his pew. Wooden shrapnel flew. He knew he was the target and about to die.

"Engage!" came a command from the van. "Engage!"

A pistol appeared from the choir loft.[65] Two shots were fired at the assailant below. The gunman pivoted. A torrent of bullets shattered the balcony. Thunderous. Shell casings ejected and danced on the floor. Terror reverberated from the organist and soloist as the thirty-round magazine was emptied. The assailant began reloading. The FBI agent jumped up again for a kill shot. Fired once. Missed.

A roar of firepower from a second assassin blasted from behind the altar, down the nave and toward the choir. A chandelier shattered. Organ pipes shrieked with distorted notes. Stained glass cracked and imploded. The balcony was disintegrating as the gunmen fired their modified automatic weapons in unison at the task team member. Odorous clouds of gunpowder drifted through the cathedral.

Another FBI agent appeared from a side aisle, kneeled at the far end of Chris's row, took aim toward the altar and squeezed the trigger. Two bursts rang out before his position was riddled with gunshots. The assault rifle had him pinned down and outmatched. Chunks of a marble column exploded above his head as he slithered in retreat.

The terrified woman eulogist did the unthinkable. She bolted into the center aisle and stumbled toward the opposite pew. She was too slow, too vulnerable and about to be killed. Chris leaped out, grabbed her waist and yanked her to safety as bullets slammed the tile floor behind them. She kicked, scratched and cried as Chris shielded her from death.

The lead agent from the van burst through a side door,[66] crouched as he fanned out across the north transept and fired his Glock at the first gunman. The assailant's finger never left the trigger as bullets sprayed toward the new threat. Blasts were relentless. The agent in the choir unloaded his 9mm. The attacker convulsed as a round struck his vest. A second pierced his leg. Erratic gunfire sent ceiling tiles crashing as the assailant spun and collapsed. The headshot was fatal.

Odds were shifting. Now three agents triangulated their pistols on the altar. The shooting stopped as the second assassin dropped to the floor, dragged the prone bishop, sucker-punched him, and laid the assault rifle across his hip. The terrified clergyman was a human sandbag.

"This is the FBI," the lead agent declared. "You're surrounded. Give yourself ..."

A hail of bullets was the defiant response.

The other agent from the van crawled out of the sacristy with an outstretched Glock. He inched forward for a better angle. He fired a single bullet above the gunman, who instinctively raised his head to reposition the AR-15. The second shot shattered the assailant's brainstem. Blood splattered the cowering bishop. The agent jumped up and kicked away the weapon. "All clear!" he shouted in victory.

The pallbearers ran toward the side door. One survivor from

the law firm stood in a daze, two wept over the bleeding body of their colleague, and the others remained hidden. Chris helped the eulogist to her feet. She slapped him. "How dare you grope me like that, you pervert. Go to hell." She stomped off in an indignant huff.

As Chris stepped into the center aisle, the flood of fight-or-flight collapsed into a chilling reminder of mortality. He was lucky and grateful to be alive but knew the danger was far from over. Wolfgang would be more determined than ever to keep sending assassins.

Chris looked down and noticed cremation ashes covering his pants. Irene Shaw clung to him in a final act of dominance and control.

Chapter Twenty-Seven: Philadelphia, Pennsylvania

Photos 62–66

CHAPTER TWENTY-EIGHT

Friday

Raspberry Island[67] resembled a giant green barge floating beneath the Wabasha Street Bridge along the glistening Mississippi River. This panoramic view from the fifteenth floor on a sun-drenched afternoon should've been calming, but Michelle's stomach was acidic. Her knuckles cracked. She couldn't stop fidgeting while pacing the hotel room in downtown Saint Paul.[68]

The prospect of seeing Dr. Nathan Yasin again had been distressing when Special Agent Sloan Hamilton mentioned it yesterday in Philadelphia. Now, with the meeting — she checked her watch — twenty minutes away, she was terrified to face the father figure she admired.

Dr. Yasin had taught her medicine and pharmaceutical science on the Amish farm in Lancaster County. During her sixteen-year career as a silentcide assassin, he'd remained a steadfast mentor, advisor and confidant — always wise, patient and supportive. She loved the seventy-eight-year-old man as an orphaned daughter.

But she had betrayed him. During the siblings' exhaustive quest to stop the senator killings and seek vengeance on Irene, they had lured him into helping. No, that was a lie to deny her culpability. She alone had promised he wouldn't be implicated. She alone vowed his grandsons would be safe from Irene's threats.

She was wrong. Dead wrong.

Soon after Irene uncovered Yasin's involvement in the plot against her, the bloated bodies of his son, daughter-in-law and the twin boys were found inside the family car dredged from the muck of the Mississippi River.

Irene's wrath had spared Yasin's life but not his will to live. He was rotting in the nearby Adult Detention Center[69] while awaiting trial for co-architecting the assassin network. A life-in-prison verdict seemed assured. There was no doubt he hoped to die before a jury pronounced him guilty.

The looming confrontation was unnerving.

Where the hell is Hamilton? They were supposed to have breakfast together to discuss the Dr. Yasin interview. The agent had pushed back the time twice, then cancelled. An hour ago, Michelle texted to ask about Irene's funeral. There was no reply. Chris's cell phone rolled to voicemail. The silence was ominous.

Michelle picked at the lunch delivered by room service. The salad was swimming in vinaigrette dressing, the veggie wrap was soggy, and there was lipstick on the water glass. She nibbled on overpriced candy from the minibar while waiting to hear from Hamilton. Michelle was being ghosted.

As much as she dreaded the meeting, Michelle refused to be late. She could try calling Hamilton again or knock on her hotel room door. Both risked further delays. *Screw it! Just go.* Besides, privacy with Yasin was better than Hamilton's irksome interference. She sent a text: Meet you there.

Michelle bolted out of the hotel, dashed across four lanes of traffic and hustled along a promenade perched high on a bluff. The four-acre Kellogg Mall Park[70] featured herringbone brick pavers, tree-lined allées and green spaces. From the wrought-iron railing and park benches were spectacular views of the skyline behind and the river below.[71] Yet she was oblivious to the scenery as tension ravaged her chest.

She was the first to reach the rendezvous point. The large circular water fountain had eight jet streams and a semicircular arbor with cascading vines.[72] The wait wasn't long. A half block away, two men wearing identical blue windbreakers left the Warren E. Burger Federal Building.[73] They walked with purpose. After crossing the street, they approached and opened leather wallets. Inside were miniature golden shields and ID photos next to the letters "FBI."

Special Agent Rochefort was the elder by at least two decades. Contempt was the prominent feature of his hardened complexion. His stance was adversarial. "You're Michelle Barton," he declared in a terse, husky tone.

"That's right."

Following a judgmental stare, he said, "I've got to tell you, I spent months investigating you and your murderous brother when you lived in this state. We almost had your asses too. Then, for no goddamn good reason, the case moved to Philly." His step forward was intimidating. "Now I hear you got a cushy plea deal with the promise of immunity. That's an outrage!" He pointed an accusatory finger. "You should be rotting in a hellhole. And to add insult to injury, we have to babysit while you chitchat with Minnesota's biggest serial killer in a lovely park, for God's sake, instead of a cell where you both belong."

Michelle maintained eye contact. "So you're saying you're not a happy camper?"

The younger agent tried covering a snicker but failed. Rochefort pivoted, gave him a hostile glare, and resumed the dogfight with Michelle. His protruding chin twitched with anger. "And where the hell is Agent Hamilton? She finagled our orders from DC. She could at least have the decency to show up on time."

"She's busy but'll be here soon."

"That's nice. We were playing checkers before we left. We've got all the time in the world to wait for that prima donna."

Michelle took the offensive without being argumentative. "Special Agent Rochefort, I get why you're upset and appreciate your arranging this meeting. Could we agree to co-exist for the next half hour until this is over?"

Rochefort acted ready to hurl another jibe. Instead, he scoffed, pocketed his hands and leaned against a lamppost. The conversation ended in a stalemate.

A rotund man – maybe early thirties – wearing an inexpensive suit raced toward them. His thinning hair was matted. Crooked horn-rimmed glasses balanced precariously above chubby cheeks. "Are you all here for Dr. Yasin? Good. I'm Simon Carpenter, his public defender. His court appearance ended ten minutes ago. Somebody should deliver him soon."

After the introductions, Carpenter began spouting rules and restrictions for the meeting. Much of the legalese was unintelligible.

Michelle nodded politely while peering over his shoulder for Hamilton. Where was she? This disaster was her brilliant idea. She should be running interference, not hanging Michelle out to dry. There was no excuse for the agent's absence.

A Ramsey County Sheriff transport van pulled up along the curb. The light bars began flashing and the backup alarm started beeping before the vehicle maneuvered up a handicap ramp on the sidewalk. One deputy with a clipboard confirmed identities and required signatures while the other opened the back door and disappeared.

Michelle gasped when they wheeled out Dr. Yasin. His appearance had deteriorated since their meeting three months ago. He slumped over despite the seat harness securing his emaciated waist and chest. The suit was too big. The red tie was soiled and frayed. Sores riddled his bald head, and liver spots covered his transparent wrinkled skin. The blanket slid to reveal shackles. Worst of all, those eyes behind the trifocals were lifeless.

Michelle fought the urge to cry. She choked down the torment.

The deputy pushing the wheelchair asked, "Where do you want him?"

She pointed to the narrow walkway bisecting the circular

fountain. In mid-stride, she activated the recording app on her cell phone. "Testing. One, two, three, four."

The lawyer walked alongside his client. "Dr. Yasin? I'll stay right here beside you the entire time."

Yasin coughed up phlegm and tried to spit. The glob dribbled down his chin. "Get lost, Carpenter."

During a tenuous retreat, the lawyer advised, "Remember, you don't have to answer any questions. Don't incriminate yourself."

Yasin flashed an arthritic middle finger.

The sheriff's deputies stood guard at opposite ends of the fountain, just out of earshot. Michelle battled trepidation, knelt, and wavered before confronting her mentor. His focus riveted on the phone. He shook his head in disgust yet remained silent. With a guttural sigh, she mumbled the apology she dreaded to make. "I'm sorry. I'm so, so sorry."

Thin lips clenched across yellowed teeth. "I don't give a shit." The voice was raspy. "I begged you, over and over again, not to endanger my grandsons. You gave me your word. Now they're dead. My son and his wife are too." His final condemnation was slow and measured. "You … killed … my … family."

She tried holding his brittle hand. He yanked it away. She considered blaming Irene for ordering the car accident. They both knew that was true. But Michelle held herself accountable for putting them in harm's way. That was inexcusable and unforgivable. Making amends was impossible.

She lowered her head to his knees and wept. Shoulders shook. Lungs heaved. The sorrow and guilt poured out for over a minute.

A finger touched her hair. At first featherlight, the touch evolved into a caress and became an embrace. The gesture was comforting. Yasin struggled to cup her chin to lift her face. "Please stop," he said paternally.

Her voice quivered. "What else can I say? I'm so sorry."

"I know." He wiped her cheeks as tears rolled down his. "I hated your betrayal. I hated you." Compassion softened those hollow eyes.

"But that's not fair. You're not to blame. I am. After thirty-six years with Irene, I got what I deserved."

"But your family didn't deserve it."

"No, they didn't. But that's on me, not you. Hear me?"

Michelle was speechless.

Dredging up reserved strength, he screeched, "I asked if you heard me."

She nodded.

"Good." He leaned back in the wheelchair. "Please don't forget you're not to blame … ever. In fact" – he paused – "I should apologize to you."

"For what?"

Gnarly fingers clenched. "For destroying your life. I earned your trust, maybe your admiration, then turned a vulnerable young girl into a killer." His chin trembled. "That's unconscionable. Evil. I'm truly sorry. Can you forgive …" A coughing fit rattled his chest. He reddened. Every limb convulsed. Michelle froze in helpless fear.

The lawyer rushed over, stared down with concern, held his shoulder and confronted Michelle. "What did you do to him?"

"Nothing. I swear."

As Yasin recovered, he barked, "Get the hell away from me, Carpenter." The lawyer backed off. "Not far enough. Move away, goddamn it."

"Are you okay?" she asked.

With heartbreaking sadness, he said, "No, I'm dying. But that's okay. Soon I'll be playing with my grandsons again." A tenuous happiness emerged and faded. "But before I go, I ask – no, I hope – you'll forgive me. My precious Michelle, you're my only family now."

She was dumbstruck. He'd never said she was that important. She leaped up, wrapped her arms around his frail neck and whimpered with joy.

"I love you," Yasin whispered. "I love you. I love you. I love you. Always remember that. And forgive me if you can. Please."

"I love you too."

One of the sheriff's deputies called out, "Ten minutes, Ms. Barton."

She pushed back, relished his unbridled affection and kissed his forehead.

The doctor struggled emotionally. He sniffled and smiled – the warmest smile she ever remembered – then became serious. "All right, let's get down to business." He wiped snot from his nose. "You didn't come here with this circus to watch an old man blubber. What do they want from me?"

Michelle sat at his feet and fidgeted. "Chris and I are on an FBI task team for two years to help dismantle and prosecute Irene's network. They've promised us full immunity. Now our boss wants a big score. But I feel like a traitor asking you. So if you don't want to …"

"It's okay. I understand. What else can they do to me? Give me a second." A blank stare suggested he was reliving decades of atrocities. He struggled to sit upright before talking. Soon he was the articulate man she remembered. "Do you know what stop loss is?"

"No."

"Well, many businesses self-fund their group health benefits because the cost of fully insured programs is outrageous. But they also want protection against catastrophic claims."

"Like what?"

"Like a lung transplant costs a million. Getting a heart runs over one point five. Hell, a single treatment for hemophilia can be three million or more. You get the idea. A stop-loss policy protects the company from these huge expenses over a certain limit."

"What's this got to do with Irene?"

"She's had a stop-loss client for, well, let's see, for almost twenty years." He shuffled in the wheelchair as if dreading his pending confession. "They gave her the names of chronic patients who they wanted to die by silentcide to avoid the high medical costs."

"Oh my God, that's awful. Immoral." Her outrage dissipated as she considered all the people she had killed. How many of them were innocents?

"I agree, but it's commissions like this that made her rich."

"Were Chris and I ever assigned to a patient?"

"No, I forbade it. You'd never live with yourselves. Listen, I'll give your boss or whomever all the details. I'll also tell them anything else they want to know if, and only if, it guarantees your freedom."

"Thank you. I don't know how to tell you how helpful this is."

His anxious expression eased. He seemed at peace. "I'm glad to hear I'm finally doing something good."

"Speaking of freedom, I have a gift for you." She pulled a bronze replica of the Liberty Bell from her jacket. "If you remember, I tried giving you this a few months ago when we thought Irene was dead. Now she is. I want you to have it."

He studied the souvenir, handed it back and cupped her hands in his. "Keep it. My life is over, but your new life is just beginning. I hope it reminds you of the good in me and not all the horrible things I've done, especially to you. I'm truly sorry."

When they hugged goodbye, Michelle knew it was for the last time.

I'm losing the closest thing I've ever had to a father.

Chapter Twenty-Eight: Saint Paul, Minnesota

Photos 67–73

CHAPTER TWENTY-NINE

The tray of dirty dishes from the uneaten lunch was still in the hallway when Michelle returned to the hotel room. The last mental image of Dr. Yasin was bittersweet. She was thankful they had reconciled but would always be haunted by his feeble wave while being loaded back into the sheriff's van. She wanted to remember him as the vibrant mentor she admired, not the dying old man he had become. Michelle shuddered, resisting the urge to cry again.

There was no answer when she tried reaching Chris. *Why's he avoiding me? He's really annoying sometimes.* Her text was simple: Call me.

She phoned Hamilton. No answer. *This woman is beyond annoying.* The agent texted back: Busy. Late checkout 3. Meet lobby. Call cab for airport.

Now I'm her gopher? What a shithead!

Michelle began listening to the Yasin recording. The water fountain garbled some words, but the essence of the conversation was audible. Reliving the meeting was painful. As instructed, she emailed the M4A file to Hamilton. After arranging the cab, she went to the hotel restaurant in search of edible food. The veggie quiche had too much salt and odorous cheese. The coffee cream curdled.

Of course, Hamilton was late. The cab driver was all too happy to keep the meter running while playing Candy Crush. By the time the agent arrived, Michelle was livid. "Where were you?"

"I was busy" was the icy response. The agent's cheeks were gaunt, her hair was uncombed, and a shirttail hung untucked from her black skirt. The stable, straitlaced and uptight woman was an unprofessional mess.

"Doing what? The Dr. Yasin meeting was your idea."

"We'll talk later," she snapped before criticizing the cab driver for being careless while loading the luggage.

After a couple of miles, Michelle asked, "How'd Irene's funeral go?"

"Can't talk now." Hamilton was heads-down typing on the phone. Her thumbs were in a frenzy.

Michelle fumed. While staring out the window, they crossed the Mississippi River[74] and passed the Memorial Chapel at Fort Snelling.[75] Memories poured in.

Prior to visiting the historic fort three months ago, she and Ansel had spent all night and most of that day intertwined in bed. For the first time, they were free from Chris's judgmental eyes and Irene's dominating control. Ansel's sensual touches were soft and stimulating. His kisses were electric. Their passion was orgasmic. Michelle had never been happier.

This utopian illusion had been shattered when Dr. Yasin announced at Fort Snelling that Irene was still alive. That was when everything went to hell. Now Ansel was dead, Dr. Yasin was dying, she and Chris were oppressed by not one but two masters, and they were being hunted by Irene's successor. She longed to be back in the cocoon with Ansel.

At the airport, Hamilton became a diva. She bypassed the long line at the Delta counter, declared there was a loaded gun in her purse and got snippy when the ticket agent didn't process the paperwork fast enough. At TSA check-in, she badgered a young security officer who didn't know the protocol for approving an armed FBI agent. When she began arguing, passengers rubbernecked.

The final straw was the message board at the gate. The two-hour delay was blamed on mechanical problems. Hamilton spewed profanities. She headed across the aisle to a bar,[76] lifted her skirt, climbed on a stool, slapped down a credit card and demanded a double of Johnnie Walker Black on the rocks. "And keep 'em coming."

Michelle asked for light beer. She sipped in solitude until Hamilton slammed down the phone, tossed back the liquor, shuddered, ordered another and directed her outrage at Michelle. "Why the hell did you copy Agent Rochefort on the Yasin recording you emailed me?"

She hesitated before answering. "Because he said that was standard bureau procedure."

"That's a crock of shit. Rochefort's been gunning for me since I was assigned his case files on you and Chris. Now he's got carte blanch to do my job."

"What's that supposed to mean?"

"It means the FBI's assistant deputy director just gave him approval to start interrogating Yasin before, and I quote, 'the old coot croaks.' It'd be bad enough if Rochefort's authority stopped at that disgusting stop-loss scheme. But oh no, Pandora's box is wide open. He has the green light to investigate anything that comes out of Yasin's mouth about Shaw's network." Hamilton held up the phone. "Here, look at this."

The text read: Hey Sloan. Payback's a bitch! Your St. Paul buddy.

"See? That bastard stole my entire mission thanks to you."

Michelle's muscles tensed. Her pulse rose. "Don't blame me. If you'd bothered to show up, none of this would've happened."

Hamilton clutched the empty glass as her voice filled with despair. "I couldn't."

"Why not? Because you were 'too busy,'" Michelle said with a sardonic bite.

The agent hollered across the counter, "Hey, barkeep! Where the hell's my next drink?" She accosted a man on the adjoining stool. "Stop eavesdropping, dirtbag." When he got defensive, she flashed her FBI credentials. "Back off or I'll arrest your ass." He scurried away to an empty table.

Michelle had enough of the tantrums. "What's really your damn problem?"

"Everything." She threw off her jacket. Her blouse armpits were soaked. "I'll soon be lucky to get a mall security job."

"I'm sure you're exaggerating."

"No, you don't know the half of it. You might want to order something stronger than that wussy beer while I tell you what happened." She proceeded to summarize the cathedral shootout.

Michelle's worry spiked. "Is Chris okay?"

"Yes, he was shot at, but he's fine."

"Was he the target?"

"Frankly, I don't know. He's under strict orders to remain quiet until debriefed by an independent investigator. But surprisingly, my guys called him heroic for shielding a woman who panicked."

"I'm not surprised." She was proud of Chris. "That's the way he is."

"Well, he might be the only hero today. As for me, I'm doomed."

"Why? You weren't even there."

"Exactly. But I'm getting all the blame because it was my operation. According to the FBI director, 'This is a fuckup of biblical proportions.'"

"Is it really that bad?"

"Worse than bad. It's not like an FBI TV show where everything is forgiven and forgotten after the next commercial. This gunfight unleashed a firestorm."

"Like what?"

"You really want to know? Okay, you asked for it. First, Philly cops swarmed in, followed by an arm-wrestling contest with the

FBI for jurisdiction. When the press showed up, their stories went viral. There're breaking news reports all over the national media. I'm sure the video of the coroner wheeling out the body bag was a huge boost for ratings. And antigun radicals announced a protest march tomorrow from the Museum of Art to the cathedral. Oh yeah, and of course, the governor and mayor lost no time grandstanding with phony condolences and demands for someone's head on a spike."

"That sounds ugly," Michelle said, feeling genuine sympathy.

"Oh wait, girlfriend. I haven't even gotten to the ugly parts yet." Hamilton twirled her thin wedding ring. Her frown displayed torment. "Meanwhile, back at the ranch, my boss called me every name in the book while belittling my critical-shooting incident report. For sure, he'll push me under the bus to save his sorry ass."

Hamilton pounded down a handful of peanut pub mix and said with her mouth full, "The damn things are stale." She swallowed and continued her tirade. "As for the rest of the bureau, well, it's a goddamn hornet's nest. From what I've been told – let's see if I can remember the numbers – three levels of directors, four division heads, a gaggle of lawyers, the Department of Justice and a partridge in a pear tree are all in the fray. Meanwhile, my entire team was sent home with pay until cleared of wrongdoing. And during the next six months or more, a review group will analyze and second-guess every damn bullet that was fired."

A new cocktail arrived. Hamilton lapped at it like a thirsty dog. Michelle had never pictured her as an alcoholic. She was meticulous, demanding and obsessive about following bureau policy. That's hard to pull off as a drunk. No, Sloan was spiraling into a crippling meltdown while numbing her distress.

Hamilton kept rambling, more to herself than to Michelle. "They're also blaming me for all the lawsuits that'll be filed. Our general counsel expects the Catholic diocese will sue for damages. Everyone in the cathedral will claim emotional distress. And Shaw's former lawyers will litigate for the wrongful death of their managing partner. I was told in no uncertain terms, 'They'll love screwing over the feds who shut down their law firm.'"

"But aren't federal agencies immune from those kinds of lawsuits?"

"Usually yes, but maybe no. Even defending against them can cost millions."

Hamilton's cell dinged twice. She shoved it across the bar with disgust. The phone skidded across a wet spot like an air hockey puck before hitting a beer tap and spinning to a stop. Michelle tried talking the woman off her emotional roof. "I'm sure things look bad now. But they'll take your full career into consideration, won't they?"

"You mean the twenty-three years of blood, sweat and tears I devoted to the bureau? Not a chance. In a few hours" – she threw up her hands – "poof, it's all gone. So is the full pension I'd have had in less than two years. And I didn't even do anything wrong. But you can bet your ass I'll be the sacrificial lamb if the worst part happens."

"What can be worse?"

"Politicians. As you know, Shaw's involvement has been kept under wraps. The seizure of her assets was justified for tax fraud, not because she ran an assassin network. So Senator McLoren and Oakley got all the blame for poisoning the senators. But after their deaths and today's fiasco, the bigwigs fear some eager-beaver reporter will uncover the truth about Shaw and learn my office authorized immunity to two of her assassins. Hell, I can see Rochefort leaking all that just to put the final nail in my coffin. Then DC politicians will scream bloody murder in televised sound bites. They'll convene a full-scale witch hunt during congressional hearings. Imagine the shitstorm that'll be."

Michelle envisioned outraged senators holding up mugshots of her and Chris while blaming them for decades of Shaw's atrocities. They'd become scapegoats led to the slaughter. "What's all this mean for us and our deal?"

Hamilton gasped in defeat. "Frankly, Michelle, I don't know. And I won't have a job long enough to do anything about it. But you can assume things don't look rosy for you either."

A flash of anxiety reddened Michelle's face.

We're screwed.

She stuttered while ordering two shots of tequila with extra limes.

Chapter Twenty-Nine: Saint Paul, Minnesota

Photos 74–76

CHAPTER THIRTY

Friday

The cathedral was chaotic after the shootout. Legions of Philadelphia police, EMTs and FBI resources swooped in like locusts. The media outside was a circus. The gawking crowd would've been a decent-sized congregation for a Sunday Mass.

All the witnesses, including Chris, were segregated in the basement and questioned by detectives. He gave candid answers but didn't disclose his affiliation with the FBI. When the special agent in charge – the highest-ranking FBI agent managing the Philadelphia field office – located Chris, he was told to shut his mouth and get his ass back to headquarters.

For hours, he and other members of the task team were grilled separately. Before a formal recorded interview, Chris was coached on how to respond as if the team's stories were being blended into a cohesive spin. The brass also wanted to imply the dead lawyer was the intended victim. There was a lot of manipulative butt-covering going on. This was surprising.

From his perspective, the task team agents had been courageous and acted by the book. He wasn't a big fan of most of them – and the feelings were mutual – but he respected their professionalism. When dismissed, Chris was told to stay home but remain available 24/7 for follow up. He was physically drained and emotionally comatose.

Thank God that hideous day is over.

At the blue door of his rowhouse, he paused before inserting the key and entered with exhausted trepidation. Anna must have read his text; she was waiting in the cramped and dated kitchen. The table was set for two, and the deep-red cabernet was decanted. Beef stroganoff simmering in a crock pot smelled delicious.

And Anna had transformed. Her olive skin was radiant, her brown eyes sparkled, and her lips were an inviting shade of pink. Although wearing ripped jeans and a faded short-sleeved blouse, her athletic figure was alluring. She resembled the intelligent and humble woman he had become infatuated with on the cruise back in mid-June. Although he was undeserving, both then and now, her presence was consoling after the harrowing shootout. He worried his emotions were transparent.

"Hi," she said with renewed energy. "I've got a treat for us." She poured two glasses of wine, gave him one, and raised hers. "Cheers."

The Cakebread was rich, smooth and delicious, reminiscent of the previous two bottles they'd shared. Those were happy times together. That was eons ago.

She shattered his memories when asking, "How was Irene's funeral?"

He considered minimizing what happened because he didn't want to upset her. But after seeing the sensational stories on the internet while walking home, he decided the unabridged version was the best approach. She'd learn the details anyway, and rebuilding trust was based on candor.

With every sentence, Anna became more traumatized. By the end of his description, she was pale again with watery eyes and a quivering chin. "Were you the target?"

"Yeah, I think so. There's no other logical explanation."

She rushed over, threw her arms over his shoulders and buried her face in the crook of his neck. She trembled.

With hands at his side, he remained rigid, trying to appear strong. "I'm okay." Hesitantly, his head leaned against hers. "Really, I'm fine." A hand comforted her back, followed by the other, leading to a marvelous embrace. He savored the affection. "Please don't worry. I'm safe."

She pushed back a few inches with darting eyes of dread. "How can you just stand there looking so calm after being shot at? You always do that."

"Sorry, but that's how we were trained. We've, uh, become numb to death, either when someone else dies or when we almost die ourselves. I guess it's our mental defense mechanism."

Her wide eyes burrowed into his. "You can't just keep burying trauma like that. It's unnatural and unhealthy."

"Well, that's what we do," he said, but knew she was right. Regressing painful memories had begun tormenting his subconscious. "Besides, it's over now."

Her temper flared. "But it's not over and you're not safe. Neither am I. Jesus, when is this going to end?"

He reluctantly told the truth. "Only when Wolfgang is stopped."

"Is your task team any closer to finding him?"

"No, but they're still looking."

"That's not good enough." She was furious. "Our lives are at stake." Her anger peaked. "Screw it, I'll find him myself."

"How you going to do that?"

"I don't know, but I will," she said with determination. "I promise you that."

There was no doubt she would.

Anna drifted away and took a sip of wine for solace. Her demeanor had reverted to when she had first walked in the door yesterday. Her foot tapped, her brow creased, and she grasped the glass stem with two fists.

Watching her become vulnerable again was dreadful. He struggled for a way to comfort her but drew a blank. Why was he always at a loss for words and letting her down?

"What's that all over your pants?" she asked.

He had tried cleaning them with wet paper towels. Instead, the stains had spread. "Now don't get grossed out when I tell you." Chris swallowed his apprehension. "Those are Irene's cremation ashes."

"Eww, that's disgusting." She checked her jeans for ashes. "How'd that happen?" His explanation made her cringe.

"Listen," he said. "I hope you don't mind, but I'm going to shower. Having Irene on me for most of the day has been creeping me out."

"Are you going to need fresh clothes from your bedroom?"

"Of course," he said with confusion. "I'm not putting these back on."

"Well, I'll go up with you. It was a surprise for later, but there's something I want to show you."

The 12x12 room was unrecognizable. She had removed most of the furniture and his framed photographs. The double bed was pushed to the side. In the center was a card table with her laptop. Adjacent was the nightstand with his photo printer from downstairs.

A makeshift evidence board was spread across one wall. On top were pictures of the four senators who had been poisoned, co-conspirators Steven Oakley and Senator Vickie McLoren plus President Starling. Below some were handwritten Post-it® Notes. In the middle was Irene Shaw with a big red X across her face.

"Do you like it?"

"You've been busy today. I'm impressed."

"I'm just getting started using the research you did when we were trying to identify Senator Rosa Phillips. There's a lot of good stuff on your spreadsheets about the senators and potential silentcide clients. Then I'll follow my own trails. Speaking of which …" She grabbed a black marker, wrote *Where's Wolfgang?* and slapped the yellow sticky next to Irene. "There! Enemy number one. Screw you, jerkwad. You're going down."

"I'm proud of you," he said with conviction.

"You mean it?"

"Absolutely."

"Good, because I'm sick and tired of being a victim. Sitting around all day worrying has been driving me crazy. I always tackled problems head-on, so taking action now feels great."

"I saw the change when I walked in. You're back to your old self again."

"You implying I'm old?" she asked with a tease.

"No, I think you're amazing. I always have."

His heartfelt response was unintentional. The words had just popped out of his mouth. They created a spark of mutual attraction that was palpable. Her gaze was receptive. His fingers twitched. She moistened her lips. He had to circumvent this before it was too late.

"How 'bout if we do this together?" *That was a stupid thing to say.*

"Do what?" She leaned closer while stroking her neck.

He hurried to reply, "I mean the research. The FBI sent me home indefinitely. I have plenty of time now to work together if you'd like."

"I'd like that a lot," she said with a seductive whisper.

Anna stepped forward, tilted her head, hesitated, closed her eyes and kissed him. Her lips radiated passion. He tried resisting, but God, the feeling was great. He drew her closer. Their body heat rose. Heart palpitations tingled. Breathing became erratic. Her fingers began unbuckling his pants.

Chris jumped back. "What are you doing?"

With a nervous laugh, she said, "I was just trying to get Irene out of the way."

He shook his head in refusal. "No, I'm sorry. I can't do this. I just can't."

"Why not?"

He resisted confessing his feelings. Admitting the inner secret would make him vulnerable. But it had to be said. "Because you've rejected me too many times. And it hurt. A lot." He struggled to finish. "I can't do this knowing I'll lose you again."

She reached for his hand. Her palm was soft and warm. Her expression was reassuring. "I respect that, Chris. I really do. But you know why I rejected you before, right?"

"Of course I do. It was always my fault. Frankly, I'm surprised you stuck around after everything that happened."

"Yeah, if I remember correctly, there were a few challenging moments." They shared a nervous laugh. "Okay, listen, you told me your reason. Now let me tell you mine." She squeezed his fingers. "The first time we were together on the cruise was one of the best times of my life. I think about it often. It always makes me smile. Believe me, that memory has gotten me through some hard times. Well, I want that feeling again. You know, to be happy for a change, to feel alive without fear ... and to be with you."

"But ..."

"Shh, let me finish. Can I make any promises about the future? No, neither of us can. I just want to enjoy being together as long as we can. Does that make sense?"

"Yeah, it does." He refused to make eye contact. "But we can be together while being platonic. Now I'm going to shower."

He rushed down the hall, slammed the bathroom door, turned on the shower and disrobed. He threw his clothes in the laundry basket and stomped them down in a rage.

Goddamn you, Irene. I despise you. You ruined me and still won't let go. You're even plaguing me from the grave. If not for you, I'd have a life. And maybe, just maybe, I'd be worthy of someone like Anna. But you've taken away everything and everyone that's good. There's nothing left worth having.

He stepped into the shower and turned up the heat. The water was too hot but felt better than hate.

I was gutless running out of the bedroom like that. Maybe Anna has accepted me — not for who she thought I was when we met or as a protector later but for who I really am. Can I expect a life together? Not a chance. Will she reject me again? Maybe. Get real. Yes, probably as soon as things are safe and she goes back to the work she loves in Boston. Besides, her family and friends would never approve. Do you blame them? No, I wouldn't either. So face it. This is temporary. Maybe a day, a week. Longer if you're lucky. Then it's done. You're going to lose her either way. You're a fool if you waste this time together.

He stepped out of the shower, dried off, and wrapped the towel around his waist. He plucked up the courage to walk into the bedroom.

Anna lifted her eyes from the desk with apprehension. "I'm sorry if …"

"Stop. We're done talking about it. I came back because I forgot to get fresh clothes. See …" He dropped the towel. "I have nothing to wear."

◆◆◆

Four hours later, Michelle knocked on the bedroom door. "Hi, it's me. Can I come in?"

"No," Chris said while Anna snuggled, stroking his chest.

"Everything all right?" she asked with concern.

"It's more than all right." The lilt in his voice signaled his happiness.

A protracted, judgmental silence followed. "Oh, I get it. We'll talk in the morning." After a downbeat, his sister added, "Good night, Anna."

"No," Anna replied, "it's a great night."

CHAPTER THIRTY-ONE

Saturday

Anna's head tilted on the pillow as her eyes fluttered open. Chris was inches away. His blond hair was mussed, his breathing was shallow, his lips and brow were relaxed, and he appeared content for the first time since they'd slept together on the cruise. Their toes touched in mutual affection. The shared warmth was sensuous and comforting. This moment, and the night before, would be a memory to cherish.

She blew him an air kiss and slipped from beneath the sheets, hoping to let him sleep. While putting on his robe, he reached across the bed as if sensing she was gone. The unconscious gesture was amorous. She lightly kissed his bare shoulder, causing the boyish grin she adored to inch across his face.

You're awesome, Chris Davis. I was lost without you. Thank God you weren't hurt at the cathedral yesterday.

The bathroom mirror was revealing. Sure, her pixie cut was a rat's nest, and the makeup was faded or smeared. But her eyes twinkled, her skin glowed, and the upward edges of her mouth reflected a forgotten happiness. Maybe, just maybe, joy and hope could replace her crippling fear and dark despair.

There's a better future ahead. I know it. We'll get there together and leave the past behind.

Anna sauntered barefoot down the stairs with renewed energy

and purpose. Michelle was working at a small desk in the living room. Her posture was stiff with an unsettling vibe. Anna tightened the robe, pulling the lapels across her chest. She struggled to utter a guiltless "Hi."

"Hi." Michelle's salutation was flat. She remained fixated on the laptop screen.

Anna tried again to get engagement. "Welcome back."

"Thanks" was the unreceptive response.

"I'm going to make some coffee. Want some?"

"The pot is already on, assuming it hasn't shut off by now." The implication was clear. Michelle had been waiting a long time to confront them, or maybe just her.

Anna retreated to the kitchen. Quivering fingers caused her to overfill the mug. *We've done nothing wrong.* She used a paper towel to clean the spill. *Face this head-on.* With a sigh of resolve, she returned to the living room. "How was your trip?"

Michelle swiveled in the desk chair. Her mouth was pinched with disapproval. "What are you doing with Chris?"

The abruptness was unsettling. She tried levity as a defense. "I thought that was obvious when you knocked last night."

"Oh yeah," she said with rolling eyes. "You made that part very obvious. But the why escapes me."

"What's that supposed to mean?"

Michelle stood in a contentious stance. "When you came back a couple of days ago, you know I welcomed you with open arms. You wanted protection. That made total sense. But it never occurred to me in a million years that you'd seduce my brother."

Anna scoffed. "It was hardly a seduction."

"Was that your intention in the first place?"

"No, it just happened." Anna's weak justification shifted to indignation. "But what's your problem? I was totally supportive of you and Ansel when Chris disapproved."

"That was different."

"How?"

"It just was. At the time, we expected things to last."

"Maybe you did," Anna countered with spite. "But I seem to recall he was betraying you the entire time."

Deflecting the jab, Michelle insisted, "And we both know you'll dump Chris again as soon as this is over."

"Why don't you mind your own damn business and let us decide what happens."

A creak on the staircase silenced the clash. When Chris reached the bottom step, the tension was palpable. Michelle ran over for a sibling hug, thankful he was alive and unharmed. Their affection would've been heartwarming if not tainted by the argument. Why was Michelle being so territorial?

Chris made eye contact with Anna and mouthed the words "Are you okay?"

A shrugged shoulder said it all.

After an extended embrace, Michelle held his cheeks while studying his face. "How you doing?"

"A bit rattled, but I'll be fine."

"Are you sure?"

Chris gave his sister a reassuring smile and stepped aside. "Yeah, don't worry. I said I'll be fine."

"Were you the target?"

"One hundred percent. There's no doubt Wolfgang ordered the hit."

Anna piped in, "And we've vowed to find him soon."

Michelle ignored her comment. The shun was infuriating.

"From what Hamilton told me, the whole thing sounded terrifying."

"How would she know?" Chris asked. "She was watching from over a thousand miles away. But I'll tell you one thing. I wouldn't be standing here without her team."

"Hamilton said you were also a hero," Michelle said with pride.

Anna interrupted, "Wait, what happened?"

"Well, in the middle of things, a woman panicked and tried to run, so I tackled her until the smoke cleared. No biggie," he said with modesty. "Hamilton's guys were the real heroes."

His bravery and humility impressed Anna. He had displayed both many times yet never wanted the credit.

"They were terrific," Chris continued. "But then afterwards, Hamilton's boss started spinning the story. It was really weird."

"I know why." Michelle took several minutes to explain the political disaster the firefight had caused. She concluded by saying, "Hamilton is convinced she's toast."

Chris clapped his hands. "That's great. It takes the bloodhound off the 'Who Killed Irene?' case."

Anna was also excited but remained quiet. It felt like the siblings forgot she was in the room. Being ignored stung. She sipped the bitter coffee.

"Maybe," Michelle said. "But we're not in the clear yet. Hamilton said our plea deal could be at risk."

Chris contemplated the ramifications before dismissing them. "If that happens, and it seems like a stretch, I hope Webber will back us up. In the meantime, if Hamilton is gone, then good riddance."

Michelle sank into the desk chair. "In a way, I feel sorry for her."

"For Hamilton? What the hell for?"

"I don't know. She tried doing everything right for over twenty years, she never got recognized for her hard work, and now she's being thrown under the bus."

"Well, she's a big girl. She should've looked both ways before crossing the street. Now are we done listening to her tiny violin?"

"I guess so." For some odd reason, Michelle still seemed empathetic to the special agent.

"Good, because I have a bigger issue to discuss."

"What's that?"

"Us!" Chris put his arm around Anna's waist, drew her close and kissed her cheek. She was thrilled with the affection and support. They were now a united front. "I heard part of the cat fight coming down the steps and, I'm here to tell you, I don't approve. So I'm going to rip the bandage off this real quick. Ready?"

Michelle knew what was coming but didn't object.

"I vividly recall someone saying they're free to make their own decisions about partners, even if they might be wrong. When you were with Ansel, you kept telling me 'Let it go, Chris' and 'Drop the attitude, Chris.' Well, I did. Now I'm asking you to do the same. Can you do that?"

"You're right. It's none of my business." Surprisingly, she said to Anna, "I'm sorry. I hope you're happy together."

"Thanks." Anna bent down to give her a side hug. The reception was chilly.

"Okay," Chris said while sitting on a worn paisley couch across from his sister. "Now that's settled, how did things go with Dr. Yasin yesterday?"

Michelle's voice had a residual edge of irritation. "If you had called me back, you would've known in real time." Obviously, she resented being dressed down. Her passive-aggressive response would no doubt fester. Anna sensed their conflict was far from over.

Chris was oblivious to the tense body language between the women. "I couldn't call," he said. "The FBI had everyone on radio silence. When I finally got out, I assumed you were in the air. So what happened?"

While Michelle described Yasin's failing health, Chris cringed. Anna had never met the man but knew he was important to Michelle and to a lesser extent to Chris. Chris got angry when hearing the doctor blamed her for killing his family. He shuffled to the edge of the couch and held her hand when she recounted their emotional reconciliation. They were both misty-eyed.

"I'm thrilled for you," he said. "Seeing him again could've gone wrong in so many ways. But you faced your fears and made amends.

If you hadn't, you'd always think he resented you. This way, you had closure and the chance to say your final goodbye."

Anna was proud of Chris's compassion and tenderness. This was another example of why she found him attractive. He had a great heart.

Everyone's mood shifted when Michelle started explaining the stop-loss scheme. Anna was horrified. She thought about all the cancer patients – the type Longfellow was dedicated to saving – who had been victims of this greed.

A painful image appeared: Jamie's last breaths before dying in her arms. For two years, her five-year-old little brother had battled a brain tumor with countless rounds of chemo and radiation, even experimental treatments, until he was skeletal and blind. Her parents had spared no amount of money to save him. Those extra two years together were priceless. Jamie was the type of precious loved one Yasin had killed for money.

"That's outrageous!" Anna screamed at Michelle. "How can you possibly admire someone who did that for decades to sick people?"

"I never said I condoned what he did. In fact, I told him it was immoral."

"Yet you still admire him? That's unbelievable."

Chris stood up to intervene. "Okay, guys, that's enough."

Unabated, Michelle yelled, "How dare you judge me. You have a super-rich family that gave you everything. My stepfather raped me and killed our mom. Then Irene controlled us since I was eight. He's the only loving father I have, and now he's dying. So have some empathy."

"Are you kidding? He deserves to die for what he's done."

Chris tried again. "Please stop." He was ignored.

Michelle took two threatening steps. Her face was flush. "No one deserves to die."

Anna stood her ground. "That's really rich coming from an assassin."

"Well, screw you, princess. See if I lift a finger to save your ass again." She slammed the laptop shut, yanked the cord from the wall and stomped toward the door. "I'm going to the FBI office."

Chris hustled in front to block her exit. "On a Saturday?"

"Yes, so get out of my way."

"Listen, this got out of hand. Let's all take a deep breath, then talk it out."

"I'm done talking. Now move it. And I hope you two enjoy a lovely day in bed."

CHAPTER THIRTY-TWO

Monte Carlo and Monaco City, Monaco

Sunday

Wolfgang dragged luggage into his suite at the elite Hôtel Hermitage,[77] pulled back the plush drapes and struggled to open the glass French door. "Son of a bitch," he muttered when bumping his splinted pinky finger. He stepped onto a narrow balcony, grasped the ironwork railing, savored the sunshine and breathed deep.

The Mediterranean breeze was heavenly. Seabirds circled in the crystal-blue sky. The superyachts docked in Port Hercule were an ostentatious display of wealth. The realization that over twelve thousand millionaires and twenty billionaires lived within less than a square mile[78] was intoxicating. They could afford the utmost of luxury, ranging from opulent condos to designer clothes, extravagant jewelry, rare wines, three-star Michelin restaurants and, of course, the world's most expensive cars.

He belonged in this haven of affluence. His destiny was to be super-rich. According to Irene Shaw's financial spreadsheet, she had a complex web of offshore and Swiss bank accounts worth over $205 million, all held under different aliases. When the FBI began raiding her criminal network, she had transferred her illicit net worth into bitcoin. The wallet had grown to $222 million. That much money was orgasmic.

There was one major problem. To access this cryptocurrency

fortune, he had to find the twelve-, eighteen- or twenty-four-word seed phrase. If she were extra paranoid – which was one of Shaw's core competencies – he'd also need passphrases she may have created for extra security. They had to be written down somewhere among the fifty-five gigabytes of her files he had transferred. He'd also search her laptop's system files if necessary. All he needed was persistence, lots of time, and to finish this last goddamn assignment for The Commander, whoever the hell she was.

Wolfgang had tried recruiting a European pro to join him in Monaco, but no one answered the bell. And Shaw's former bodyguard Frank was AWOL after not being paid. Wolfgang was stuck with Jacob Conners, the teenager he was mentoring. The twerp demonstrated a natural talent for silentcide but was a doofus whenever he opened his mouth.

Using a burner phone he had purchased at Nice Côte d'Azur Airport, Wolfgang asked, "Have you checked in yet?" The teen had flown in on an earlier flight from New York City and was staying at a different hotel. They could not risk being seen together.

"Yeah, like this place is dope, right?"

You're a friggin' dope. "Do you still have the names of the men's fashion boutiques I gave you?"

"Yup."

"Good. They close at seven. That gives you three hours to buy the clothes I listed. You must blend into the Monte Carlo lifestyle. Got that?"

"Yeah, bro."

Wolfgang cringed. He hoped his decision to bring this twerp wouldn't bite him in the ass.

He disrobed down to boxer shorts, plodded into the bathroom, checked the adhesive beneath his gray hair, mustache and beard, and reapplied makeup to intensify the forehead creases, crow's feet and bags below the eyes. Adding rouge to his nose and cheeks telegraphed "Here's a man whose lover is liquor." The contact lenses with a reddish tinge completed the rich drunk disguise. After scrubbing his armpits with a wet washcloth, he dressed in linen pants, a crisp blue dress shirt and polished loafers. He'd be overlooked and forgotten in this disguise.

Walking three blocks along Avenue d'Ostende and Avenue de Monte Carlo was thrilling. This was part of the street circuit for the annual Monaco Grand Prix, one of the most renowned Formula One car races. When he reached Place du Casino,[79] the square at the geographical heart of Monaco was abuzz with sightseers of every age, shape and nationality. Someday he hoped to visit again as a tourist or, better yet, as a resident, but not as an assassin.

He placed three miniature cameras for a 360-degree view. There was a ninety-minute wait for a table on the terrace of Café de Paris Monte-Carlo.[80] The world-famous brasserie had an elegant Belle Époque exterior, an impressive Art Nouveau interior and palatable food that was criminally expensive. He nibbled on crème brûlée with Sicilian pistachios, sipped two espressos and watched news reports about yesterday's shooting at Shaw's funeral with disgust.

Damn morons. Big guns, no brains. Whatever happened to killing with finesse?

People shrieked and jumped aside as horns blew and headlights flashed on two racing Ferrari convertibles. The pair of glistening 812 Superfast coupes – one cherry red, the other metallic blue – were sleek, stunning and phallic. Wolfgang googled the stats. The V-12 under the hood could generate 789 horsepower, accelerate to 138 miles per hour in about ten seconds, go 211 miles per hour, and fuel surging testosterone in any male with a heartbeat.

The sports cars came to a screeching stop in front of Casino de Monte-Carlo.[81] Two valets hustled down the stairs, greeted the honored guests with a slight bow, and discreetly pocketed a fistful of euros. The drivers resembled models dressed for a *GQ* magazine cover story.

As if choreographed, the valets opened the passenger doors and held out their hands. Two women in their early twenties stepped out with long legs punctuated by flashy high heels. One was a bleached blond, the other a brunette. Fake boobs strained to escape skintight dresses. Several men standing nearby were photographing or recording the spectacle to show the boys back home.

As the foursome sauntered away — their struts screaming of entitlement — the chain in front of two empty parking spots was pulled aside. Soon their cars would be on display beside a Bentley, a Bugatti and a Rolls-Royce Phantom.[82]

Wolfgang compared the two men to the bio photos on his phone. The brothers were almost identical: mid-thirties with dark skin, lush black hair, mustaches and beards featuring a triangular patch below their full lips. Bushy brows overshadowed jet-black eyes, and their aquiline noses protruded. The eldest had pronounced distinguishing features. Prince Muhammad bin Faizan was taller, had a paunch and a port-wine stain on his right cheek.

The crown prince had groomed his sons into royal wealth and power since their birth. One had a PhD in energy science and engineering from Stanford University. The other had a DPhil in economics from the University of Oxford. Despite their relative youth, they commanded significant positions of influence in the kingdom.

The Commander's instructions were explicit. She didn't care which Saudi Arabian died, but the death must appear to be from natural causes and happen in two and a half days. When Wolfgang had complained about the unreasonable deadline, he was reminded how his foolish refusals to accept the assignment earlier had cost precious time. He was also told the price for failure was dire. The euphemism did not require clarification.

The two couples were boisterous and laughing while walking up the stairs into the lobby of the five-star Hôtel de Paris.[83] The show was over, but not the exhilaration. Wolfgang always got a visceral rush at the first sighting of his prey. But in this case, maybe fate would decide which prince would die.

The reconnaissance was far from over. He paid his bill, ambled toward the Prince Charles III's entrance[84] to the Salle Garnier opera house and stared up at the Round Tower of the Hôtel de Paris.[85] One prince was on an upper balcony and oblivious to the Mediterranean Sea. He was kissing and fondling the blond.

Wolfgang snapped a photo to document the room's location and placed another camera near the hotel's service entrance. The challenge was to find a discreet, elevated position to conduct surveillance. He ignored the moored yachts along Jetée Lucciana and focused on the two-hundred-foot-tall promontory known as the Rock of Monaco.[86] A location in Monaco City's Old Town might be workable.

He made a pit stop at the hotel room for equipment before the short drive around the harbor. The northeast end of the peninsula proved to be an ideal observatory of the Monte Carlo skyline half a mile away. However, finding a hiding place after nightfall was challenging. He wedged into bushes below a terrace and above a small amphitheater, part of an early eighteenth-century fortress.[87] This position would be undetectable at night but could be compromised after sunrise when tourists returned.

Wolfgang struggled to screw a Swarovski STS-80 spotting scope onto a mini tripod. The damn throbbing little finger made the simplest task difficult. He found Hôtel de Paris and sharpened the focus. The 20-60x80mm magnification was perfect. He was transported inside the room as Prince Muhammad bin Faizan proceeded well past foreplay on a king-size bed. His brother was entertaining the brunette in a jacuzzi.

According to the floor plan from the hotel's website, the princes were sharing the Diamond Suite. The 1,900-square-foot, semicircular space had two bedrooms, two walk-in closets, three baths and a central living room for a nightly rate of twenty-one thousand euros. Yes, life was grand when you were stinking rich.

Live it up, boys. Time is short for one of you.

He checked his watch, called Jacob, gave him a status report, told him to place GPS trackers beneath the Ferraris and remain vigilant from Place du Casino. "And while you're standing around, why don't you learn how to gamble on your phone?"

The teenager's unintelligible response was "Hop off. Like, I'm here for this."

Wolfgang grumbled with disdain.

Half an hour later, when Muhammad finished his lascivious acrobatics, he bent over a table. Judging from the way he held his nostrils and shook his head, it appeared he had snorted cocaine. When the naked blond followed the same routine, Wolfgang's assumption was confirmed.

Excellent! Druggies can be easy marks.

Soon afterward, the foursome got dressed and left their suite. Jacob texted: out hotel 2 big gards folowng. Wolfgang chastised himself for not spotting the bodyguards earlier. A follow-up text ten minutes later read: at restrant. From Jacob's bodycam, Wolfgang saw the entourage being seated on a private balcony overlooking the glittering lights of the harbor and The Rock. The maître d' rejected the teenager for not having a reservation. The twerp would have a long wait out on the street.

Wolfgang packed up, returned to his hotel, ordered an overpriced sandwich from room service, longed for a nap to recover from the sleepless red-eye flight but took a long hot shower instead. He studied the videos of the princes from the hidden cameras in the square and Jacob's bodycam. They revealed Muhammad smoked cigarettes. That habit might prove helpful.

His cell phone dinged. A new text arrived: left restrant ☺ Wolfgang watched in real time. The princes and women were tipsy. The bodyguards followed close behind. The image was crappy, dark and jumpy, but he saw when they entered the casino. He messaged Jacob to follow them in and he'd be there within the hour.

Time to suit up for close-quarters recon. The casino would be full of cameras, so he needed a different disguise. Step one was to inflate a silicone beer-belly suit. Heavy makeup created a weathered complexion. He adhered a shaggy black wig, sideburns and beard. Blue contacts and tinted glasses hid his eyes. The black suit, white shirt and drab striped tie would blend into the crowd unnoticed. What would stick out like a sore thumb, however, was the splinted little finger. He hid that inside a full arm sling. Not ideal, but what else was he going to do?

Stepping into Monte Carlo Casino[88] was a boyhood fantasy come true. The James Bond theme song played in his head while admiring the two-story atrium's marble floor, onyx columns, golden walls and ornamental vaulting. The nineteenth-century elegance glistened. Each successive room was kinetic, with gamblers playing different games of chance surrounded by décor worthy of the Palace of Versailles. His favorite was Salle Europe, featuring French paintings of maidens, crystal chandeliers and an oval glass ceiling over craps tables, roulette wheels and a blue lounge bar. Las Vegas was a crass and garish imposter compared to Europe's most prestigious casino.

When entering Salle des Amériques, Wolfgang initially didn't recognize Jacob perched at a blackjack table. The transformation was astonishing. His curly red hair and trimmed beard matched his New York City alias passport. He wore a purple paisley silk sport coat with a tux shirt, black bow tie, crisp white pants and black tassel shoes without socks. God only knew how much the outfit cost, but the teenager appeared chic, rich and twenty-five.

Yet designer clothes couldn't hide stupid. Wolfgang cringed as Jacob split a pair of sixes and stood on sixteens with the dealer showing an eight. When the dealer busted, the teen added four hundred euros to his sizable stack of chips. The adjacent players cursed his dumb luck.

To get his attention, Wolfgang approached the caisse window, converted large euro bills into smaller ones, and eyed Jacob while pretending to count the money. The teen subtly pointed toward Salle Blanche, the lounge reserved for high rollers.

Wolfgang sat at a slot machine near the roped-off double door. The princes and their female friends were whooping it up at a French roulette wheel. They repeatedly covered the green felt with high-denomination rectangular plaques, watched with anxious anticipation as the wheel spun, then cursed or cheered when the croupier slapped the dolly on the winning number, followed by endless sips of champagne. Tens of thousands were in play every few minutes.

By the time Wolfgang lost two hundred euros at the slots, Muhammad had squandered three hundred thousand euros, maybe more. Whenever he'd deplete his stack, he'd storm off to a mosaic bar, order a drink, pretend to sneeze while sticking a golden snuff bullet up each nostril for a quick snort, and bitch to his bodyguard. Then he'd chain-smoke on the outside terrace until the manager notified him that a new rack of chips had been delivered to the roulette table.

Wolfgang had seen enough. He now knew the who and the how. What was missing was the opportunity. He was convinced Prince Muhammad bin Faizan would die on schedule.

Satisfied with the progress, Wolfgang approached Jacob's blackjack table, stood behind a player as if watching the action, mouthed the words "Leave now," left the casino, and waited near a water fountain in Jardin du Casino. He placed a call when Jacob exited.

The twerp began rambling in teenage language. "Bro, why'd you make me dip? Like, I was slaying it."

"Shut the hell up and listen. Keep watch until the princes return to their hotel. If they go to a club, follow them. Otherwise, get some sleep. At five o'clock, take a taxi to Saint Nicholas Cathedral, then walk to the coordinates I texted you. You'll find a spotting scope under a bush. Use it to monitor their room in the photo I've also sent. But be careful. After sunrise, tourists will swarm the area. Got that?"

"I suppose," Jacob whined. "But, like, what are you doing?"

"Now I'm going to bed. In the morning, I have an errand to run. I'll meet you after that."

"Like, what kind of errand?"

"I'll tell you later. Goodnight."

Wolfgang felt no sympathy for the teenager. If the princes got amorous again in the morning, Jacob would learn some valuable lessons.

Chapter Thirty-Two: Monte Carlo and Monaco City, Monaco

Photos 77–88

CHAPTER THIRTY-THREE

NICE, FRANCE AND MONACO CITY, MONACO
Monday

Experiencing the French Riviera[89] had long been on Wolfgang's wish list. Even the words Côte d'Azur sounded enchanting. Yet neither name portrayed the beauty of France's hundred-kilometer southern coastline. Dramatic seascapes, plunging cliffs, pine forests, inviting beaches, quaint villages and famous resort towns were all bathed in endless days of sunshine nestled between the rolling Maritime Alps and the aquamarine Mediterranean Sea.

Wolfgang could sample his fantasy in the short distance from Monte Carlo, Monaco, to Nice, France. But he refused to squander the opportunity by driving along the A8 Motorway. Instead, he left before sunrise and savored every marvelous panorama along Corniche Inférieure, a serpentine coastal road. He had not felt this peaceful in a long time. Too bad such a glorious morning had to be ruined by business.

On the approach to Old Nice, irritation grew as traffic clogged. He tried tempering his frustration by appreciating the old, bright-colored tenement houses facing the moored sailboats and yachts at Port Lympia.[90] His first glimpse of the stunning Bay of Angels[91] was tarnished by a tailgating jackass. A car horn interrupted him enjoying an artist painting the pebble beach of Opéra Plage.[92] By the time he found a place to park, Wolfgang was seething.

He grabbed a plastic bag he found in the hotel wastebasket and set off on Rue Saint-Francois de Paule. Early tourists were strolling the limestone pavers of the pedestrian-only street. Some were exploring the boutiques, galleries and souvenir stands while others were having breakfast at outdoor cafés or nibbling on calorie-laden pastries from a bakery. A few history buffs were admiring the opera house[93] and the eighteenth-century mansions or trying to determine where Napoleon Bonaparte stayed in 1796.

Wolfgang couldn't care less. He had one objective: find a flashing neon-green cross. When spotting the French sign for a pharmacy, he bolted through the sliding glass door, down an aisle filled with a dizzying array of cosmetics and lotions, and headed toward the customer service counter.

"Bonjour, monsieur." The young woman wore a white lab coat and a welcoming smile. "Comment puis-je vous aider?"

At times like this, it would've been helpful to be multilingual like the silentcide assassins trained on the Amish farm. He raised his phone, tapped the microphone symbol and said into Google Translate, "I'm here to see Jacques Truffaut."

She seemed accustomed to the app, probably after helping international travelers for years. Her French response came back as a computerized voice. "Mr. Truffaut is busy now. Can I help you?"

"No." His abrupt tone and hostile posture were a universal language. "Tell him Wolfgang König is here. I must see him."

The clerk became flustered. Her eyes darted with indecision.

"I said now!"

"Oui, monsieur."

She dashed into the back room. He worried she might call the police. If she did, he'd be in jeopardy. But so far he had come across as rude, not dangerous. He waited patiently but kept a close eye on the front door.

A distinguished man emerged wearing a white lab coat. He

paused to assess Wolfgang. The pharmacist was perhaps in his mid-sixties with snow-white hair, intelligent eyes, a lanky frame and slight curvature of the spine. He pushed thick glasses above his creased forehead while shuffling forward. The clerk cowered in a corner.

"Monsieur König?" he asked in a monotone. His glare signaled he knew Wolfgang's reputation.

He was led into a cramped office surrounded by three-ring binders, medical and pharmaceutical books, filing cabinets, a few personal mementos, a desk and credenza drowning in paperwork, and a stained coffeepot on a hotplate. The air was hot and stale.

Truffaut locked the door. The men confronted each other. The pharmacist was the first to engage. " Qu'est-ce que vous voulez?"

"Speak English," Wolfgang demanded.

"Je ne parle pas anglais."

"Bullshit. Speaking English was a requirement to be one of Irene Shaw's sanctioned pharmacists. So stop the act."

The man's lips tightened before he said, "Fine. But you're not following protocol by just showing up."

"That's impossible since the feds confiscated our computers."

"Yes, I heard they shut you down, jailed lots of people, and Shaw is dead. It's over."

"No, Shaw's business was crippled but is still very much alive, which is more than I can say for you if you don't cooperate." Wolfgang lifted the plastic bag he was carrying and grabbed the middle. The gun outline was obvious.

The pharmacist wasn't flustered. According to his bio, he had dealt with seedy underworld types for decades. His legs spread in defiance. "How do I know this isn't a trap?"

"You don't. But my friend here can vouch for me."

With a wry grin, he said, "It seems your credentials are in order. What do you need?"

"I need ten milligrams of fentanyl mixed with an equal amount of pure cocaine in both powder and liquid form."

One white eyebrow rose. "Curious combination."

"Why?"

"Because of course those drugs will be detected in a postmortem tox screen."

"Based on the mark's habits, nobody will be surprised."

"You know best. There're some dealers nearby who will happily fill your order."

Wolfgang removed the plastic bag and racked a 9mm round. "Look, you can either have this or the euros in my pocket."

He wasn't intimidated. "Okay, three hundred for the drugs and another two hundred for the compounding."

That amount was outrageous. On the street, a gram of the drugs cost one hundred euros apiece. He was being gouged about a thousand times more. But he didn't want to mess with back-alley drug dealers who might sell him crap, and there was no way he'd mix the toxic drugs himself. Convenience, safety and assurance came at a price.

While Truffaut had a brief phone call in French, Wolfgang read the English translation on the app. After disconnecting, he said, "The pharmaceutical rep will deliver your order in about fifteen minutes."

Smart-ass.

Truffaut did paperwork and Wolfgang played solitaire until there was a knock at the back door. A teenage plug with torn clothes and reeking of incense held out two baggies with white powder identified by scribbles on masking tape. He grabbed the cash and ran off.

The pharmacist moved to a clean room and dismissed the staff before putting on a bunny suit, goggles, a respirator and blue nitrile gloves. Wolfgang watched from a safe distance as Truffaut stood at a sterile cabinet with a hood fan. Within minutes, he finished preparing two mini syringes of the lethal compound. One of them would seal Prince Muhammad bin Faizan's fate.

✦✦✦

He drove back to Monaco, parked at the base of The Rock, rode an elevator up to the Oceanographic Museum[94] and walked the short distance where he hoped to find Jacob. The teen was well camouflaged. He lay in a shallow trench beneath a bush and a fallen tree branch. Nobody would see him from the terrace if they weren't looking.

Wolfgang waited until a Japanese tour group left the area. "Hey, Jacob. It's me. Come on up."

The teenager emerged from his cocoon, stretched, brushed off his clothes, slid down an embankment and bounced up stairs two at a time. He wore black jeans and a T-shirt for concealment, but his exposed neck, arms and ankles were dotted with welts resembling chickenpox. "What the hell happened to you?"

"Bloodsucking mosquitos," he said while itching a cluster of bumps. "They're like black with white spots and, you know, real nasty ass. Those suckers are friggin everywhere."

Wolfgang wanted to laugh but didn't. The twerp appeared miserable. "What's happening with the princes?"

"They stayed at the casino til 'bout, I don't know, 'bout two somethin', then crashed. They looked effed up. This morning, that Muhammad dude, like, oh my God, he's like extra."

"He's what?"

"Like what you old folks call a stud. Then he and that blond babe got room service on their, you know, their balcony, then went back to smashing."

Sure enough, Jacob had gotten an eyeful. "What about the brother?"

"Just slept late. So did the brunette. Then got bed rot."

"Bed rot?"

"Yeah, like watched TV in bed. Like boring."

"How'bout the guards?"

"At least one, sometimes both, like don't do nothin''cept sit in the living room. Extra boring." Jacob wiggled while pulling down the crotch of his jeans. Hopefully, he hadn't been bitten there.

"Where are the princes now?"

"Out drivin' their 'raris. I've been like tracking 'em." He took out his phone and opened an app. "They're at some fancy-ass hotel in Cannes.[95] That's like thirty-five miles from here."

"Okay, good. Now listen up." Wolfgang explained the contents of the two mini syringes, then gave him the key fob and parking lot ticket. "Here's what I want you to do. Follow them at a safe distance. If they stop again, see if you can plant the drugs on Muhammad."

"Not a chance. Those guards are like shadows."

"I understand, but you might get lucky. When they get back to the hotel, call me and we'll discuss tonight's recon."

"Yeah, okay, but I'm like cooked. I need Zs."

"No time to sleep. Tomorrow's the deadline. Hear that? Dead … line."

Jacob snarled yet didn't complain. Maybe there was hope he'd become a professional one day. He turned to leave, then did a one-eighty. "Like, what are you gonna do?"

"I've got other business." Wolfgang hoped he'd have quiet time to start searching through Shaw's transferred laptop files line by line.

"Like what?"

"You do realize I'm the only one running the whole network now, right?"

The teenager smirked as if shouting "What network?" but wisely held his tongue. He ambled down the sidewalk, turned a corner and disappeared.

Rideshares were banned in Monaco. Wolfgang hoped to catch a taxi at Palais Princier de Monaco,[96] the residence of the royal family and the most popular tourist site in Monaco-Ville. After a one-third-mile walk, he reached the crowd-infested Palace Square.

His cell phone rang. Caller ID showed it was The Commander. Wolfgang's blood pressure surged. He flashed a finger, rejected the call and shoved the phone into his pocket. Within seconds, he got a text: That's not polite. Answer my call! He did when the phone rang again.

"My, my, my," the scolding synthesized female voice said. "You need better manners for your top client. Ms. Shaw would never be so rude."

Wolfgang resented being talked to like a child. He wanted to sound irritated and in control. "What do you want?" he barked.

"Just seeing how things are going. Have you picked the lucky prince yet?"

"Still working on it."

"I see. Well, there's still plenty of time. By my watch, you have just about thirty-six hours."

"You'll be the first to know."

"Excellent. Excellent. Say, I hate bothering you like this – I know you're busy – but I have another assignment for you."

"Sorry, but this was a one-and-done."

The Commander's tone shifted from upbeat to ominous. "Yes, you will be sorry if you don't continue to cooperate."

Wolfgang became emphatic. "No, after this, I'm done with your assignments and your threats, and I'm done with you. Got that?"

"There's no need to get testy. But it would be such a shame to traumatize all those wonderful tourists standing around you at the Prince's Palace."

Wolfgang's head swiveled, searching with dilated pupils for a killer.

"I see I now have your full and undivided attention. So where were we? Oh, I know. For encrypted details on the next assignment, go to the same URL address and type in the code 'livingthedream.' That's all one word and lowercase. You have sixty seconds before it expires. If you fail to accept it, you'll expire shortly. Rest assured,

I'm always at your side. Have a great day."

Chapter Thirty-Three: Nice, France and Monaco City, Monaco

Photos 89–96

CHAPTER THIRTY-FOUR

PHILADELPHIA, PENNSYLVANIA

Monday

Chris woke at sunrise to the sight of a voyeur peering through the bedroom window. "Churr, churr, churr," the red-bellied woodpecker called before drumming on the rotting windowsill. Wood shavings chipped away as the beak hammered deeper in search of prey. The pounding was relentless.

Annoying little cuss.

He threw a Kleenex box across the room. It frightened the bird but also startled Anna. She bolted upright in bed, gasping, with terrified eyes and flailing in defense. The crippling fear she struggled to suppress had erupted again. Her constant vulnerability was painful to watch. He always fell short of providing comfort. Worse yet was his corrosive guilt for destroying her life and spirit.

"It's okay," he whispered with reassurance. "You're fine. I was just scaring away a woodpecker. Sorry if I scared you too."

The tension melted and her eyes softened as she lowered back onto the pillow. She inched closer, draped an arm across his chest and smiled with affection. Their shared warmth was amorous. "Good morning. I like waking up with you." With a naughty grin, she added, "But then I like everything we do in bed."

He leaned over for a kiss. She turned away. "Cottonmouth," she explained. "Please give me and my toothbrush a moment of privacy. I'll be right back. Promise. Can you wait that long?"

"Nooo" was his childish pout.

She slid his forefinger between her lips, fluttered her tongue and kissed the tip. "There. That'll give you something to think about while I'm gone."

The tease quickened his pulse. He was transfixed while she crawled over him and lingered before putting on a robe. *God, she's gorgeous.* With an impish giggle, she pulled the robe open for a quick flash and swayed her hips while walking out. Chris was mesmerized.

Excited anticipation was all-consuming until his gaze wandered toward the evidence board on the wall. They often got distracted during their two days of working together. Impromptu playing was lots more fun than disciplined focus. But they had made some progress. They had added several more Post-it® Notes below the bio photos. On each yellow sticky were large black keywords plus tiny numbers corresponding to detailed information in a growing database.

Yet they still had no clue who had commissioned the poisoning of the four senators. Sitting President Starling now seemed like an unlikely villain. Two of the killed senators were among his strongest supporters in Congress.

Maybe Chris was overthinking this. Maybe Steven Oakley and Senator Vickie McLoren were the only co-conspirators. Irene must have ordered their simultaneous murders to hide her role in the carnage. That was a logical conclusion. But his instincts screamed otherwise. He sensed a larger plot. His intuition knew something his logic couldn't decipher.

He leaped out of bed to examine the wall. The elusive answer was hiding somewhere in plain sight. He knew it. But where? Frustration festered.

His attention drifted toward the words *Where's Wolfgang?* One thing was certain. In retaliation for killing Irene, her number two had ordered the hits on Anna in Boston last week and on himself in the cathedral two days ago. He'd keep trying until they were dead.

Anna was right. Finding Wolfgang was imperative if they wanted to stay alive. But how do you find a ghost?

He was oblivious when Anna returned and dropped the robe, but flinched when she patted his bottom. "Cute tush."

"Thanks" was his monotone reply. "I'll be back in a minute."

He yanked on yesterday's boxers, scurried out and encountered his sister in the hallway.

Michelle was dressed for work. "For God's sake," she said with a sneer. "Have the decency to wear some pants, will you please?"

"Yeah, whatever." He escaped into the bathroom.

From the other side of the door, she yelled, "I'm leaving soon. Then the two of you can prance around naked for all I care."

He mumbled under his breath, "Glad to know I have your permission."

Chris performed his morning routine on autopilot while his cognitive skills searched for insight. Halfway through shaving, a novel idea appeared. *That's it!* The hypothesis seemed viable, but only time would tell. He washed off the excess shaving cream, skipped the shower, patted his face dry and hurried into the bedroom.

Anna was curled up in bed. With an enticing smile, she pulled back the covers. "I kept your place warm."

"Be there soon" was his distracted response. He grabbed a black pen and a yellow note, wrote *Irene's Dog*, and slapped it on the evidence board next to *Where's Wolfgang?*

Anna sat up, covering her chest while lowering her feet to the floor. "What're you doing?"

Chris bubbled with excitement. "I know how to find Wolfgang, at least I think I do. The answer is Irene's dog."

"Sorry, but you've lost me."

"Think about it. Her one true love was her Afghan hound, right? She'd do anything to protect that animal. Even while luring us into that death trap in Seville, she had that Jacob Conners teen walk a doppelgänger rather than risk a precious hair on the dog's head."

"So?"

"So, knowing Irene, I'll bet the dog wore a GPS tracker in case he got lost. If I can find the device, I can find the dog."

"So what? Irene is dead."

"You're right. I wish I had thought of this earlier when we were hunting her. But if the dog is still alive, maybe Wolfgang is taking care of it."

"That sounds like a stretch to me."

"More like a Hail Mary," he admitted. "But it's worth a shot unless you have a better idea."

"I did a couple of minutes ago." After emitting a sigh of disappointment, she added, "But I sense your mood's changed. You owe me a make-up game."

"You've got it," he said with a roguish twinkle.

"Fine. Then let's get dressed and go back to work."

Chris wasted no time. A quick search on Google revealed that implantable GPS trackers did not exist. The technology was restricted to collars. Hoping to see the correct brand and model, he reviewed the hummingbird drone video of the dog in the courtyard at Irene's mansion. No device. Strike one. He watched the video from the first time he saw Jacob walking the dog in Seville. Strike two. "Goddamn it!"

Anna lifted her head from the laptop next to his. "What's the matter?"

"Nothing." He moped around the room, deep in thought, snapped his fingers, and rushed back to the Seville videos. He selected the earliest ones recorded by Jack Olsen, Ansel's childhood roommate from the Amish farm in York County. At Ansel's bequest, Jack had started surveillance five days before Chris and Michelle arrived in Seville. "Bingo!" he shouted.

"Find something?"

"Kinda, sorta, maybe."

"That's not very definitive."

"Bear with me. I'll explain later."

The resolution was fuzzy, but something hugged the dog's neck on day one but not on day six. Somewhere in that timeframe, Irene had left Seville, took her dog and replaced him with a fake. Chris spent the morning studying the tapes — often in slow motion and frame by frame — but couldn't identify the device. But at least one existed. Now the hard work was ahead.

Finding the top brands of GPS dog trackers, and their most expensive models, was the easy part. Irene would never settle for second best. But determining how to hack their computer systems might be challenging. They had to open an undetectable Trojan horse, giving him full administrative access to their real-time customer database. He needed a ruse.

Step one was to search for dog influencers. The results were laughable. The top ten were specific dogs with millions of followers on Instagram and TikTok. They featured endless videos, photos and worthless merchandise destined for future garage sales or the trash can. Lonely dog lovers had too much idle time and money.

An alternative step was finding dog product reviewers. Again, the field was flooded, ranging from Consumer Reports and Amazon to illiterate morons with bad grooming, worse diction, and rambling, often incoherent opinions. In the words of Goldilocks, he wanted a product reviewer who was "just right."

Hours later, he found Good Dog Stuff. The influencer posted legitimate weekly product comparison reviews, had over seventy-two thousand followers and an impressive website that didn't disclose her email address. You had to fill out a contact form. This was perfect.

Chris created an email account called gooddogstuff@outlook.com. He wrote an enticing cover letter along with an elaborate questionnaire asking about dog collar features, benefits, technical specifications, warranties, price points, product availability and customer satisfaction. Any manufacturer's marketing department would salivate over the chance to participate.

He opened the sophisticated hacking toolbox he'd purchased on the dark web about three months ago from OdinOne. He had used the software before to infiltrate the corporate computers of people he suspected of hiring Irene to have Anna killed by silentcide. Chris embedded a root access tool into an Excel version of the dog collar questionnaire. All someone had to do was click, and he could sneak undetected through an installed software back door and rummage around to his heart's content.

Anna agreed to review and edit his material on one condition. As soon as he finished sending the emails to the dog collar manu-facturers, it was time for the make-up game he promised. What an excellent suggestion.

At seven o'clock – thirteen hours after they began working – he pushed Send one last time and announced, "Done," with libidinous glee. "Let the game begin."

They reached for each other's belt buckles.

The front door opened. His sister was home and walking up the stairs.

CHAPTER THIRTY-FIVE

The scheme for killing Prince Muhammad bin Faizan was simple in concept, brazen in method and glutted with ways to fail.

Wolfgang didn't have time to find a better alternative. He focused on the Saudi Arabian's greatest vulnerability: when his suite was unoccupied. The challenge was circumventing the hotel's tight security.

The plan had three steps. One, gain access to the prince's restricted floor by using a service elevator. Two, slip an angled rod with a steel cable beneath the door to pull down the handle from the inside. And three, taint with the toxic drugs something only the prince would use to ensure his death by overdose.

After getting The Commander's phone call yesterday, Wolfgang had mapped out the steps, identified the needed props, created a to-do list and delegated a share of the work to Jacob. Although the preparation was intense, that was the easy part. The Achilles' heel was that the plan's implementation relied on the rookie skills of Jacob Conners. His naivete, sense of immortality and ego made him overconfident he'd succeed. That was worrisome.

Before dawn, Wolfgang settled into the observation post on the Rock of Monaco, trained the scope on the Diamond Suite of Hôtel de Paris,[97] and lathered on insect repellent. For hours, nothing happened. The princes and their girlfriends slept, while the bodyguards rotated between napping and watching TV. Wolfgang idled away the wait agonizing over how to implement The Commander's next assignment. It made this one look like a no-brainer.

Prince Muhammad woke up first. He jostled the blond, gave her a lecherous smirk, jumped out of bed – naked, of course – and headed to the bathroom.

Wolfgang called Jacob on the burner phone. "The prince is awake. Are you ready?"

"Yup, and I'm like so pumped. And this hotel is like really boujee."

"Goddam it! Stop that teenage bullshit and talk like an educated adult or you'll blow your cover in seconds. Got that?"

"Yup."

"Try 'yes, sir.'"

"Yes, sir."

"Good. Now turn on your bodycam and show me what you've done."

The video of Jacob's hotel room appeared on Wolfgang's phone. The teen had booked into the Hôtel de Paris yesterday. They charged his alias the full, in-season rack rate, but the excessive cost was justified.

The video picture wobbled as Jacob walked. "'Bout three hours ago, I ordered a standard breakfast for two from room service and, like, they delivered it on a cart with a white tablecloth just like you hoped. I think, like, it's perfect."

"Get closer, then stop moving so I can see what you've done."

The presentation on the cart was decadent. Yesterday, Wolfgang and Jacob had spent eleven hundred euros at high-end retailers and at a farmer's market to create the elaborate prop. The French crystal was Baccarat. In a large cut-glass bowl was an array of red fruits: pomegranates, dragon fruits, rambutans, strawberries, Bing cherries and passion fruits. In the center were a yellow banana and a butt-shaped pear. The suggestive connotation was impossible to miss. Accompanying the bottle of Dom Pérignon 2015 Brut was a pair of champagne flutes. As a finishing touch, Jacob had arranged hotel silverware, linen napkins and two china serving plates on the cart that room service delivered this morning.

"That'll work," Wolfgang said without enthusiasm. "Now go into the bathroom and show me what you look like."

Jacob had rented a black cutaway tuxedo with a white piqué bib shirt and a white bow tie centered in the wing-tip collar. His reflection in the mirror proved the adage that any man looks distinguished in a tux. Wolfgang compared the outfit to the surveillance photo of a restaurant server he had snapped the day before. They were a close match.

"Your clothes seem fine," Wolfgang said, "but your tie is sagging."

"Like, I don't know how to tie the thing."

"Go online and learn. You don't have much time. Now let me look at your face."

Jacob had checked in under his redhead alias from New York City, but now his hair was short and black. Eyeglasses and tinted contacts helped a little, as did some makeup to age his appearance. But they ruled out facial hair because it seemed against restaurant policy.

In short, the disguise was minimal. Security cameras could easily identify him. That might be a problem. If Jacob messed up, he'd bear the consequences and Wolfgang would leave him hanging. But if the prince died as planned, there probably wouldn't be an investigation. His ashamed family would want to avoid a scandal, and the hotel would be eager to sweep the overdose of a high-profile druggie under the rug.

"You look good," Wolfgang said. "I'll let you know when it's time to go."

With raging teenage excitement, Jacob asked, "Is that FBOI like smashing that snack again?"

Wolfgang peered through the telescope. The prince was putting on another show. "Stay focused, Jacob. Goodbye."

For two hours, Prince Muhammad and the blond repeated

yesterday's routine. They romped, showered and ate breakfast on his private balcony before the brothers and their playmates left the suite. Minutes later, the minicams in the central square showed them leaving the hotel.

Wolfgang called Jacob. "It's time. Any last-minute questions?"

"Yup, you got anything better than like this calamine crap? These bug bites are effing me up."

Damn idiot. "Go! Now!"

Jacob's video feed showed him entering a public elevator. On the top floor, he nonchalantly wheeled the dining cart into Le Grill restaurant, past a hostess and two waiters who were scurrying to open for lunch, and into the kitchen aflutter with cooks and wait-staff. The camera panned left and right in search of the service elevator.

"Arrêt!" came a stern off-camera voice. A stately man in a tuxedo entered the screen and demanded, "Qui es-tu?"

"Oh shit," Wolfgang mumbled while turning on the Google Translate app so he could follow the conversation.

"I'm André Bertrand, sir," Jacob said in French with confidence. "I just started at Alain Ducasse."

The man was unimpressed that Jacob claimed to be working on the ground floor for Monaco's only three-star Michelin restaurant. He eyeballed the dining cart. "What the hell do you think you're doing?"

"I'm delivering this to a guest room, sir."

"Not a chance. Hotel policy forbids serving guests food we didn't prepare."

"I learned that, sir. But the concierge told me their policy is that guests can have anything they want if the price is high enough."

The elder frowned before seeing the handwritten note on hotel stationery that read, *Happy passionate anniversary, my love.* After scanning the fruit bowl again, he belly-laughed. "It looks like some horny rich guy is willing to pay a lot to get laid."

"Yes, sir," Jacob said with respect.

Smooth. Very smooth.

"But wait." The man raised an index finger. "You need a champagne bucket."

Jacob checked his watch. "But, sir …"

"This will only take a second."

The extra time allowed the teenager to locate the service elevator. He ambled forward, pushed the down button, peered inside and discovered a showstopper. There was a security keypad on the panel.

Damn it. Now what?

As the man positioned the bucket on the cart, Jacob said, "Sir, I just realized I left my badge downstairs. Could I …"

The man angered. "Continued mistakes like that will get you fired, young man. We expect only top performance."

"I'm sorry, sir. It won't happen again."

"It better not." The elevator reopened and the man swiped his badge across the panel.

"Thank you, sir. Please don't tell Chef Lefebvre. Please. I really need this job."

Wolfgang breathed a sigh of relief. *He's a natural. Cool, calm and collected. Just don't get cocky and screw up act two.*

Chapter Thirty-Five: Monte Carlo, Monaco

Photo 97

CHAPTER THIRTY-SIX

Monte Carlo, Monaco and Èze, France

Tuesday

Jacob exited the elevator into a housekeeping room filled with linen, cleaning supplies, and a dripping washbasin. He put on a pair of white service gloves, threw the love letter, banana and pear into a trash bin, covered the food with a tablecloth hidden on the bottom shelf of the dining cart and pulled a folded paper from his pocket.

Wolfgang peered into the spotting scope and said into Jacob's earpiece, "The suite's still empty. Proceed."

The teenager entered the hallway and approached the main door of the Diamond Suite. All he needed to do was kneel, reach for the break-in tool taped to the dining cart, and he'd be inside in ten seconds.

He began bending down. There were unexpected footsteps. His bodycam swung to reveal a maid approaching with towels. While tying his shoe, he said to her in French, "Good morning."

The harried elderly woman flashed a disinterested smile. She walked past and stopped at a nearby guest room. "Room service," she announced.

Jacob was quick to adapt. He stood, knocked on the door and called out in French, "Hotel concierge." He was stalling until the maid left before resuming the break-in.

A gruff, unintelligible voice boomed. Wolfgang's head snapped back with surprise. The scope revealed a lethargic bodyguard stand, stretching from a nap on a couch. Wolfgang yelled into the comm, "A guard's coming. Abort."

From the perspective of Jacob's bodycam, a Neanderthal opened the door, wearing a cannon in a shoulder holster.

"Bonjour, monsieur. Avec les compliments de l'hôtel." Jacob handed him a letter on hotel stationery. In Arabic, the message said the champagne had been hand-selected from their cellar containing the world's largest hotel collection of wines. The gift was a small token of appreciation for being their honored guests. The hotel general manager's forged signature appeared at the bottom of the letter.

The brute grunted and yanked the cart into the room.

Jacob held on to the other handle and scurried inside. He pointed at the champagne and said in French, "May I place this on your table, sir?"

The bodyguard's eyes narrowed with suspicion. He pulled off the tablecloth and surveyed the fruit. He grabbed a Bing cherry, sucked it into his mouth, pulled out the stem, devoured the flesh and spat the pit into his meaty palm. His stance was menacing. He towered over the teen.

Wolfgang tensed. Jacob seemed unfazed while giving the guard a handful of cherries. He then retrieved the linen from the floor, draped it over the food, lifted the champagne bucket and motioned someplace off camera. "Please, sir, may I?"

The savage seemed unyielding. Jacob remained quiet and subservient. The standoff ended when the guard huffed, returned to the couch and turned on the seventy-five-inch flatscreen TV.

The bodycam video did a slow one-eighty as if Jacob was searching for a point of vulnerability. The living room was huge and luxurious, featuring a chevron-patterned hardwood floor, an inset ceiling encased in elaborate white molding, a crystal chandelier, lush golden drapes, plus leather-upholstered club chairs and matching couches. Jacob took his time arranging the champagne on the dining table set for six.

Wolfgang was losing patience. He said into the comm, "Too dangerous. We'll find another way. Get the hell outta there."

Wolfgang got livid when Jacob went to the wet bar, grabbed the coffeepot, approached the bodyguard, refilled his cup, removed used plates from the accent table and stacked them on the bottom shelf of the cart. He proceeded to the main balcony and started clearing the bodyguards' breakfast dishes.

"I said abort!"

"I got this," Jacob whispered.

Goddamn that twerp.

The teenager reentered the living room with the final armload. He stopped and pointed toward the prince's bedroom. The man grunted, too engrossed in the action film to care. Jacob left, pushed the cart down the suite's hallway and entered Muhammad's bedroom. His pace quickened.

Okay, I guess it's game on.

The bodycam showed two lines of cocaine on a marble vanity. "No," Wolfgang said. "Might kill the girl." On the desk was a bong filled with water. "No, might get emptied. Look for a backup bullet." Jacob rummaged through the dresser drawers and uncovered a package of Narcan nasal spray. "That could counteract Muhammad's overdose. Take it and keep looking."

The first nightstand contained makeup, jewelry and scarves. "Move!" The video image blurred as Jacob raced around the king-size bed. "Go, go, go!" Sex paraphernalia filled the second nightstand. "No, damn it."

Inside the bottom drawer was a half-empty carton of Marlboro soft packs. "Yes! That's it."

Jacob pulled out the mini syringes. Wolfgang heard two beeps and a door opening. One syringe fell to the floor and under the bed skirt. Loud voices in Arabic. On his knees, the teenager searched, found it, and struggled with the cap of the vial filled with powdered drugs. Boisterous laughter. He stabbed the needle into the bottom of a cigarette pack, tapped the plunger and ran onto the balcony.

"Madha tafeal?"

The camera rotated. With demonic eyes, Muhammad started screaming what sounded like Arabic obscenities. Spit flew from his raging mouth. Jacob mumbled apologies in French while clutching a half-empty carafe of orange juice. The blond cowered in a corner. With clenched fists, the prince poised to charge.

The bodyguard rushed in to intervene. He tapped the prince on the shoulder and said something to calm him down. The guard waved Jacob back into the room, shoved him toward the dining cart and began escorting him out. Muhammad yelled a final time as the bedroom door to the central hallway slammed shut with a rattling bang.

Wolfgang peered through the scope. The blond was consoling the prince by stroking his chest and standing on her toes to give him a kiss. The bodyguard retreated to the living room, plopped on the couch and resumed watching the movie. Jacob had averted the immediate crisis. However, an investigation into the prince's death could be problematic.

Wolfgang switched back to the bodycam video. Jacob was pushing the cart out of a public elevator. "You idiot! What the hell were you thinking? I told you to abort."

"I'm sorry." The teen's voice quivered between labored breaths.

"Are you okay?"

"No, I was stuck with the needle."

"Were you injected?"

Jacob fumbled with his room key. "Maybe. Some. I don't know."

His hands were shaking. "I'm feeling kinda weird. Like everything's spinning."

"What's that mean? Talk to me."

The teenager gasped for air as the door swung open. He rushed in. The cart wobbled before collapsing. Red fruit, dirty dishes and shards of French crystal scattered across the floor. He stumbled to the bathroom, dropped to his knees and hugged the porcelain bowl.

Wolfgang's priority was clear. "Jacob, flush the syringes down the toilet."

The marble walls magnified chest-wrenching coughing. "I'll try." One syringe plopped in and sank. Animalistic gags preceded the second syringe. As the evidence swirled away, a torrent of vomit followed. Two more rounds of explosive retching refilled the bowl.

Jacob squealed. "Oh my God. Oh my God. Oh my God."

"What?"

"My heart. It's exploding."

Wolfgang tried to sound calm. "Listen to me. You're overdosing. You gotta act fast."

"Help me" was his pathetic plea.

"I am, but you've got to listen. You've got Narcan in your pocket. Use it."

Trembling hands encased in white gloves struggled to open the box. He sobbed in alarm. Scratching. Clawing. A long string of saliva dripped into the toilet after horrific dry heaves. His breathing became faint as if falling asleep.

"Stay with me, Jacob. Open the damn box."

He convulsed with tremors. The box shredded. The medicine's plastic tray plunged into the repulsive water.

"Go get it!"

A puke-covered glove fished it out. He used his teeth to pull back the cellophane.

"Stick the nozzle in your nose. Now! Then push the plunger."

Jacob never snorted. Instead, a gruesome wail. The room spun. A thundering crash. The ceiling appeared. There was silence. Dead silence.

"Jacob!" Nothing. "Jacob!" Still nothing. "Goddamn it, answer me!"

Wolfgang exhaled a mournful sigh. He was certain the teen was gone. Anger and pity crushed his chest and burned his heart, a toxic feeling he hadn't had since his brother died. They were both too young – in the prime of life – before fate stole their souls.

He cowered in defeat. Recovering the body was impossible. A horrified maid would soon discover the corpse, sparking an investigation. Authorities might assume the imposter died during a drug robbery gone bad. But when the prince suffered a similar overdose, they'd suspect murder. Weeks later, matching toxicology reports would confirm their conclusion. This was a homicide, not a silentcide as intended.

Wolfgang was confident he wouldn't be implicated. They had been cautious maintaining their distance. There was only one connection. He pried open the burner phone, broke the SIM card and buried the remains beneath a bush. "Goodbye, Jacob," he said while pushing back the dirt.

His life was screwed. He was the king of a collapsed network without people, resources or respect. If he ran now, Shaw's bank account plus his own, and The Commander's down payment, would last a few years, maybe longer if frugal. Poverty was no way to live. If he could recover Shaw's bitcoin, he could hide rich and hope The Commander never found him. But if he didn't finish this assignment first, The Commander would retaliate. And if Wolfgang kept following orders, the next assignment would probably prove fatal.

Any way he turned was a dead end. There was one viable option: string The Commander along until he found the pot of gold. To demonstrate his continued compliance, he needed to supply proof of death. With luck, the entitled son of a bitch would smoke his last cigarette before Wolfgang's early morning flight back to Philly. Wolfgang didn't feel lucky.

With a sigh of resignation, he peered through the scope. The Diamond Suite appeared empty. He checked the surveillance cameras. The Ferraris weren't parked in front of the casino. He opened the tracking app. The boys were joyriding along Moyenne Corniche, one of the twisting scenic routes called Les Corniches in French and The Cliff Roads in English. He was compelled to follow them.

Wolfgang struggled to stand. His back spasmed, his finger throbbed, and mosquitoes had bitten his neck and ankles. Red welts began itching. He went to the Oceanographic Museum, took the elevator to the parking garage, turned on the engine and consulted the app again. The princes were visiting Éze, France,[98] a small medieval village that clung to a mountainside. They were about a fifteen-minute drive away.

On the approach to their location, traffic slowed to a stop. Complete deadlock. In frustration, he pulled into a neighborhood of Èze-sur-Mer and began walking. Ahead were the flashing lights of police cars and an ambulance. A crowd of people in a parking lot was wedged among tour buses and gawking over a cliff. He elbowed his way forward and stared down.

At the bottom of the 260-foot ravine was a twisted blue Ferrari, charred from fire and smoke. On a bridge, Muhammad and the blond stood shell-shocked beside their dented red sports car and a disintegrated railing. The wrong prince had died. The Commander might get a twofer.

For his proof of death report, Wolfgang snapped a few photos before asking an idle bus driver if he knew the name of the bridge.

He replied, "I think it's called Devil's Bridge."[99]

Karma's a bitch. He laughed. *And then you die.*

Chapter Thirty-Six: Monte Carlo, Monaco and Èze, France

Photos 98–99

CHAPTER THIRTY-SEVEN

Wednesday

It was the fifth day of self-imposed isolation, and their emotions oscillated from elation to determination to frustration in the 12x12 space that doubled as a love nest and war room. The evidence board now consumed two walls with tentacles of crooked yellow notes reaching down to the floor. Stacks of research printouts encroached on work areas and walking lanes around their side-by-side card tables. The wastebasket was overflowing with discarded ideas and empty food cartons delivered by DoorDash. A box fan circulated oppressive air.

Despite their dedicated teamwork, Chris and Anna were still clueless about the identity of the plot mastermind or Wolfgang's location. They weren't ready to admit defeat. But constant disappointments, lack of sleep and the confining proximity were sapping their endurance and grating on their nerves.

There were a couple of bright spots yesterday, but they were fleeting. When the first GPS dog tracker manufacturer clicked on the spurious questionnaire, Chris tried in vain to circumvent their zero-trust security. He then solicited the help of OdinOne, his black-hat resource. The crook charged him a thousand dollars up front with no guarantees. When he failed, he typed into a chat box, "Sorry dude."

The second manufacturer was more promising. The RAT installation gave him administrative access to their customer database. Fifteen minutes later, however, he learned Irene did not have an account. Hoping she might've used an alias, he did simple searches by dog breed and pet name. Nothing. He also used artificial intelligence to script a query of the eleven thousand accounts in Pennsylvania. Still nothing.

Midafternoon today, another alert flashed on his laptop screen. The third and final vendor's unsuspecting marketing department had entered the spider web. His heart quickened, yet his brain remained skeptical. He decided against telling Anna this time. Why get her hopes up again, only to disappoint? The expectation rollercoaster was demoralizing.

The hacker's toolbox penetrated the cybersecurity of BestFriend, the top-rated provider of GPS dog trackers. Within five minutes, he had total remote system control while remaining undetected, at least for the short term. That's all the time he would need.

"I've got it!" he screamed the moment he discovered Irene Shaw's name listed as an active premium member. He jumped up and did a happy dance.

"What? What? What?" Anna asked through her precious smile.

He bent over and gave her an exaggerated loud kiss. "I've found Irene's dog tracker account."

"Oh my God. That's awesome. Does that mean you know where Wolfgang is?"

"Not yet, but we're a huge step closer. Just give me a minute." He sat down with renewed enthusiasm. While clicking through Irene's account profile, he sensed Anna monitoring every keystroke and reading every screen. "You're kinda cramping my style. You'll be the second to know when I hit the mother lode," he promised with a whimsical grin.

She went back to work, but he could tell she was unproductive while hovering for more good news. That took a while. He scoured a database containing details like customer number, username, model type, package plan, purchase date, payment status and past service activities. There was no live or interactive information. He leaned back, rubbed his neck and sighed in frustration.

Anna's foot started tapping, echoing like a snare drum in the silent room. "Sorry," she said. "I'll go get us more coffee."

When she left the bedroom, he pulled up the BestFriend website to get familiar with the collar's features. The market leader's list was impressive. The most valuable was the ability to locate the pet within twenty-five feet and a year's worth of global tracking history. But they were useless without logging in as a customer, and Irene's profile didn't show a password. He suspected it was locked down in a separate encrypted database.

The Sharing feature caught his eye. It allowed the user to "add trusted family and friends to your pet's profile." Chris couldn't be trusted, nor was he family or a friend, but this sounded promising. He found the profile for Brutus. Three people were listed: Pierre Brassel, whoever the hell that was, Jacob Conners and Wolfgang König. His skin tingled and his breathing quickened while using AI to write the code to add him as the fourth person in the database.

His cell phone dinged within seconds. Excitement surged while clicking on the email account icon. There was an invitation to join the "BestFriend Community of Dog Lovers." Signing up took a long two minutes. Then he was "a co-guardian of Brutus, Irene Shaw's Afghan hound." Attached was an out-of-focus photo of the mangy mutt.

Immediate disappointment. The collar status indicator read OFF. He tapped on Location History. The last entry from two hours ago showed a forty-two-minute route in Harrisburg. "Gotcha!" Out of curiosity, he entered the date range from mid-July to the present and scrolled through the results. Irene's elusive travel path was clear as day, from her escape from Elkins Park, Pennsylvania, to Seville and then Granada, Spain, to a couple of weeks in London, until hiding for a month on State Street in Pennsylvania's capital city.

So the dog's alive, but who has custody? If it's Wolfgang, he's a dead man walking.

In an instant, Chris transformed from a determined sleuth to a primal hunter. He grabbed his Glock 19 from the nightstand, checked the magazine, slammed the fifteen rounds back into the polymer grip, and pocketed two extra mags in an abundance of caution. He doubted the extra firepower was needed. One well-placed hollow point would end Wolfgang's life in less than four milliseconds.

At the end of the bed, under a pile of clothes, he found Anna's runner's waist pack and slipped the semiautomatic pistol inside. As he reached the bottom of the steps, she came out of the kitchen holding two cups of coffee. With one glance at his hardened expression, her cute face twisted into concern. "You found the dog, didn't you?" The question sounded like a statement.

His tone was sullen. "Yeah, he's in Harrisburg."

She stared at the runner's pack and asked with trepidation, "You're going to turn Wolfgang over to Hamilton, right? And, you know, let her handle it."

"Why would I let her handle it? She's incompetent. Besides, he'd make bail in a day and we'd never find him again."

Coffee slopped over the rims as she put the cups on the bottom stair, stabilized her rocking by grabbing the handrail, and pleaded, "But you can't just kill him. I thought you were done with that."

"I was. But I promised to protect you and Michelle. And sometimes protection looks like this. Besides, if I don't stop him, he'll keep coming after us. It's kill or be killed. Understand?"

"But if you're caught, you'll go away for life."

"Maybe, but at least you two will be safe."

Anxiety dilated her brown eyes. "Chris, please don't do this."

He realized for the first time that she was frightened for him, not for herself. Her affection for him was real. Maybe she could love him someday. Perhaps they had a future together, but not until this threat was neutralized. He had to act with conviction. "Listen, I gotta move."

"Please be careful," she begged as he walked out the door.

He didn't dare look back or he might not go. Staying was safe, at least for a while. Leaving risked losing his life or freedom, or worse, losing her respect and admiration. She might abandon him again. That prospect was torturous. But if he failed to prevent her death when he had the chance, remorse would corrode his essence forever.

Every town, truck and green mile marker he passed heading west on the Pennsylvania Turnpike increased his self-doubt. For over ninety minutes, he vacillated between shooting Wolfgang, killing him by silentcide, telling Hamilton, doing nothing, or running away with Anna.

He pounded the steering wheel. What was his problem? He'd never been this indecisive. Were his feelings for Anna clouding his judgment and making him risk-averse? Had he lost his nerve?

His cell phone rang. Caller ID read Michelle. He resisted answering but knew she'd keep calling for the remaining thirty minutes of the drive. When he swiped Accept, she began ranting. "What the hell are you doing?"

"Apparently, Anna's already told you."

"You're damn straight she did. Why didn't you ask for my help?"

"Why should I? You vowed never to kill again and someone's got to do this."

"No, Chris, you don't. I agree with Anna. Let Hamilton arrest him. Otherwise, you could blow everything. The scumbag's not worth that."

"No, if I don't do this, I'll blow my only chance at keeping you and Anna alive. And that's definitely worth it."

"Just don't do something stupid."

"Thanks for that wonderful vote of confidence."

He ended the call and solidified his resolve.

Wolfgang must die. Today.

CHAPTER THIRTY-EIGHT

Harrisburg, Pennsylvania

Wednesday

Wolfgang had always envied people who slept on long flights. He had spent most of the nine hours from Nice to Philadelphia reading through files he had transferred from Shaw's laptop. One bright spot was finding passwords in a Word document called Strawberry Rhubarb Pie Recipe. His excitement was fleeting. The list was for online retailers, utility companies and streaming services.

Pierre opened the door of Shaw's safehouse in Harrisburg before Wolfgang reached the front porch. "Welcome back, Mr. König," he said with a professional smile while grabbing the handle of the roller bag. "Will Mr. Conners be returning soon?"

Wolfgang didn't have the heart to tell him Jacob's fate. The butler had begun self-medicating after the deaths of Shaw and her chauffeur John. His cheeks were gaunt, his amber eyes were hooded, and his uniform drooped over his emaciated frame. One more loss could send him reeling into crisis mode. "No, Jacob flew to our next assignment."

"I see. Please give him my best. For your flight tonight, I've laid out attire for your consideration. And I'll launder these soiled clothes. Any other requests?"

"Yes, pack my lucky boxer shorts. And no starch this time."

"No problem, sir. Please come in."

On the other side of the front door was the Afghan hound. Brutus bared his teeth, growled, and launched into ferocious barking. His long blond ears shook with aggression. Wolfgang did a threatening side kick. "Get away from me, animal."

Pierre grabbed the dog's collar. "I'm sorry, sir. Brutus hasn't been himself since Ms. Shaw passed. I'll let you get settled, then I'll bring you something to eat."

Pierre's meals were the best perk since assuming Shaw's role.

He trudged up the creaking staircase, undressed in Shaw's former master bedroom, and washed away stress and travel fatigue under the gold-plated heads of the thermostatic shower. The enormous walk-in closet dwarfed his half rack of clothes. He got dressed, put on a leather coat to conceal the shoulder holster, and swapped out two shirts laid out on the silk duvet cover of the canopy bed.

The study was immaculate as always. Dust didn't stand a chance from Pierre's obsessive cleaning. Wolfgang opened the wall safe behind a Marc Chagall painting and removed Shaw's laptop, jewelry, credit cards and bitcoin hardware wallet. He had watched a video about a hacker who claimed he could recover private keys from crypto wallets. As a last resort, Wolfgang was confident he could persuade the braggart to unlock Shaw's fortune, either with a promise of a huge cash reward or the promise to spare his life.

He put the items into a knapsack, along with his own laptop that Pierre had brought up for him. This collection represented all his valuable possessions. Someday soon, however, they'd be a rounding error of his net worth.

The smell emanating from the cherrywood desk was mouthwatering. On a polished silver serving tray was a pulled-beef, open-faced sandwich drenched in brown gravy piled high on mashed potatoes and fresh sourdough bread. The sides were homemade kettle chips with onion dip and a dollop of cottage cheese garnished with paprika and a parsley sprig served with a frosted mug of root beer.

Wolfgang had just put a linen napkin on his lap and lifted a fork when an explosion rocked the first floor.

In an instinctual second, he extracted his SIG P229, swiveled in the executive chair and stared at the center security monitor behind the credenza. Three masked assailants wearing FBI vests and brandishing M4 carbines rushed through the breached door. A single bark was silenced by rapid fire from an assault rifle. The word "clear" was heard at different volumes until ending in a terrified shriek. An ominous mix of whimpers and heavy boots thundered up the steps. The commotion stopped on the landing.

Wolfgang was ready. He took cover behind the desk, aiming his handgun at the study doorway. His 9mm was a poor match against a 5.56mm weapon, let alone three of them. But with superior marksmanship and an iota of luck, he'd down one, maybe two of the attackers before being shredded apart.

"Oh, Wolfgang." The assailant's tone was condescending and sinister. "We're back. How's your pinky? I'll bet it still hurts like a son of a bitch."

Wolfgang's breathing was calm, his focus was intense, and he refused to be intimidated. "Doing just fine. Thanks for asking."

"That's great news. Say, remember how I said our next visit wouldn't be as pleasant. Well, we're here to prove I'm a man of my words."

Wolfgang considered sending a few rounds through the wall but worried he might hit Pierre. "I never doubted your intentions, only your IQ."

"Oh my. Let's not get into insults or I might get mad. And you wouldn't want that to happen, would you?"

"No, what I want to happen is for you to leave before you get hurt."

A peal of laughter roared down the hallway. "Okay, let's stop screwing around." The assailant's inflection became dark. "We can either throw in another flashbang – and you remember how unpleasant that was – or you can drop your gun and let us in."

"Come on in," Wolfgang dared while pulling back the hammer into single-action mode and slipping his finger onto the trigger.

Pierre was shoved into the doorframe, handcuffed and trembling. His gagged mouth twisted with fear. Bulging eyes pleaded to be saved. The barrel of a Glock dug into his temple. He had wet his pants.

On cue, two assault weapons jutted into the threshold. The shielded gunman behind Pierre said, "I see you didn't lower your gun. There are penalties for disobeying." He shot the butler in the foot.

Pierre's muffled scream was bestial. He almost collapsed while contorting in pain. Tears of horror gushed down his cheeks when seeing the muzzle move toward his other foot.

"It'd be a real shame to make this boy a cripple. Only you can stop that. Now put your gun on the floor, stand up slowly, kick it away, then have a seat so we can chat."

Wolfgang hesitated before complying. That was the one viable way to save Pierre from further disfigurement. He was innocent in all this. Wolfgang alone should suffer the consequences.

"I'm glad you wisely decided to play nice." While he pushed Pierre into a guest chair, the two henchmen rushed in, flanked Wolfgang and assumed a shooter's stance.

"So what do you want this time?" he demanded with arrogance, resolved not to display his dread.

"Just be patient. You'll know in a minute."

While they waited, the only sounds were Pierre's moans and sniffles. Wolfgang was getting impatient with the theatrics until the cell phone rang in his pocket.

"Answer that and put it on speaker."

It was no surprise The Commander's name appeared on caller

ID. Wolfgang considered being brash but was conciliatory instead. "Good afternoon, ma'am."

"There's nothing good about it." The previous whimsical elegance of the synthesized female voice was now outraged. "Why the hell is your ass in Harrisburg and not flying to the next location?"

"Just picking up a few things," Wolfgang said, trying to sound calm. "But don't worry. I'm booked on a red-eye flight tonight. Everything's under control."

"No, it's not. You botched Monaco."

"Apparently you didn't read my proof of death report."

"That was complete and utter bullshit," The Commander screamed. "Troy, show Mr. König what happens when he lies."

The Glock erupted, blowing out Pierre's kneecap. The butler convulsed, clutching the gaping wound as blood gushed between his fingers. His body rocked. Terror and torment spasmed his youthful face.

"So let's try a little honesty here, shall we, before your friend ends up in pieces. You had nothing to do with the prince's death on Devil's Bridge, did you?"

"No, ma'am. That was an accident."

"And your handiwork was the overdose of Prince Muhammad bin Faizan, correct?"

At least that part of the debacle succeeded.

"Yes, ma'am."

"Were my instructions not clear? I specified the death of one prince that must appear from natural causes. So enlighten me. What part of leaving a dead accomplice behind did you misconstrue as seeming natural?"

"That was an unfortunate complication."

Pierre seemed grief stricken when realizing Jacob was dead.

The Commander continued her tirade. "No, that was a major fuck-up. You've unleashed a snake pit of investigations that are spiraling into an international incident. And I warned you the price for failure was dire, remember that?"

"Yes, ma'am," Wolfgang said, expecting to die.

"Troy, are you ready to show Mr. König what the price for failure looks like?"

"Ready, ma'am."

"Then I suggest you …" The Commander stopped mid-sentence. An excruciating silence followed. The assailants glanced at each other in confusion. Wolfgang riveted on the raised handgun. Pierre was quaking in uncontrolled sobs.

The Commander returned with alarm. "Gentlemen, you've been compromised. Wolfgang, I expect you'll implement my next assignment flawlessly. Is that clear?"

"Yes, ma'am."

"And, Troy, show Mr. König what to expect if he fails again."

Pierre was shot in the head. A jet of red mist splattered as his body hurtled over the chair and slammed into the floor. Lifeless eyes registered horrid surprise.

"Now, all of you, get the hell out of there before it's too late."

CHAPTER THIRTY-NINE

Wednesday

According to the GPS on the car's dashboard, Chris was five minutes away from confronting Wolfgang. His goal was clear – to stop the threat and protect Michelle and Anna – but his plan was murky.

Would he kill him, detain him, or take the women's advice by calling Hamilton to come arrest him?

He hated his uncharacteristic indecisiveness. Being hesitant could get him killed. Being rash could ruin the potential for a new life. Doing nothing would make him a coward.

The magnificent lime-green, terra cotta tile dome of the Pennsylvania State Capitol Building was in his rearview mirror as he drove across the Soldiers and Sailors Memorial Bridge.[100] The modest homes along State Street,[101] all built at the turn of the twentieth century, had less square footage than the six-car detached garage on Irene's palatial twenty-acre estate in Elkins Park. She must have missed the grandeur of her multi-generational mansion while hiding in a puny safehouse. He hoped she was miserable spending eternity in a burial plot.

At a stoplight, he reached below the driver's seat, pulled out the Glock 19 and rested it on his lap. The firearm wouldn't have long to wait. The hideout was two blocks ahead. Soon it would be "game time" as Michelle always called an imminent kill. In retrospect, he should've asked for her help. They were strong when working together and weak when separated by an inconsequential argument.

The light turned green. He drove through the intersection, flicked on the emergency flashers and inched along, hoping impatient drivers would pass. The Waze app on his phone was counting down the feet. He took stock of CCTV and home security cameras. There was some traffic but no pedestrians. Exit routes by car and on foot flashed on a mental Google Maps. The response time from the main police station was about seven minutes tops. An elevated pulse began responding to diaphragmatic breathing. He twitched at the cheery voice announcing, "You have arrived."

He surveyed the porch on the first level, the bay windows on the second, the dormers on the third, and the narrow walkways between houses. One of them was gated. His radar zeroed in on the entrance again. He had to squint to be sure. The blackened front door dangled on the hinges. The safehouse had been breached.

Chris accelerated into a U-turn and came to a screeching halt in a narrow driveway. He ejected, examined and reinserted the loaded magazine, racked the slide back, opened the car door and bolted out. He was two steps into a dead run before stopping in his tracks.

A tall man wearing a tactical vest with the yellow letters FBI stenciled on the chest came out the front door carrying an M4 carbine.

What the hell? How did they get here? Did Anna tip off Hamilton? Maybe Michelle? Or did they collaborate against him? Goddamn them! They'd better hope to God the FBI arrested Wolfgang.

He had to find out.

He pushed the pistol back under the car seat and walked past the neighboring duplex. The agent was staring, getting edgy and raising the assault rifle. When Chris turned toward the house, the agent shouldered his weapon and took aim. "FBI. Stop!"

Chris froze.

Had Hamilton instructed them to arrest him too?

"Hands behind your head. Down on your knees. Now!"

Chris followed the instructions, yet his temper flared. *Why did my two best friends betray me?*

The agent was leery on approach. He pointed the muzzle at Chris's chest and demanded, "Who are you?"

"I'm Chris Davis, special advisor with the Sicarius Task Team at the FBI Philadelphia field office."

"Do you have identification?"

After viewing Chris's FBI credentials, the agent lowered his weapon and relaxed his shoulders. He reached out to help him stand. "I'm sorry, Mr. Davis. Special Agent Hamilton said you might be coming. We're from the Harrisburg field office and just got here a few minutes ago. We're still kind of jumpy because there's a real mess inside."

"What happened?"

"There's a Caucasian male with multiple GSWs on the second floor. He's DOA. From the looks of it, he hasn't been dead long."

Please be Wolfgang. Please be Wolfgang.

"Do you know who it is?"

"No, sir."

"Maybe I can help. I'm here because we suspect this is a safehouse for Wolfgang König, a major fugitive we're after."

"Yes, that's the name Agent Hamilton gave us. Maybe you could ID the victim."

"If I can, sure," Chris said, trying to sound detached while concealing his excitement.

While walking up the stairs, Chris scanned the remains of the reinforced front door. Judging from the burn patterns, remnants of duct tape, and scattered chunks of wood and steel on the porch, someone had used a detonating cord. "That looks like a professional breach," Chris said.

"That's what we guessed too."

Brutus was sprawled on the foyer floor. The lifeless Afghan hound was wearing the BestFriend dog tracker. Chris was awash in sympathy. He rarely felt remorse after killing a scumbag but was always saddened by the death of a pet, especially one that someone shot. Losing the love of her life would have traumatized Irene.

Anticipation escalated on each step of the staircase. Hope plummeted when entering the study. The bloody corpse appeared tortured before the fatal headshot. Two nickel-plated brass casings on the floor suggested the weapon was a 9mm handgun. Chris speculated this was Wolfgang's handiwork. But why?

"Do you know who this is?" the agent asked.

"Judging from the uniform, I'm guessing the butler. Sorry, but I don't know his name."

"Hey, David, you're going to want to see this," an agent said while sitting at the desk, focused on one of the three security monitors.

After Chris was introduced, the agent swiveled back and began pushing buttons inside a pop-up panel on top of the credenza. Chris noticed the uneaten food. The sandwich seemed fresh, maybe still warm. The condensation on a mug convinced him. This crime and the murderer's escape happened minutes ago.

The security video was conclusive evidence. The playback showed three hooded men wearing FBI vests rushing out the front door, followed by a fourth unarmed man carrying a knapsack and pulling a roller bag.

"Stop the tape." Chris pointed. "That's Wolfgang König."

"But those aren't FBI agents," David said. "It looks like König and his crew must've burst in here, tortured the butler for some reason, then shot him when they got what they wanted." He asked the other agent, "When did this happen?"

"Based on the timecode on the video frame, about eight minutes ago."

"Check to see if the cameras captured them entering a vehicle, will you? In the meantime, I'll call Agent Hamilton with an update."

Chris pretended not to listen as David gave Hamilton a status report. When the agent finished, he turned toward Chris. "Agent

Hamilton said she appreciates your help, but the scene is now restricted to official bureau personnel. She'll call you tomorrow if she needs anything else." With a shrug, he added, "So I guess it's time for you to leave."

Chris nodded politely but wanted to scream in frustration. *Why did Anna and Michelle blow my chance to keep them safe?* There was no doubt Wolfgang would keep tracking them down.

A female agent walked into the study and gave Chris a passing glance. She carried a plastic Ziploc bag as if it were toxic.

"What's that?" David asked.

"I found this in the freezer," she said with disgust. "It's a human hand. According to the plastic ID bracelet, it belonged to an Irene Shaw."

Chapter Thirty-Nine: Harrisburg, Pennsylvania

Photos 100–101

CHAPTER FORTY

Wednesday–Thursday

For over two and a half hours, Michelle worried at the kitchen table with Anna, waiting for news about Chris's fate like family members who prayed for the best yet dreaded the worst during the life-saving surgery of a loved one. Half a bottle of red wine and two shots of tequila helped to numb their anxiety while lubricating their candor.

Michelle apologized for doubting Anna's romantic intentions, confessing she was overprotective of Chris and didn't want to see him emotionally hurt again. But she conceded Anna made her brother happy for the first time since childhood; he had never been in a meaningful relationship with a woman. She had no right to deny him that pleasure. She promised to be supportive.

Anna admitted to sometimes acting entitled. It was unintentional and she vowed to stop. She profusely thanked Michelle again for taking risks that had kept her alive. She also regretted criticizing her love for Dr. Yasin and empathized with the pending death of her surrogate father.

That led to heartfelt toasts to the people they cherished who had died prematurely. Michelle shared a few heartwarming stories about her mom. She also reminisced about her infatuation and affection with Ansel before his betrayal and explosive death in Seville.

Anna described her younger brother's infectious smile, the bond with her friend Jessica, the early love of her ex-husband, and the acute mourning for her miscarried child. She struggled against tears while recounting how each of them had died.

The memories were bittersweet, drawing them together in shared grief.

What began as a common concern for Chris's safety morphed into a reconciliation among troubled sisters. They hugged and laughed and worried until Chris walked in the door. Then they jumped off the chairs with elation and relief.

He was furious. With raging eyes and a spasmodic brow, he shouted, "Wolfgang escaped, and the FBI was waiting for me. Which of you sold me out?"

Michelle bristled at the allegation. "What are you talking about?"

"Don't act innocent," he seethed while pointing an accusatory finger. "You were all sympathetic to Hamilton after your girl chat in Saint Paul. So you decided to give her a big break by telling her where I found Wolfgang and that I was driving there."

Outrage reddened Michelle's neck and cheeks. "That's insulting. And even if I wanted to tell Hamilton, I was clueless where you were going."

He swiveled toward Anna. "Didn't you tell Michelle I was going to Harrisburg?"

She recoiled, stepping back until bumping against the stove. "Yes, but ..."

"So when she wouldn't call Hamilton, you did?"

Anna's lips twisted. "No, why d'you think that?"

"Easy. You gave us up to the FBI when we were in Seville."

"That was different."

"No, it's exactly the same."

Anna regained her fortitude. "Chris, stop ranting for one second and listen to me. I'd never betray you now. You should know that."

"I thought I did, but obviously I was wrong."

With a calm and convincing tone, Anna said, "No, your anger is blinding your judgment. Think about it. I was out of the bedroom when you found Wolfgang's address, remember?"

"You could've found it by retracing my steps. And soon I'll know the truth." He bolted out of the kitchen.

The women shared perplexed stares. "What was that all about?" Anna asked, digging her fingernails through her short black hair.

"I have no idea, but I intend to find out." Michelle poured a generous ounce of tequila, pounded it back, winced, slammed the shot glass on the table, and sucked a lime wedge.

She raced up the stairs and burst into the bedroom with raging intensity. With a clenched jaw and combative posture, she yelled, "What the hell's your problem? We've been worried sick about you, then you storm in here calling us traitors and liars."

His head was buried in remorse in front of the laptop. "You were right," he said, not daring to face her. "The last login timestamp on my hacker's toolbox was five hours ago. You couldn't have known Wolfgang's address. I'm sorry."

"That's not good enough, Chris. You owe us a huge apology. I know you're a horse's ass, but I'm stuck with you as a brother. But if you accuse Anna like that again, I wouldn't blame her if she left you in the dust."

Chris raised his head, showing panicked sorrow. "God, I hope not. She's the best thing that's ever happened to me. I'd be lost without her."

"I feel the same way," Anna said, walking in with renewed confidence. "But we need to get a few things straight. Stand up." When he did, she cupped his chin and met his conciliatory gaze. "First, never, ever question my loyalty again, got it?"

A long blink signaled his understanding.

"Second, remember I've never lied to you, and I don't plan on starting now. Third, we're glad you're back safe, but don't go running off half-cocked again. And finally" – her voice softened – "I'm not going anywhere, Chris Davis, even if you are a horse's ass sometimes. Any questions?"

"That mean you forgive me?"

"I'll have to think about that." A teasing pause preceded a tender kiss, followed by a long embrace.

Their passion was embarrassing. "Okay, break it up before I throw cold water on you two."

They disengaged yet kept their arms around each other's waists.

Michelle asked, "Now you going to tell us what happened?"

They listened without interruption. Changing facial expressions and uncomfortable body language revealed their reactions. At the end of the description, he said, "Now you can see why I thought one of you tipped off Hamilton."

Anna asked, "Could she have tapped your phone?"

"Maybe," Michelle said.

"Absolutely," Chris countered. "That'd explain how she knew the address and when I'd arrived, so she called in the local boys to intervene. What really pisses me off is I missed Wolfgang by about ten minutes."

"Consider it a blessing," Michelle said. "Had you gotten there before the FBI, they probably would've arrested you for going after the bastard or blamed you for shooting the butler."

"But now he's in the wind again. I may never find him."

"Let's hope the FBI tracks him down," Michelle offered as a consolation. "He couldn't have gone far. I'll ask Hamilton about it in the morning."

"I wish someone competent were at the helm," he said with disdain.

Michelle considered defending Hamilton's capabilities but didn't. Why risk rekindling Chris's ire? The best idea was to change subjects before he began brooding over his perceived failure as their protector. "I love what you've done to the bedroom," she said with a razzing twinkle. "It looks like a pigsty in here."

Chris bantered back, "I'll convey your compliments to the interior designer."

"What is all this?"

"This is our war room and that's our evidence board," Anna said with pride.

"We've been trying to answer two things," Chris added. "Where's Wolfgang and who besides Steven Oakley and Vickie McLoren masterminded the plot against the senators?"

"You succeeded on the first question." Michelle wanted to sound uplifting. "Your idea about the dog collar was brilliant."

"Thanks, but I still failed."

She didn't respond to his self-admonishment. Doing so might send him reeling into a funk. "And your second question seems to be an elaborate version of your Name That Client game you always love to play."

"Don't belittle it, Michelle. We've been working our asses off in here for days."

She considered making a joke about what else they were doing in here for days but didn't. Chris's temperament was fragile at best. She approached the first column of Post-it® Notes. "So your oil theory didn't pan out?"

Chris tilted his head. "What are you talking about?" He gave off an irritated vibe.

Michelle pointed. "This top-left sticky says the first senator, Richard Tomlin, died in Ottawa during an oil pipeline meeting."

"That's right," Anna said. "It happened the same day as the Québec City shootout. I remember seeing it on the news just before the video clips about our being ambushed."

"That's not what I meant," Michelle said. She pulled out her cell phone and used ChatGPT to summarize the senator's involvement with oil.

"What are you doing?" Chris asked with growing impatience.

"Looking something up. Hang on." She paraphrased the AI results. "It says here Tomlin was a four-term, hardline Democrat. He was best known for his staunch environmentalism. He authored over fifty bills for stringent regulations on oil, gas and mining, and frequently chaired congressional hearings on fossil fuel's impact on climate change. He also lobbied aggressively for increased funding of the EPA. And Anna was right. He died unexpectantly in Ottawa while leading a contingency to block the Keystone XL Pipeline construction permit."

Michelle lifted her head to see Chris and Anna staring in awe. "It seems to me any oil company would be delighted to see Senator Tomlin retire prematurely," she concluded.

"Holy shit!" A cheesy smile spread across his boyish face for the first time in ages. "How the hell did you do that?"

"Do what?"

"You just walked up there and found the Holy Grail in less than a minute."

"I didn't do anything. I just read the first sticky of the hundred plastered around the room," she said with a sweeping gesture. "I assumed you already examined and rejected an oil plot."

Anna acted embarrassed to admit, "No, we've been so buried in information overload that we never made that connection."

His eyes danced with excitement. "But now it's like someone pointing out the hidden figure in an optical illusion. Once you see it, it becomes blatantly obvious."

"I might be jumping to conclusions," Michelle said, hoping to lower his expectations to cushion the fall if they failed again.

"But we'll never know unless we try, right? Are you willing to help us prove your theory?"

It's about time he asked for my help instead of ghosting me.

"I'd love to," she said before turning to Anna, "assuming you're okay with that."

"Oh my gosh, why wouldn't I be? We can use all the help we can get."

Chris's slapping palms sounded like a starter pistol. "Then let's get to work."

The rest of the evening and into the wee hours of the morning was exhausting yet exhilarating. The room reeked of pepperoni pizza, cheesy garlic bread and ranch dressing. Errant pieces of popcorn crunched underfoot. They had moved the kitchen coffeepot upstairs to keep them awake, augmented by Mountain Dews, Diet Cokes, occasional showers and catnaps. As the woodpecker's irritating pecking announced sunrise, the threesome stood back and examined what they had done.

Spread across the top of the third wall were index cards listing the stages of oil production: Exploration, Drilling & Extraction, Transport, Refining, and Distribution. Below each were rows of yellow notes showing how the three poisoned Democrat senators represented costly roadblocks. Senator Classon – a Republican who died of a silentcide-induced heart attack while having sex with his intern – seemed an exception. He was just old. After analyzing the voting record of his gubernatorial appointed replacement, they discovered a pro-oil champion. They also factored in what Senator McLoren could have done by executive order if elected president.

A clear picture emerged. An oil company wanted to expand exploration and drilling on federal land and offshore waters, expedite transporting crude, reduce regulations, increase subsidiaries and tax breaks, weaken and acquire competitors, and maximize profits while dominating the US market, the largest producer and consumer of oil in the world. Killing political adversaries was faster, cheaper and more effective than spending $150 million on federal lobbying.

But one frustrating question remained. Who? There were five major integrated oil companies domiciled in the US. Any of them might aspire to control every stage of the oil process.

"I think that's pretty good work for one all-nighter," Anna declared.

"I'd call it awesome," Michelle said.

Chris added, "I'll up your awesome and say it's outstanding." He displayed his exuberance with a passionate kiss on Anna's lips and a sibling peck on his sister's cheek. "Now let's get some sack time before tackling the who."

"Sorry, but count me out," Michelle said.

Chris frowned. "Why?"

"'Cause I have to go to work. Hopefully, Hamilton will have some good news about Wolfgang."

Michelle hadn't yet reached her bedroom before getting a text from Mason Webber. The message from the mysterious operative read: Chris & Michelle – DO NOT go to work today or call anyone at the FBI. Instead, report to the Betsy Ross House at 6:00 tonight. Attendance is mandatory.

Chris ran down the hall. "Did you just get a text from Webber?"

"Yeah."

"What the hell's that all about?"

"I don't know, but it sounds serious." Her mind raced through possibilities. None of them were good.

Chris asked in a hushed voice, "Do you think there's a connection between the US oil plot and rescuing the Russian oligarch in Montenegro?"

"I've been wondering the same thing all night but didn't want to mention it with Anna around. But I guess we'll find out during another delightful meeting with Webber." To sound cheerful, she added, "On the bright side, my day just opened up. I'll be available in a few hours to help answer our next big question. Let me know when you two are done with your sack time."

She winked, giggled and closed her bedroom door.

CHAPTER FORTY-ONE

Thursday

Michelle approached the Betsy Ross House with trepidation. She and her brother were clueless about the meeting agenda, but there was no doubt Mason Webber would make unreasonable demands. Any assignment worthy of immunity had to be perilous. Her palms were moist and she shivered in the raw wind, yet she faked a posture of confidence.

The front door of the narrow, Pennsylvania Colonial-style brick house was locked. After knocking twice, a Betsy Ross impersonator appeared in an adjacent courtyard.[102] The costumed young woman[103] waved them over. While holding up her billowing skirt and petticoat, she hustled down a side corridor, into the house, past a parlor filled with period furniture and up to a door marked Staff Only.

The entry code was ridiculously obvious: 1776. At the other end of a narrow office that doubled as a changing room was a high-security keypad. Her fingers entered a flurry of numbers as fast as a virtuoso, followed by an iris scan.

The thick steel door opened like a bank vault, revealing a cramped room dominated by two workstations with computer towers, monitors and headsets, plus cell phones and laptops connected to a spiderweb of wires. A small refrigerator and a veneer dining table for two were pushed against the other wall. The stench resembled a locker room.

Webber sat at a desk with outstretched legs and an intimidating smile. His wrinkled white shirt was open at the neck, and his sleeves were rolled up to the elbow. A black suit coat and red power tie were draped across the back of his antique captain's chair. His eyelids drooped with exhaustion.

Shawn stood rigid and attentive. His chiseled body was on full display beneath a Nike golf shirt and tight black jeans. Michelle never cared much for buff bald men; they tended to be narcissistic. But she found Shawn attractive, not for his rugged good looks but for his ability to orchestrate the elaborate scheme to fake the Russian oligarch's death. He was fiercely competent yet surprisingly humble. She admired those traits in a professional.

With an uncharacteristic saccharine voice, Webber asked, "Did you miss us?"

"Hardly," Chris said while pocketing his hands. Michelle knew her brother was acting relaxed but wasn't. A subtle cheek twitch betrayed his nerves. "It's only been a week."

"Eight days actually, but who's counting?"

"Apparently you are. What do you want this time?"

Webber's authoritarian expression returned. "Sit. Get comfortable. This is going to take a while. And as always, everything we discuss is classified, comprende?"

This doesn't bode well. Michelle nodded. Getting comfortable wasn't likely. The hardwood chair could've dated back to the eighteenth century, and Webber's aura was unsettling.

He rolled over to the table, removed his tortoiseshell glasses and studied Chris. "How you doing after that cathedral shootout?"

Michelle was surprised by what sounded like genuine concern.

Chris appeared equally taken aback. "I'm fine, thanks."

"Good." He placed a hand on Chris's shoulder. "I heard you were heroic saving a panicking woman. That's impressive. Glad you didn't get hurt." As he slipped the glasses back on, the fleeting veil of kindness disappeared. "Now, let's get down to business, shall we? First, congratulations for not disclosing anything about Montenegro to Hamilton or Anna."

"You're right. We didn't," Chris said. "But how do you know that?"

Shawn shuffled his footing. "You're not going to like this, but I've been monitoring your laptops and phones since you picked them back up after our trip."

Chris slapped the tabletop. "Son of a bitch! Why the hell did you do that?"

Webber was unfazed by the outburst. "Because we had to be sure you could keep classified secrets."

Michelle struggled to suppress her fury, hoping to sound calm and rational. "But after violating our privacy and lying to us before, how are we ever supposed to trust you?"

"Fair point. But I assure you, this was the last test. Once again, you passed with flying colors. So if you agree to keep working with us, that's great. If not …" He sighed. "If not, I understand, but then your chance for full immunity is off the table."

Emboldened by her disgust for Webber's repeated deceit and ultimatums, she said, "That's okay. We'll just keep the FBI deal we've got."

"Nope, that's gone too."

Chris's back arched in defiance. "That's bullshit. Why?"

"Because the Sicarius Task Team has been disbanded. If you don't cooperate, then you'll be arrested tomorrow, go back to prison and be prosecuted on all previous charges."

An eddy of fear twisted her gut. Her quest for freedom was disintegrating. There had to be a way to salvage it. In desperation, she asked, "But you can stop that if we work with you?"

"Yes," Webber said, crossing his ankles.

"And no more killing?" she asked.

Shawn answered. "Our goal is to prevent them. We need to neutralize a national security threat. We could really use your help." His appeal was directed at her. Shawn seemed sincere, but he was also a master of deception.

Chris remained skeptical. "And if we agree, Hamilton won't try to arrest us anyway?"

"Don't worry about her," Webber said with a flick of the wrist. "She's out of the picture."

Hamilton's premonition must've come true. "You mean she was fired?"

"No, she tried hanging herself at the FBI office."

"Oh my God!" Michelle muttered while clutching her mouth. "Is she okay?"

Without showing an ounce of sympathy, Webber answered, "Doctors don't know the extent of her hypoxic brain injury, but the damage seems severe."

"Why'd she do that?" Chris asked.

Shawn responded, "We've spent the last twenty-four hours trying to answer that, but the tipping point came when you found König's location on that dog-tracking app."

Webber continued, "That's when I called Hamilton to warn her. By the way, what did you plan to do when you got there?" His vertical frown lines deepened in judgment.

Chris agonized over an acceptable answer. He tried being emphatic. "I had to stop his attacks on Anna and me, and I knew Michelle might be next." He lowered his eyes and voice. "The best way was to kill him. But frankly, I was wobbling all over the place."

"Thanks for your honesty," Webber said. "I understand your motive, but I'm glad you didn't get the chance. You could've really screwed the pooch."

Chris didn't respond. He stared at the floor. Michelle knew her brother would risk anything for them and didn't care about the consequences. She loved him for it.

After allowing the admonishment to linger, Webber resumed talking. "Anyway, I gave Hamilton the address on the condition she got her people there first, detained König, and allowed me to question him about an incident in Monaco."

Shawn sat down at his desk. "Then we listened to your phone at the safehouse and learned that the fast exit of the assailants and König happened less than two minutes after the Hamilton call. That seemed an unlikely coincidence."

"And it pissed me off," Webber said. "I called her SAC to explain our suspicion when he said Hamilton had just been wheeled out by paramedics. He refused to keep talking, saying the FBI's Office of Professional Responsibility would launch a full investigation. Of course, that was utter crap. I asked the Director of National Intelligence to intervene. That sparked a mud-wrestling contest in Washington. For over five grueling hours, bureaucratic egos and their nitpicking lawyers debated jurisdiction of domestic crime versus foreign intelligence, then argued over rules, roles, procedures and communication protocols."

"Finally, very early this morning," Shawn said, "I got access to all of Hamilton's devices and have been analyzing them ever since."

"And I spent the day interviewing her team and combing through case files."

Webber's clout continued to amaze Michelle. "What did you learn?"

"A while back," Webber said, "Hamilton's SAC threatened to terminate her team if she didn't score something big very soon. First she got desperate, then she went rogue."

"What's that supposed to mean?"

"It started a couple of weeks ago when one of her agents traced fingerprints from the Lancaster farm to a William Mathews."

"Who's that?"

"He was a decorated soldier and then a mercenary in Afghanistan. Eleven years ago, he went missing after a deep-sea fishing accident, yet his mother kept cashing large checks. Using age progression software on his military photo and facial recognition, the agent found him going into the downtown Philly Barnes & Noble[104] for magazines. Can you guess his new name?"

Chris stated the obvious. "Wolfgang König."

"Exactly. Anyway, Hamilton saw this as her golden ticket to find Shaw. She ordered her agent to stand down, turn over his files, and she'd handle it. She got König's credit card info and email address from the bookstore, used CCTV to locate his truck, affixed a tracker, and then bugged his cell phone and house, all without a warrant. She tracked him like a hunting dog, hoping he'd lead her to Irene Shaw. We think her SAC suspected Hamilton wasn't following protocol but did nothing because he wanted a big win. That's why he tried covering his ass after the cathedral shooting."

"I knew that douchebag was trying to twist the facts," Chris said.

"Hamilton's lead agent felt the same way. Lance told me if they had arrested König when they had the chance, the cathedral shootout would've never happened."

"All that sounds like grounds for a reprimand," Michelle said, "or maybe to be fired. But why hang herself?"

Webber stroked the facial hair on his pronounced chin. "Because it was worse, much worse."

Chapter Forty-One: Philadelphia, Pennsylvania

Photos 102–104

CHAPTER FORTY-TWO

PHILADELPHIA, PENNSYLVANIA

Thursday

Michelle was distressed. She cursed Hamilton for not arresting Wolfgang when given the chance, thus endangering the lives of Anna and Chris, yet felt compassion for the agent's attempted suicide. Equally disturbing were Webber's continued deceptions and his promise to deliver worse news. The bombardment of revelations was sucking the air out of the claustrophobic room concealed deep inside the Betsy Ross House. She squirmed in anxious anticipation.

Webber cleared his throat while scanning the faces to make sure he had everyone's attention. "Okay, here's what we've learned so far. After Shaw died, Hamilton focused every resource on proving you two were the killers. In her mind, you ruined her career."

"That's hardly a news flash," Chris quipped.

"Well, here's something that is," Webber said, irritated by the interruption. "Hamilton simultaneously stopped pursuing König. Instead, she began texting his info and location coordinates day after day to someone called The Commander and getting big paychecks in the Caymans."

What a slimeball. And to think I felt sorry for her. "Do you know who The Commander is?" Michelle asked.

"No, and so far the phone number is untraceable. But we believe it's someone we've been after for nine months. We have a handful of domestic and foreign suspects, but nothing concrete." Webber swiveled toward Chris. "But one thing's for sure. This is probably the same person you keep calling the plot mastermind."

Her brother's cheesy smile returned for the second time in two days. "You mean Senator McLoren and Steven Oakley weren't acting alone?"

"No, McLoren's goal was to be president, Oakley wanted to grow defense contracts and …"

Michelle finished, "And a third person wanted to control oil."

Webber nodded. "Give that woman a prize."

"Damn, we're good." Chris exchanged a high-five with his sister.

"Frankly, the three of you are a great team. We learned a lot from your analysis. But, Chris, an insider's tip … you might want to consider moving the bed out of your war room."

He jumped out of his chair. "You damn voyeur!"

Michelle and Shawn laughed.

"Relax," Webber said, gesturing for him to be reseated. "We stopped monitoring whenever things got frisky. Besides, we're impressed with Anna."

"Very impressed," Shawn added.

"We see why you like her. You make a great couple."

"We do," Chris said with defensive conviction.

To deflect her brother's embarrassment, Michelle changed the subject. "So you want our help to neutralize the oil plot?"

"Yes, but it's bigger than you realize," Webber said. "But before I explain, you must answer two questions. Ready? One, are you willing to follow my orders like a soldier? And two, do you promise to keep everything confidential? I need a verbal yes from both of you."

The siblings locked eyes. She could tell Chris was vacillating but leaning toward agreement. Two conditions held her back. "Sorry if I'm repeating myself, but I want a couple things made perfectly clear. If we do whatever it is you want – one more time – you'll stop dangling the carrot and grant us full immunity?"

"Yes," Webber said with hands folded in his lap. "But as I said before, you have to earn it."

"And you're not asking us to be assassins?"

"That's right."

Chris asked, "Anna is going to be curious about what happened to Hamilton. Can we tell her?"

"Sure, no problem. Just be mum about what you're doing with us."

"And you'll be straightforward with us and stop your sneaky-ass bullshit?"

"I promise." Webber raised his hand. "No more games."

Chris studied Webber before committing. "Then you've got my yes, but only if Michelle agrees."

This is your last chance, girl. Take it. "I do. Let's go."

"Good. Welcome back to The Club." He shook their hands. Shawn leaned over and did the same, flashing a smile she couldn't interpret but considered charming. She was eager to work with him as an equal and hoped to learn some of his skills.

Webber leaned forward, becoming intense. "Okay, let me explain the things that are not on your evidence board. First, remember me telling you about Dimitri Yegorov's twin brother who fell from a building? Everyone assumed he was one of about thirty high-profile Russian businessmen, including six energy executives, who've unexpectedly died in the last three years."

Shawn added, "It's jokingly referred to as sudden oligarch death syndrome."

"That's right," Webber said. "But Dimitri claimed it had nothing to do with Russian politics this time. Instead, he said his brother was being extorted. We verified the claim by matching a fingerprint on the scene with the Middle Easterner who fired the Russian drone during McLoren's presidential rally in Washington, DC. In short, Fyodor was killed by one of Irene Shaw's assets. Then Dimitri was threatened. That's why he was eager to make an asylum deal."

"What did he give in exchange?" Michelle asked, hoping Webber wouldn't say "it's classified" again. This was the first test of his promised candor.

"For five years, Iskop, Dimitri's oil company, had been secretly mapping potential reserves in the Arctic in direct violation of an international treaty under the ruse of creating shipping channels. They found over ninety billion barrels of recoverable oil. That's about thirteen percent of the world's proven oil reserves. The day Dimitri safely arrived in the US, he gave us the seismic data and released a wiper malware that destroyed all the records at Iskop. Imagine how your plot mastermind could've benefited from this information."

Holy Christ! No wonder there was so much cloak and dagger.

"Another recent victory was that we, along with Mossad, foiled a plan to simultaneously destroy Iran's Abadan and Isfahan refineries. The goal was to cause an Iranian war against Israel. This would've been a bonanza for Oakley's arms sales, while also lowering oil supply and boosting prices."

Webber shifted in the chair and adjusted his glasses. He appeared uneasy. "Those were our only Ws. Unfortunately, we've failed more often than we've succeeded. Besides the murdered US senators, there've been eight suspected silentcide deaths in major oil-producing countries. The latest was a couple days ago when someone killed the two sons of the crown prince in Monaco. They were the left and right hands of the Saudi Minister of Energy. Shawn, show that photo of the suspected assassin in Monte Carlo, will you?"

Shawn leaned over the workstation, clicked on a file, scrolled through JPEGs and clicked again. The monitor displayed a dead waiter sprawled across the bathroom floor.

Webber asked, "Do you know this man?"

"Jacob Conners," they said in unison.

Chris elaborated. "He was Wolfgang's protégé."

"Okay, well, that confirms it. König has been hired to finish what Shaw started. And he's not done yet. Just for giggles, let's show that other family photo."

Shawn replaced Jacob's photo with a close-up of a man with blood seeping from his temple.

"This is Frank Polaski. Do you know him?"

Chris said, "That's Irene Shaw's former bodyguard."

"We knew there had to be a connection. Ballistics from the slug matched the 9mm that killed the butler in Harrisburg. And we found Frank's address among Hamilton's texts sent to our mystery plotter."

The growing body count was sickening.

Chris implored, "Please tell us you know where Wolfgang is?"

"Well, no surprise, Hamilton didn't issue a BOLO or lift a finger to find him. And his phone is off, so we can't track him in Hamilton's system."

Chris kicked the table. "Goddamn it! You mean he's in the wind again?"

Webber smiled, the one genuine smile Michelle could remember. "I didn't say that. Early this morning, his truck was found at a PHL lot. So we had one of our techies work with major airlines to cross-reference their lists of passengers arriving from Nice, France, two days ago with those departing on flights from Philadelphia since yesterday." Webber squinted at his diver's watch. "About two hours ago, she reported a match. Shawn, bring that photo up, will you?"

A man in his early sixties with gray hair, mustache and beard appeared. The disguise was convincing, but the deep-set cruel eyes canopied by heavy eyebrows were unmistakable.

"Meet Maynard Fry," Webber said, "one of König's many aliases. He boarded a red-eye last night to Quito, Ecuador."

"Why Quito?" Michelle asked.

"Because they're the host city for an OPEC+ meeting that starts in four days. That means the oil ministers of twenty-two countries will be under one roof for two days. And our assignment is to keep them alive."

That sounds next to impossible … and dangerous.

"So go home, pack light and be back here in sixty minutes. Wheels up at McGuire Air Force Base at 2200 hours."

CHAPTER FORTY-THREE

Anna bristled with frustration when Chris and Michelle returned from their clandestine meeting. They didn't explain where they had been and, even worse, they wouldn't tell her where they were going or how long they'd be gone. Chris only said their trip was sanctioned and critical to their futures.

Every unanswered question raised Anna's anxiety. He kept apologizing for being secretive and assuring her they'd be safe. The more he tried putting her at ease, however, the more her intuition screamed she'd never see him again. Their last kiss was long and emotional. She didn't want to let go. Watching him walk out the door was like watching a loved one go off to war.

Before the siblings left, they shared the disturbing news about Hamilton. Michelle got the inside scoop from a disgruntled task team member. The bottom line: if Hamilton had arrested Wolfgang a couple of weeks earlier when she had the chance, then the Boston and cathedral shootings would've never happened. Wolfgang would now be in jail, and they'd be free from his vengeance. Anna cursed Hamilton's greed and was unsympathetic to her plight. The bitch got what she deserved.

One positive thought flickered in Anna's despair like a firefly in the darkness. Perhaps Hamilton's betrayal was serendipitous. If the Boston shooting hadn't happened, Anna would've never reunited with Chris, they would've never rekindled their romance, and she would've never realized he was the man she wanted to be with. Perhaps she owed Hamilton a modicum of thanks. The agent's traitorous actions had altered Anna's life for the better. But the pain would be unbearable if she lost Chris now.

An hour later, wads of damp Kleenex lay across the kitchen table. She considered calling Mom and Liz – just to hear their voices – but knew if their phones were still tapped, a few minutes of comfort wouldn't be worth the risk of disclosing her location to Wolfgang or one of his assassins.

Anna felt her mental demons on the precipice of a full-scale attack. If left unchecked, the profound sorrow of losing so many loved ones would haunt her again. The PTSD from all the attacks would add to the toxic mix. Together with the distress about Chris, she feared being swallowed into the bowels of crippling depression. There was one antidote: immersion into critical problem-solving.

She ran up the stairs, into the war room, and stared at all the new Post-it® Notes on the fourth wall. Near the ceiling was the word *WHO?* Listed down the left column were the perceived benefits of the oil plot. Along the top row were the names of the six major US oil conglomerates. Chris, Michelle and Anna had each focused on two companies and spent the day quantifying how they might benefit. No clear suspect had emerged, but the analysis was far from finished.

Anna's goal was obvious. Find the *who* and end the plot. She was desperate to learn the answer and prove her worth to Chris and to herself. She emptied the sludge in the coffeepot, spooned dark roast into a new filter and went back to work.

Thirty minutes before sunrise, she succumbed to exhaustion. While clutching Chris's pillow, she savored his smell and imagined he was lying next to her. Three hours later, she woke in a cold sweat of dread. There was no text from Chris to ease her worry. The slithering demons had to be abated. She laced up her pink Asics, inserted earbuds, turned on her favorite playlist and secured the waist pack containing the snub-nosed revolver.

Bolting out the front door was like being released from a cage. Each pounding footstep along Arch Street pumped more endorphins into her bloodstream while passing the Betsy Ross House, Ben Franklin's grave and Independence Mall. She spewed expletives at the FBI office. By the time she reached the African American Museum,[105] her mind was clear and the anxiety was gone. The tranquility was euphoric. At The China Gate,[106] a decorative paifang at the entrance to Chinatown, she skidded to a stop.

The who is not a company but a person. And the oil plot mastermind has to have some traceable connections to Steven Oakley and Senator McLoren. Find the nexus and you'll identify the culprit. Start by digging where the co-conspirators were first uncovered, the Republican National Convention.

Rejuvenated, Anna sprinted three-quarters of a mile back to the siblings' house.

+++

Anna grew impatient in the war room. With elbows on the card table and palms propping her head, she stared at the words on the laptop screen, "Waiting for host." Kathy Linhoff was twelve minutes late for the Zoom call Anna had requested. Being tardy was disrespectful and rude. Or perhaps the former *Des Moines Register* cub reporter turned podcaster superstar enjoyed making the little people wait. Linhoff probably felt exalted by her national acclaim for exposing Oakley and McLoren and sensationalizing every detail of their prosecutions and deaths.

The screen flickered. Kathy Linhoff appeared. The long black hair and frameless glasses resting on chubby cheeks depicted demure naivete, yet her narrow eyes and uplifted nose portrayed cocky superiority. "What do you have for me?" Linhoff asked instead of a salutation, introduction, or apology for being late.

"Hello to you too," Anna said, trying to contain her annoyance.

"I have exclusive information about who killed Steven Oakley and Senator McLoren."

"Let's have it."

"Not so fast. I need something in return."

"No cash for tips," Linhoff said with a brash tone. "I get hundreds of worthless leads a week."

Anna had to break through the young woman's arrogance. "How many leads come from an FBI whistleblower?"

Linhoff's expression morphed from impatience to curiosity. She leaned toward the camera while adjusting her headset. "Who are you?"

Anna knew her email and phone number were untraceable thanks to Chris's encryption. She said with confidence, "That's not important."

"It is to me."

"No, what's important to you is that you're the first person to report the next big bombshell on this case. Otherwise, your podcast audience will drop like a rock now that your golden geese are dead."

Linhoff's thin lips disappeared in anger. "Do you know who you're talking to?"

"Sure, a recent grad student from Iowa who got lucky with one big story. Is that the way you want to be forgotten? Or do you want to become a respected investigative journalist?"

The silence was tense. The outcome would be binary. Either Linhoff was going to disconnect or swallow her ego and pursue Anna's offer. "You said before you wanted something. What is it?"

"I assume you took lots of photos and videos during the Republican National Convention while trying to trip up Senator McLoren."

"Sure. Four days of documentation. What good is that to you?"

"Because Oakley and McLoren weren't acting alone. There's a third conspirator. I'm trying to learn who it is."

Linhoff got as excited as a puppy seeing a squirrel. "If you find out, can I get an exclusive on that too?"

"Yes, but let's start with baby steps until we trust each other.

Send me the first two days of your visual media and I'll give you the first clue. When you upload the second half, I'll tell you more."

Two rounds of visual media transfers took forty-five minutes. Before the conversation ended, Anna told Linhoff about Irene Shaw. She explained the Philadelphia lawyer didn't have her assets seized by authorities for tax fraud, but because she had operated an assassin network for decades. Shaw was the culprit who orchestrated the poisoning of the senators and the fake bombing in Washington, DC. She also had Oakley and McLoren killed as a cover-up.

There was no doubt the industrious reporter would delve into Shaw, her murder and the shootout during her funeral. If Linhoff were diligent, she might also uncover Hamilton's suicide attempt and the implosion of her Sicarius Task Team. Somebody was bound to connect the dots someday. It might as well be Kathy Linhoff who got the glory.

Anna hoped the gambit would pay off. She began the laborious task of reviewing the visual media. With perseverance, and maybe an iota of luck, she'd soon discover the oil company executive who colluded with Steven Oakley and Senator Vickie McLoren.

Chapter Forty-Three: Philadelphia, Pennsylvania

Photos 105–106

CHAPTER FORTY-FOUR

Quito, Ecuador

Friday

Wolfgang was wretched in the gutted room near the La Ronda neighborhood[107] of Quito. The landlord was thrilled to rent out the six-hundred-square-foot space until he resumed his renovation project in a couple of weeks. A wad of US hundred-dollar bills circumvented prying questions.

The Incas had probably walked on the dirt floor, and the stripped walls exposed its seventeenth-century Spanish construction. Two portable handlamps dangling from yellow extension cords hung from rotting ceiling joists. Folding chairs surrounded a sheet of plywood suspended by sawhorses. The damp, musty ambiance reflected the wet season in Ecuador's capital city. Everything about the hideout sucked, yet it was functional and tolerable for another five days.

Yesterday, when Wolfgang placed mini cameras around Plaza Grande[108] – the epicenter of Old Town Quito – nothing had seemed amiss. Locals chatted or napped on benches while foreigners meandered among the historic buildings encircling the square. A tour group stood below the Independence Monument, listening to a boisterous guide, and a pair of bored policemen patrolled. An occasional child threw a temper tantrum or chased pigeons. Two Tarqui grenadiers standing at attention resembled nutcracker soldiers. Their ceremonial lances didn't pose a threat. The target looked too easy.

Conditions began changing this morning. He frowned at the laptop screen as traffic barriers were moved in front of the block-long Carondelet Palace,[109] the office and residence of the Ecuadorian president. Wolfgang wondered if the ten small shops etched into the first-level façade would be closed during the OPEC+ meeting starting Monday. A young man in green Army fatigues followed behind a German shepherd sniffing the Doric colonnade on the second-floor loggia. The palace suspended public tours.

Each time a limousine arrived with a dignitary at the adjacent Hotel Plaza Grande,[110] an entourage of staff and bodyguards followed them. Wolfgang maintained a tally sheet of which oil ministers checked in at this five-star hotel, and at the prestigious Casa Gangotena Boutique Hotel[111] a couple blocks away on San Francisco Plaza.[112] Posted at the main entrance of each hotel were two men posing as hotel staff with pistols below their suit coats. Their posture was stiff, but their eyes never stopped surveying the surroundings.

Wolfgang cursed The Commander. This assignment felt increasingly dangerous, maybe impossible, but it was too late to abandon the plan.

When his cell phone dinged, he rolled up the rusting steel door. Navigating down the narrow cobblestone street was a full-size Foton pickup truck covered with dust and mud. The headlights flashed once. Wolfgang gave a thumbs-up. Five burly men jumped out, pulled back a canvas over the cargo bed and carried three large wooden crates into the room. Stenciled on the sides were the words Café Colombiano. Four of the men drove off, headed toward a cheap hotel on the outskirts of the city. One man stayed behind.

Andrés Valencia was the ringleader of the Colombian mercenaries who Wolfgang had partnered with in Afghanistan to sell medical supplies and drugs on the black market to Iraqi insurgents. The collaboration had been obscenely profitable. Wolfgang's monthly wire transfers paid for his brother's education, supported his widowed mom and started building a nest egg.

The two men hadn't seen each other for eleven years, but they greeted each other like brothers. "Goddamn, it's good to see you," Wolfgang said as their right hands locked and they slapped each other's backs. "Thanks for coming."

"Ya know me. Not miss big payday." The accent had always been heavy, and his cadence was manic in Spanish. However, Andrés's pace was slow and simple when he spoke English.

Wolfgang pushed back a step. "Let me look at you, man. You haven't changed a bit."

Full lips, a broad nose and flat brow over vicious squinting eyes overpowered the mercenary's rectangular brown face and thick goatee. Unruly black hair dangled over the shoulders of his worn leather jacket. A tiny silver cross swayed on his right ear when he talked. "Ya get fat. Too much burgers 'n beers."

Wolfgang laughed but the assessment was true. His soldier's physique had given way to a dad bod. Yet Andrés was still slender with bulk in all the right places.

"Shitty office," the mercenary declared while assessing the dank room.

"Best I could do on short notice. But we won't be disturbed."

"What happen finger?"

"Slammed it in a car door."

"No shit. Must've hurt." That was the extent of Andrés's small talk. He never wasted time when there was business to be done. "Do recon?"

"Yup." As they walked over to the makeshift desk and sat down at the laptop, Wolfgang kept talking. "Yesterday I got blueprints and made a video inside the palace during a tour. And I got aerial and ground maps of Old Town. See, on this one," he said, pointing to an annotated layout on the screen, "I started a plan of attack, but I need help fleshing it out."

"¡No hay problema!"

"Well, it may be harder than we thought," Wolfgang said, trying to recalibrate his friend's expectations. "Of course I've got eyes on the target, but only outside. Too risky to put cameras in the rooms where the ministers will meet. If they found 'em in a sweep, they might cancel the conference. They've been beefing up security since this morning." Wolfgang showed him the barriers and the armed men in front of the hotels.

Andrés scoffed. "Pussycats. My boys take 'em. They like good fight. And we bring lots of toys. Wanna see?" He sauntered over to one of the wooden crates, grabbed a crowbar, and started prying the nails securing the cover. Wolfgang helped lift it off, revealing plastic bags filled with green unroasted beans. A few were open. Coffee aroma permeated the room. Andrés grinned. "Fool sniffing dogs."

Together they threw the sacks on the floor. Each landed with a dusty thud. Andrés wedged out a false bottom, revealing automatic carbines, dozens of magazines and boxes of ammunition. He pointed to the other two crates. "Tactical gear in there. That one's got two M79 shoulder-fired launchers – lovingly called The Thumper – and XM1060 40mm grenades."

"What the hell's that?"

"Thermobaric grenades, baby. They release a cloud of fuel that mixes with oxygen to cause an ass-kicking fireball. Nobody walks away from that. Happy?"

Wolfgang was miserable. The armaments foreshadowed a bloodbath. But that was what The Commander demanded and had paid a huge deposit to get. "Looks good. I knew I could count on you."

"Ya got something for me?"

Andrés was a consummate yet impatient businessman. He had

not agreed to this assignment out of friendship. Greed was his sole motivator. He wanted his electronic pockets lined now.

Wolfgang had made the first transaction of twenty-five percent days earlier. Andrés hovered over his shoulder as he transferred the second installment to his account. The Colombian stepped away, pulled out his phone, gave his index finger a workout and bent over to inspect the screen. "¡Excelente!" His grin was decadent.

Andrés popped coffee beans into his mouth, followed by loud sucking. "Need caffeine. Long trip." He mimicked the action of a steering wheel. "Twenty-two horas. Needed Clan del Golfo cartel to get crates 'cross border. I add cost to bill."

Haggling over expenses was the least of Wolfgang's worries. What he wanted was a drink, maybe two or three. But alcohol would have to wait. He must stay sharp, yet rising anxiety was reminiscent of riding the Chinook helicopter into the Afghanistan battlefield. His face contorted and his back spasmed as his brain replayed the 5.56x45mm NATO bullet twisting the body of the first person he'd ever killed while his wounded buddy screamed, "Medic!" He crawled through frigid mud as a mortar round whistled past and exploded. Relentless bullets ricocheted off rocks, promising instant death. A fountain of pulsing blood gushed from …

"Hey, ya 'kay?" Andrés asked with a wide-eyed stare.

The question snapped Wolfgang back from his vision of hell. The damp T-shirt clung to his pounding chest. "Yup, I'm fine," he said, struggling to sound in control. "Just thinking 'bout escape plan." His gut tightened. "Getting out might be a bitch."

Andrés slapped him on the shoulder. "Ya worry like old woman, amigo. Me and my boys want escape too. I've got asses covered. Trust me." The reassurance wasn't very reassuring.

Their cell phones dinged in unison. Wolfgang lifted the steel door again and Andrés rushed out to flag down the second truck. Four men carried in two more crates. One mercenary had gang tattoos covering his bald head, face and neck. Many of his teeth were missing.

Goddamn it. These animals have my back? I'm fucked.

Andrés jumped into the passenger seat and rolled down the window. "No worries. We got this. Plenty time to plan. Oh, one more thing." He reached into his back pocket, pulled out a Colombian passport, and handed it to Wolfgang. "Here. Not real but fool quick look test." He slapped the outside of the car door, signaling the driver to take off.

The weak sunlight disappeared as the steel door rattled shut. Wolfgang sidestepped the crates consuming the dingy room. He sat down. His body drooped. He covered his ears. Penetrating the screaming tinnitus, Satan was calling again to collect his soul.

I've got a bad feeling the devil's going to win this time.

Chapter Forty-Four: Quito, Ecuador

Photos 107–112

CHAPTER FORTY-FIVE

QUITO, ECUADOR

Friday

Chris had never flown on a Learjet. On any other occasion, riding in the USAF C-21A executive aircraft would've been exhilarating. The plane's sleek design and luxurious amenities were far more comfortable than the transport plane he and Michelle had flown on during their first assignment with Mason Webber and Shawn.

Yet this eight-hour overnight trip from New Jersey, including a refueling stop at Eglin Air Force Base in Florida, was grueling. The foursome fought sleep deprivation while analyzing how to thwart Wolfgang König's plans to assassinate someone at the OPEC+ conference in Quito.

A black embassy car with diplomatic plates greeted them on the tarmac of Mariscal Sucre International Airport. The sun was rising when they reached their hotel in Centro Histórico. There was no time to rest. Chris shaved, showered and wolfed down a boxed sandwich provided on the flight. He was back in the lobby in forty-five minutes.

Michelle shuffled along with her head down after exiting the elevator. She wore a conservative black skirt and jacket over a white blouse. The fresh, professional attire clung to her slumped posture. Her long blond hair was greasy and tied tight in a bun. Makeup couldn't mask her exhaustion. She mumbled she was okay, but Chris knew otherwise.

Webber and Shawn were alert. They were masters of taking frequent tactical naps, lasting only a few minutes at a time. Webber disclosed another secret: Military Energy Gum. The one hundred milligrams of caffeine were coursing through the siblings' bloodstreams by the time they were driven to Carondelet Palace[113] for an arranged tour and meeting.

An honor guard at the palace entrance escorted them down a wide corridor defined by a stone colonnade. Before entering an atrium flanked by two courtyards with gushing Neocolonial fountains, Chris noticed commemorative plaques, especially the one marking where a former Ecuadorian president was assassinated in 1875. Not a good omen.

Up a grand staircase and past a huge mural, a hallway led to the Cabinet Room where, they were told, the oil ministers would meet. While the guard described with pride the coffered ceiling and Baccarat crystal chandeliers suspended over the glistening wood table, Chris scanned for vulnerabilities and made a mental note of the balcony overlooking Plaza Grande.

The tour proceeded to the Banquet Hall. It was much larger yet similar in design, except for a parquet floor, gold leaf mirrors and portraits of historic leaders. They learned this was where meals would be served during the OPEC+ conference. The guard also pointed out the President's Hall, named for the oil paintings of every Ecuadorian president. This was the venue for a cocktail reception both nights. Chris scowled. The pattern of this meeting was far too routine and predictable.

They were ushered into the Manuela Sáenz Cabinet adjacent to the president's office. The small living room's design was elegant yet comfortable, featuring delicate wallpaper above half-panel wainscoting and antique rosewood furniture on a Turkish handwoven rug. A distinguished graying diplomat was waiting in one of the six high-back wing chairs encircling a coffee table. He had time to stand and introduce himself as the US ambassador to Ecuador before an entourage burst through a side door.

"Buenos días, Presidente Paladines," the ambassador said while shaking hands. "Thank you for agreeing to meet."

"Of course," the president said in perfect English. The middle-aged leader with a politician's black hair, practiced smile and polished fingernails exuded confidence bordering on arrogance. He assessed the foursome but didn't acknowledge them. "You said this was urgent. Fine. But make it quick." He unbuttoned his impeccable suit coat and took a position of power in the most ornate chair. "Sit," he commanded.

The five of them did as instructed. Three uniformed men remained at attention. The president introduced them as the captain of the Presidential Escort Group, the commanding general of the National Police and the admiral of the Ecuadorian Armed Forces. Their stoic silence, judgmental stares and chests heavy with medals were intimidating.

The president asked the ambassador, "And who are these people?"

"This is Mason Webber. He leads a State Department group on counterterrorism."

That's a crock of shit, Chris thought of the bogus title.

"And these three are his expert analysts on silentcide assassins."

"I've never heard of silentcide," the president said with a sneer.

"Mr. President, if I may," Webber interjected. "Silentcide is the art of undetected killing. They specialize in making their targets' deaths appear to be from natural causes. One of these assassins, Wolfgang König, was tracked traveling to Quito."

The president uncrossed his legs, leaned forward and showed interest for the first time. "Is this man acting alone?"

"Typically yes, sometimes in pairs, but we don't know for sure."

"And why do you believe he's a threat to us?"

"Sir, you've heard about the recent deaths of the crown prince's sons?"

"Of course. Tragic. That's why the Saudi Arabian energy minister is not attending. We'll sorely miss his stewardship as OPEC's largest oil-producing country."

Webber continued, "Well, König is the prime suspect for those events in Monaco. Our job is to prevent that from happening at your meeting."

"No, that's not your job," the admiral of the armed forces barked as his neck swelled. "The three of us have been working on security for months while catering to the demands of security teams from every oil country. You can't stroll in here at the last minute and start telling us what to do."

The president raised his hand, silencing the admiral without glancing back. "Listen, Mr. Webber, was it? I'm grateful for your warning. Please share any intel or suggestions you have with these men. If anything has merit, they'll act. I have full confidence in them. You and your team may remain, but only as advisors. Let us know what you need."

The president's expression switched from appreciative to demanding while eyeing Chris. "But your lilywhite faces must never be seen by the ministers. If they get a hint we're cooperating with the US – their staunch competitors with oil – they'll storm out of here. Is that clear?"

"Yes, Presidente Paladines," Webber said with respect.

Chris was amazed. He didn't believe Webber could be subservient.

The president stood, signifying the meeting was over. After shaking hands with Webber and the ambassador, he turned to leave, then pivoted. "You know, I don't think I've made myself clear. I'm proud to be hosting this two-day conference. It legitimizes my administration's investment in oil as a cornerstone of a revitalized Ecuadorian economy. As I've told these men, I refuse to turn my capital city into a demilitarized zone in the name of security. The ministers must feel welcome, pampered, and leave here with positive memories of this great country. You'll do nothing to fuck that up. Now am I perfectly clear?"

Spoken like a true, self-serving politician, Chris thought. *What a conceited jerk! Let's hope he doesn't have to eat his words.*

Chapter Forty-Five: Quito, Ecuador

Photo 113

CHAPTER FORTY-SIX

Chris had never felt more useless. During their sixteen-year career, he and Michelle had always controlled the planning and implementation of silentcide commissions. This time was radically different. Their goal was to prevent a killing, but they were mere advisors to high-ranking bureaucrats who were dismissive and treated them with scorn. The siblings were reluctantly allowed to educate the palace and hotel facility managers on increasing vigilance over food, water, air, accommodations and proximity to dignitaries. But they couldn't disclose too much information without causing alarm.

In short, trying to protect one unknown target among the twenty-one ministers moving among three locations seemed doomed to fail. Yet somehow, this didn't feel like a typical silentcide. Why kill just one person during an event with so much security? If that were the goal, there would be far easier ways. Chris suspected a bigger plot was at play.

His anxiety kept escalating. He begged Webber to leverage the ambassador to get another audience with the Ecuadorian president. The politician had to understand the danger and take radical countermeasures. However, the ambassador refused to cooperate, so the meeting never took place.

Day one of the conference was uneventful, which fueled the

bravado of the president's officers. This was day two, and half the day was over. Chris's instincts were screaming. His stomach churned with dreadful certainty. In anxious anticipation, he twirled the ends of his long brown wig into tight knots. Sweat rolled down the thick dark makeup on his temples.

"Will you please relax?" Webber asked. "Go take a break." Since dawn, they had been monitoring live video feeds from cameras placed at the entrances and public spaces of the palace and two hotels. "Just don't flirt with those cute Ecuadorian guys again." This was another of Webber's sexist jokes about Chris's disguise as a female TV reporter. None of the jokes were funny.

Chris stepped out of a TC Televisión van parked in front of Carondelet Palace. He stretched. The flow of people at Plaza Grande seemed normal except for a cluster of peaceful protesters. Their handwritten signs read, "Stop Drilling! Save the Amazon!" They were being encouraged to leave by a pair of mounted police. That's when Chris heard a commotion.

A dirty, late-model pickup truck was speeding the wrong way on a narrow street toward the palace. It crashed through a security fence and screeched to a halt. An assailant leaped from the passenger seat. A burst from an AK-47 dropped two policemen standing near the palace's south entrance. Additional bullets silenced the growling Rottweiler on a leash.

People near the carnage started running and screaming in frantic disarray. Mothers grabbed their children. Elderly cowered. A flock of pigeons took flight.

Chris riveted on the driver. Despite a partial windshield glare and a black balaclava mask covering most of his face, those cruel eyes were unmistakable. Wolfgang König was behind the wheel.

Chris ran to stop the attack but, without a weapon, was defenseless. He pulled an orange armband up his sleeve, a prearranged sign to palace security that he was not a hostile.

Wolfgang made a hard right, wedged between two bollards

installed to block traffic, and drove onto a cobblestone sidewalk in front of the cathedral.[114] The gunman covering his six swept his rifle from side to side. Judging from distant gunfire, a second truck at the north end of the palace was turning in front of Hotel Plaza Grande. The square was being surrounded.

When Chris reached the fallen policemen, he checked their pulses. Nothing. He unholstered a sidearm, racked a 9mm round into the chamber, and squatted into a shooting position with the extended Glock held with both hands. Too many panicking people prevented a clear shot.

A canvas flew off the back of Wolfgang's truck, revealing three men in full tactical gear. One combatant steadied his weapon from behind the closed tailgate. Two others jumped out. The first began protecting the truck from a possible frontal attack. The second knelt and shouldered a grenade launcher.

The ten small shop doors along the palace's lower façade opened like silos, releasing members of the Ecuadorian Army's elite special forces. The soldiers fanned out, clutching Heckler & Koch HK33 assault rifles, searching through their scopes for a target to engage.

With an innocuous thud, a thermobaric incendiary grenade sped toward the president's office. Another projectile from across the square made a direct hit on the Cabinet Room, the venue for the OPEC conference. The blasts were volcanic. The shockwaves slammed Chris to the ground, dazing him.

As the palace's pediment imploded, shards of glass flew like shrapnel. Billowing smoke and raging fire consumed the building. The flames crackled and hissed. Three Doric columns toppled, shattering into pieces. Giant stone blocks and rubble smashed the satellite dish and shattered the top of the TV van. Webber was still inside.

The Ecuadorian commandos took cover, shooting from behind concrete benches. The mercenaries retaliated. Endless bullets were exchanged. Snipers fired from the cathedral bell tower[115] and from the roofs of the hotel and Archbishop's Palace.[116] A combatant blew backward, convulsed, and collapsed onto the cargo bed. Bullet holes riddled the pickup's side panels. Only sharp edges remained of the window glass.

The double doors of the cathedral burst open. Two policemen brandishing pistols rushed through the Carondelet Arch. Before they reached the semicircular staircase, an Mk 2 pineapple hand grenade fell at their feet. The blast was horrific. They were smothered under dark green stones. Religious statues dropped headfirst from the sky and disintegrated.

Wolfgang leaned on the horn. The other truck responded with a honk. While emptying their forty-round magazines, the attackers scrambled back to the pickups. One stood on the running board. Tires squealed as Wolfgang accelerated through the plaza, dodging people, scaring a horse, demolishing a barrier, sideswiping a Policia Nacional mobile unit and disappearing down the street with a hail of bullets trailing after them.

A black cloud of red cinders rained over the plaza, igniting several treetops. Tourists and locals covered their heads and their terrified expressions while scrambling for safety.

Coughing with watering eyes, Chris struggled to stand. The drooping wig smelled burned. Fire had scorched his dress. Adrenaline propelled him toward the TV van. He used the sharp end of a mangled flagpole to wedge open the vehicle's back door. A plume of smoke escaped. Webber was unconscious in a chair. A bank of monitors compressed his chest. His breathing was shallow. His lips were turning blue.

The video monitors were deadweight. With a determined second effort, Chris pushed them aside. He nudged Webber's shoulder and called his name. No response. The stench of smoldering electronics and toxic fumes worsened. Moving Webber risked further injury but leaving him meant certain death.

Chris shoved his hands beneath the broad shoulders and yanked.

Webber's heavy body slammed to the floor. He groaned but didn't open his eyes. Chris pulled with all his strength. After a few inches of progress, Webber's foot got caught under twisted metal. Chris stretched out to dislodge it when he heard these words uttered into his crotch: "Well, this sure is romantic."

Chris rolled off and laughed, thrilled that Webber had survived.

Webber managed to crawl out before rolling into a fetal position. "I'm fine, I'm fine," he said with weak reassurance, clutching his rib cage. "I just need to catch my breath."

"Listen, I've got to go find Michelle and Shawn. You sure you're okay?"

"Yes. Go."

Chris waved over a Special Forces soldier, pointed to his orange armband and said, "He's a palace security advisor. Take care of him, will you?" The soldier smirked at the female disguise but agreed. Chris thanked him and, with the outstretched Glock, bolted toward what remained of the palace's south entrance. Two commandos initially stopped him but let him pass.

He ran down the wide corridor, dodging debris and jumping over pieces of fallen colonnade and twisted iron railings. A total collapse of the palace seemed imminent. Two grenadiers lay at the base of a double wooden door. They weren't breathing. One of the honor guards still clutched a lance.

The atrium was a blackened chimney. Flames pulsed across the ceiling. Stone walls groaned from heat and fatigue. The ornate wrought-iron gate leading to the parallel courtyards was hot. He stepped into a wind tunnel of suffocating smoke and ash. "Michelle! Shawn!" He screamed their names again, praying they would answer but fearing they were dead.

"Coming," Shawn answered, limping out of the abyss. A bleeding kneecap poked through a shredded pants leg. His T-shirt was bloodied and blackened. The hairpiece was askew, revealing a deep gash across his head.

Shawn was carrying Michelle. Her arm was around his shoulder. One leg dangled unnaturally. She had Shawn's wet shirt pressed against her nose and mouth. Soot covered their faces. They were coughing, wheezing and gasping for breath, but they were alive.

Shawn floundered while exiting the palace. His strength appeared sapped, but his teeth clenched with determination. Michelle held on tight. She winced in pain every time her leg bounced. Chris feared she was losing consciousness.

They stumbled to the middle of Plaza Grande. Shawn eased Michelle onto the steps of the Independence Monument[117] and repositioned her leg. She moaned in agony. The trio were oblivious to the chaos of first responders treating the injured.

Chris hugged his sister in gratitude. Her smile was weak yet affectionate. Shawn bent over, kissed her on the head and joined the embrace. Chris's emotions broke. "I love you, Michelle," he whispered as tears flowed down his cheeks.

Like a planned demolition, a series of explosions thundered across the block-long Carondelet Palace. The walls buckled, folded, collided and collapsed into a violent cloud of suffocating smoke, red flames and noxious fumes.

Chapter Forty-Six: Quito, Ecuador

Photos 114–117

CHAPTER FORTY-SEVEN

Philadelphia, Pennsylvania

Tuesday

Forty-eight hours of too little food, too little sleep and too much work should've drained Anna to the core. Yet she was pumped while sitting at the kitchen table in the house she shared with Chris and Michelle. The romaine lettuce in the salad bowl was wilted. The vinaigrette dressing expired months ago. Her coffee was lukewarm. She didn't care. They were enough for sustenance. Instead, Anna was feeding off a sustained adrenaline rush while staring at her phone.

Watching Kathy Linhoff's newest half-hour podcast was riveting. The Iowa reporter's opening salvo was, "Can you imagine the feds lying to us about the biggest political crime in decades? Golly, they'd never try selling us a cover-up, would they? They're always honest and transparent, right?"

The rhetorical questions prompted a sardonic snicker, followed by an outraged glare into the video camera. "What a joke! Remember when they told us the threat against US senators ended when assailants were killed in Denver and Washington, DC? I was the first to expose that as crap. Remember when they told us that Senator Vickie McLoren and Steven Oakley acted alone in the conspiracy to steal the White House? More crap. Remember the feds saying they had no idea how McLoren and Oakley mysteriously died on the same day three weeks ago? Turns out that was crap too. They knew the facts but withheld everything. Frankly, they told you bald-faced lies. But, as I always do, today I'll exclusively tell you more of the truth you need to know!"

Linhoff's inflammatory rhetoric stopped. She nudged the microphone closer to her lips and expelled a sigh of frustration. Her pause for dramatic effect was timed perfectly. "Sadly, this conspiracy and cover-up have as many layers as a giant rotting onion. And they stink just as badly. It's enough to make you cry over what's happening to our democracy."

The reporter's posture straightened. She tapped her shoulder with exaggerated confidence. "But I, investigative reporter Kathy Linhoff, promise you this. I will not rest until I peel back every single one of the sordid layers. You'll always be the first to learn the dirty secrets."

This young woman was a gifted orator. Her Midwestern aura of innocence juxtaposed with a New Yorker's accusatory tongue made her credible and titillating. Her avid fans were in a feeding frenzy over her breaking story: *Who Was the Faceless Killer?* The counter measuring views exceeded 245,000 in the first two hours since the podcast's release. The thumbs-ups were speeding past thirty thousand. The rookie's meteoric success impressed Anna.

"Take a good look at this photo," Linhoff said slowly to build suspense. "This woman looks like a refined senior citizen, right? Maybe a philanthropist? Somebody's loving grandmother? No," she said with a practiced shake of her long black hair. "This was Irene Shaw, the powerful and very rich former head of a major Philadelphia law firm. Back in August, Philly's local news reported that authorities seized Shaw's firm and personal assets for tax evasion while she was still at large. Another reprehensible example of the elite one percent not paying their fair share, right?"

Linhoff slapped the desk. "Wrong! Another lie courtesy of the feds. The real reason Irene Shaw was being prosecuted and hunted was — are you ready for this bombshell? — because she managed killers for hire. Believe me when I say, Shaw did this for decades. And not one or two wise guys from the Philly mob. Oh no. Think bigger than Murder, Inc. from the 1930s. Irene Shaw's network of assassins was international in scope. You heard that right. International! She was commissioned by Senator McLoren and Steven Oakley to …"

Anna's phone on the kitchen table rang. She rarely let a ringing phone distract her, but this was a wonderful exception. Only Chris had this number. She paused the podcast and accepted the call. "Oh my God. Hi. How are you?"

"I'm fine," Chris answered, sounding exhausted.

"And how's the trip going?"

"That's fine too."

His evasive answers were worrisome. She wanted to ask where he and Michelle were and what they were doing, but knew he'd say "I can't tell you that." She resented the secrecy. Their relationship had evolved from repeated lies when they first met to full openness and candor. Why not now? But there was also a foundation of mutual trust. She believed him when he said the trip was sanctioned and critical to their future. As difficult as it was, she wouldn't pry. At least he was safe.

Bubbling with excitement, she said, "So, I have some big news that'll cheer you up."

"What's that?" he asked in a monotone.

"Drumroll, please." Anna banged a spoon and a knife on the kitchen table. "I think I know who the oil plot mastermind is."

"You mean you identified the oil company?" he asked with sudden enthusiasm.

"Better than that. I've ID'd a person who may have conspired with McLoren and Oakley."

"That's awesome! How'd you do that?"

"Well, I found a video clip of Steven Oakley on day four of the Republican National Convention. He was standing three rows back from the podium when Senator McLoren gave her acceptance speech for being nominated as the candidate for president."

"That's not surprising," he said. "That's the night the two of them were photographed kissing in an elevator."

"I know … but let me finish. So anyway, when McLoren was done with her speech, the crowd went wild with applause and kept cheering her name. That's when Oakley did a fist bump with a guy next to him. I'm not an expert lip reader, but I think Oakley said, 'We did it.' Then – oh here's the best part; you're really going to love this – then they flashed a thumbs-up at the stage and, I swear, McLoren stared right at them with the biggest smile and a nod."

"Am I missing the punch line here?"

"Hold your horses, will you? I'm getting to that. I printed a freeze-frame of this other guy. It was dark and blurry, but I spent hours comparing it to photos of thirty-three top executives from major oil companies before getting a match." She teased him by going silent.

"Enough with the suspense already. Who was it?"

"The other guy was Vincent Wooledge, the chairman and largest shareholder of GlobalPetro," she announced with triumphant glee.

"That's amazing! Congrats. I'm really proud of you."

His praise sent her on an emotional high. He sounded elated and impressed that she had solved his case. They were finally true partners. But how could she tell him that over the phone? She hoped he knew and felt the same. "Thanks, but it's only a smoking gun," she said with a modicum of modesty. "And now I'm digging for other connections between the –"

The kitchen window shattered. A black gun barrel appeared. An earsplitting blast. The bullet exploded the salad bowl, propelling chunks of lettuce. The second destroyed the toaster behind her. She screamed and dove for cover.

Chris panicked. "What's happening?"

"Someone's shooting at me!"

"Do you have your revolver?"

"No, it's in the bedroom."

"Goddamn it!"

"Stop yelling at me, Chris. I'm scared. I'm really –"

A third bullet struck the kitchen table. Slivers of wood ricocheted. A shard pierced her shoulder. Excruciating pain blackened the room. She might pass out.

"Anna, listen to me. Can you get upstairs?"

Her voice quivered. "I don't think so." Blood seeped through her fingers while clutching the wound.

"Just do it!"

She mustered her courage, held her breath and started scrambling across the floor. Another bullet whizzed past her head and lodged in the molding. She wailed in terror.

"Keep moving!"

Anna tried standing at the bottom of the staircase. Her legs gave out, causing her knee to smash against the riser. The bolt of agony was paralyzing until the front door buckled from an explosion. She crawled up the stairs, hastened by another thunderous noise.

"He's breaking in. He's going to kill me."

"No, he's not," Chris said with strained calm. "Just keep moving and get your gun. Now!"

The front door collapsed as she reached the landing. The attacker stepped inside, brandishing an enormous weapon. He was tall, dressed in black and searching for a target. Their eyes met. She leaped before he pulled the trigger. The bullet sliced through the bedroom door, punching a hole in the wall and sending yellow sticky notes fluttering.

She pushed the lock, panicked and dropped the phone. Every nerve pulsed with fear. *Where's the gun?* "Jesus!" *Not on the tables.* "Jesus!" *Not on the research boxes or the coffee stand.* "Jesus!" She yanked back the pillow and clawed beneath the blanket while heavy boots sprinted up the stairs.

The runner's pack catapulted off the end of the bed.

Wolfgang's assassin kicked the bedroom door. His determination to kill was terrifying.

She struggled with the pack's zipper. It was stuck. Then the gun got tangled in the strap.

The door handle rocketed into the room from brute force.

She ran into the closet, tumbled to the floor and cowered. She held the snub-nosed revolver with both hands. They shook. She was hyperventilating.

The bedroom door burst open. Menacing breathing entered the room.

I'm going to die! I'm going to die!

A deafening roar. Wood fragments flew. Clothes above her head swayed. She saw his shadow through the bullet hole in the closet door.

Anna closed her eyes, ground her teeth and began pulling the trigger.

CHAPTER FORTY-EIGHT

Wednesday

Chris's chest compressed as the taxi pulled up in front of Boyer Pavilion,[118] the Level 1 trauma center at Temple University Hospital. He had dreaded this moment for over eighteen hours.

Yesterday afternoon, Chris had made a frantic request for help to the lead agent on the former Sicarius Task Team. Lance was the first to arrive on the scene. His somber words still haunted Chris. "The assassin's dead from a single gunshot to the neck. Anna's alive, but barely. She was shot at least three times, maybe four. Most don't seem life-threatening except for, uh, for the head wound. I stopped the bleeding the best I could until the paramedics arrived, but …" Lance's pause was ominous. "I guess I don't know how else to say this. It doesn't look good. I'm sorry, my friend."

The cab driver gave Chris his carry-on luggage from the trunk and drove off. Chris stood frozen on the curb. His legs shook.

The only solace was the phone call to Michelle after his red-eye flight landed in Philadelphia. She was groggy but doing her best to sound upbeat. She said the tibia surgery was a success but, with a laugh, added she'd never clear a TSA screening again because of all the screws and rods. Recovery time was "only" three to five months.

His sister then tried lessening his guilt. She claimed there was nothing he could've done by staying in Quito. Shawn and Webber were taking good care of her. His place was at Anna's side. She ended with a quivering voice, "And give her a big hug for me, will you?" Michelle disconnected without saying goodbye.

The hospital's automatic door opened as he approached. He took the elevator to the sixth floor and cringed at the Trauma and Surgical Critical Care sign. The lobby reeked of antiseptic and misery.

A woman at the nurses' station greeted him with a welcoming smile. The smile disappeared when he asked about Anna Monteiro's condition. "I'm sorry, sir. I can't disclose that information unless you're an immediate family member." But her grave expression conveyed the worst. After she gave him Anna's room number, he stood in a silent daze. "Sir, is there anything else I can help you with?"

Without answering, he turned to walk but stopped. The sorrow and remorse were overwhelming.

What can I say? What can I do? What if she's brain damaged? What if she dies? This is my fault. I failed her.

A bodyguard sat on a folding chair outside Anna's room. He resembled a barroom bouncer in a cheap suit with an ugly toupee. He was laughing at an inane video on his phone. The thug jumped up, thrust out his hand and commanded Chris to stop. "Who are you?" The question sounded like a threat.

"A friend," Chris answered without slowing down.

"You're that Chris Davis guy, right? Get your ass outta here."

Chris shoved him hard. The bodyguard stumbled, tripped over the chair and slammed to the floor. Chris opened the door.

Anna was unconscious, resembling a corpse. Her head was shaved, partially covered by bandages. A plastic strap and tape across her bruised cheeks secured a tube down her throat. The ventilator's rhythmic whoosh … click, click … whoosh … click, click … was hideous. IV bags dripped into both arms. A pulse oximeter was on her finger. A half-filled urine bag hung from the bed railing. Machines and monitors connected with hoses and cords flashed a dizzying array of numbers and graphs. She appeared to be on maximum life support. Would it be enough to save her?

He took a cautious step forward before noticing the people

surrounding Anna's bedside. He assumed they were her parents and two older brothers. They wore surgical gowns, gloves and hatred showing above their masks. Chris made eye contact with Liz Walker, Anna's best friend and boss from Boston. An agile, middle-aged man rushed forward, tackling him to the floor.

The eldest brother tried punching Chris with a flurry of fists. He easily deflected the aggression but didn't reciprocate. He considered letting the guy beat the hell out of him. He deserved a pounding, maybe worse.

The bodyguard struggled to separate them. After pulling off the brother, pushing him aside and telling him to cool off, he yanked Chris to his feet, threatening to take a swing himself. "Get the fuck outta here," the thug roared, "before I pound your scrawny little ass into dust."

Chris could've neutralized him in three moves. Instead, he acted intimidated and slinked away, dragging the roller bag behind him. The bodyguard's and brother's actions were justified. They were protecting Anna after he'd failed.

Chris got as far as the floor's central waiting room. He collapsed onto a seat and hung his head. Why did he ever leave Anna alone? It may have been warranted if he had stopped Wolfgang's assault and captured him. But that was a failure. Although three of the assailants in Quito were killed, and another three were captured, four of them escaped, including Wolfgang. Everything Chris touched turned to shit. And Anna was paying the price.

"Hi," came a soft voice. "Mind if I sit down?"

Chris assessed Liz Walker. She appeared far worse than at their first meeting over three months ago. Her ultra-white skin was devoid of makeup, leaving a sickly pallor dotted with freckles. Her curly red hair and bangs drooped over her round face pinched by distress. "Sure. How's Anna doing?"

Liz emitted an exasperated sigh. "I won't sugarcoat this, Chris. Her prognosis is touch-and-go."

Her words ravaged his heart. "What the hell happened?"

Liz's description reflected her extensive medical education. "As I understand it, the bullet pierced the right hemisphere before exiting her skull. The initial CT scan detected a large hemorrhage. Then, a seven-hour emergency craniectomy was performed."

"Meaning?" Fear gripped him while listening to her response.

"It means the surgical team removed part of her skull, cleaned out the bullet fragments and vacuumed up the blood. The skull flap will be replaced after the swelling subsides."

"Will she have brain damage?"

"They won't know until they think it's safe to end the medically induced coma and let her wake up. That might be in about a week, maybe longer." Liz placed her hand on his. "I know this is hard, but rest assured, Anna's being treated by one of the best trauma teams in the country. They're doing everything they can."

"Thanks for coming out and telling me."

"Sure." Liz stood to leave, paused, and sat down again. "Listen, I have an idea. Her family leaves her room when they eat together. While they're gone, what if I set up a Zoom call on our phones so you can see her and maybe talk to her? Maybe she'll hear your voice. I know it's not the same as being there, but it might be the next best thing."

He got misty-eyed with gratitude. "That'd be awesome. Thanks." He tried reading her motive. "But why are you being nice to me?"

Liz shifted her weight as her green eyes bored into him. "I'll admit, I resent you for what's happened to Anna. When I heard she'd been shot, I wanted you to burn in hell. And your job is utterly repulsive, but ..." Her judgmental expression softened. "Anna told me everything you did to save my company. Because of you, Longfellow BioSciences has the chance to cure millions of cancer patients. So let's just call the Zoom calls my simple way of saying thanks."

"I didn't expect anything for doing that."

"I know. That's what made it special. Your sister told Anna about how you threatened Robert Nole to do the right thing. Listen, in my mind, extortion is a crime and morally wrong. Had I known about it in advance, I would've stopped you cold. But in this case, it was for a just cause and it worked." She patted his hand. "So thank you."

They exchanged smiles. Chris sensed they were developing a bond.

"And let me tell you something else," Liz continued. "I've known Anna half my life. We're inseparable. Yet I still don't understand your relationship. But I do know one thing. If she says you're a good man, then you're a good man. I might have trouble condoning it, but I support her decision … but on one condition."

"What's that?"

"She was emotionally fragile before this happened. Now she might be physically and mentally challenged too. So do you promise to take care of her no matter what?"

"Absolutely."

"Then, if that's what she wants … well, she has my blessing." Liz's face contorted. "But don't you dare screw up again, hear me?"

Chapter Forty-Eight: Philadelphia, Pennsylvania

Photo 118

CHAPTER FORTY-NINE

Sunday

This was the fifth day Chris had waited at the hospital, hoping for encouraging news about Anna. At night, he didn't go home because it was still an active crime scene. If allowed in, he couldn't bear to see her blood all over the bedroom closet. He had rented a hotel room but always fell asleep in a family room recliner at the other end of Anna's corridor. The nursing staff often gave him a blanket and pillow. During the day, he wandered around the medical campus or sat in waiting rooms. The only highlight was the brief Zoom calls when he whispered to Anna while she lay unconscious.

Lance was nice enough to drop by once. He reported that Sloan Hamilton was still in critical condition with severe brain damage. Her family was considering pulling the plug. Lance admitted to never liking his boss, but he'd never wished her harm. But the special agent enjoyed explaining the shitshow at the FBI office since the news about Irene Shaw went viral. "The brass are still scrambling to cover their collective asses," he said with a smirk. "And there's already talk about a congressional hearing. That should be a real circus." Lance turned serious. "Oh, and one more thing. I want you to know all the boys on the task team are praying for Anna's full recovery. We know she's going to make it."

Chris's frayed nerves jumped when he got a text. It read: ETA 10 minutes. He scurried over to the hospital's main entrance[119] in time to see a black sedan pull up. The driver was the Betsy Ross impersonator wearing normal clothes. Webber emerged from the passenger seat. Shawn hovered over Michelle while she balanced on crutches. The plaster cast extended to her knee. An oversized sock covered her toes. The siblings shared a long hug. God, it was great being back with his sister. If not for Shawn, she'd be dead.

"How's the leg?" he asked.

"It's hot, itchy, and hurts like hell. Other than that, it's great," Michelle said, trying to make light of a bad situation.

"And how are your cracked ribs?" Chris asked Webber while they shook hands.

"Just peachy. They only hurt when I breathe. But, if I must say, you look like crap."

Chris hadn't shaved or showered in days. "No, you didn't need to say that. But frankly, I'm surprised I look that good."

When the awkward levity ended, Chris gave them an update on Anna. There wasn't much news to report. Their expressions were despondent while listening. Fortunately, no one offered meaningless platitudes.

Webber was the first to break the tension. "Chris, I apologize, but I can't stay long. Duty calls. Is there someplace private where we can all talk?"

"The Prayer and Meditation Room[120] is usually empty."

Shawn helped Michelle get into a lime-green chair beside Chris before sitting next to Webber in the front row. They leaned back so the four of them could huddle. Webber surveyed the empty chapel before talking. His voice was hushed. "I've got several things to discuss, so bear with me. But trust me, this is all good news for a change."

Chris wanted to quip that he wasn't always trustworthy, but he resisted the urge. Webber's demeanor was too serious.

"First, it seems Anna was right about Vincent Wooledge. Several agencies have done a coordinated deep dive on him in the last few days. They've uncovered plenty of evidence that he was the oil mastermind and co-conspirator. You'll be happy to know the Houston FBI apprehended him this morning. I suspect they'll announce formal charges soon. You should be very proud of Anna. She found the link we couldn't identify after nine months of trying."

Webber's admiration of Anna sounded heartfelt. But he didn't need to tell Chris to be proud of her. He'd been proud of her since their first conversation on the cruise over four months ago. She was an amazing, intelligent and selfless person dedicated to saving others from cancer. The thought of losing her was inconceivable.

"More good news," Webber said to Chris, continuing to tick through the agenda. "Presidente Paladines plans on granting you the National Order of Merit. That's Ecuador's second-highest decoration. He's invited you back to Quito for a knighting ceremony."

Michelle's eyebrows rose, obviously impressed by the honor. Chris couldn't care less. "Fat chance I'll ever go back there. Tell him to stick the ribbon in the mail. If that dumbass had really listened to my advice, he would've armed Plaza Grande like a fortress or, better yet, just cancelled the whole damn OPEC+ conference."

"But at least he moved the meeting to the attached Ministry of the Interior Building,"[121] Webber said. "As a result, none of the oil ministers were injured."

"Of course I was happy about that. Everyone was. But I'm still pissed you didn't tell us in advance that you convinced the US ambassador to make the warning call to the Ecuadorian president."

"I'm sorry, Chris. As I said before, the change of venue had to be kept secret among the highest echelons for security reasons. But here's another secret. The ambassador didn't make that call. He's a gutless, incompetent simpleton who should've retired years ago."

"Then who did? You?"

"No, my boss passed along your advice. He can be very convincing. And he appreciates what you both did. So much, in fact, he'd like you to become full-time members of The Club. Unless of course you have other plans for your unemployment."

"We're not looking for a job," Michelle piped in. "If your boss is so damn appreciative, tell him to start with our immunity. And don't you dare go pushing that off again. You promised." Michelle's quest for freedom was unrelenting. She refused to be denied.

"I did promise, and here's the best news. You ready for it? He agrees. He plans on granting you both a full pardon."

"Wait a minute," his sister said with wide-eyed bewilderment. "You just said pardon, not immunity. Did I hear that wrong?"

"No, you heard me correctly. And your pardons will be signed in nine days. He wants it to happen on election day so they fly under the radar of news reporters."

Chris was incredulous. "Are you saying your boss is President Starling?"

"Yes," Webber answered with a rare, delighted grin. "And based on recent polls, he's confident he'll be reelected. That's why he wants you both to work with Shawn and me, plus a dozen others, during his next term. The Club is his baby for special covert projects."

"Holy shit!" Chris exclaimed.

Michelle echoed his surprise. "Seriously?"

The siblings shared shocked disbelief. Shawn appeared eager to hear their response or, judging by his focus, to hear Michelle's response.

"Can we think about it?" Michelle asked. "That's a huge commitment."

"Sure, talk it over and let me know. There's no hurry. But there is one more thing. And this one thing must happen soon."

Okay, here it comes, Chris thought. *A new laundry list of conditions, caveats or more broken promises.* "Now what?"

Webber displayed a full-face grin. "We've located Wolfgang König."

"Oh, this just gets better and better." Chris shared a triumphant smile with his sister. "But how?"

Shawn spoke for the first time. "I've been monitoring Irene Shaw's phone number listed on that dog tracking app. It's been off since the day she died. But we just got a ping."

The hunter in Chris flared. He wanted revenge against that son of a bitch for what he did to Anna. "Where is he?"

Webber said to Shawn, "Go ahead. You found him."

"He's in Havana, Cuba."

"How the hell did he get there?"

"We're not sure."

Webber added, "But what we are sure about is that Cuba ignores our century-old extradition treaty. In fact, they often harbor US fugitives, so we can't get him back to the States that way."

Chris's temper flared. "You saying he's untouchable?"

"Not necessarily. Since 2017, the Cubans have shown some co-operation with transnational crimes. But if we pursue König on that basis, we'd need to send a delegation from our State Department, Justice Department and maybe Homeland Security. Soon the Ecuadorian government would get involved, and probably the OPEC countries too. To say it'd get messy is an understatement."

"Then what the hell are you saying?" Chris asked.

"What I'm saying is …" Webber searched the empty chapel and lowered his voice. "President Starling has agreed to look the other way if someone were to … silently … take care of this problem within the week before his reelection, comprende?"

Chris struggled with the gravity of Webber's statement.

Holy shit! Has the president of the United States just given me permission – no, maybe an order – to find and kill Wolfgang König?

Chapter Forty-Nine: Philadelphia, Pennsylvania

Photos 119–121

CHAPTER FIFTY

Tuesday

Chris followed other arriving passengers through the jet bridge, toward the Chequeo de Inmigración sign and down an escalator at José Martí International Airport in Havana, Cuba. A health inspector scanned the QR code on the D'Viajeros form before he approached the immigration window.

Although his Theodore Robert Collins alias had worked in Italy, Belgium, Canada and Spain during the summer, there was always a residual "what if it's uncovered as fake?" in the back of his mind.

The customs official held up the passport and compared it to his short brown hair, sideburns, well-trimmed beard and brown eyes behind thick, tinted glasses. She asked questions already answered on the Tourist Card. With a bored grunt, she stamped the passport and waved him on. He should've never doubted the Cuban entry documentation Shawn had prepared in less than twenty-four hours. He had come to admire Shawn's quiet confidence but was trying hard to ignore his subtle attraction to Michelle.

With luggage in tow, he walked toward the double sliding doors and into a furnace of humidity. Whiffs of steam rose from the concrete after a recent sun-shower. Perspiration formed before he reached a handwritten sign for Mr. Ted Collins. The aging man with receding gray hair flashed a dental-challenged grin, mumbled "Bienvenido," and loaded Chris's bag into the trunk.

The half-hour ride to Old Havana was abruptly cut short. The driver veered onto a side road and said for reassurance, "No need for concern, Mr. Collins." After splashing through two blocks of potholes, the car skidded to a stop at a small community garden at the edge of a putrid river. "Please wait here," he instructed. "The chargé d'affaires wishes to meet." He left with the keys.

Chris stiffened. He searched past the manicured rows of cabbage, lettuce and red peppers for signs of an ambush and paths for an escape. His mind spun with scenarios of what might happen. Instincts screamed he was defenseless and vulnerable.

A chubby, middle-aged man emerged from a thatched shed wearing an off-the-rack black suit. Mud covered his dress shoes. His expression seemed more perturbed than dangerous, but his eyes were impossible to read behind the sunglasses.

The man sat up front and turned toward Chris. Without a greeting or offering his name, he launched into a tirade. "I run the US embassy here. I'm not sure who the hell you are or what the hell you're doing here, but I've been told to cooperate."

"That's nice to hear," Chris said with an insincere smile, sensing the guiding hand of Mason Webber.

"There's luggage in the trunk filled with the stuff you ordered. That includes a Glock 19 and an extra magazine." He whipped off the glasses, revealing a menacing glare. "But let me tell you something. Owning a gun has been banned since the Cuban Revolution. Violators get life in Combinado del Este prison, and you wouldn't survive a week in that shithole. And if you're caught doing anything illegal – and I mean anything – my embassy, and the State Department for that matter, will disavow you. Nobody will lift a goddamn finger to save your butt."

"Message delivered."

"Screw you," the man said, confusing Chris's compliance with arrogance. "Thomas will take you to your hotel now. But one last word of advice. Do what you need to do, do it discreetly, then get the hell out of this country fast. And don't you dare jeopardize our fragile diplomatic relations with Cuba or I'll have my security people hunt you down like a rabid animal."

"You make a charming welcoming committee," Chris said, brushing off the threat. The career diplomat was all bravado with no balls.

Two hours later, Chris stepped out of a former mansion turned hotel[122] and onto the bustling Plaza de San Francisco facing Havana Bay.[123] An elderly couple drifted across the cobblestones. While the wife gazed at the namesake basilica[124] and the husband read aloud from a German travel book, taxi drivers and tour guides flocked toward them like pigeons diving for breadcrumbs. A stealth pickpocket pretended not to covet the man's protruding wallet. Someone was going to get their money soon.

No one seemed to notice Chris, a positive sign his disguise was convincing. His bushy brows and curly goatee were peppered gray. The clothes from the embassy were quintessential Cuban: frayed cotton shirt and pants with scuffed black shoes, a worn straw hat and bent wire glasses. He hoped the dark bronzer with a setting spray was sweatproof.

He began walking with a slouched posture[125] and hands behind his back, shuffling like a man with nowhere to go. Yet he inspected everyone without making eye contact. His mission was clear: kill Wolfgang. Hopefully, the bastard would surface soon. But Chris lacked motivation. For the first time in his career, the inner burn to neutralize a target was a flicker.

What consumed his mind and tortured his emotions was the omnipresent image of Anna, lying unconscious in a hospital bed thirteen hundred miles away, struggling for life without a skullcap. The constant gloom of worry and guilt was all-consuming. He'd longed to be at her side, holding her hand and whispering words of affection and encouragement until she opened her eyes. She had to recover. The alternative was inconceivable.

Chris shuddered, forcing himself to concentrate. There were

only two ways to find Wolfgang. One was blind luck. It was unlikely Wolfgang was wearing a disguise because he probably felt safe in Cuba. Chris might spot him somewhere within the two-square-mile radius of the city center.

The second way was hard work. Wolfgang would've been required to present a passport when checking into accommodations. Yet there were over one hundred hotels in Havana, plus more than a thousand casas particulares. Contacting them all was a daunting task. And that assumed Wolfgang registered under the Maynard Fry passport used in Monte Carlo and Quito. He could've used another alias. Or his real name. All of this was based on the premise that he was still in Havana. He might be elsewhere in Cuba or already off the island.

No, finding Wolfgang wasn't just daunting. It was improbable.

Determining how to kill him was also challenging. His options were limited. He had no resources, technology, surveillance equipment or backup, nor access to pharmaceuticals. Even street drugs were rare in Cuba. A gun would be fast but wouldn't be a silent killing. Staging an accident would be tricky because Wolfgang's radar was always on high alert.

Chris had just arrived. There were five days left before the deadline. He was already despondent and sensed he was going to fail.

He began soaking up the ambiance of Havana's neighborhoods with a photographer's eye. The decaying charm[126] of Baroque, Neoclassical and Art Deco architecture hinted at Spain's four centuries of prosperity and when Havana had been "America's Playground" for the rich and social elite during the first half of the twentieth century.

However, after Fidel Castro seized power in 1959, virtually everything had been frozen in time. While some landmarks struggled to maintain their glamour, most buildings were in a state of crumbling disrepair. Pastel colors of peeling paint[127] couldn't conceal people struggling to exist in squalor and poverty. The city resembled a former beauty queen now in geriatric hospice, gasping for breath after more than sixty years of oppression.

Oppression. Chris had suffered a lifetime of oppression, first by the drunken rage of his stepfather, and later under Irene Shaw's dominating control. He had no regrets about killing them. They had decimated his potential and robbed his soul. They warranted his hatred.

But maybe, just maybe, he should accept some responsibility for the assassinations he committed. He always blamed Irene for his actions. Was that a cop-out? Being compliant was always safer than being defiant. Perhaps he had free will but was too weak and too afraid to make the right choices. The conclusion was chilling.

His meandering search for Wolfgang continued before stepping into Plaza de la Catedral. He admired the asymmetrical twin bell towers of Havana Cathedral,[128] then remembered Christopher Columbus had been interred here for a century before they moved his body to Catedral de Santa María de la Sede in Seville, Spain.

A gruesome flashback from three months ago erupted in his mind. Once again, Chris was spread-eagle and handcuffed by the FBI in front of Seville Cathedral. A submachine gun pressed against his face. The building where they thought Irene Shaw was hiding exploded. The roar was deafening. The heat was intense. The inferno consumed Ansel Meehan in a cloud of embers and smoke. His body was burned beyond recognition. Authorities needed dental records to identify him. Michelle still mourned the loss of their former foster brother and the one person she trusted enough to be her lover. Now he shared his sister's pain with the potential death of Anna. Was the cost of vengeance too high?

Chris had an alarming realization. He had always shielded his guilt behind a target's anonymity, never allowing himself to personify them. His sole purpose was to complete each commission as required, avoid detection, hone his skills, and strive to be the best. Now, for the first time, he understood the pain he must have inflicted on the loved ones he killed.

He felt dizzy. Breathing was rapid and erratic with a pounding pulse. Was the searing Cuban sun the cause? Or shame and remorse? He needed air. Hopefully, there was a breeze coming off Canal de Entrada. He rushed toward the waterfront.

Along the way, he encountered a row of adorable, uniformed schoolchildren.[129] They were laughing, smiling and holding hands while skipping along a cobblestone street behind their teachers. The essence of innocence. He was envious of their purity. He waved to a little girl with pigtails. She waved back and giggled. The child had no idea how her simple gesture lifted his spirits.

The sun would soon drift below the horizon. Before Chris reached the promenade along the canal, a father and his teenage son had anchored their old fishing boat.[130] The small vessel was an obvious source of pride. The wooden panels glistened with bright blue paint. His calloused hands were wrapping the fresh catch with care. Within the hour, the fried fillets would probably be on the kitchen table.

To Chris, they were inspirational. The fishermen had no money and suffered under total communist control. Yet they showed him freedom wasn't granted. Freedom was a state of mind, sharing purpose with someone you love.

The cell phone rang in his pocket. He flinched. Liz Walker had promised to give him a daily update on Anna's condition. A surge of dread consumed him. Would the report be positive or neutral? He feared a decline and refused to consider the worst.

Nervous anxiety clogged his throat. "Hello," he answered with apprehension.

"Hi," Liz said with tired enthusiasm. "How's the business trip going?"

"Fine, fine. What's her status?"

"Good news. Early this morning, the doctors determined her cerebral edema had declined enough to perform a cranioplasty."

"What's that?"

"It was a three-hour surgical procedure where they replaced the missing bone flap on her head and secured it with plates and screws."

Chris quivered at the image of Anna's decimated skull.

"Her vitals were good during postoperative recovery, so they removed the ventilator and reduced the sedation."

"C'mon, Liz. Get to the point."

"The point is – here's the best news – she woke up briefly about an hour ago and talked. She'll need months of intense rehabilitation and therapy to regain some motor skills, but her cognitive functions appear intact."

"Are you saying she's going to be okay?"

"Well, her doctor said she's young, strong and a fighter. He's cautiously optimistic for a full recovery."

The exuberance was overwhelming. "Oh, thank God!"

"Hey, wait a minute. She just opened her eyes again. I'll give her the phone." There was a shuffling noise while Liz said, "Here. It's Chris."

Sounding horse and groggy, Anna mumbled, "Hi."

He took a deep breath, struggling to control his feelings. He said with tenderness, "Welcome back. I was so worried about you. Liz says you're going to be fine."

"Uh-huh," she managed to say. "Where are you?"

He vacillated, not wanting to lie.

Somehow, she knew the answer. "Stop. Don't do it." Her voice was weak, yet her plea was emphatic. "I need you here."

"But your family doesn't approve."

"You're family too. We belong together. Come home."

Words failed him as her breathing became shallow. "Anna?" There was no response.

"Hi, Chris. Me again," Liz said. "She's fallen asleep. I'll call you with another update tomorrow. But for now, everything is looking great."

"Thank you. Thank you so much." He disconnected and dropped to his knees, covering his head. His chest heaved and his lips trembled. He sobbed. The pain, worry, guilt and relief wouldn't stop flowing. Anna was alive, she was going to recover, and she wanted them to be together. He now had everything he wanted but never expected to get and didn't deserve.

As the wave of emotions subsided, he stood, sniffled, and wiped away tears. He was at a loss for where to go or what to do. He was flooded with gratitude.

Then he saw him, or what appeared to be him, walking along the watchtower of La Punta Castle[131] at the harbor entrance. He rubbed his eyes to clear his sight. Now there was no doubt. A short distance ahead was Wolfgang König.

Instinctively, Chris began stalking his prey.

Chapter Fifty: Havana, Cuba

Photos 122–131

CHAPTER FIFTY-ONE

A royal palm tree in Parque Central shadowed the Cuban sun but was defenseless against the oppressive heat. Wolfgang tugged on his sweat-soaked shirt in a vain attempt to cool off. His skin was hot and clammy. His mouth was parched. On the left, boisterous men argued. On the right, annoying Europeans gawked at a marble monument. A passing bus belched black exhaust. Wolfgang stared at the filthy concrete while reaching a conclusion: he was screwed.

Andrés Valencia, the Colombian mercenary he had partnered with in Quito, had described Havana as the idyllic Caribbean hideaway. "Costs are low, beaches are great, and girls are happy to please rich daddies," he had said with a salacious wink. "And Cuba has no extradition treaty with Ecuador or the States, so ya safe. And when ya wanna go home, I'll give ya a name. His go-fast boat will get yah to the Keys, no problema."

Wolfgang had been a fool to believe that bullshit. Havana was a hellhole. There was one redeeming quality. He admired the pastel-colored 1950s convertibles parked in front of the palatial Great Theater of Havana.[132] They were not an exhibit. Classic cars were the norm on Cuban streets. He had learned there were over sixty-thousand American cars dating from the 1930s to the 1950s because of Fidel Castro's 1959 auto embargo. Many had pristine exteriors but were held together with handmade or black-market parts.

Wolfgang was envious, but he might as well scrap his dream of collecting vintage cars. He had no job, no network, no assets and no future. He hoped to have enough money to get off this godforsaken island.

Andrés Valencia's escape plan from Quito was masterful. Within three minutes after their attack on Carondelet Palace, they had ditched the truck in a car park, changed clothes in the La Ronda hideout and driven away in a rental car. After dropping off their two accomplices at a pre-arranged safe haven, Wolfgang and Andrés were stopped at a police roadblock. Fortunately, their Catholic priest disguises were convincing, augmented by falsified documents regarding missionary work.

Four hours later, Wolfgang was entrusted to Clan del Golfo, Colombia's largest drug cartel. During multiple handoffs, he was smuggled over the border, flown on a prop plane from Ipiales to Cartagena, and boarded a cargo ship bound for Cuba, where he was taken ashore by a rubber dinghy and driven to Havana.

The four-day trip was well-coordinated yet terrifying. Colombians had a distinct method of debt collection: a gun pointed at the head. Andrés was the first and, by far, the most expensive. He had no sympathy that The Commander had stiffed Wolfgang because all the oil ministers survived. Andrés insisted on getting paid in full. He also added exorbitant expenses and "suggested" a contribution be made to the families of his crew who were captured and killed. Other members of the Gulf Clan joined the feeding frenzy like piranhas in Colombia's Amazon River. To a man, they demanded double the pre-agreed price for services.

One of Irene Shaw's pearls of business wisdom played in his ears. "Enough money can buy you anything or anyone."

But outta money, outta luck, he thought.

Wolfgang was desperate. US citizens were prohibited from using credit cards, ATMs and banks in Cuba. Turning to the US embassy for financial assistance was a non-starter. There was one option left.

He cupped the velvet bag in his pants pocket, grimaced at the back spasm while standing, and adjusted his crotch so the boys could breathe. *Hope to God this works.*

He walked a few blocks, mimicking the gait of locals to blend in while searching for patrolling police who might ask to see his passport and Tourist Card. When reaching the small jewelry store, there was a moment of apprehension before entering.

The cold air was divine, a rarity in Havana. The walls displayed flashy link chains, necklaces, earrings, bracelets, charms and souvenirs. Most were probably crafted on-site. Two glass showcases contained modest diamond rings, other artistic pieces with multicolor gems and a few gaudy watches. With the average Cuban making less than $250 a month, he questioned how much of the glitter was gold.

A twenty-something woman approached wearing a formfitting dress plus too much makeup and bling. "Bienvenido, señor. ¿En qué puedo ayudarle?"

"I want to talk with the store owner," Wolfgang said in a monotone.

She responded in perfect English. "May I tell him what it's about?"

"An appraisal of a family heirloom."

Soon an elderly man with the facial wrinkles, drooping jowls and sad brown eyes of an English bulldog emerged from behind a curtain. A tattered leather apron failed to conceal his girth. "My assistant says you want an appraisal."

"Yes." He removed Irene Shaw's ring from the velvet bag and held it in an outstretched palm.

"¡Ay, qué cosa!" The jeweler bent over for a close inspection. His admiration was hushed. "¡Es exquisito!" He faced Wolfgang. "There haven't been rings like this in Cuba since the Revolution. May I?" His long, graceful fingers caressed the stones as if they were enchanted. "It's a bit dirty. Mind if I clean it?"

Wolfgang followed him into the back room. The ring was bathed in solvent, scrubbed with a toothbrush, blasted with steam and polished with a cloth. After hopping onto a ragged swivel chair and adjusting the workbench lighting, the jeweler pushed a finger-held loupe near his eye and purred while rocking and tilting the ring.

"Any idea how much it's worth?"

Without looking up, he said, "I'm guessing the three-carat diamond is forty to fifty thousand USD, maybe more. That doesn't include the surrounding accent stones and those along the band."

He tried to conceal his excitement. The good feeling was short-lived.

With a piercing glare, the man said, "You're American, right?"

Wolfgang nodded.

"Then why in Christ's name are you bringing this to me?"

Wolfgang sensed the man had scruples. There was no way he was going to help him sell it, regardless of the cut. "I was just curious."

"Uh-huh. And who did you say this belonged to?"

"My grandmother."

"I see." The jeweler knew he was lying. "Then who's Brutus?"

Wolfgang was dumbfounded and struggled to recover. He stuttered, "My, uh, grandfather. Why?"

"Because his name is laser-inscribed on this diamond's girdle."

"Where?"

Using tweezers to point, he said, "Right there. And it includes some kind of serial number."

"Can I see that?"

The jeweler handed him the ring and the 10X loupe. The flashing colors and fluctuating focus made the inscription difficult to see.

"Here," the jeweler demonstrated. "Hold the loupe over your eye and press your thumb knuckle against your cheek. Then, move the ring about an inch away and rotate slowly so you catch the light just right."

BRUTUS-X8ZP2#5 came into view, sparking a jolt of dopamine.

The jeweler's expression was condemning. "Do you have proof of ownership?"

Wolfgang floundered. "Yes, but, uh, the paperwork's back home."

"Then I suggest you get the hell out of my store before I call the policía."

"Sure, no problem. But before I leave" – as Wolfgang reached into his back pocket, the jeweler recoiled – "let me give you a hundred dollars for this loupe." He slapped the bill onto the workbench.

When there was no response, he added another C-note. That amount was within the man's ethics. He pocketed the bills, showed Wolfgang out and locked the store's front door.

Wolfgang would've worried the jeweler was calling the cops if he wasn't so jazzed. He power-walked half a mile and was breathless after bolting up three flights of stairs to his Airbnb loft.

Sweat covered his face as he used the loupe to try reading the inscription on Irene's ring. The lighting sucked. He pulled up the window shade to make the room less insufferable. He didn't need to write down BRUTUS, but the gobbledygook of letters, numbers and symbols was challenging to get straight.

He opened the closet safe, pulled out Irene's cryptocurrency cold wallet and pushed the On button. He sensed the fortune hidden deep within the thin metallic device resembling a small cell phone. The treasure would soon be his.

Immediate disappointment. The touchscreen PIN pad only displayed zero through nine. This had to be a password to something else. But unless it unlocked hundreds of millions of dollars, he couldn't care less.

His neck and shoulders throbbed after inspecting the ring, bracelet, earrings and watch. The damn splinted pinky finger hindered his ability to hold the jewelry steady. He didn't find other inscriptions. A gloom of failure was pervasive while removing Irene's necklace from the safe. This was it. The last chance. All or nothing. King or pauper.

With twitching eyes, he hunched over the first of the dozen large center diamonds. The word *butter* appeared like a mythical creature rising from the mist. *Oh God!* On the next stone was *alpha* and on the third was *patient*.

"Jackpot!" he screamed, followed by a booming, uncontrollable laugh. This had to be the seed phrase that unlocked Irene's wealth in cryptocurrency. He recorded all dozen words on a slip of paper using perfect penmanship, then triple-checked their spelling.

Enthusiasm crashed as the next problem arose. He needed a new wallet device to start the recovery process. Fat chance of finding one in Cuba. He didn't risk a factory reset of Irene's wallet. One mistake meant her money would be gone forever. That left one unsecure option.

Downloading a cryptocurrency app to his laptop from the vendor who made the cold wallet took forty-eight minutes. The spinning icon was torturous. If the damn Airbnb landlord was charging him three times the room rate for not requiring his passport, the least the bastard could do is supply a fast router.

The moment of truth. The screen prompt asked for the first word. He typed *butter*. After entering the last word, he hovered the cursor over Submit. A trembling finger left-clicked the mouse.

The laptop dinged. He opened his eyes. At the top of the screen was "Welcome, Irene." The balance read over $225 million. His fingers traced the nine digits to verify the amount.

At first stunned, then ecstatic, he leaped up, danced around the room with waving arms, went back for a second look, and cheered with unbridled joy. He was rich! No, stinking rich! He owned Irene's entire fortune. He blew a kiss to the sinister shrew. He hoped to God she was doing cartwheels in her grave.

He must celebrate. Wolfgang went to the rooftop bar at Hotel Nacional de Cuba, the famous five-star hotel in Cuba. He was unimpressed. The prices were outrageous, the drinks were watered down, and the atmosphere and customers were stuffy. Downright boring. He also resented that Americans couldn't rent a room. Not his kind of place.

Next stop was El Floridita,[133] the hangout of Ernest Hemingway for twenty years when he lived in Cuba.[134] Once named the world's best bar, the joint was packed. A flirtatious woman shook maracas, and another tapped bongo drums while swinging their hips and belting out an infectious Cuban song.

He sipped a daiquiri – a cocktail invented here and Papa's favorite libation – next to a full-size bronze of the author.[135] Tacky, sure, but what the hell. He wanted to shout, "All drinks on me! I'm rich!" In fact, he could buy the whole damn bar with pocket change.

Two hours and four sweet concoctions later, he had to take a leak. While hopping off the barstool, he lost his footing. No match for Hemingway's drinking prowess, especially on an empty stomach. *Need fresh air. Now.*

He stumbled along El Paseo del Prado, a tree-lined boulevard nicknamed The City's Living Room until reaching Malecón, a waterfront esplanade. The slight breeze was refreshing.

Two musicians sitting on wooden stools played a Cuban love ballad on their guitars.[136] They were ecstatic when Wolfgang dropped a fifty-dollar bill into their straw hat.

A pair of men chatted on the seawall.[137] They appeared to be close friends. Life's simple pleasures.

He weaved along the sidewalk, passed the bastion of La Punta Castle, and rested on a knee-high wall with a battery of smoothbore cannons[138] behind him. A golden hue bathed the lighthouse atop El Morro Fortress[139] on the other side of the harbor mouth. Beautiful. Mesmerizing. The perfect setting for a new life. He was rich and free. The euphoria was surreal.

He pulled a fat Cuban cigar from his shirt pocket, gnawed off the end, spat, and picked tobacco specks off his tongue. A match flared. Several puffs. The tip glowed. A deep inhale and exhale. Smoke drifted in the breeze. He stared at the stick. Fine cigars were aristocratic and manly, but this one tasted like shit. Bitter, harsh and dry. From now on he'd only buy the best of everything.

From now on …

What did the future hold? Anything he wanted. Too bad Dad wasn't alive to witness his success. His brother would be proud too. Maybe he'd find a way to buy Mom a new house. She'd be delighted to learn he was alive. He missed his family. He wished there was someone he loved, and who loved him, to share his future with.

There was movement in his peripheral vision. He spun. A shadowy figure was crouched. An old man? But he was stealthy like a cat on the hunt. The predator froze.

Wolfgang's heart rate surged. Muscles tensed. He squinted. The body shape was familiar. Those eyes.

Chris Davis? Can't be. Goddamn it, it is!

Wolfgang leaped, stumbled, and made an evasive move by bolting across the street.

A car horn blasted. Screeching tires. Horrific impact. Twisted metal. Scattering glass.

With his final breath, the last thing Wolfgang König saw was the rusted undercarriage of a pink 1953 Plymouth Belvedere.[140]

Chapter Fifty-One: Havana, Cuba

Photos 132–140

If you enjoyed Silentcide 3: Freedom Quest,
then please …

- **Write a review** on Amazon, Goodreads, Barnes
  & Noble, or where you purchased the book.
  Favorable reviews and ratings are essential to
  authors.
- **Tell your friends** and family so they can enjoy
  the novel.
- **Buy** *Silentcide: The Art of Undetected Killing* and
  Silentcide 2: Vengeance, the first two novels in the
  Silentcide trilogy.
- **Send email** to Author@RichardEbert.com.
- **Sign up** at RichardEbert.com to be updated
  about future books and author events.

**Chris, Michelle, Anna and all the dearly departed
characters thank you for allowing them to entertain
your imagination.**

ACKNOWLEDGMENTS

I am excited to have finished the Silentcide trilogy after more than four years. What started as a distraction from COVID evolved into a renewed passion for writing novels. But I didn't accomplish this alone. Several people helped transform my stories into marketable novels. I appreciate all of you. Here are the major contributors to *Silentcide 3: Freedom Quest*.

To my subject-matter experts: Kathy Jonsrud, Matthew L., Tom Emmerich, Tim Hatcher, Don Reid, Jackie Couette, Jim Giefer, Derek Gilboe, Jim Miller, Joy Turner and three others who asked not to be named. Your expertise added realism and nuances to my novel. You were also so much fun to work with.

To my editors Ryan Steck and Megan McKeever, plus my copyeditor Lisa Gilliam and proofreader Sarah Grace Liu. You collectively corrected, enhanced and polished my early drafts.

To my beta readers. Thanks for your insightful observations and suggestions. Your feedback improved all three novels.

To Kraig Larson for ten years of technology, design and creative support for Encircle Photos and Encircle Books. Your partnership is invaluable.

To relatives and friends who provide words of encouragement and congratulations. Your cheerleading is more important than you realize.

To the bookstores – especially Barnes & Noble – who shelve my novels and host author events, plus to the booksellers who welcome me and recommend my novels to customers. A huge thank you. You're awesome!

To Michelle, Bobby, Ali, Charlie and Daniel. You're a wonderful family. I love you all.

And to Mary Beth. You've been my companion and best friend for fifty-five years. You are also a spectacular wife, mom, grandmother and decades-long advocate for students with adversity to help them realize their higher education dreams. Words can't express my gratitude for the life we've shared. I love you always.

ABOUT RICHARD EBERT

Richard Ebert started as a photographer and cinematographer. Then he was president of two advertising agencies before becoming president of a consulting firm serving Fortune 500 companies in the US, Canada, Mexico and Chile. Since retiring, Richard has pursued three passions: writing, travel and photography. He lives in Saint Paul, Minnesota, with his wife and has two adult children plus two grandsons.

Contact the Author

Author website: RichardEbert.com
Author email: Author@RichardEbert.com
Travel guides website: EncirclePhotos.com
Travel photos Facebook: Facebook.com/EncirclePhotos

Sign up at RichardEbert.com or send me an email for updates on my novels and events.